THE FALCROIX LEGION

ETERNITY'S HOURGLASS BOOK TWO

E.A. BLACKWELL

GALMEDEA PUBLISHING

ISBN: 9781956703030 (e-book)

ISBN: 9781956703054 (paperback)

ISBN: 9781956703061 (hardcover)

Cover illustration by Gaia Cafiso

Galmedea Publishing
Miami, FL

Visit the author's website at www.eablackwell.com

For my friend, Dawnielle—the first person to ever cry over something I'd written. It's only right for the book containing that scene to be dedicated to her.

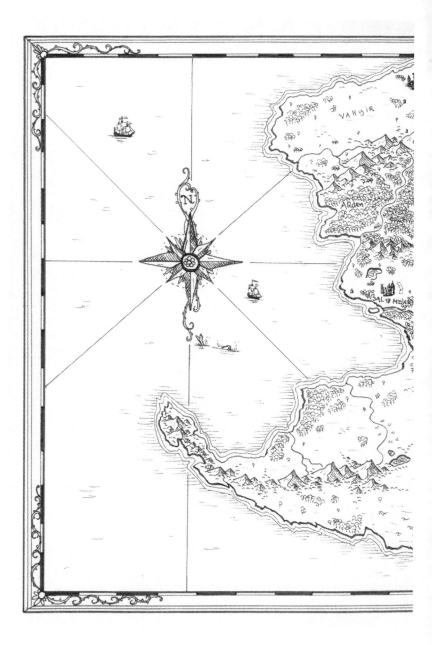

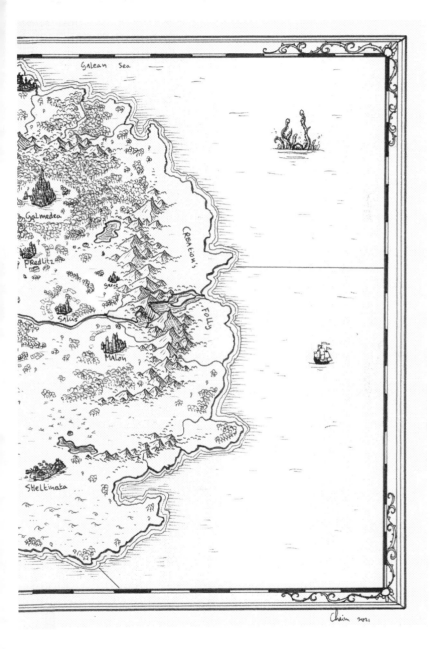

DARKNESS FALLS

THE GIRL'S legs burned as she wove through the trees. She tossed the basket she'd used to gather mushrooms by the wayside, and no more than a moment passed before the wicker snapped under the weight of the monstrosity chasing her.

Her lungs screamed as she pushed them harder. She should have listened to her father. Whispers of dark beings from the south had filled the markets and flooded into his bakery. He'd insisted for weeks, it was no longer safe to leave the lights of the city after dusk. And to think, she'd laughed and called him a gullible fool that morning. What she wouldn't give for the chance to apologize.

Her spirits lifted as the lights of Galmedea twinkled through the trees. Maybe she would get the chance after all. She broke through the tree line in a dead sprint, hoping the thing behind her would stop at the forest's edge as the stories foretold. She glanced over her shoulder as she ran toward the towering city gates, horrified the lumbering beast was still giving chase. If she looked at it just right, she could believe it had once been human, but it was simply too massive, too twisted, its ash-colored veins pulsing and straining beneath every last inch of visible skin.

"For the love of the Creator, open the gate!" she screamed as she closed in on the wooden barrier whose safety she had always taken for granted. How cruel that it might be the death of her, as the two soldiers atop the gate made no move to open it.

Arrows whizzed past the girl's head, thumping into the ground behind her. An animalistic screech shattered the night as she reached the gate and banged her fists against it. She had a moment to hope the beast had been downed before her legs were ripped from beneath her. Her head bounced against the ground as the monster dragged her back toward the forest, and her fingers sank into the grass, clawing for purchase as her fingernails tore from bleeding flesh.

The beast stopped and bent over her. Endless pools of black stared down as it sniffed in the direction of her wounded fingers. Broken fangs jutted over thickened lips, and no less than six arrows were buried in its flesh. A thick grey sludge, that in no way resembled blood, leaked from the wounds.

Another arrow whistled overhead, this time finding a home in the girl's chest. She bucked and gasped. When she coughed, a thick red froth bubbled from her lips. An angry snarl rose from the creature as it grabbed her by the legs and flung her toward the trees. Her last sensation was the freedom of flight, and she smiled as her world darkened, taking it as a sign the Creator would see her home.

~

Alara stared into the dead eyes of her most recent meal. The chill of death had overtaken this one long before it was brought to her. She snapped the arrow protruding from the young girl's chest and tossed it aside. Her finger dipped into the pool of congealed blood surrounding the wound, and she sucked it clean before tossing the bloodless husk down from her perch. It toppled over gleaming white bones intermingled with corpses in various stages of decay. A group of her servants converged on the body, ripping it apart to claim their pound of flesh.

Carrion would never sate Alara's hunger. Centuries had passed since she last tasted the blood of a god. Mere drops of Michael's blood had kept her content for weeks, but he'd all but vanished after her rebirth. She'd spent these last centuries in an endless search to quench the agonizing thirst clawing at her from within—a thirst he had damned her with.

Humans worked well enough. When alive, the blood of one mortal could satisfy her for a day or two before her soft brown irises cracked and the darkness flooded her eyes. But the blood of the dead was all but useless. Draining ten corpses a day would bring her no closer to peace than a score of lower animals, and living in constant thirst was madness. She'd once decimated a dozen servants while plagued by the insanity that overcame her when she had gone too long without a decent draught of blood. Not that it helped. Drinking from the creatures she created was akin to feeding from her own vein. She didn't need grey blood or even dark, clotted blood like what she'd pulled from the veins of her last victim. What she wouldn't give to have a new, rapid pulse beneath her lips on a daily basis.

Soon.

The mortal race had done well for itself over the years,

and larger cities now dotted the realm. She'd worked her way up through several of the smaller southern towns, but their populations ebbed and flowed with the seasons. What she needed was a city flush with thousands, where she could feast to her heart's content while maintaining a healthy stock of breeders—a city like Galmedea.

She crouched low and jumped, clearing the debris surrounding her makeshift throne with little effort. She walked the twisted halls of the caverns that had sufficed as her home for the past few years, taking stock of the army she'd amassed. Three thousand to a man, if one dared to call them such. In the beginning, she'd been more discerning when creating her brood, but as time went on and the thirst strengthened, she took most of the mortals who came to her with breath in their lungs.

Her lips curved into a wicked grin at the thought of her last creation. The boy had fought so hard, invoking a creator who had long since abandoned him. His cries were a delicacy as she forced her blood into him, and the darkness bled through his sky blue eyes.

Humanity clung to him for a day or two, as it always did. On his third day, She'd sacrificed her only meal for the satisfaction of watching him ravage the poor mortal in every way imaginable. By the end of the week, she couldn't tell him from any of her other servants.

She was drawn away from her thoughts as the wind played through her hair, signaling the cavern's exit was near. The hulking shadows of her guards milled about where stone gave way to the lush green of the forest. One of them bowed low and held out a scarlet cloak as she approached. Snapped arrow shafts stuck out from his chest at odd angles. This one had brought her the dead girl, and now she was forced to venture out in search of sustenance.

She snatched the cloak from him and twirled it around her shoulders, fastening the clasp at her neck and tucking her long, dark locks beneath the hood. A few steps beyond the cavern, she turned back to the guards, and her eyes slid from one creature to the next before settling upon the one who had disappointed her.

"His life for the horde," she rasped, and the sound of flesh being rent from bone filled the air as she turned back to the forest and took her first steps toward Galmedea.

The guards at the gate were easy enough to pass. They stumbled over themselves to allow her through while insisting on her good fortune. After all, no monsters had lumbered out of the woods at her heels. They boasted of downing one earlier that evening, and despite the blatant lie, there was no shame in their self-congratulatory remarks. One of the men even slid a heavy hand down her arm and hinted at a reward for safe passage. It took every thread of self-control to keep from dragging him into the dark, but his friends would miss him. Sounding an early alarm would not only be unwise, but likely lead to an empty stomach.

Alara slipped free of the guards and strolled through the lower dregs of the city, eying the gleaming tiers that rose above her. The metalwork Galmedea was so well known for shone in the moonlight, stretching across the bannisters separating each of the five tiers of the city. At the top, the smallest tier was packed with royals and visiting dignitaries. Servants ran from place to place doing everything short of wiping the asses of the opulent. To tumble from one rung of the city to the next was akin to a fall from the blessed realm. The closer one was to the ground, the less likely they were to prosper. The opposite was true for one's likelihood to breed.

Alara pushed through the unwashed masses in a part of

the city so depraved, that had there been a prison, more souls would have been inside than out. She despised coming here, each time hoping her next visit would be the one during which she claimed the city as her own instead of snatching a few foul-smelling bodies to drain before returning to the dank recesses of her current home. It had been nearly thirty years since her last visit, and despite Alara's disgust, the mortals did not disappoint. The highest tier of the city had been erected only two decades earlier, and the once scantly populated lower tier was now bursting with life—and death.

She came up short as a sign hanging above an open door caught her eye. The image of wings pinned to the ground with a sword creaked on rusty chains as it swayed in the breeze, a single word scrawled beneath it. *Bleak.* Raucous laughter and the clinking of glass filtered into the streets from the glowing portal beneath it.

The symbol was well-known throughout the realm, a stigma of the unclean and forsaken. It applied as much to those employed within as the vermin who frequented such places. Death likely whispered through the establishment often enough that a naked, pulseless body or two discovered at dawn wouldn't even raise an eyebrow.

Alara crossed the threshold and breathed in the life teeming within the grimy brothel. Men and women alike wove through the tables delivering drinks and brushing their largely uncovered bodies against the patrons whenever a chance arose. The number of scars marring their skin spoke more to the time they'd served than their age, but the one similarity between them was the angry red brand embossed over their left breasts, a replica of the image on the sign outside.

She took stock of the room as she made her way to the

bar, and her heart raced when her gaze lit upon the man sitting at a table in the far corner. He looked up as if he'd sensed her reaction, his sapphire eyes narrowing in recognition before he turned back to his half empty glass.

Alara's instinct to run was strong, but her thirst won out as she took a seat at the bar and used the dingy mirror behind it to keep an eye on Michael. If he'd lost interest in killing her, perhaps she could come away from this trip with more than a day's worth of sanity.

Staring into the mirror, she had a difficult time reconciling the disheveled man at the table with the godly being she'd worshipped so long ago. Aside from his lack of wings, the stubble covering his face caught her off guard more than anything else. Michael had never appreciated his wings, anyway, but in centuries together, she'd never seen him lift a razor, yet his face had remained smooth. Now, there was easily three days' growth on his cheeks. His hair hung shaggy about his shoulders and stuck up in various directions, although that was likely due to the three women fawning over him from behind. They ran their fingers through his hair as they took turns kissing his neck and massaging his shoulders. Despite their efforts, he remained decidedly more interested in glaring at his drink than affording them the slightest attention.

"Only paying customers sit."

Alara's gaze shifted to the man standing in front of her. His bald head shone bright in the flickering torchlight, and a short, macerated ginger root hung between cracked lips.

"Bleak." Michael's voice startled Alara enough that the hood of her cloak slipped down her back. In a moment of inattentiveness, he'd moved within arm's reach. It served as a much needed reminder that despite his appearance, he was still a threat. "You'll never keep new customers with greetings like that."

"I prefer to keep my doors open," Bleak shot back, but his expression softened as Michael slid a silver piece across the polished wood. He grabbed the coin and brought it partway to his pocket before his hand stalled, and he placed it back on the bar. Bleak glanced at the three women sitting at Michael's table before shifting his pale grey eyes back to him. "You're paid up."

Michael turned the coin on edge and flicked it with his finger. It spun back across the bar, and Bleak caught it before it fell to the floor. "Get this woman a drink, Bleak, before I change my mind."

Bleak scurried away and came back with a tall glass of bubbling gold liquid and a bottle of grey sludge. He set the glass in front of Alara and slid the bottle to Michael without a word, before disappearing down the line of patrons.

Michael leaned against the bar and absently twirled the bottle on its edge. "So, I take it you're the monster the locals are raving about."

"Hello to you, too, dear." Alara smiled and took a long draw from her glass. It should have tasted delicious, but her lesser senses were the first to go when the hunger took hold. "And I assure you, I am not the monster you seek."

Michael shrugged. "I seek nothing. Your sins are no longer my concern, but you reek of death."

"In the future, I'll strive for the scent of liquor and whores, to better please my maker." She smirked at the flicker of anger in his eyes. So, he was still in there. Somewhere. "All things being equal between us, are there any women in particular you'd prefer I not kill this evening?"

"They're all the same in the end." He tipped the bottle

to his lips and sucked down a third of it. His body shivered as he set the bottle on the bar.

"You don't believe that."

"I don't believe anything anymore. It makes the passage of time a lot easier." He took another swig from the bottle and cringed. When he faced her again his eyes were half-closed and glassy. "Are you here after a woman?"

"I'm here after whomever will have me." She stood and toyed with the front of his shirt before pulling him down to her and whispering in his ear. "That could mean you."

She crushed her mouth against his, but he pushed her away when her teeth sank into his bottom lip. Her pulse thundered in her ears as she savored what little blood she'd stolen, the thick coppery liquid coating her mouth and setting her senses aflame. She wiped a wayward drop from her chin and sucked her finger clean, her eyes never leaving Michael's. When she lifted her glass to her lips, the golden fluid not only threatened to dull her wits, but dazzled her tongue with hints of pear and honeysuckle.

She stroked a hand down Michael's arm and gripped his wrist when he attempted to pull away. "We could raze this city, you and I."

"I just want to be left alone." Michael finished his bottle and tossed it behind the bar, where it shattered against the floor. Bleak glanced from Michael to the glittering remnants of the bottle with little interest.

Alara's eyes narrowed. Michael was the last person she'd expected to find in Galmedea, and while the prospect of having him as an endless supply of blood was tempting, if he wasn't going to cooperate, she needed him gone.

"Oh, please," she scoffed. "If you really wanted to be alone, why reside in one of the realm's most populous cities?"

Michael waved her comment away. "It was a mistake talking to you. Do what you want tonight, but leave me alone." He headed for the stairs, and the three women from his table hurried to follow.

Alara ordered another drink as she beckoned a man with dark bronze skin who had been eying her while she spoke with Michael. A rush of words and exchange of coins later, he was leading her up the stairs to his deathbed, but the smile on Alara's face had nothing to do with the promise of sex and blood. It was the questioning spark in Michael's eyes before he retreated to his own sins that kept her spirits high. Knowing him as she did, it was doubtful he'd finish out the month in Galmedea. And then the city would be hers.

The spires of Galmedea flared so brightly Morghan would have sworn the heat from the smoldering buildings warmed her cheeks. She crouched in a main street of the top tier amidst a wealth of twisted, bloodless mortal husks.

Alara stood not far in front of her, the fingers of one hand threaded through the tawny locks of a woman who had little life left within her. Alara waved her free hand toward a contingency of her hulking, orc-like minions and barked orders to them before bringing the woman's ravaged neck to her mouth and draining the last bit of light from her eyes. Tendrils of mahogany flared through the swirling black orb in Alara's chest as she tossed the body aside. Her eyes caught on something in the distance, and a devious grin spread across her face. She whipped her scarlet cloak around the back of her shoulders and strode down the street, walking straight through Morghan without paying her the slightest attention.

Morghan gasped and grabbed her chest. Her vision of the city faltered, and granite walls shimmered into view as she awoke in Luke's bed, thankful for the interruption. Luke could watch people for weeks without surfacing to do so much as stretch his legs, but she couldn't handle being a ghost in someone else's world for more than a few days at a time.

The fingers of Morghan's left hand were loosely threaded between those of Azrael's right, and her head rested on his shoulder. She toyed with the idea of tightening her grip and disappearing into the burning city once more but decided against it. In a few days, it would be two centuries since her unfortunate run-in with Nikoli, and there was no point in spending more time haunting a place to which she would soon be exiled.

The bed creaked as she untangled her hand from Azrael's and sat up. Azrael remained motionless, his left hand still linked with Luke's right. The past two-hundred years had moved fast, especially once they'd learned she could share Luke's visions through Azrael. Without the buffer, any attempt at watching Michael ended with Morghan being unable to look at food for the next several days. At least she'd talked the guys into laying in a bed while they watched. Granted, they were fully clothed, but a win was a win, because there was no way she was spending days at a time sitting motionless in those stone chairs. Her back hurt just thinking about it. She stood, and the net of energy Azrael had woven around them flashed as she walked through it. Her chest tightened as a chilly, all-too-familiar aura slithered across her skin.

"It's about time you woke," Nikoli purred from where

he'd appeared against the wall. "You've overstayed your welcome."

She turned back toward the energy field, intent on taking the pain in order to wake Azrael, but her legs wouldn't cooperate. Instead, she walked to Nikoli and stood by his side, while every fiber of her being screamed in protest.

"Better." Nikoli grinned.

"You're cheating me," she seethed. "I have a few days left."

Nikoli shook his head. "You had a few days left a week ago. I was generous enough to give you an extension."

Generous her ass. He'd bided his time until the opportunity arose to rip her away from those she loved without the luxury of goodbyes. She looked down at her bare feet and sighed. "Can I at least get my things? I don't even have any shoes on."

"Stay," he commanded, and she did, despite the urge to grab her sword and run it through his chest.

Nikoli grabbed her coat and boots and shoved them into her chest. "Put them on."

He collected her daggers, katana, and a shoulder holster before dumping them at her feet as she tied her boots. He quirked an eyebrow, as if to ask if there was anything else.

Morghan rose to her feet and nodded to the dresser. "Second drawer from the top. Sunglasses." She stumbled forward and fell to her knees as Nikoli released his hold on her.

"The only thing of Lucifer's that I want to touch is you," he said. "And trust me, if I could avoid touching you, I would."

She glared at him from the floor before her gaze shifted back to the bed.

"You won't be the one to pay the price if you cross the barrier and wake him."

She rose to her feet and swiped her glasses from the dresser before shoving them onto her face. "One day, you son of a bitch."

Nikoli took her chin in his hand and made her to face him. "That barrier isn't a solid, defensive one. If I wished it so, I could force you to walk through the net of energy and take the pain as you ran them through. They wouldn't even have time to acknowledge the danger. So, forgive me if I find your empty threats amusing." He let go of her chin and pushed her toward the corner of the room, where her ranking sword lay abandoned against the wall. "Pick it up and be quick about it. Your grandson is lost. Let's see if you can find him."

2

WELL, THAT ESCALATED QUICKLY

MICHAEL ROLLED his shoulders as he knelt beside a river and splashed water onto his face. The air was stifling, and though the crisp, cool water trailing across his skin was refreshing, it did nothing to ease the tension that had come to fit him as a second skin.

He was being watched. When the nagging feeling first surfaced a few months earlier, he began a haphazard journey, hoping to lose whoever was trailing him. But no matter the erratic his path became, the unorthodox presence continued to tug at his mind.

He'd almost gathered the nerve to turn back and track it in return, but he balked at the idea of tracking anything without the advantage of an aerial view. He closed his eyes and groaned. The thought of flying brought the loss of his wings to the forefront of his mind like a festering wound.

Enough generations had passed that all save a few of the older settlements only viewed him as a descendant of the winged creator in their religious texts. Michael hated the idea of being singled out more than his longevity already caused, but after more than a century without his wings, he would have traded any amount of ridicule for the ability to take to the skies again.

He turned back to the water and scratched the back of his neck as the nagging sensation of being watched attacked him with renewed force. A shadow fell over him, and he spun around to find a strange figure lording over him.

"Are you growing another head back there?" The voice was female, but Michael could barely tell by the look of her as he squinted into the sun. "You sure do scratch it a lot."

The woman's hands rested on her hips, and jagged scars ran under her chin and along her left cheek, adding an edge to the annoyed expression hanging on what he could see of her face. Though her clothing was anything but typical, it was the dark, reflective lenses of her glasses which drew Michael's attention. Sunglasses. Which made no sense at all. The woman standing over him was wearing something that, as far as he knew, had yet to be invented in his world.

She smiled and tapped the side of her glasses. "You like 'em? Pretty bright around here most of the time. I know damn well you can make clouds."

Michael backed away, and he went careening into the water as his foot slipped on the muddy riverbank. He came up sputtering for air, but a sharp yank on his shirt set him flat on his back in the grass.

"Someone should be paying me for this." His stalker frowned. "I can't believe you managed to create an entire civilization. You're a fucking mess."

Michael's eyes widened. She knew who he was. "Who are you? What do you want?"

"World peace." She laughed. "Sorry, standard answer."

She offered him a hand up, but he only stared at it.

"My name is Morghan Windstarr," she said. "And I'll be playing the part of your guardian angel."

"Wait, you're an angel?" Michael grabbed her hand and hoisted himself to his feet. His excitement died a moment later. "Where are your wings?"

"That's my question to ask. You shouldn't be ashamed of them, Michael. They're part of who you are."

Michael took a hasty step back, nearly forgetting the river. He steadied himself and glared at Morghan. "You're one to talk. Hiding behind dark glasses and a long coat. My clothes are soaking wet, and the heat is still stifling."

Morghan sighed and shrugged out of her coat. She draped it over her shoulder before removing the glasses from her eyes and situating them on her forehead. "Better?"

He gawked at the arsenal of daggers draped about her waist, which absolutely did not make him feel better. A longsword hung on her right hip, and a long, thin blade was held at her back by a strap that looped from shoulder to hip. But it was the gun secured in a holster beneath her right arm that decided it—Morghan may have looked to be somewhere in her late thirties, but she had to be much older. If she came from his original world, as her attire suggested, it meant she was at least as old as he was. It also meant she was more dangerous than she looked, if that was at all possible. He couldn't quite decide if he should run or throw his arms around her and sob with joy over finding someone who shared his plight.

Morghan took a step back and held up her hands. "I don't do the touchy-feely thing, especially not with new people, but I won't hold it against you if you cry."

"You read my mind!"

"It comes and goes. Mostly goes lately." Remorse flashed across her face. Michael understood why she wore the glasses; her green eyes were unusually expressive. "I'm not very good at controlling it, but my superpowers have about run out by now anyway. You'll get used to it."

"I'm not going to get used to it." While Michael thought it would be a good idea to keep in contact with the woman and learn more about her origins, if she thought she'd be tailing him the rest of his days she had another think coming. "I'm not interested in a travel companion. Definitely not a woman."

She raised an eyebrow.

"It would complicate things, and no offense, but you don't look like my type."

"Good," she said, "Because I wouldn't sleep with you if you were the last man on Earth. Speaking of which, did you have to use the same name? You could have called this place anything. My friends and I were really disappointed by the lack of creativity."

"There are more of you?"

"Oh no, I'm one of a kind." She smiled. "My friends are angels, and though I seem to attract the bastards like sticky-fingered kids to a candy shop, what I am is slightly less fantastic: immortal brand B, just plain human. But you're stuck with me."

He turned away and stalked along the riverbank. "I'm not stuck with anything. I already told you, I travel alone."

"Well, the way I see it you have two options."

Michael stuffed his hands in his pockets and concentrated on the ground as she fell into step beside him.

"You can either accept that I'm not going anywhere and try your hand at being civil, or I can trail you from a distance and pop in to scare the shit out of you every now and again."

"Neither of those works for me." Michael turned away from the river and picked up his pace as he passed beneath the forest's canopy. Much to his dismay, Morghan had little trouble keeping up with him.

"Neither wasn't a choice," Morghan said.

"You'll find I prefer to make my own choices."

"And you'll find I am exceedingly stubborn." She poked him in the back, and he turned on her with narrowed eyes.

"Touch me again without permission, and I might just kill you."

"Oh, I would like to see you try." Her lips curled into a smirk Michael was already coming to despise. "You may trump me in a lot of areas, but the only thing you've ever tried to kill with your sword is a tree. And, if memory serves, and it always does, even that did not go very well. You've gotten by because you're a ranking immortal, but you need a ton of fucking work."

"A what immortal?" His pulse pounded in his ears; how in God's name did she know about the tree? He shook his head and waved a hand in dismissal before continuing deeper into the forest.

Morghan jogged beside him and nodded to the sword at his hip. "Your sword wasn't made by any human blacksmith in this realm. It means you can only be killed by another person with a similar sword. A wound from a ranking sword will remain open and heal at a normal pace. Otherwise, it's eternity or bust. Listen, I know you're skeptical, but I can help you fill in a lot of gaps."

"Like how you have glasses from my old world? It was destroyed ages ago, but those sunglasses look brand new. Was it all a lie?"

"Oh no, our home dimension is toast. These sunglasses are almost as old as you are, but they're time-locked. Neat little trick—stops all forms of decay, well, for inanimate

18

objects. You don't want to time-lock something alive; I hear it's brutal."

Michael's eyes widened. "You can stop something from aging?"

"Not personally, but I can help you with other things."

Michael put his head down as he walked. "I don't need your help, and stop pretending to know me."

"Michael Bradley Kavanagh, born October twenty-second of 2212. Your mother was a psychotic bitch who abused you. I'm sorry for that." The lines collecting on her forehead suggested she truly was. "When you were sixteen your world was destroyed. You lost everything you cared about, including the girl some of us suspect was your soul mate. An impossible amount of time later, after being thrown into a desolate dimension, you created your own race of humans in an attempt to stave off the loneliness. But you feel like you've failed your people because of a few careless mistakes. In the end, the new civilization only reminded you of how different you really are, and despite all your efforts you ended up an outsider in your own world."

Michael stopped walking and stared at her in disbelief.

"And you should probably stop frequenting brothels, especially if you're going to cry yourself to sleep afterwards," she added, but the way her face contorted, it was unlikely she meant to say the last part aloud. "Shit. Sorry."

He turned away in shame, and his jaw tightened as he fought to keep his emotions in check. In a matter of seconds this strange woman had lain his life bare, and not even his most private moments had been spared.

"What do you want from me, really?" He gathered the nerve to look at her again and was relieved to find she had replaced the glasses over her eyes.

"I'm here to help. We're a lot alike." She tapped the sword at her hip, and Michael noticed the letter embossed on the hilt, much the same as on his. "I doubt watching everyone around you grow old and die is fun. We can keep each other company."

"You wouldn't be very good company. I don't trust you, and you strike me as particularly unlikable."

"Well it does take a special kind of crazy to like me." Morghan hooked her thumbs into her pockets and rocked back on her heels. "I'm a pretty big pain in the ass."

Michael didn't doubt that at all, but despite his best intentions of holding on to his sullen mood, he was unable to suppress a snort of laughter. He opened his mouth to make a witty comeback, but a high-pitched scream tore his attention away.

"That can't be good." Morghan craned her neck to look through the trees.

Michael didn't bother answering. He sprinted through the trees, and it wasn't long before he came upon a small settlement. Chaos reigned as flames leapt from one thatched roof to the next and bloodied villagers scattered along the dusty road around which the town was built.

Morghan stood beside him a moment later, her coat clutched in one hand as she leaned over her knees to catch her breath. "You can't just take off without warning me. Fuck. I haven't run in forever."

Michael glared at her before turning his attention back to the village. He hadn't used his powers in ages, but if he could conjure a storm strong enough, it would quench the flames. But that would take turbulent emotions he currently didn't feel. It had been so long since he felt much of anything.

He thought back on the way Morghan had summed up

his life in a matter of moments. His failures and triumphs. Shameful secrets. And his futile wish to belong in a world that had outgrown him shortly after he created it.

A few clouds formed overhead, and he coughed a spray of blood into his hand. He wrinkled his nose and wiped the back of his hand beneath it, coming away with a thin streak of crimson. A hard punch to the shoulder reminded him of his unwanted companion, and the sun reappeared as his thoughts slipped back to the present.

"And another thing," Morghan said. "I'm not putting up with this masochistic bullshit."

"It's just from using my powers." Why did he feel the need to justify himself to her?

"No, it's from you being careless." She shoved her arms into her coat and pulled it around her as if the sun wasn't strong enough to fry an egg on a rock. "If you don't know how to use your power correctly in your human form, don't."

"Then help me do something about this." Michael started forward but turned back when Morghan didn't follow. "What's wrong? Are all those weapons just for show?"

"Yes and no," she admitted. "What are we doing here? I thought you were a lonely vagabond who didn't give a shit about his people anymore."

"I reserve the right to change my mind." He covered his ears and cringed when glass shattered behind him. "Listen, you think you'll be a good travel companion? If you really want to help me, then prove it. Save these people."

Morghan glowered at Michael before shrugging out of her coat again and shoving it into his chest. She mumbled a few colorful words as she stalked past him and headed toward the line of burning buildings.

Morghan wasn't sure if Michael was the patron saint of indifference or lost causes. There was no happy medium with him.

She reached the first building, and its thatched roof was a mess of flames. That wasn't necessarily a bad thing. Her telepathy may have been waning, but she still had firepower in spades. Maybe tapping into that power reserve would wow Michael enough to shut down his uber-dick attitude and make him act like a normal person.

A stack of abandoned crates worked well enough as a vaulting point, and she grabbed the edge of the roof, using the momentum to swing onto it. She cracked her knuckles and smiled, walking along the edge of the first roof, sure to keep her feet over the outline of the wall so she wouldn't fall through. Her thoughts turned to Luke and her ever-present rage over being unceremoniously ripped from his arms. The flames responded, licking toward her and stretching to follow as she passed. The charred skeletons of buildings appeared in her wake, and by the time she came to the last roof, the only thing left aflame was her.

She breathed in the warmth playing across her skin. It was possible this was as close as she would ever get to Luke again. A tired sigh escaped her lips; maybe spending time with Michael would soothe the hollow ache the last few months had carved in her chest. The thought brought her back to the task at hand, and she quashed her emotions, ordering the flames to die along with them.

The flames wavered before roaring back to life.

Anxiety washed over Morghan as the fire danced across her arms and chest. She fully expected to lose this gift in the same manner as Azrael's, but unlike the telepathy, there had been no signs of waning control.

Pain crackled over her arms, and she took a step back, forgetting the brittle remnants of thatching behind her. It gave way beneath her feet, and her back screamed as she crashed into a wooden table, breaking it asunder. Blisters shined along the length of Morghan's arms, and the only positive she could find in her current clusterfuck of a situation was that the flames had extinguished themselves during her fall.

"What's all this now?" a rough voice called from behind her.

Morghan twisted her neck around until she spotted two men hovering in the back corner of the room. Their hair was so matted with dirt and blood that the colors were anyone's guess, and their skin was in no better shape. Daggers gleamed in their hands and at their hips as they rifled through the belongings of those who lay lifeless at their feet.

"Women falling from the sky, Kit." The other man chuckled, abandoning the drawer he was looking through and starting toward Morghan. A thick scar ran from the right side of his forehead down to his cheek, and his right eye was fixed and pale. He glanced up to the hole in the ceiling and grinned. "Fire's out, too. Creator's with us today."

Kit stood, a vase rolling off his fingers and smashing against the floor. "Well, hurry it up then. The boss wants us outta here in time to be in Malon before dusk. Get your fill of women there."

"But then we have to pay," the scarred man sneered. "And I know those bitches charge me more."

Morghan wished the dumbass would hurry up already. Her hands itched to use the daggers tucked behind her thighs. If he hadn't been put off by the fact she was sporting triple the number of weapons as he and his companion combined, she doubted he would think twice before giving her a clear path to his neck. Or maybe she'd wait for him to drop his pants. A quick flick of her wrists could take out both femoral arteries and veins; he'd bleed out in seconds. It was ages since she'd taken a life, since she'd even felt the compulsion to do so, but being away from Luke and Azrael didn't bring out the best in her.

Morghan was so busy deciding how to kill the man, she paid him little attention until his dagger slid under the top buttons of her shirt and sliced it open.

"Seriously?" She scowled. "This is my only shirt!" Neck it was. She brought her daggers around, but they sliced through air. The man's body flew across the room. It slammed into a wall and crumpled to the floor.

Michael loomed over her. He swiped the man's dagger from the floor and stalked across the room to where he lay.

Kit ran to help his accomplice, but Morghan pulled the gun from her shoulder holster, and red blossomed between his eyes as the gunshot echoed around the room. His body dropped to the floor with a thud, and Morghan holstered the gun. Her nostrils flared. All that forethought on how to kill that other jackass for nothing.

She rushed to Michael's side, where he was struggling with the man who should have been her first kill. Arms and legs flailed for purchase as Michael held him at arm's length. The dagger's broken blade stuck out from a shallow wound in the center of the man's chest.

Morghan punched the bandit hard in the side of his face. Bones shattered beneath her fist, and his body went limp. "Of all the places you could have stabbed him, you tried to go through the sternum?"

"I thought the chest was a good idea," Michael said. He glanced at where Kit lay in an expanding pool of blood.

"The chest was a great idea," she agreed. Her brow furrowed when Michael let go of the man and headed for the door. "What are you doing? He's still alive."

"He's not trying to hurt us anymore."

"That's because he's unconscious." She nudged his body with the toe of her boot. "What about when he wakes up? If we're not here, he'll do all this again elsewhere." She gestured around the room and to the remainder of the village outside.

"We can tie him up," Michael suggested.

Morghan knelt over the man and ripped the fabric from the front of his shirt. "And what, drag him behind us as we walk the world over? No, thanks."

"What are you doing?" Michael knelt and put a hand on her shoulder, presumably to stop her.

"I'm going to show you the right way to stab a chest."

His gaze slid from Morghan to the dead man across the room and back again. "The only difference between good and evil is one believes in redemption and the other believes in murder."

Morghan pushed him away. "There is so much wrong with that statement I can't even begin to correct it. Besides, did you think the dagger in his chest was going to tickle?"

"That's different. I did what I had to do to save you."

"You did it poorly." She pointed to the man's chest. "On the left side of the chest count four rib spaces down from the top," she instructed, plunging her dagger between the man's fourth and fifth ribs before Michael had a chance to stop her. The body convulsed as the blade sank deep, and the heartbeat pulsed up the hilt. "About halfway between where your dagger went in and the shoulder. Angle a little bit toward the middle if you want, and there you are. Quickest way to a man's heart." She twisted the hilt and the mechanism within her dagger fired, splitting the single blade into three and shredding what was left of the struggling muscle. "You'll develop an eye for the right spot."

"Doubtful." Michael stood and walked out the door.

"Wait!" Morghan followed him, but she hadn't made it to the door before he ducked back in and blocked her from leaving.

"There are more of them," he said. "Three men holding horses. I think they're waiting on these two."

"Do they also look like they need a hug and some redirection?"

Michael's eyes drew down to slits, but he didn't say a word.

"We can stand here glaring at one another until they come find us, or we can go kill the assholes and get some free transportation out of it," Morghan suggested. "Your call."

Michael looked around the doorframe. "I'll take the two on the left. You're in charge of the one on the right."

Morghan pushed past him, turning toward the three men at the edge of the settlement. When they noticed her, two drew swords and the third grabbed a bow from around his chest. She pulled a more conventional dagger from her belt and flipped it over, weighing the blade in her hand before letting it fly toward the archer. It buried to the hilt in his chest, the momentum throwing his body into the horse he stood near. The beast startled and trampled his corpse before sprinting away.

"If you want any of them, you'd better hurry."

The sword-wielding men charged her, but she wasn't worried. This could have been over in a moment if she used her gun again, but as it stood, she had seven bullets left and had yet to devise a way to make more. So, she grabbed the hilt of her longsword and freed it from its sheath. It was warm in her hand and offered a clarity she hadn't felt since before Nikoli had stripped her of one family to force her into creating another.

At least the two men had the sense to attack her simultaneously—not that it saved them. Morghan parried one swipe and dodged the other. She turned and rammed the hilt of her sword into the neck of one, sending him careening into the blade of his counterpart. They fell to the ground, one run through and the other trapped beneath the squirming body.

Morghan placed a booted foot against the cheek of the man on the bottom, forcing his face to the side.

"Stop!" he begged, his eyes wild. "I have gold. Horses. I'll give you anything."

"You can't give me what I want," Morghan rasped, bringing her sword down hard across his neck. She kicked the severed head away from the body before wiping her sword clean on the grass and sheathing it. "No one in this fucking dimension can."

3

IF IT AIN'T BROKE DON'T—NEVER MIND, IT'S ALL BROKE

KRISHNA SLUMPED against the wall of the control room and struggled to keep his eyes open as he stared across the room without focusing on anything in particular. His mind barely registered the momentary darkness as the images on the walls blinked out and struggled back to life. He'd long ago lost count of how many times the system had restarted.

Nikoli and Winstin stood over one of the main consoles engaged in an endless debate on the finer points of why the monstrosity wasn't working. To be fair, Winstin was being very diplomatic with his side of the argument, interjecting a point here or there and claiming Nikoli had led him to each conclusion. Whether it was Nikoli or Winstin who came up with the ideas didn't seem to make any difference, as the problem remained—it used too much energy to locate the souls in Michael's realm, and being restricted to one soul at a time rendered the room obsolete.

Since the destruction of the previous mortal realm, Winstin had remained largely useless. As it stood Winstin was good for exactly two things, looking in on Michael and plotting to betray them with Lucifer's harlot. Krishna didn't understand why Nikoli had chosen to spare Winstin. Krishna was certain if it had been he who betrayed their master, his head would have been on a pike.

Krishna sighed and slid down the wall into a crouch, studying his hands as the lights went out again.

Nikoli slammed his fist into the console and blue sparks scattered around the room. He knelt in front of it and pried the metal cover from the part of the machine closest to the floor. Spirals of blue light shone from the metallic cavern. Nikoli threaded his fingers together and stretched them until the joints cracked. Pale blue sparks lit at the tip of each finger as he reached inside and grabbed one of the spirals, bending it until it more closely resembled a cube. The screens flickered again, but when they lit this time one screen showed a blurry picture of a mortal tending bar while another focused on a woman goading children into bed.

By the way Nikoli and Winstin went on about their progress, one might have thought they solved a great mystery of the universe. Maybe they had, but did it really matter?

Krishna absently banged his head against the marble wall, trying to stay awake. His breath caught when Nikoli's shadow loomed over him.

"Are there invisible chains holding you to this wall?" The annoyed edge in his voice made Krishna cringe.

He turned his eyes up to Nikoli and shook his head. "No, Master."

Nikoli made a sweeping gesture toward the door with one arm. "Fantastic. Then by all means, relieve the room of your presence."

"But—"

Nikoli held up a finger to silence him. "Your boredom is a distraction. Take a nap. Or a walk."

Krishna half expected him to add "off a cliff" to the last sentence. He stood and gave a short bow before turning to leave.

Nikoli grabbed Krishna by the arm and spun him around, giving him a quick kiss on the lips. "Not off a cliff." A grin slid across Nikoli's face as he nodded toward the door. "Not today, at least. Go."

Krishna couldn't keep a smile from spreading across his face as he left the control room. He decided to take Nikoli's advice and sleep. Maybe when he woke Nikoli would be done.

His smile vanished as he came up to Nikoli's door and heard a voice on the other side. Lucifer's voice.

"Well, then go back." Lucifer sounded annoyed. "You shouldn't even be here."

"Neither should you," Azrael said as Krishna leaned against the door. "This is a mistake."

"How can you be okay with what he did? With never seeing Morghan again?"

"I never said I was, but this is not the time. We should play this card when it makes a difference."

"What are you doing?" Lucifer asked, and in the next moment the door opened, spilling Krishna across the threshold.

Krishna looked up at the man standing over him. He had only met Azrael a few times during the destruction of Earth, but it was hard to forget someone when you'd spent your entire life living in their shadow. Nikoli and Azrael had been together longer than Krishna could fathom being alive, and despite the relationship ending millions of years earlier and Nikoli bleeding Krishna as his hybrid in the meantime, Nikoli continued to watch Azrael with a fervor bordering on obsession.

It wasn't fair. Krishna would have died a thousand deaths for Nikoli without ever being asked, and Azrael, the two-toned, wingless angel bastard, turned down every last bit of charity Nikoli offered.

Lucifer swooped in and grabbed Krishna off the floor by the back of the neck. His arm wrapped around Krishna's shoulders and the weight of a blade pressed against Krishna's stomach.

"Really, Lucifer, is that necessary?" Azrael sighed. "He's harmless."

Krishna wasn't sure if he was more upset over Lucifer's threatening posture or Azrael's dismissal.

"Did you miss the ranking sword at his hip?" Lucifer spat. "You know damn well he's Nikoli's hybrid. You would have stood there, inches in front of him, waiting for him to kill you."

Krishna flinched when Azrael moved in front of him. His head throbbed and bringing any thought to the forefront of his mind was an uphill battle. Azrael's golden eyes glowed so brightly Krishna worried they would burn straight through him. If nothing else, those eyes would haunt his dreams for years to come.

"Let him go, Lucifer. I have him."

Krishna blinked through the haze as Lucifer released him and stepped away. Azrael remained within arm's reach, which was far too close for his liking. Azrael was off limits. Nikoli wouldn't allow anyone to think about him without permission, let alone touch or attempt to kill him.

"Nikoli is in our old room." Azrael looked away and ran a hand through the dark blonde hair he no doubt kept short because Nikoli preferred it otherwise. "Are we really doing this, or can we go home?"

Lucifer glared at Azrael before heading down the hall without a word.

Azrael followed, and Krishna's body fell into step behind them despite his mind screaming for his feet to stop moving.

"Don't fight it." Azrael turned back to him as they left Nikoli's quarters and entered the sun-drenched hall. "It will only make it—" Azrael stopped short and Krishna slammed into him, toppling to the floor.

"Worse." Azrael's final word came as a whisper.

There was no chance of rising from the floor, but Krishna's eyes were already turned up to Azrael, who stared at the sky in abject horror. Krishna shifted his eyes to the sky in confusion, as the day remained as sunny and cloudless as ever.

"Azrael!" Lucifer grabbed his arm. He glanced at the sky and back to Azrael. "What's wrong?"

A schooled expression of indifference Krishna recognized all too well replaced Azrael's original reaction. "Nothing." He turned his eyes from the sky and forced a smile. "Let's go. The sooner we talk to Nikoli, the sooner we can leave."

Krishna's puppeteer had him up and walking again as they made their way to the control room. Krishna should have been happy they were taking him to Nikoli, but allowing himself to be used as a pawn was unlikely to please his master. Not to mention the last thing Krishna ever wanted to witness was an interaction between Nikoli and Azrael. Without it, he could go on believing Nikoli hated the traitor as much as he let on. Everyone the realm over knew the truth was not so simple, or as Krishna feared, all too simple.

Nikoli turned from the console when they walked into the room. Anger flashed in his eyes as they lit on Krishna before turning to Lucifer and finally landing on Azrael. The anger faded as he leaned back against the malfunctioning relic and smiled. "All three of my favorite mistakes in one room. To what do I owe the honor?"

Lucifer drew his sword and pressed the tip against Krishna's neck until a thin trail of blood spilled onto his chest. "Give me permission to go to Michael's realm and see Morghan without consequences, or I swear I'll kill him."

Nikoli's eyes remained on Azrael for a few more moments before he half-heartedly turned his attention to Lucifer. "Why bother? Killing him will get you nothing."

"I'll be happy to take something irreplaceable from you, like you have from me."

Nikoli laughed. "When you walked into this room I was afraid you'd finally acquired the intelligence to match your strength. Somehow, you managed to bring insurance and payment, but you don't even understand which is which, Lucifer, or that they may be one and the same."

Krishna's heart sank. He tried to convince himself Nikoli was pretending indifference to move Lucifer's attention elsewhere, but as Nikoli's gaze shifted back to Azrael, he couldn't quite bring himself to believe it. If this much time had gone by and Nikoli still couldn't let go of the past, then what hope was there for the future? Not that it mattered. He would love Nikoli until the end, even if his was the sword that brought him there.

Azrael took a step back, and the haze covering Krishna's thoughts rolled away. Lucifer's sword remained at his neck, but he tested his fingers, relieved he could move his body again.

Lucifer's gaze darted from Azrael to Nikoli. "That's not why he's here."

"Isn't it, though?" Nikoli raised an eyebrow. "Do you want to see your life mate again or not?"

Lucifer didn't respond for what felt like an eternity. In the end, he sheathed his sword and slammed the palm of his hand into Krishna's back so hard it sent him stumbling across the room. He fell against Nikoli's chest, but instead of catching him, Nikoli pushed him aside and let him fall to the floor.

Krishna turned around in time to see the confused look on Azrael's face when Lucifer grabbed his wrist. And then they were gone.

Nikoli stared at the emptiness where they had stood for an impossibly long time before he turned around and started manipulating the console once more without affording Krishna the slightest glance.

Azrael fell to his knees in front of the thrones in the labyrinth's main hall. He clutched his stomach and hoped his head would stop spinning before his last meal repeated on him. No wonder Morghan hated shifting with Lucifer.

He glanced to where Lucifer stood beside him, staring down the hall at nothing. Lucifer ripped the sword from his hip, sheath and all, and flung it into the darkness with a feral scream. He crouched and briefly laced his fingers together behind his neck before collapsing onto his back, his unblinking eyes reflecting the flames overhead.

"You didn't have to—"

"Shut up, Azrael." Lucifer's concentration on the ceiling never wavered.

"We can go back. It's a wonder he didn't insist on punishing me for stepping foot in his realm, anyway." Azrael sat down on the floor and rubbed a hand over his chest. "I'll be fine. We didn't even hear Nikoli's proposal."

"I said shut up. We're not going back."

Silence stretched between them until Azrael placed a comforting hand over Lucifer's. "You will see her again. I promise. We both will."

"You can't know that." Lucifer's voice was so quiet his words were almost indecipherable.

"Have you looked at my sword lately?" Azrael smiled. "Knowing things is my entire job description. I tried to scratch knowledge out and replace it with wisdom, but it clearly didn't work."

The lines on Lucifer's face softened, and he let out a short chuckle.

"The joke was worth more than that," Azrael insisted.

Lucifer sat up and pulled Azrael into a tight hug. He pressed their foreheads together before releasing him. "I'm going to lay down for a while. Should I come get you when I wake up? We can watch her together."

Azrael nodded, his heart pounding so hard he thought it might leap from his chest. As Lucifer disappeared into his room, the weight of the day fell on Azrael's shoulders, and a bone-deep weariness overcame him. He crawled into Morghan's seat and curled up there, his thoughts drifting from Lucifer to Morghan and back again as the cool granite chilled his skin.

"Azrael." Lucifer stood in his doorway, one hand rubbing along the back of his neck. He abandoned the nervous gesture and held out his hand. "Maybe it's better if you're in here with me. I mean..."

Azrael sat up, and his brow furrowed.

"I'd feel better if you weren't alone. For safety's sake." There was a long pause before Lucifer let out a frustrated sigh. "I don't want to be alone, either."

The spires of Malon grew steadily closer as they melted into the blood red horizon. Michael shifted uncomfortably in his horse's saddle. He could have walked faster than this. His ass was numb as shit, and he could really use a drink. He glanced at Morghan, who continued to fiddle with her bare arms, which were raw and bleeding, mostly because she wouldn't stop scratching them. It was bad enough he had to watch her strip the blisters from them one thin, slippery piece of skin at a time when they had first left the settlement, but now that the wounds were scabbing she had to torture him with this. He wasn't sure why she didn't heal as fast as he did. Sure, the settlement was less than a day behind them, but with wounds like that, and being healthy when they were scored, the burns would have been a memory before he ever mounted his horse. He forced his eyes from her arms, instead concentrating on the steady descent of the sun.

"Faster?" Michael offered, hoping she would agree. The sooner they got to Malon the sooner he could get off this damn horse.

Morghan shook her head. "The first and last time I rode a horse was on a family vacation when I was ten. Bastard walked into the shallows of a river and laid down. My brother never let me forget it." She glanced over at Michael.

"I'll learn, don't get me wrong, but today, I'm taking it slow."

Michael had a hard time picturing her as someone's sibling. "Your family sounds like it was a lot nicer than mine."

She shrugged. "It was until it wasn't."

"What, they turned out to be assholes in the end, too?"

"No, it's just hard to be nice once you're dead." There wasn't a hint of emotion in her voice.

"Oh, sorry."

"No reason to be sorry. It took less than a minute for them to go from a loving family to rotting corpses, but it was kind of like ripping off a bandage. Didn't have much time to dwell on it back then. Being thirteen in the foster system was like clawing your way up through Dante's Inferno, and focusing on the past would have sunk me."

Michael wished he had the ability to forget his past. Life would be so much simpler.

"Forgetting your past is dangerous, but so is dwelling on it. Your problem has always been balance, or lack thereof. You need to learn to use your past to make you stronger without letting it consume you."

"That's easy for you to say." Michael was about sick of her picking his thoughts out of thin air. "The horrors in your past are far removed and not your fault. Mine stick to me like a shadow, and I have only myself to blame."

"I gave you a ten second excerpt from a life spanning over half a million years. Granted, most of what shaped me into who I am happened when I was mortal, but that's still forty-three years you know fuck all about. You're not the only one with problems, Michael, but not everyone wears them on their sleeve like a badge of honor. The sooner you realize that, the better off we'll all be."

Michael cut angry eyes to her before urging his horse faster, relieved when she didn't pick up her pace. She could continue the slow ride to Malon alone. If she found him when she made it, which he had no doubt she would, at least he'd have a full stomach and a blissfully swimming head to aid him in dealing with her.

He entered Malon through one of the many open archways that led into the heart of the city. There were no gates needed here. Sinner and saint were welcomed all the same, and an unspoken law that the territory within the arches remained neutral was known throughout the realm.

The spires of the central keep towered endlessly upward, and though they stood black against the evening sky, Michael knew them to be as crimson as the horizon they'd shown against earlier that day. He brought his horse to a small stable not far from the city center and handed the reins to the woman leaning against the wall outside it. He brought a copper coin out of his pocket and tossed it into the dented tin cup at her feet.

She bent down and picked through the coins before plucking out the one he had thrown and tossing it back to him. "Free boarding, my lord. The matriarch would have my head if I took your coin."

Michael opened his mouth to protest, but the woman had already led the horse toward a stall. His teeth slid angrily across one another, but he turned toward the keep without a word.

Laughter and foul language met his ears in equal measure as he stepped into the front hall of the stone giant. Torchlight bounced around the room from every angle until dark corners disappeared and the room shone like a midsummer's day. Men and women in various states of undress flitted about the cavernous room and occupied enormous tables that could be used for so much more than the mundane act of eating.

Michael made his way to the bar and took an empty seat before banging a fist on the polished wood to signal the barkeep. His eyes roamed as he waited. Unlike most cities in the realm, where brothels were hidden away in the darkest alleys as houses of ill-repute, Malon glorified in what it was. The city thrived on lust and satisfying the most imaginative carnal desires. When dealing in their trade, supply was always the problem, because only the end of the human race could threaten demand.

"You're a bit overdressed, my dear."

The familiar voice brought a smile to Michael's lips.

"Tyrra!" he cried, turning back to the bar. His smile faded when his eyes met the woman on the other side. Silver shined in her hair and skin gathered at the corners of the spritely brown eyes he knew so well. The skin covering her bare chest was still bronze and flawless, but everything stretched toward the floor a little more than he remembered.

Tyrra's face turned down, and she muttered a short prayer before raising her eyes to his. "Thirty years, Michael. You haven't aged a day. Mother was right."

He forced a smile. "How is Tena these days?"

"Long ago in the ground." Sorrow flickered across her face before a practiced cheerfulness replaced it. She leaned across the bar and engaged him in a long, leisurely kiss. "The city is mine now, and one day, when you stride in here still shining as the epitome of youth, it will belong to my daughter.

"But all that unpleasantness aside." She retreated across the bar and made a beckoning gesture with her hand. "Your shirt, love. You know the rules. No one is served fully dressed."

Michael pulled off his shirt and slid it across the bar. He opened his mouth to order but she silenced him with a finger to his lips. "I know what you like." She winked before turning and walking away with his shirt held tight to her chest.

He would have sworn he half loved the woman not long ago, but had it really been thirty years since he'd been to Malon? His thoughts were interrupted as Morghan collapsed in the seat next to him, chest heaving.

"Fucking horse." She left it at that. When she turned to face Michael her eyes slid past him to a man smoking a hand-rolled cigarette a few seats down the bar. "Holy mother of God! What body part do I have to sell to get one of those?"

"You'll have to ask him," Michael answered as Tyrra returned with a large glass of crystal clear liquid that had a tight swirl of blue floating within it. She leaned over the glass and bit the tip of her tongue. A single drop of blood fell into the drink, and as it hit the fluid and diffused through it the blue swirl exploded like a thousand tiny, multicolored fireworks, turning the liquid into a rainbow of colors before they ultimately joined and darkened.

"Amazing!" Morghan's eyes were wide as they moved from the now black drink to Michael, and across the bar to Tyrra. "I'll take whatever that is."

"It's called an Edge of Eternity," a silvery, masculine voice answered as a slender man with long platinum hair and not a stitch of clothing took a seat on the other side of Morghan. His light grey eyes glittered in the torchlight, his skin so pale it was almost translucent. "An Evenstar specialty. Very exclusive."

Morghan's chair screeched against the floor as she hopped it closer to Michael. "What the Hell are you?"

The man's eyes flashed before his gaze slid to Michael. He inclined his head. "Maritch, we have much to speak of. I'm thankful my search for you is finally at an end."

"It's been too long, Valerian." Michael raised his drink toward the Evenstar Clan's leader and nodded in kind, although he could have done with a few more centuries without laying eyes on him. It wasn't that he felt remorse over creating the Evenstars, but they were beyond long-lived, and, despite his insistence, refused to treat him as an equal. He was certain their deference and constant use of the title they had bestowed upon him was the reason humanity continued to treat him as other.

The heavy tapping of Tyrra's finger against the bar broke into their greeting. She held another Edge in one hand while pointing to Morghan with the other. "You're not exempt, honey. Take that coat off and let's see what's underneath."

"A ruined shirt," Morghan grumbled. "And I'm good, thanks."

Michael nudged Morghan's shoulder. "Being completely clothed in here is considered rude to the matriarch." He nodded toward Tyrra. "Which is her. If she tells you to take your clothes off, you just do."

"I just don't," Morghan insisted. She crossed her arms over her chest and turned back to Tyrra. "I don't undress on command. Isn't that's your job?"

Glass shattered as Tyrra dropped the Edge and leapt over the bar. She grabbed Morghan by the hair and dragged her across it. The two disappeared to the other side before Michael knew what was happening.

Michael stood so fast his chair toppled behind him. He leaned over the bar until he had a clear view of them. Tyrra lay on her back, her chestnut hair flooding the floor behind her. One of her arms wrapped around Morghan's neck, the thin, gleaming stiletto that served as her hairpin pressed hard against the back of Morghan's ear. Morghan's arms were crossed above her head, a dagger in each hand with the blades resting against either side of Tyrra's neck.

"Morghan, what are you doing!" Michael vaulted over the bar.

"Trying to be diplomatic? She's not dead, is she?" Morghan winced when Tyrra pressed harder in response to the quip, causing blood to spiral down the thin blade.

"Enough!" Michael's voice boomed, echoing off the walls. His eyes burned, and he saw the white-hot light within them reflected in the widened eyes of Tyrra and Morghan. Thunder rumbled outside, and the room fell silent.

Both women opened their hands, the weapons clattering to the ground.

Michael turned back to the room and groaned. Every last person was on their knees, foreheads to the ground. He jumped back over the bar and stalked out of the building, fists clenched at his sides.

Morghan scrambled to her feet and followed Michael. Rain beat down from the sky in sheets, soaking through her coat the moment she stepped outside. She could barely see him ahead, and he was gaining distance on her.

She mumbled a curse under her breath and picked up speed, her boots sloshing in the mud. She had centuries of practice dealing with brooding angels, and she still hadn't learned when to hold her tongue; so much for wisdom coming with age. Maybe she should have taken her coat off, and what she imagined would have ended up as a request for her shirt as well. It was only skin after all, but if she was honest with herself, if she had it to do over again it would have ended no different. She'd only willingly undressed for two men before, a skeevy little son-of-a-bitch from her mortal life, who had at least given her a son, and Luke. This far in, she was unlikely to become nonchalant about putting her body on display for strangers.

Her thoughts were so scattered she didn't notice Michael standing in front of her until she ran into his chest. Morghan backed up and glared at him. White sparks wove through his irises, cracking the sapphire flames that burned there. Blood ran in rivers from his nose and the corners of his mouth as the rain grabbed each gathering drop and forced it toward the ground.

"Your sword!" he pointed to her hip, apparently not at all concerned with how many inches of rain he poured onto a city that was ill-equipped for it. Standing water was quickly turning into a moving entity as mud slid down from the steeper alleys nearby.

"Turn it off!" she screamed at him, waving a hand at the sky. "Calm down and let the storm pass!"

"I can't!" His brow creased and he bent over, coughing a large clot of blood onto the ground. "I haven't been angry or strong enough for this in centuries."

"Just let your wings out, for God's sake," she pleaded. "It will help ground you. I promise."

He shook his head, and his face twisted into a mask of pain. "My father took them away. They won't come back."

No wonder they hadn't seen him use his wings since Nikoli had shown him how to shape shift them away. He never learned how to release them. Morghan added another page to her mental "death to Nikoli" folder and took a step toward Michael. "We can figure this out."

He took a step back and pointed to her sword again. "Show me!"

Michael had clearly lost his mind, but if she didn't figure out how to calm him down soon, half the city would wash away. "Show you what?"

"Your sword. What does it say?" Michael put his hands to the sides of his head and grimaced before looking back at her. "In the settlement earlier, I agreed to let you follow me to Malon because of what I thought I saw on your sword. But there's something so wrong with you. The way you act, the things you do. You killed five people today without blinking, and you enjoyed it. You almost killed Tyrra. Just show me I was hallucinating so I can forget it and be done with you."

Morghan steeled her expression against his words and filed them away to mull over at a later time. She popped the hilt from the sheath with the thumb of her right hand and drew it with her left before spearing it into the ground in front of him.

Michael stared at her sword, and the light shining in his eyes illuminated the word inscribed on the blade.

Redemption.

Angry eyes moved from her to the blade and back again before softening.

Her muscles tightened when he took a step forward and wrapped his arms around her. He tucked his face against her neck and sobbed.

"Where have you been?" Even with her enhanced hearing his words were barely audible.

His knees buckled as he passed out in her arms, and she struggled to remain standing when his weight hit her full force. She shifted his weight to make him easier to hold, but her boots slipped in the mud and she landed flat on her back with Michael laying bloody and unconscious across her chest.

Morghan closed her eyes and let out a long, slow breath, thankful that, if nothing else, the rain had stopped.

～

Michael swam up from the abyss, his eyes protesting as they opened to a dimly lit room. He turned onto his side and his muscles screamed despite the soft mattress whispering against his cheek. A deep, dull pain rolled within his abdomen, and when he tried to sit his stomach reeled. He bent over the edge of the bed and vomited into a large copper basin on the floor.

"Damn, I love being right," Morghan chuckled. "Now, I don't have to pay the Queen of Whoreville for any of this stuff. Not like I have money anyway."

Michael wiped his mouth with the back of his hand and cringed at the acrid red mess staining the basin. He looked up at Morghan. Could someone like her really be who he was waiting for? When Jessimine had given him his sword so long ago, the last thing she had said was that redemption would find him. He'd clung to those words for ages, never knowing what he was looking for until Morghan's sword had flashed in the sunlight the day before.

A low curse brought his attention back to the present.

Morghan sat in a chair across the room, intent on using a dagger to dig out the sole of what looked to be a new pair of boots. A clean white linen shirt covered her chest and black leather leggings trailed down to her bare feet.

"Don't do anything with that." Morghan looked up from

the boot and pointed to the basin with her dagger. "I told Tyrra we'd need that thing for you to puke in. She thought I was crazy, but blood never sits well on the stomach. We made a wager, and I'm sure she'll want proof I won."

"Why—" A hard knock on the door cut off his question.

Morghan rose from the chair and waved the boot in his direction before setting it on the ground. "I'm giving them better tread." She headed for the door. "This will be the shimmery asshole from downstairs. He's been banging on the door every five minutes demanding to talk to you about Galmedea. I don't think he understands the word unconscious."

Michael stretched his arms. Most of his body still throbbed, but his stomach felt better. "He doesn't understand patience. No one keeps the leader of the Evenstars waiting."

The angry banging repeated and Michael gestured toward the door. "Let him in. He'll tell me whatever about Galmedea and leave."

"I'd imagine the only thing to talk about is how it doesn't exist anymore," Morghan said as she reached for the doorknob.

"It what?" Michael was sure he heard her wrong, but as Valerian strode into the room, pushing past Morghan as if she didn't exist, a dark foreboding washed over him.

"Maritch." Valerian bowed low. "You're looking...well," he finished with a strained smile.

Michael glanced down at the specks of drying blood on his hands and shirt. "Lying doesn't suit your people, Valerian. It's not necessary to throw groundless compliments at me."

Valerian nodded, his gaze sliding to Morghan as she

returned to the chair and slipped the boots onto her feet. "Might I speak with you in private?"

Michael was surprised and a little dismayed the glare Morghan threw Valerian didn't cause him to burst into flames. She clearly had some control over the element, which he still needed to discuss with her.

"No, she stays."

Morghan sat back in her chair and threaded her fingers together, a satisfied grin plastered across her face.

"I come to speak of death, destruction, and the likelihood of war." Valerian frowned. "None of which are suitable topics for a woman."

"Unbelievable," Morghan said. "You live in a realm where women were created first, and currently stand in a city run by women, where I can only imagine you've come to discuss an invading horde led by a woman, yet you still somehow manage to be a misogynistic asshole." Morghan waved her arm in Valerian's direction while looking at Michael. "Can we go ahead and throw this guy out already?"

"How did you know I came to discuss the Falcroix Legion?" Valerian's eyes narrowed.

"The what?" Michael asked.

Valerian pulled a small, ragged piece of cloth from his pocket and handed it to Michael. The fabric was a shade of grey that begged the question of what color it had once been. The image of the forsaken that marked every brothel the realm over save Malon stood out from it in such a way Michael was certain it had been dyed in blood. "Galmedea is a memory. Alara has amassed an army of thousands and stolen it out from under its people. They call themselves the Falcroix Legion and have renamed the city in kind."

Michael turned the cloth over in his hands. "Thousands of what? Men?"

"Blood drinkers, like herself," Valerian answered.

"Flesh-eaters," Morghan corrected. "From what I can tell Alara is the only one who needs blood."

"Do not interrupt me, woman!" Valerian seethed.

"It's Windstarr. Not girl. Not woman. Windstarr," Morghan bit out. "And I'll interrupt you if you're wrong. Alara makes men into those creatures by feeding them her blood, sure, but they don't drink it afterwards." She turned to Michael. "Trust me, my friends and I have been watching this evolve for years. They're basically this world's version of orcs."

Michael made a mental note to ask more about her friends at a later time. Soon, he'd have to start writing all these questions down or he'd forget them, especially since he was having a difficult time wrapping his head around anything that had been said in the last few minutes.

"I don't understand." Michael shook his head. "Galmedea is gone? Did they destroy the entire city?"

"No," Valerian answered, shifting his eyes to Morghan for a moment as if daring her to challenge him. "As best we can tell, they ravaged it from the inside. Most, if not all life in the upper three tiers was lost. The lower two remain intact as a slave state." He pointed to the cloth Michael held. "They fly this as their banner."

"But I just spoke with her not three months ago," Michael said, mostly to himself. He thought her comment about razing the city had been tongue-in-cheek. And then she had taunted him about wanting to be alone. His breath caught as he realized his error. His heart pounded in his ears, and his gaze flew to Morghan. "She wanted me to leave. I could have stopped this."

"I think it's time for you to go," he heard Morghan say, presumably to Valerian, although he'd lost focus on what was happening in the room. His mind continued to run over every word and mannerism from his short meeting with Alara.

Out of the corner of his eye, he saw Morghan stand, and he barely registered the unsheathed sword hanging at her side.

This was his fault in so many ways. He had created Alara and allowed her to live, knowing full well what was necessary for her survival. He had imbued the most honorable of his creations with power in the hopes they would counter the darkness he'd spawned, but the Evenstars had grown into a proud, fickle people. Instead of protecting the humans, they looked down on them, treasuring their own ways above all else. He had no doubt what brought Valerian to him now had nothing to do with the tragedy in Galmedea and everything to do with his kingdom being a stone's throw from the once great city.

"Hey!" Morghan's voice sounded distant, despite the fact she was kneeling in front of him. "Get it together!"

Pain erupted across his cheek, and the world snapped back into focus. He brought a hand up to the side of his face.

"Welcome back," Morghan said, shaking her left hand out and blowing on the palm.

"I have to go to Galmedea." He attempted to stand, but Morghan pressed down firmly on his shoulders.

"It's Falcroix now, and no, you don't." Morghan held him in place for a long moment before dropping her hands to her sides. "Your power is unpredictable and still worse, uncontrollable. You've never killed a man, and you don't even know how to use the sword you carry."

"I can't die, Morghan," he said. "I can deal with them all myself, sword or no sword. Power or no power."

"They can't kill you, but they can hurt you." Morghan stood and stared down at him in a way that made him feel like a small child. "Alara would bleed you dry and keep you as a trophy, harvesting every drop of blood your body produced. Do you want to be an empty shell on her wall for eternity?"

"No," he whispered. The thought of being kept prisoner had never crossed his mind. "This is my fault, Morghan. I need to fix it. How do I make it right?"

"Oh, we'll make it right." The light that sparked in Morghan's eyes was at once brilliant and chilling. "But first, we need an army."

Alara drummed her fingers on the armrest of her gilded throne. Her glazed eyes moved from one end of the spacious throne room to the other, marking the dull crimson of the floor at her feet. In the beginning, her floor had gleamed red and shimmered in the sunlight that filtered through the towering windows. There were days she could have lapped the blood of her enemies from those floors, giddy with the lingering warmth of their life force as it caressed its way down her throat and spread through her body.

By now, the pair of guards milling around the entrance was more for show than anything else. There hadn't been a challenge from within the city for weeks, and the fields beyond the walls of Falcroix remained silent. She had no doubt other cities were teeming with conversation and worry over the fall of Galmedea, but the problem with deci-mating one of the largest cities in the realm was it made those who might oppose her loathe to tempt fate. After being thrust into the dregs of humanity and spending two centuries yearning for a kingdom of her own, one would have hoped to find victory slightly less boring.

The double doors at the far end of the hall creaked open, and a bald man with a solid build shuffled through them.

"Bleak, you've kept me waiting for ages," Alara purred, smiling into the man's pale eyes as he neared her. She'd been feeding on him for days, bleeding even the washed out grey from his tired eyes. With a wealth of mortals to feast on, while killing them in a single feeding was fun, it was no longer necessary. She could sip their life away one day at a time, their eyes fading to blank, shining white orbs that conveniently signaled the end of their usefulness. Bleak had two or three small meals left in him before she'd snap his neck and offer him as a gift to her soldiers. A shame, as he'd lasted far longer than most, easily twice as long as the remainder of his family combined.

"My apologies for displeasing you, my queen," he droned, bowing low as he reached the base of her dais. He lifted a squirming lump of cloth above his head. "I was procuring a gift."

Alara leaned forward, craning her neck for a better look. Bleak refused to take the hint to move closer, and the gift remained just out of reach. She snapped her fingers and pointed at the parcel. Guards rushed from their posts, falling over one another to reach the dais first.

The victor snatched up her gift and a screeching cry emanated from within the cloth before morphing into a steady wail. In his shock, the guard fumbled the contents, and a human infant fell through his hands. It hit the cold stone floor with a crack, its cries reaching a crescendo.

Its neck bent at an odd angle, and the majority of its once squirming body remained still. Alara's hand deftly moved to hover over her womb, or rather, the place her womb should have been. Centuries had passed since she had pined for a child. Michael's child. Memories of a different life flooded in, and her eyes narrowed as they returned to Bleak. "A baby?"

"I hear the blood of the new affects you most," Bleak stated noncommittally. The slightest smirk touched the corner of his mouth, and she would have sworn his eyes darkened a shade.

She unwrapped herself from the throne and nudged the baby aside with her foot before beckoning Bleak forward.

His once again pale eyes remained unblinking as he mounted the steps and stood before her. Alara snaked a hand around the back of his neck and pulled him closer, her lips whispering against the skin below his ear.

"You dare mock me?" Her teeth scraped his earlobe, and the first drops of blood rolled over her tongue before she bit down hard enough to sever it from the rest of his ear.

Bleak screamed and fell to his knees, clutching his ear. He turned angry eyes up from the floor, and Alara took a step back, appalled that they had returned to their original hue. "The Maritch will rise, and you will be no more than a stain on the memory of our people."

Rage swept through her, and her vision dimmed. Alara had every intention of making him suffer. He would scream and beg for mercy as she stripped him of his skin.

Why then, was his head in her hands, his spine wagging below it like a clock's pendulum while his body lay crumpled on the other side of the room? She blinked away the haze of anger and tossed Bleak's severed head to the floor. It rolled down the steps before coming to rest at the base of the dais, and even in death his expression taunted her.

Alara returned to the infant struggling on the floor, its cries now reduced to a gurgling whimper. She wrapped the cloth around it and cradled it in her arms. Her hips swayed as she walked toward the balcony, humming under her breath and gently rocking her arms.

The sun warmed her face as she stepped through the open windows, and the metal bannisters of the lower tiers gleamed red below her. She imagined for a moment that the child was hers, that Michael hadn't vehemently opposed every request she'd made for him to give her one. She had stayed faithful to him for so many years, but when it became clear he wouldn't give her what she wanted, she'd gone looking for it elsewhere. By the time Michael had caught her, she'd started to think it was her fault no children had been conceived.

While her sins had been many, she hadn't deserved this accursed thirst.

Bleak's words echoed in her mind. *The Maritch will rise.*

Oh, how she hoped he would.

She had ravaged his city and made a feast of his people, but still he had not come. She would take her time ripping his precious realm apart piece by glorious piece until the injustice was so great he would have no choice but to face her.

And then she would have him. With Michael as an endless fount of blood, she would never have to worry about losing herself to the madness again.

Alara stepped to the balcony's edge and stared down into the pained expression of the child in her arms. "The world is so dark, little one," she whispered, caressing a wisp of hair from its forehead. "And you have only your maker to blame."

She brushed her lips across the child's wet cheek and tossed it over the side. Alara turned back to the throne room and slammed the doors behind her, deciding it was high time to pull more souls from the lower tiers and paint the floors anew.

4

THOSE FOOLS DIDN'T DIE IN A
SNOWDRIFT AFTER ALL

MORGHAN HUNCHED FORWARD as she led her horse through the outskirts of Vahyir. Nearly five years had passed since they'd first visited Malon, and she was beyond tired of traveling from one city to the next kissing the asses of royals in a vain attempt to garner support against Falcroix. For someone who complained so much about being revered as a god, Michael found few in his realm willing to risk their lives for him.

A wealth of severed heads from the Falcroix Legion stared down at them as they passed through the gates and entered the city proper. Fields of soldiers running through drills fanned out beyond it, and still farther out, the Galean Sea glittered in the sunlight, scores of ships rocking in the gently rolling waters. Goods and passengers shuffled between the vessels and shore like so many ants.

Michael cleared his throat, pulling Morghan's attention away from her surroundings. "Vahyir is different from the other cities we've visited."

"You mean they're going to say yes?" she sniped, running a hand over her face in frustration. "Sorry."

"No, you're not." Michael tugged harder on his horse's lead and pulled ahead of her.

Morghan didn't feel like going faster. She didn't feel like going anywhere except the one place she could never go. Home. She gripped the leather reins in her hand more tightly as she trudged ahead to catch up with Michael. Stalking him when she'd first come to the realm had kept her mind occupied enough she could half convince herself this stretch of time was no different from her stints in Nikoli's realm. These days, she had nothing to do but think on the long trips from one place to the next, and it was hard to ignore that this time there was no scheduled homecoming to look forward to.

For a while she'd hoped Luke would refuse to accept the way Nikoli had forced her to leave. She'd dreamed of waking up to his warm embrace, even if he couldn't stay long, but the monotonous passage of time had warped those dreams into something vile. Instead of looking forward to them, she feared sleep, more often than not opting to doze fully clothed and armed in the cramped corner of a room instead of using a bed. Each time her dreams brought Luke or Azrael within arm's reach, it was that much harder to face reality when she woke.

"No, really," Morghan said, attempting to smooth things over with Michael. She caught up with him in front of a large wooden building that reminded her of something out of Norse mythology and tied her horse on a hitching post next to his. "Tell me what's different about the leaders here."

Michael looked up, but when he opened his mouth a voice boomed from the front steps of the building.

"Michael, I was beginning to wonder if you'd forgotten us." The man standing on the top step had hair and skin as pale as Valerian's, but his dark eyes shone in stark contrast to the rest of him. The armor he wore was laden with overlapping scales of thick grey metal that clanked against one another as he descended the stairs, and the rich purple cloak draped over his shoulders waved in the breeze. A longsword hung at his left hip, and although well-worn leather strips covered most of the ivory hilt, it was topped with an intricately carved, one-eyed eagle.

"Kayne." Michael inclined his head. "How could I forget a great city such as yours?"

Kayne gave a half-smile. His gaze slid to Morghan for a moment before returning to Michael. "It's only that I imagine if someone was looking for an alliance to assist in waging war, they might visit the strongest military power in the realm first. Do you think so little of me and mine?"

The disappointment hanging on Kayne's features told Morghan the one way this city would not be different was in its answer to their request for assistance. In the end, it was her fault for not taking charge of their itinerary after the first few rejections. Kayne was right; they should have made it to Vahyir long ago.

"Come," Kayne beckoned, mounting the steps. "It's not fitting to talk of war in the open, let alone on an empty stomach."

When Kayne reached the door he barked an order in a language Morghan had never heard before, and the double doors opened wide, revealing a large room with several long tables and a trinity of thrones clustered at the far end. The large throne in the middle stood empty, but the two smaller ones flanking it were filled by children, their pale skin and dark eyes an echo of Kayne's. As they approached the thrones, Morghan noted each child, one boy and one girl, wore their own set of scaled armor and carried a short sword with a hilt not unlike their father's, despite her guess that their ages were well under double digits. Servants milled about the room with trays of food that were largely ignored.

"Twins are revered here," Michael whispered. "They've been born into the royal family every generation for over two-hundred years. Birth order matters little. The line of succession comes down to which heir sires a set of twins first.

That had to make for a healthy family dynamic. The reverence of twins would have been intriguing in almost any other light. If her mother was to be believed, Morghan had been a twin for the most part of a trimester. Luckily for the rest of the world, there ended up being only one of her.

Kayne took a seat in his throne and gestured to Morghan. "I heard tell you traveled with a woman these days. Shall we excuse her while we discuss this messy business?"

Morghan scuffed her boot against the floor and glared down at it. She was so sick of the casual misogyny. For the past few centuries, she had been isolated from misogynistic bullshit. Every bit she had experienced came from short interactions with Krishna or Nikoli, and who gave a shit what they thought? Now it was everywhere. She wasn't a person here. She was Michael's companion, and she could guess what type of companion they painted her as in their narrow little minds. Case in point, this condescending jerk thought she was less competent than the children seated at his side.

She longed to take him down a notch, but she held her tongue. Michael had begged her again and again not to speak when they were in the presence of royalty, since each time she did they were invariably thrown out on their asses with nothing to show for it. She took a deep breath and started a slow count to ten, one of the few tactics she employed that worked. Sometimes.

"No," Michael said. "She is my general. If there's a plan to be made, she's to know of it."

Morghan breathed out slowly before looking up at the thrones once more. The girl to Kayne's right beamed at her, and Morghan smiled back before thinking better of it.

"Kayla!" Kayne barked, and his open hand came down hard against the back of the girl's head. He turned back to them and frowned. "My apologies. She has yet to learn to school her expressions. Creator willing, that will be remedied before she takes the throne."

Morghan cut her eyes to Michael. She was pretty sick of hearing the creator's name invoked in front of them, especially since it was more often than not followed by an insult to the very person they asked for help.

"Also, Michael." Here it came. "I hate to be the bearer of bad news, but you need an army before appointing a general."

Morghan had brought that up no less than a thousand times, but Michael was adamant when it came to introducing her as such. He claimed it was better than his "assassin friend," but she begged to differ. Assassin friend had a nice ring to it and was a damn sight more terrifying and deserving of respect than being the general of a nonexistent army. Also, he could have just used her name.

"I was hoping you might assist me with that," Michael pressed on. One of Michael's superpowers was the ability to believe in an endeavor long after it had been beaten to a pulp and left for dead. Morghan could only hope one day he would develop something more useful, like common sense or the ability to shapeshift his wings back into existence. He would be a lot harder to turn down with wings.

59

"Clearly, the heads speared on your gate demonstrate our goals are one and the same."

"My goal is to protect my people from threats outside our borders as well as within." His brow knit together. "Of late, Falcroix demands monthly human tributes. Those heads will multiply until the requests cease. I will not send my people to slaughter, by Alara's order or yours. You may be long-lived, Michael, but you are not my Creator. I will not force my people into the service of a false god with no kingdom or following."

Morghan leaned closer to Michael. "Now would be a great time to break out some thunder and lightning," she whispered.

Michael's jaw tightened, but he refused to even look at her.

"Excuse me?" Kayne inquired, his eyes narrowing.

Morghan pointed to Michael and back to herself before waving a hand in dismissal. "General stuff."

Kayne scowled. "I have given you my answer. That does not mean Vahyir has forgotten that you helped build and name this great city, and you are, as always, welcome here. Her." He pointed to Morghan. "I do not trust. I have a strong suspicion she revels in chaos, but since she is yours, she may stay as long as I have your word my city will remain safe."

"I have her under control," Michael assured him. "She's harmless."

Morghan cut her eyes toward Michael before looking back at Kayne. Had her under control? He wished.

～

Michael watched the golden bubbles floating through the mug of ale on the table in front of him, jealous of the progress they made in their quest to the top of his drink. This was it. Now he'd have to take on Falcroix alone. Morghan wouldn't be able to convince him otherwise. They'd crisscrossed the realm, and he'd begged every leader on the planet to join him, with only a few of the smaller, more superstitious kingdoms agreeing. Valerian had become relentless in his pursuit. Evenstar clansmen hounded them at every turn, begging him to do something about Alara and her ever increasing demands for goods and sacrifices.

He had a hard time understanding why Alara hadn't expanded her borders since claiming Galmedea. Threats abounded, and although many cities cooperated in full to stave off invasion, it still didn't make sense. Arden was the closest city of any consequence, only a week's ride from Falcroix, and they had reportedly not cooperated at all. Alara's forces could have easily swooped in and swallowed the city whole, rendering the Evenstars little more than a memory. Valerian was right about one thing: it was only a matter of time before Alara got bored with however she currently busied herself and pushed harder to spread her influence.

Morghan burst through the door of the tavern, and her eyes shone like emerald flames when she spotted him. She slid into his side of the bench seat, getting far too close. After her mouth ruining their last chance at a useful alliance, he didn't feel like being in her company.

"I've got an idea," she said.

Michael raised his glass to his mouth and drained it without taking a breath. "I'm sure you do."

"Look at this." She slammed a rolled up piece of parchment on the table in front of him, unfazed by his indifference. That was the thing about Morghan: it wasn't that she didn't recognize social cues, she simply didn't give a shit about what anyone else thought.

Michael closed his eyes for a long moment before opening them and unrolling the parchment. The faster he did what she wanted, the sooner she would leave him alone. His brow furrowed as he looked down at the most intricate map of the realm he'd ever seen. Most of it was drawn and labeled in thick black strokes, but a few cities, some he'd never even heard of, were in a gleaming, smeary red. Galmedea had been struck through and Falcroix scrawled beneath it.

"Bal Mek is fairly new." Morghan pointed to one of the red cities before moving her finger southeast and tapping Malon. A large X with a circle around it had been placed between the two cities. "Before it was built, leaving Malon meant more than a month to get anywhere worth going, and there are several equally spaced options." She pointed to Predlitz, Sheltinata, and Grenz. I've been told if you ride your horse so hard it dies beneath you on the last day, the trip from Malon to Bal Mek can be made in less than a fortnight. Do you know what that means?"

"Someone has been needlessly killing horses to see how fast they can travel?" Michael signaled the barkeep and a fresh glass appeared before him a few seconds later.

Morghan glared at him and turned back to the map. "Bal Mek is now the preferred travel route from Malon. Its population has exploded since being built, mostly because it provides a resting point between Malon and Predlitz." She pointed to the X with the circle around it. "This is roughly halfway between Malon and Bal Mek. About a week's ride, slightly more if you're traveling heavy. I don't know about you, but after three or four days sleeping on the ground, I'm sick of it."

"So stop following me around." That would be best for everyone, because although she tried his patience, he didn't want to drag her into whatever bleak fate awaited him in Falcroix.

He slid the map back to her and reached for his drink, but she snatched it and downed the ale before slamming the glass on the table so hard Michael wondered how it didn't shatter.

"Pay attention!" She jammed her finger at the X again. "This spot is roughly a week from Bal Mek and Malon. Nothing there but rolling hills and forest. There's even a river nearby."

"And?"

"Really?" Morghan asked, exasperated. "Kayne was right; you need an army. Maybe not just an army, a kingdom."

"I need a lot of things." He signaled for another drink, intent on holding it close to his chest when it came. "A kingdom isn't one of them."

"It is, and we can build one. A large city at the very least." Morghan pushed the map toward him again. "This place is perfect. It's in the heart of the realm with mild weather and would fill out part of a great trade route. Depending on the lay of the land, it's possible we could even use the river to irrigate crops."

"Sure, we'll irrigate crops we don't know how to grow in a city we don't know how to build. Brilliant."

"It is brilliant. You're not thinking large scale." She glanced toward the tavern entrance and made a beckoning gesture with her hand before turning back to Michael. "Building something takes planning, strength, and time.

We're stronger than any of these people, and all we have is time. I know we could put our heads together to plan a city more advanced than anything this realm currently has. Once we build it, irrigation is a pull no one else in your realm has yet. We don't need to farm the land, Michael. Someone else will come do it for us."

"I don't want a kingdom, Morghan. Or a city. I can't even control myself, let alone a city full of people. Trying to gather an army was a mistake."

She ignored him and turned to the middle-aged man who approached their table. He rubbed a hand over his arm, the mahogany skin beneath it rough from wear. His eyes, their irises so dark brown they blended into the pupils, darted from Morghan to Michael before landing on the parchment. Well, that solved the mystery of where she got the map.

"Meet Rothert." Morghan pointed to the bench on the other side of the table, and Rothert dropped onto it. "He comes from a long line of merchants, one of whom was the driving force behind the founding of Bal Mek. Now he's looking for a venture of his own."

Michael reached across the table and shook Rothert's trembling hand. With the hand away from his arm, it was more obvious both his arms were unsteady, and Michael noted even his head trembled the slightest bit. "Morghan, you've scared the man half to death."

Morghan kicked him under the table.

"I'm not afraid." Rothert frowned, his voice as unsteady as his hands. He nodded to Morghan. "She's the only person who's bothered listening to me."

"If you could share the secret of getting her to listen, I'd appreciate it." Michael's newest drink was almost gone again, but he wasn't feeling any effect. He either had to pick up the pace or switch to something stronger. He hated that it took so much alcohol to numb his senses, but even if he wasn't revered enough to gather an army, he held enough clout to allow for an infinite bar tab in most cities whether he had the money to pay it or not. In the end, he preferred the latter, anyway. "And I'm sorry to waste your time, but building a new city doesn't interest me. I helped build dozens of the ones already standing, but it took hundreds of people several years to accomplish. We have three people and no resources. You would be dead and buried long before any semblance of a city we built was livable."

"Living to see it finished was never my intention." He moved his hand back to grasp his arm. "I have six grown sons and strong family ties that can provide most resources, the rest of which we can take from the land. If we build a tavern first, it will serve as a place for travelers to rest. We can employ their help instead of charging for their stay. Money is no problem, but security is. My sons are smiths, tailors, and alchemists. We would start this ourselves, but the last thing I want is to get partway through and have someone sweep in and steal it out from under us." He nodded toward the map. "My family has been working on this map for generations. It's time to add another new city. This will be our legacy."

Michael opened his mouth to apologize, but Morghan shoved a hand in his chest. She pulled the map out from under his hand and pushed it across the table to Rothert.

"Thank you. You're free to go." She nodded to the door. "We'll discuss this more, and I'll have an answer for you by morning."

Rothert tucked the map into the inner lining of his cloak and shuffled away without a word.

"It's nearly two months' ride to the spot on his map,"

Michael complained. Which was only made worse by the fact they would have to give Falcroix a wide berth on the way there.

"We could always go to Bal Mek first." Morghan leaned over the table, resting her head on threaded fingers. "Neither of us has been there, and it would probably be a good idea to check it out."

"That's even farther out of the way." Michael scowled. "We just got here. It's the tail end of spring and Vahyir has everything we could possibly need."

"Including a leader who despises us."

"You. He specifically said you. Kayne may be a pompous ass at times, but he's a good man and a better leader."

"Fine," Morghan huffed. "It will take Rothert some time to get word to his family anyway. We'll stay here through the summer to give the couriers a head start and then head south again. I refuse to be stuck here when the snow hits."

Michael pinched the bridge of his nose. "I didn't agree to any of this."

Morghan rose from the bench and pulled a cigarette from her pocket. She lit it with the candle in the center of the table, and the tip glowed when she shoved it between her lips. Smoke streamed from her nose. "But it's been a good five minutes since you said no."

Michael hung his head and gave a weak nod. One day he would figure out how to wipe that smirk off her face. But not today.

5

THE BEST LAID PLANS

Two months had been a pipe dream. Michael glanced at Morghan, who was half asleep on top of her horse despite the sun being high in the sky. Maybe if she slept more, or at all, she wouldn't practically fall off her horse every few days when exhaustion overwhelmed her. They were well into their fourth month of travel, and while they had bypassed Falcroix over a month ago, this all-important spot where they were to build a city was nowhere to be found.

Rothert insisted they were close, but he'd been saying that for days. Not to mention the fact he rode slow and needed frequent stops to rest. It was like traveling with a small child, if the child had to stop to piss every hour and then fell asleep under a tree for half the day.

Morghan had been no help in that regard. She provided zero pushback when he asked to stop. When it came to Rothert, the woman he had come to know over the last several years was nowhere to be found, replaced by someone with infinite patience Michael couldn't hope to match.

"Morghan, wake up." He moved his horse closer to hers

and nudged her leg with his foot. She opened her eyes and sat up straight in the saddle. "Don't want you falling off the horse. Again."

She mumbled something under her breath. He didn't catch it, though he could guess the gist. He was so bored, a low drone buzzed in the back of his mind, and as they continued on it only grew stronger.

Rothert rode to his side. His lips were moving, but Michael couldn't hear anything over the sound in his head. Rothert pointed in front of them and mouthed a word again. Michael looked ahead and brought his horse to a halt. There were only a few hundred feet left before the ground sloped down and dropped out from under them. Rothert stopped with him and continued to point frantically toward the cliff. Morghan was slumped over in her saddle again and showing no signs of stopping as she headed for the cliff.

Michael's heart pounded as he gunned his mount. While her horse was unlikely to walk over the edge, with her being half asleep it could easily stop short and throw her. He passed her and made a quick turn to put himself between her and the cliff. His horse's back legs slipped on loose stones and it scrambled for a moment before the crumbling edge gave way.

Michael sprang from the horse as it fell. He clawed at what was left of the rocky ledge, but nothing he grabbed would hold. A hand locked around his wrist, and Morghan's face appeared over the edge as his weight pulled her forward. Just as he felt they would go over together, Morghan winced, and they stopped, hanging in midair. He looked down, and his eyes widened when he spotted the churning whirlpool far below. A torrent of water flowed from a jagged mouth in the side of the cliff, and a massive river fed by the falls snaked through the trees below. It wasn't until then that he realized the sound in his head wasn't in his head at all.

Morghan squeezed his wrist harder, and he looked up into eyes glassy with pain. She gestured the way they'd come with a sideways nod of her head, and he could pick out "Any time now" from the movement of her lips.

Using the side of the cliff and more than a little of Morghan's body, he made his way back onto solid ground and pulled her up after him. She had cut one side of her reins and wrapped its end around her right wrist. It was a makeshift anchor that had served its purpose, though not without consequence. Blood trailed down Morghan's right arm, and her hand, fingers curled loosely around the leather strip, hung at an awkward angle above a wrist lain open to splintered bone.

The horse lay on its side, its flanks twitching. Michael cut through the side of the reins attached to the horse and knelt beside Morghan. She smiled and patted his knee with her uninjured hand as if unaware the other one was barely attached to her body. He picked her up and started back the way they'd come.

Rothert pointed down the hill that ran alongside the cliff, and Michael changed course. When the roar of water had faded enough he could hear himself think, he set Morghan on the ground and tried for a better look at her hand, but Rothert kept going without a word.

Morghan glanced at her wrist and sighed. "Might as well hack it off and start over. I doubt I'll ever get those bones to set well."

"And that's how I know you've never regenerated anything," Michael said. "We'll try salvaging it a few times before it comes to that." He started unwrapping the leather strap, but Morghan stopped him.

"Don't. It's probably keeping me from bleeding everywhere."

"You won't bleed out, and you can't keep this lashed around your wrist forever. It'll never heal."

She brought the arm up in front of her and turned it in various directions before holding it against her chest and slamming her good hand into a deformed part of her wrist. A litany of curses flew through the air, but the wrist flattened and looked less alien. "You can unwrap it. Slowly. Rewrap it into something more like a splint. Go from mid-forearm, around the wrist, and finally between my thumb and first finger. Secure it against my palm if you can."

Michael had almost finished unwrapping her wrist when the thunder of approaching horses echoed through the trees. Rothert appeared first, followed by six other men who bore a striking resemblance to him.

"This is Raelik, my eldest." Rothert nodded to a man who carried a large satchel over his shoulders. "He's a healer and an alchemist. He can tend her wounds."

Michael held pressure on the wrist and gave Morghan a questioning look.

She seemed less skeptical. "What do you have for pain?"

Raelik jumped from his horse and shuffled through his bag, finally coming out with a small stick. "Chew this."

Morghan assessed the stick for a moment before smiling and taking it. "Don't worry, you can let him do it," she assured Michael before shoving the stick partway into her mouth and munching on it. "Looks like a willow branch. Aspirin."

Relief washed over Michael as Raelik took his place. Michael wiped his hands on his pants and backed away until he was standing next to Rothert's hors, but his eyes never left Morghan. "Thank you, Rothert. The only person I'm any good at healing is myself."

As Michael stood and watched Raelik work whatever medical magic he'd been trained to do, several more men wandered through the trees and gathered around them. Many had the same dark complexion as Rothert and his sons, others were fair-skinned and still more somewhere in between. All were equally covered in sweat and sawdust. By the look of it, they had finally arrived at their destination.

Morghan adjusted the sling holding her arm and rolled up her sleeve before scoring another line on her skin with the charcoal stick in her good hand. That made three. She rolled the sleeve down before taking another step and starting the count over.

"Morghan!" Michael jogged through the trees in front of her. He was shirtless and covered in grime, as was his baseline state for the past few months. "I've been looking all over for you. What are you doing?"

"Measuring. Give me a minute." She kept walking, counting steps as she went and changing course only the slightest bit when a tree stood in her way. Michael followed, and by the time they reached the doors of the makeshift tavern her count was just short of two-thousand. Several men hauled trees through the grass while others cut them into beams. "We're roughly four miles from the falls. It's mostly downhill to the tavern."

"Is that good or bad?" Michael leaned against the wall and wiped sweat from his forehead. It wasn't all that hot. In fact, winter would be upon them before they knew it, and then they'd see how mild the winters in this part of the realm really were. Morghan guessed Michael had been on the hauling end of most of the trees stacked for the lumber mill.

"Good. Redik and I have been working on a few new toys." Rothert's youngest son, a blacksmith by trade, was forever interested in any idea she threw his way. She could still hear his squeals of glee when they'd put together a lathe and he realized what it could do.

"We can make screws now, better cutting edges on hand drills, and take a look at this." She dug in her pocket and tossed Michael a small metal object.

"What's this?" He turned the metal tube over in his hand. "It looks like a mini pipe, maybe for under a..." He trailed off, and his eyes lit up. "No!"

"Sink? Toilet?" Morghan couldn't help but smile at his reaction. "How would you like to give this place running water? That's a model, obviously, but making it bigger, much bigger, isn't so hard now that we have it down. The hard part was learning how to make screws, nuts, and bolts that seated well. Not to mention the tools to use them, but that's done now."

"Do you think it will really work? Morghan, we could take real showers!"

"I'm more interested in working toilets, but showers are a nice bonus." She readjusted her sling again and winced. "And yes, I think it will work. We can start at the river and run pipes of varying sizes to the city. Between the hill and the size differences of the pipes, it should give a kick to the downstream water pressure. There's enough land between here and there that we can clear the trees and plant crops along the course of the pipeline. Small tributaries branching off the side should be sufficient for irrigation. It's not an overnight job, but it's doable."

Michael tossed the pipe back to her and pointed to her injured arm. "How's the wrist?"

"Shitty." She scowled. This was the fourth time breaking and setting the bones, but they still weren't healing right. Last time she couldn't move three of her fingers. This time her last two fingers were eternally numb and alight with pain simultaneously, not to mention she couldn't tell the difference between touching a needle or a pillow. "Pretty soon, I'll just cut the thing off my damn self. I told you before, the bones were all comminuted and wouldn't heal well. They're irritating if not entrapping the regenerated nerves. There's no point in having a useless hand when I can grow a new one."

"How in the world do you know so much about this stuff? All the metalworking, sure. It's easy, hobby type stuff, but medicine? I don't even understand the words you use half the time when you talk about it." Michael's hands settled on his hips. "Are you sure you weren't a nurse back home?"

The skin on the back of Morghan's neck prickled, and her hand curled into a fist at her side as she remembered the countless times a similar question had been directed at her in her mortal life. She could have been elbow deep in a trauma patient's chest, scalpel in hand, and some idiot would still ask where the doctor was. There was nothing wrong with being a nurse; she'd certainly gotten along with them better than many of the other physicians. Still, she knew damn well if she had been sporting a penis, Michael would have asked if she was a doctor. But he hadn't, and so her answer was easy enough. "I think I'd remember."

She turned toward the tavern door, deciding she needed a drink. Knowing what Raelik could concoct under a half-built roof, she looked forward to seeing his full potential when the place was done and the bar fully stocked.

Michael started following her again, and her temper flared. She spun around, stabbing a finger into his chest as he nearly ran into her. "And another thing, what Redik and I do is not easy. If you think you can hobby your ass into building a plumbing system from scratch or making struts for better building support, then by all means, the forge and lathe are yours."

Michael raised his hands. "I didn't mean to offend you."

"Minimizing anyone's work is offensive. I majored in two different branches of engineering, Michael. You know, back in a time and place where there were colleges and cars and fucking painkillers you didn't have to chew off sticks! Almost everything I learned is useless here beyond my critical thinking skill set. So, don't be a patronizing asshole. It doesn't suit you."

"What do you want me to say? I already apologized."

"Not really, but that's not the point. I think you might have missed it." Morghan pushed through the doors and took a seat at the bar. She smiled at Raelik and attempted to ignore Michael as he sat down beside her. "Surprise me."

"Morghan, we still haven't talked about why I came to find you," Michael pressed. He really had no concept of when to leave people alone. The thought that maybe the trait was her minuscule genetic contribution to him made her smile in spite of herself.

"What do you need?" She turned to face him and relaxed against the bar. He might get on her nerves sometimes, but whenever she looked into his sapphire eyes, the gaping hole in her chest filled the slightest bit.

"A couple things. First, Rothert wants me to come up with a name for the city. It's somewhat of a realm tradition if I'm involved, but I can't make up my mind. I thought maybe you could come up with something."

"Salus," Morghan said without having to think. "Next issue."

"Okay, so clearly you've thought about it. Does it mean anything?"

"Yep."

"And that is?"

"I was under the impression you were asking me to name something, not submit it for your approval. It means safety, salvation, and whatever other bastiony type word you want to throw into the mix. If you can name an entire group of people after a Tolkien character, I can name a city after a Roman goddess."

Michael blushed. "I didn't realize you knew."

"Please. I was a lot closer to Tolkien's time than you were. It's a good name and a great fit for them."

"I thought so." Michael beamed. "When I was a kid, escaping into that world was the only way I stayed sane sometimes. I had a real copy of it, not the electronic books we used for everything else. It cost a fortune, but I begged my father for weeks when I saw it was going up for auction." He slouched over the bar and stared across it. "I always thought my father was the good one."

Morghan wasn't sure how to respond. She should have probably hugged him, or at least given him a consoling pat on the back, but in the end she took too long deciding.

Michael sat up straight and shrugged off the memory. "Anyway, getting back to the point. Rothert, the boys, and I wanted to sit down with you and talk about the city schematics again."

Raelik set a glass filled with what looked like blood infused with steam on the bar. He lingered on the other side and shook his head. "It's been a while since anyone called me a boy," he chuckled. "Besides, I don't want to talk to her about anything. I'm all for her plan. Bigger is better!"

"See." Morghan pointed at Raelik. "Listen to the guy who will be inheriting this place one day. We've been through this before—no downscaling." She picked up her glass and toasted Raelik before taking a sip. She couldn't pinpoint what it tasted like, but it was somewhere between strawberries and the halls of Valhalla. "You've outdone yourself, as usual."

Rothert sidled up to the bar and sat on Morghan's other side. "It's too much." He brought out a large parchment and opened it. Raelik moved dry, empty glasses to the edges to keep it flat so his father's shaking hands didn't struggle to do so.

Morghan's eyes roamed the schematic; it was a master-piece. The wooden frame of the tavern that was currently being built was only temporary, until the stone for the construction of the real walls arrived from whatever quarry Rothert had procured it.

The entirety of the city would be constructed as a circle of stone on the outside. The tavern would serve as one of three entry points for the city. From that entrance, one would have easy access to the bulk of the city, including living quarters and the open air markets that would eventually occupy its heart. The second entrance was to be constructed as a gateway to military training grounds with the barracks and armory housed beyond. The third entrance was Morghan's personal favorite, and thus, the part every argument revolved around. It was also the part she was least likely to concede. The entrance was a towering gate leading to a series of roofless halls that wound through the city, filling the architectural gaps of the circular structure and ultimately leading nowhere. Of all the entrances, this one would be the most heavily guarded, and she planned on scheduling guard shifts that didn't overlap every once in a great while just to mess with whoever might be keeping track. The halls to nowhere would be easily accessible from the rooftops of the remainder of the city, and it was doubtful anyone would ever leave them once they entered.

"It's perfect," Morghan said. "I don't see the problem. You were all for the stone walls and said you had quarries at the ready."

Rothert ran a shaky hand through his greying hair. "At the ready, yes, but this is monstrous. It will take years to haul all the stone here, let alone cut it and begin the city walls. If we removed this one section..." He pointed at the third gate. Always. None of these men understood a damn thing about killing or being killed. Even Raelik only wanted the city as big as possible to bring in more customers. He saw the third gate as an enigmatic attraction, since it was well understood between them that the third gate and the halls behind it were not to be spoken of beyond their close circle of planners. Morghan didn't even want to give the entirety of the plans to those building it. They would build it piece by piece and she would make certain those constructing it were switched out regularly.

If Michael and whatever army he gathered was really going to use this as a stronghold, then sooner or later someone would attack. The people of Salus would sure as Hell be thankful for the third gate then. Any idiot with a scout would salivate over the monstrous, heavily guarded gate that every so often went unattended.

Michael pointed to the third gate. "Can we make it smaller? The dimensions are huge. The gate outside is three times the height of the inner halls, which are already taller than the rooftops of the rest of the city. And the halls are designed to press up against everywhere else in the city, when we can easily compress it all if you're so set on having them."

"I tell you what." Morghan leaned against the bar and took another generous swig from her drink. She removed her injured arm from the sling and laid it across the bar before pulling a dagger from her belt and tapping the broad side against her forearm. "You can change it if even one of you can keep a straight face while I saw through my arm to get rid of this useless hand."

She flipped the dagger so the sharp edge bit into skin, but she allowed Michael to swipe it from her before she could make the first deep cut.

"Fine, we'll keep the plan as is, but I'm not giving this back to you." He shook the blade at her.

"You know damn well I have more. Maybe, I'll be more efficient and use the one that splits into three blades." She finished her drink and tilted her head toward Raelik. "That one's my favorite. You'd be cleaning blood off the walls for weeks."

Raelik gave her a playful punch in the shoulder and replaced her empty glass with a full one.

"Stop hitting on me, Raelik." She started in on her new drink, and the pain in her hand dulled. He'd probably slipped in a homemade painkiller. She had no idea what could work so fast, but for a moment, she may have just loved him. "Don't forget that family in Bal Mek you never stop talking about."

"I have the good sense not to go to bed with someone who handles a blade better than I do."

Rothert mumbled something under his breath. He

collected the schematics and left the bar. The man was wise enough to know his end of the conversation was settled.

Michael flipped Morghan's dagger in his hand and slid it across the bar to her hilt first. "No worries, Raelik. She doesn't like men. Or women. Pretty sure she's asexual."

Morghan snatched the dagger from the bar and slammed it into her belt, unable to hide her annoyance. "Fuck off, Michael. What I am or am not is none of your fucking business. Besides, we can't all be world class man-whores. There are probably little Michaels running rampant all over the realm."

"There aren't." The humor in Michael's eyes dimmed. "I kept track for a long time, and I don't think we work like that. We have to want a child to make one."

"That seems far-fetched," Morghan scoffed. Not that she would know. Luke was infertile, and Azrael was off limits for any number of reasons. And who knew if she was even able to have children? As far as she could tell, no part of the female reproductive cycle applied to her since becoming a ranking immortal.

Michael shrugged. "The one time I seriously considered it, Tyrra fell pregnant. I left Malon and didn't know until over a year later, but her mother slipped her an abortive tonic early on, so it didn't matter in the end."

"Shit," Raelik said under his breath, as he finished wiping a clean glass.

Morghan didn't know what to say since Raelik had stolen her expletive.

"Like I said, it doesn't matter." Michael's forced smile said otherwise. "Tena had no idea it was mine. She thought Tyrra had started taking customers behind her back."

"Instead of in front of her?" Morghan raised an eyebrow.

"The matriarchs in Malon choose a mate, Morghan. They appear ever available, but it's a show. I was her first choice, and I thought it was what I wanted, too. After that, I changed my mind. It wasn't fair to her, but my head was a mess." He sighed, and his eyes came back to the present. "In all honesty, I've cut back on the debauchery a lot since you showed up, but we can't all be holier-than-thou celibates like you."

Morghan slid her left fist across the bar toward him before turning it over and lifting her middle finger. "I'm in a relationship, jackass."

At least, she imagined she still was. She wasn't certain of the logistics behind having a life mate you were forbidden to see.

Michael made a show of looking around the room. "With whom?"

That question was both easy and infinitely difficult to answer. "Is it hard to regrow teeth? If you don't know already, you're close to finding out."

Michael relaxed and draped an arm over the back of his chair. "That's not an answer."

"He's trapped in a different dimension at the moment." Morghan pointed to her nearly empty glass and Raelik scurried away to comply. "Stronger."

Michael looked skeptical. "And he's trapped for how long?"

"Given historical precedent, forever?" She finished the rest of her drink in one long draw. Raelik really needed to hurry up with the new one. "Or at least until he feels it's worth the risk to break the rules."

"If I were you, I'd wonder why my partner didn't think I was worth the risk."

"I am the risk. He breaks the rules, and the asshole who

makes them murders my ass." She pushed her empty glass across the bar to Raelik and grabbed the fresh one from his hand. In a moment's time the new glass joined the old as it slid back across the bar. "Can we talk about something else? Like how despite all this talk of our various levels of sexual promiscuity, there's nothing in the city plans for a brothel? It's pretty much a staple of cities in this realm. I think I'd miss it."

"There won't ever be a brothel here," Michael said, his expression darkening.

Morghan highly doubted that. And it was only a matter of moments before Raelik began to protest the city's marketability without one.

6

A LONG WALK OFF A SHORT CLIFF

MORGHAN DROVE her shovel into the ground, and it thumped against metal. Finally. She leaned back against the side of the hole she'd dug herself into and concentrated on slowing her breathing. The midsummer sun beat down from a cloudless sky, and while the winters in Salus were mild enough to rarely include snow, they paid for it with sweltering summers. Over the last forty years she'd come to accept that men in this part of the realm simply didn't wear shirts half the year. That turned into year-round if they were doing manual labor—which was everyone with a healthy pair of legs. She didn't mind the view but found it horribly unfair she had to sweat her ass off fully clothed.

She pushed off the wall and changed the angle of her shovel, uncovering the enormous pipe and the series of levers that should have been supplying water to the fields beyond. It had been over thirty years since they'd finished burying the pipelines, and she didn't remember any of them being this deep. Maybe this one had been laid during the four million some-odd seconds it had taken to grow a new hand once she'd finally tired of Michael's pleas to salvage the original one. Counting was the only thing that kept her sane during the process, and she was never afforded the luxury of sleep. Apparently being a ranking immortal meant it took catastrophic amounts of pain to pass out, and she hoped to never test that threshold again.

She looked down at her hand and flexed it. Sometimes she would swear the nerves were still regenerating, but since the memory alone stole the breath from her lungs, she doubted the pain was real. Still, Michael had been right about the pain of regeneration, infuriatingly so. Yet he had remained by her side throughout the process without a word of criticism. When it was over and her hand was perfect again, he'd left the room and avoided her for the better part of a week.

In the future, she would approach the idea of salvaging limbs with a little more respect.

"Morghan?" Michael loomed over the edge of the hole. He was wearing a shirt today. All of Salus was likely wearing a shirt right now. "What are you doing out here?"

She crouched and concentrated on the levers in front of her, picking minuscule pieces of dirt from them for no reason. "The crops are dying in the eastern fields. They're not getting any water, and I think the problem is at the earliest takeoff." She pointed to the levers. "Here."

Michael crossed his arms over his chest. "This is someone else's job now. Salus is full to bursting with an endless list of people trying to move here. There's no reason for you to be working on this right now. We just buried one of your closest friends, and you weren't there."

"Raelik wasn't my friend." Morghan tried moving one of the levers, and when it didn't budge, she lashed out with her foot. It broke off and flew across the hole, lodging in the dirt wall. "I've taken naps longer than half of these fucking people live. They're like goldfish. You don't make friends with a goldfish; you just feed it and watch it swim around in its cramped little world until it's time to flush it."

Michael jumped into the hole. If he knew what was good for him, he'd keep his distance.

His arms circled her shoulders from behind, and he pulled her back against his chest, resting his head on hers. "I know it's hard. It will never get easier, but it will be so much worse if you don't face it now."

Morghan didn't face her emotions as a general rule. It was probably why she was such a bitch to everyone. Not to mention all the time she spent huddled in a corner of her room hating her life and everything associated with it. "He's just rotting meat in the ground now. Him, Rothert, and any day now Redik will join them. I can't even look at their children and grandchildren anymore. All I see is death, and death is so much easier to deal with when I'm wielding the weapon."

"Raelik might not be here anymore, but he's somewhere," Michael said. "They all are. Maybe one day you'll pass someone and see a familiar smile on an unfamiliar face."

Morghan pulled his arms from her chest and turned to face him. She wasn't sure if reincarnation was even a thing in this realm. "Has that ever happened to you?"

Michael gave her some space. "I've convinced myself of all sorts of things over the years. Real or not, it helps me get by."

"With my luck the first person I'd notice would be someone I killed." She looked up at the edge of the hole, which was a few feet higher than her head. Claustrophobia was sneaking up on her, another tell her anxiety level was ratcheting toward critical. "Let's get out of here."

Michael boosted her up and she pulled him out after her. "How were you planning to get out of there?"

"I hadn't thought that far ahead," she admitted as they walked back to the city. "Someone is going to be pissed about that lever. Seriously though, most of the others are above ground. Whose idea was it to bury the cutoff valves closest to the river?"

"Probably yours," Michael reminded her.

"Well then, me of forty years ago was a dumbass."

Morghan picked up her pace when the tavern entrance came into view. A large gathering of men stood outside in a circle. Their words were unintelligible as the screams of one blended with several others. She caught a gleam of metal between bodies and drew her sword as she sprinted toward the group.

She broke through the mob before Michael. The guards at the front moved aside for her, and she came up short when she saw Valerian standing in the middle, his eyes wild and a gleaming scimitar in his hand. Several other members of his clan stood at his back, their stances similar. None of them looked to have slept or bathed in days.

"You!" he rasped, pointing his weapon at Morghan. "My kingdom is in ashes because of you." He glanced at the men surrounding him. "You put off fighting Alara for decades, and now that I'm homeless the dregs of your city refuse me entrance."

Michael stepped into the circle and faced Valerian. "I haven't refused you entrance. Yet. Continue to talk about my people that way and you can camp on the other side of the river instead of sleeping in a warm bed tonight."

Morghan didn't know what bed Michael was referring to, seeing as every residence in Salus was full, and last she'd heard the inn was packed.

Valerian relaxed and sheathed his sword. The men behind him did the same.

Morghan kept her sword out, anyway. No matter how beaten and broken Valerian looked, she didn't trust him. The guards remained at her back, their postures similar.

Valerian glared at her before turning his attention back to Michael. "What I come to discuss is far from civil, but perhaps we can pretend and adjourn to a more private place?"

"Stand down and let him pass," Michael ordered. No one moved. "Morghan, now!"

Morghan slammed her sword into its sheath, and the guards followed suit. She took a step back and gestured toward the city with her arm. The circle parted, revealing the tavern entrance. Valerian and his men made their way through the doors as the gathering dispersed.

Michael dropped back to Morghan's side as she fell in behind them. He bent toward her and spoke in a voice so low only they could hear it, but the venom in his tone wasn't lost on her. "If you want me to raise and lead an army, you have to, at the very least, act like I am in charge."

"I want you to lead a strong army, not a doomed one," she replied in kind. "Rothert's children and grandchildren are feeding and clothing us for a service. I take pride in holding up my end of the deal."

Michael moved to the front of the group without another word and led the Evenstars into the residential halls that stretched from the back half of the tavern like spokes from a hub. "We can talk in my quarters. If the inn is full, you're welcome to my bed, and I'll stay elsewhere."

Morghan didn't like the idea of turning over one of the few centrally located rooms to the Evenstars. Of all the rooms in Salus, it was one of only four with a window and access to the rooftops. "And where will you stay?" she asked.

Michael stopped in front of his door and turned to her with a wicked grin. "With you, of course. Don't act like we've never shared a bed."

Morghan tensed, and heat rose in her cheeks. The satisfied, denigrating gleam in Valerian's eyes threatened to drive her mad. Michael's words weren't a lie; they'd shared a bed a few times when inns were full and he'd pestered her to the point of abandoning the floor, but the underlying implication was damning.

Michael ushered the Evenstars into his room and turned to Morghan with a questioning look when she didn't follow. "Aren't you coming in?"

Coming in? At the moment she was slowly counting backward from one hundred to keep herself from both saying and doing things she was bound to regret. The way he kept staring at her expectantly convinced her she should start over from a thousand. Maybe if she did so while reminding herself he was family, she wouldn't slice the smug grin right off his face.

"I'm not coming in." Her knuckles blanched around the hilt of her sword. "I'm likely never coming in again."

"Morghan, I'm sorry." He took a step toward her. "It wasn't funny. I'll tell them it was a joke. A poor one."

Morghan shook her head. "You can't close that door once you've opened it. You act like it hasn't been a whisper behind us at every turn. Now you've legitimized it."

He reached back and closed the door, leaving the Evenstars alone inside. "Is it really so terrible? We're adults with an infinite lifespan. Who cares if people think we're sleeping together?"

"I care, for several reasons." She let go of her sword and

flexed her hand to dull the numbness that had gathered in her fingers. "You fuck me, and people pat you on the back for taming the shrew. Then they look at me, and it finally makes sense why I'm second in command."

"You're overreacting."

"Well, I'll be overreacting in the tavern. Depending on how drunk I am when you finish with the Evenstars, I may or may not accept an apology."

Morghan retreated to the tavern, and true to her word she immediately ordered a drink in the hopes of getting smashed by the time Michael was done. Hours later her first drink remained on the table in front of her. The liquid within it had once danced with red and blue sparks, an attempt by Raelyn to lift her spirits. While he was almost as good as his father when it came to drinks, it didn't seem right to enjoy someone else's work when her friend was fresh in the ground.

Because he was her friend. Had been her friend. No matter how much she wanted to downplay the loss.

She slumped in her chair, and her eyes fluttered shut. The sun had long since disappeared, and Michael still hadn't emerged from his quarters. Her muscles ached almost as much as her chest, and for the first time in months she was looking forward to climbing in bed.

Her eyes opened when a chair scraped across the floor in front of her. Bael, one of the guards who had stood at her back earlier, sat across from her. She'd charged him with keeping watch outside Michael's quarters while he spoke with the Evenstars. Morghan might have been too proud to engage in the conversation, but she sure as Hell was going to know what was said.

"So, did Alara really destroy Arden?" Morghan wondered.

Bael shifted uneasily in his chair and nodded. When he moved, his armor caught the light, flashing the image of a waterfall flanked by wings with a whirlpool churning below it. Morghan was particularly proud of Salus's crest. It had been a joint effort that was at once a reminder of the city's beginnings as well as the reason behind its inception.

"And what now?" she asked.

"They're discussing it, but I caught Merrick in the hall and had him take my place so I could speak with you." The "before Michael does" was strongly implied, but Bael had enough tact not to say it. "The underlying theme is war, sooner rather than later. Very soon." He huddled over the table, and his voice lowered to a whisper. "You can't let them take us to war with Falcroix. We barely have a thousand men, and that's if we strip the city of every last soldier and leave it unguarded."

"I'm well aware of how many men I command." She leaned back in her chair. "Michael can count. I'm sure he knows what would happen if we attacked Falcroix alone."

"He said as much, but Valerian accused him of sitting idly by while the realm burns to the ground." The ever-present lines on Bael's forehead doubled in number. "The Maritch was silent far too long afterwards. I don't know what to expect from him when he leaves that room."

"I expect him to realize when to risk the lives of his people, and when to bide his time and ask for help. We need Vahyir at the very least, and even then we'd be outmanned."

Bael's feet tapped uneasily on the hardwood floor. "I think we should gather more men and prepare to defend ourselves here, but I don't know where we'd get them. Predlitz and Bal Mek will be looking for the same, since they're closer to Falcroix than we are, and the only men in

Malon aren't fit for battle. There isn't anywhere else close enough to recruit from on such short notice."

Morghan was starting to regret her choice not to drink. "This place wasn't built to weather the storm while everyone else is blown away. War is inevitable, but I won't march us to a slaughter."

If the cities in this realm weren't so spread apart, maybe they could have found a way to raise an army faster. Even still, as well known as Salus had become in the past few decades, Michael's position commanded only so much respect. As the figurehead and protector of a city that was owned and operated by humans, he was unlikely to garner enough support to make others abandon such self-serving plans as the one Bael had set forth. No one but Falcroix would benefit if the entire realm erred on the side of defense. Not when every loss in battle was a potential addition to the Legion's numbers. Morghan didn't even want to think about what Alara's blood gift could do to beings such as the Evenstars. If their forest stronghold had already been razed, Morghan expected Falcroix would have a few surprises for them when they met in battle.

There was only one way to make any of this work. They needed Michael's wings, and it was high time she stopped screwing around when it came to coaxing them out of him. Her eyes moved to where Raelyn sat on a stool barking orders to his son over the usual organized chaos of demanding customers.

"How old is Raelyn's granddaughter?" she asked.

Bael gave her a questioning look before turning to look at Raelyn. "Which one?"

"The blonde one, with the mother from Vahyir. What is she, seven or eight by now?"

"That one is married with a child of her own." Bael eyed Morghan's drink.

Damn. She sat up straighter in her chair and shook her head. "I'm not drunk, just oblivious to unimportant details."

"His youngest granddaughter is about seven. She plays with my daughter on occasion."

"She'll work." Morghan stood up and pushed her drink toward Bael. "Valerian has fucked with Michael's head long enough. Drink this. Slowly. When you're done, bang on the door and tell them the child was abducted."

"By who?" Bael looked at the drink and then at Morghan.

"Someone fast." She smirked. "Your men saw them heading for the falls but lost the trail."

Michael couldn't wait for this day to be over. When he laid Raelik's body in the ground earlier that morning he never would have guessed it would be the least stressful part of his day. Now, he was running along the riverbank faster than any mortal could ever hope to in an attempt to keep from burying two people from Raelik's family in the same week. He had no idea who he was looking for or where they were headed aside from a general direction. It wouldn't be long before he reached the whirlpool at the bottom of the falls, and if he hadn't found them by then, he wasn't sure what to do.

He slowed and let out a sigh of relief as Morghan came into view, her hand on the small girl's shoulder. His brow furrowed as he came closer and noticed the child was sobbing, her eyes wide with fear. The guards had said Morghan was nowhere to be found, so how had she rescued a girl she hadn't even known was abducted? He stopped several paces in front of her. "What are you doing?"

"Good of you to finally emerge from that circle jerk with the Evenstars." Morghan ignored his question. She pulled the girl closer. "We can't go to war without allies. You'll get everyone killed."

Had she really drawn him out in such a way just to talk about this? He tried so hard to look past her volatile nature, but it was getting out of control. "Let the girl go, Morghan. She's terrified."

He took a step forward, but Morghan had a dagger at the child's neck before he could think of taking another.

Thunder rumbled in the distance, and Morghan smiled. "Might want to reel that in or you'll be puking blood in a bucket before you know it. The least you can do is look professional while leading your people to their deaths."

"I don't know why you're doing this, but you need to let her go. Now." He couldn't believe his eyes when she slung the child over her shoulder and bolted uphill, away from the river.

Michael sprinted after her, and even with a head start he knew he would catch her. She should have known that, too. Had Morghan lost her mind? Was she doing this to prove a point, and if so, what? He hadn't told her anything about the Evenstars or his plans for Falcroix.

He caught up with her as she turned toward the cliff above the falls. When he drew his sword, Morghan dropped the girl and lunged at him. She caught him around the hips, and they both hit the ground.

"Really?" Morghan was on her feet and kicking Michael's sword out of his hand before air returned to his lungs. She drew the sword from the sheath across her back and held it to his chest. Strange markings he couldn't read were etched into the thin, gleaming blade. "You were going to stab me in the back with your ranking sword? You could have killed me!"

Shame washed over Michael for a moment before anger replaced it. He hadn't planned on killing her or even hurting her. He didn't want to do either, but he'd unsheathed his sword to be ready in case she forced his hand. And right now, she was doing just that.

Michael grabbed her sword and attempted to yank it away, but she held fast to the hilt. The blade bit deep into Michael's palm before he abandoned the move and released it.

Morghan sheathed her sword and kicked him hard in the side, lifting his back off the ground and sending him rolling down the hill away from the cliff.

Michael scrambled to his feet and back up the hill, not bothering to pick up his sword. The roar of the falls assaulted him as he climbed closer to the cliff. There had to be an explanation for Morghan's behavior. They'd been friends for decades, long enough the few others he counted as such were dead and gone. Morghan was a never-ending fount of ideas that transformed into journeys, projects, or both. They kept him preoccupied enough that beyond Salus, he hadn't made any personal connections in years, but he also no longer spent his nights staring at the ceiling and wondering why he was alive. For once, his life didn't feel like an eternity of nothing punctuated by unconscionable mistakes. All of that would change if she murdered this child. He wanted to believe that alone would be enough to leave their friendship in ruins and force him to banish her from Salus. If he wasn't so selfish, he might have believed it.

When the cliff finally came into view, Michael's heart

sank. Morghan stood there, inches from the edge, her dagger back at the girl's throat. So she would try his resolve after all, and he would find out if he was willing to sacrifice his morals to keep faith with the devil who held his demons at bay.

He approached her slowly, hands held above his head. With the deafening sound of the falls, there was no point in trying to communicate until they were within arm's reach of one another. If she let him get that close, maybe he could grab the child. His eyes slid to the dagger gleaming in the moonlight; then again, maybe not.

Morghan dropped the dagger from the child's throat as Michael approached her. She took a step backward and Michael's chest tightened when loose pebbles shifted beneath her foot. "If you can save one, we can save thousands," she said, as she shoved the girl into his arms and flung herself over the edge.

Michael didn't think, he reacted. A moment later he was hurtling through space after her. Even without his wings, he still knew how to dive. She wasn't far in front of him, and the way she was tumbling end over end, he was certain to catch her before hitting the water. But then what?

He needed his wings now more than ever. If he didn't catch her, she would heal, but how long would it take? A fall like this would rupture organs and pulverize bone. She already healed more slowly than him, and something this devastating would take him weeks if not months to heal. Months Alara could run rampant throughout the realm unchecked. His eyes shifted to the quickly approaching whirlpool. What had he done?

Pain speared through his back and cloth shredded as wings expanded behind him. His once graceful dive turned into a haphazard somersault when his wings caught the air.

Michael slammed into the side of the cliff and grabbed at the rocky outcroppings before propelling himself back into free fall. He'd lost all the ground he'd made up, and even speeding toward her with his wings tucked behind him it would be close.

Michael was well into the misty spray of the falls before he reached Morghan. He wrapped his arms around her waist and spread his wings, angling them up as quickly as possible. For all his efforts, he wasn't fast enough, and as Morghan's leg skimmed the water she was ripped from his arms and disappeared.

Michael tucked his wings and rolled, hitting the water with enough upward momentum that he skipped across the surface like a stone. He slammed into the riverbank and rolled uphill several feet before coming to a stop.

When he was finally able to discern up from down, he rushed to the edge of the whirlpool, his breathing fast and ragged. Morghan was in there somewhere, injured and being flung around in an infinite spinning nightmare. Even facing it with only minor injuries, he was unsure if he would be able to escape, but he couldn't leave her down there alone.

Michael tucked his wings flush against his back and jumped in, the current hauling him under in an instant. After only a few trips around, the whirlpool spit him out, and he sputtered to the surface of what appeared to be an underground river. The current carried him through the darkness, with only the light from his eyes illuminating the cavernous tunnels through which it flowed.

He called Morghan's name but resolved not to fight the river until he heard a response. In all likelihood, if she was unconscious, she would be wherever the water changed course or moved above ground.

"Michael?" He barely heard Morghan's voice over the sound of rushing water, and had she not coughed after saying his name, he would have thought he imagined it.

Michael swam to the side of the river and grabbed a passing stalagmite. He climbed out and called Morghan's name again, although the way everything echoed made it difficult to pinpoint the origin of any sound. He walked back along the course of the river, wishing for nothing more than a torch. When he found Morghan, she was leaning against the cave wall. What little light their eyes provided was enough to see the blood gushing from the base of her skull. It matted in her hair, gluing it to the back of her neck, and her right leg had grown an extra knee above the original one.

Morghan gestured to her head and the hand that wasn't pressed against the wound. "It's about time you showed up. Can you put pressure back here? I need to reduce my femur before it starts healing like this, and I'd like to do it without passing out from blood loss."

Michael knelt beside her and put his hand over the back of her head, but he wasn't sure if it was doing anything. Blood pulsed through his fingers, and he wondered how much she would have to lose before passing out. Michael looked away from Morghan's leg until after he heard a loud pop and a sufficient number of curses had echoed off the walls to convince him the worst was over. When he turned back, the joints of her right leg were once again correct in number and spacing.

Morghan batted his hand away and replaced hers over the back of her head. "You're going to have to carry me."

With the adrenaline fading, Michael was left feeling frustrated and more than a little betrayed. "After what you pulled, I should make you crawl."

"Those wings look good on you. A simple thank you would be sufficient."

"You realize I left a terrified child at the edge of a cliff? A child you abducted and threatened just to lure me into something that could have easily ended with both of us incapacitated for months."

"I've been thinking about this plan for years." Morghan chuckled. "You've tried everything short of being in a life or death situation where your wings mattered. And calm down, I'm sure the kid is fine. Raelyn was close by, and he knew where to pick her up. If anything, I should be the one pissed at you. First, you tried to stab me in the back, and then you didn't even save me!" She gestured to her head and leg. "Seriously, Michael, what the fuck?"

Michael ignored her complaints. "Raelyn knew what you were going to do, and he was fine with it?"

"Well, he knew I was pretending to abduct his grand-daughter for the good of the realm. I was less than specific about the details." She shifted against the wall and sighed. "C'mon, Michael, it's cold and dark down here. I want to go home and get a real splint on this leg. I'm hoping Raelyn will stitch up my head, because I doubt I could do a very good job, even with mirrors."

Michael situated Morghan against his chest and picked his way through the dark, following the river. "You're impossible."

She rested her head on his shoulder and relaxed against him. "But you love me anyway."

"Is that what this throbbing pain in my ass is?"

Morghan's laughter echoed off the walls until a hiss of pain replaced it. "Stop it. And yes, that's love for you. Don't worry, you get used to it."

7

WHEN LIFE GIVES YOU LEMONS

Bael pulled himself out of the hole he and several of the other soldiers were digging in Morghan's bedroom floor. She should have been digging too. Instead, she'd been sitting in bed for the past five days. A dull throb was all that remained of her head wound, but she didn't trust her leg yet. The last thing she wanted was to destroy it and have to go through the pain of regenerating another limb. She'd lived thousands of years before having to regrow one, and she damn sure wasn't excited about doing it twice in half a century.

"What exactly are we digging for again?" Bael grumbled, brushing dirt from his hair. "That thing is already deeper than this building is tall."

Not to mention taking up half her room.

"Stone or water." Morghan grabbed an apple from the plate of food beside her and tossed it to Bael. "Eat something. Maybe low blood sugar is what's making you so bitchy today."

Bael caught the apple and scowled before throwing it back to her. "It has nothing to do with whether I'm hungry or not. I don't enjoy pointless errands."

"You better hope that hole doesn't end up being point-less. Otherwise you'll have to dig it all over again in a room on the next hall." Morghan sliced a wedge from the apple with a dagger and popped it into her mouth.

Bael raised an eyebrow. "Haven't you killed people with that blade?"

"Not recently." Morghan sighed and cut another piece. Sometimes she missed being the bad guy. She'd never had to justify much of anything, and it had paid better, too. Not that she had any use for money. Everything in Salus she could possibly need was provided with no expectation of payment.

Bael rested a hand on the hilt of his sword. It was likely subconscious, but it entertained her all the same. "So am I hoping for water or stone?"

"We hit rock!" A voice cried from the bottom of the hole.

Morghan pointed her dagger at the hole and gave Bael a thumbs up.

"Uncover it for the entire length and width of what you've dug out so far," she shouted down to the men before turning back to Bael. "See, now you don't have to dig another hole. Well, not today. Go get Redik and tell him we need black powder. A lot of it."

Bael's expression morphed from annoyance to fear. "But—"

Morghan wagged her dagger back and forth like a disap-proving finger. "I like you, Bael, but you're a little too vocal lately. Don't think an injured leg would keep me from killing you where you stand if I thought it necessary, and the more bored I get, the more flexible my definition of necessary becomes. Now go get Redik, and then clear all the people from the rooms to either side of this one."

Morghan leaned back against the wall as he trudged out of the room. She shouldn't have threatened him. Bael had a good head on his shoulders, but he tended to err on the side of self-preservation. She was so far to the opposite extreme, his opinions often sounded ridiculous, but that didn't mean they were without merit. After all, setting off an explosion in the middle of Salus was unlikely to win her any friends, but if they could link the city to the caves beneath them, it would provide an invaluable escape route. She was just glad Michael wasn't around to give her grief over it.

As it turned out, the subterranean portion of the river flowed along the same path as the one on the surface, and the two reunited above ground only a few miles west of the city. Which was lucky for Morghan, since Michael had insisted on flying back to Salus once they emerged from the caves. While she had mastered riding horses over the years, she didn't think learning to be carried through the sky by angels without freaking the hell out was anywhere in her future.

Michael had left for Vahyir not long after they returned to Salus, and he had guessed it would take about a week to fly there. Which meant he should make it any day now. If the people of Vahyir reacted to Michael's wings the way the mortals in Salus had when he'd walked into the tavern carrying her, their allegiance was all but assured.

A knock on Morghan's door drew her away from her thoughts. When she called for them to enter, Redik strode through the door. His two sons and his granddaughter lugged an enormous chest behind him. Despite being in his late fifties, Redik's hair was as jet-black as the day she'd met him, and no matter how many times he'd singed it off, it always grew back the same. There wasn't much else about him that had gone untouched by the laborious and often volatile nature of his trade, or whatever Morghan had morphed it into. He wore a patch where his left eye had once been and two of the fingers on his right hand were missing. Scars layered over his bare arms to the point normal skin no longer existed. Morghan hadn't seen him wearing a shirt with sleeves in at least a decade. She guessed he'd finally tired of them catching fire so often. Between developing explosive powders and his ongoing quest to create a bullet that wouldn't cause Morghan's gun to explode, he'd had his fair share of accidents.

"I hear you need something violently dispersed?" Redik grinned. The chest thumped to the ground behind him, and his jaw clenched before he whirled around on his offspring and gave them an earful of impressive curses. He turned back to Morghan. "My apologies, but if I die in an explosion, I'd like it to be from one I meant to start."

Redik's youngest son, Redden, sat at the edge of Morghan's bed and eyed her apple. He was in his mid-twenties, a decade younger than his brother, and about a hundred times lazier, but the man had a gift with metal that was rivaled only by his father. Sometimes.

She cut another slice of her apple and handed it to him. Despite spending most of her time in the forge with his father and brother, she'd had a soft spot for him since the first time he'd come tearing through the forge as a child.

Redden sidled closer to her, and she continued feeding him as his family members flipped open a series of fasteners on the chest.

Morghan quirked an eyebrow and gestured to it. "Black powder?"

"Nah." The gold caps covering several of Redik's teeth gleamed in the torchlight. "White. It's new and will explode when struck by, well, pretty much anything." He walked to the edge of the hole and looked down. "Trying to bust through rock?"

"Yes. There's a series of caves beneath us. I want direct access. Can you do that for me?"

"I could give you a road through a mountain if you gave me enough time. This job is insultingly easy." He walked to the chest and flipped open the final latch holding it shut before lifting out a container no bigger than his hand. It was wrapped in a water bladder, but by the way it kept its shape, Morghan guessed it was filled with air. Redik gingerly set it on the floor before reaching into the chest again and coming out with a long, hollow metal tube with screw anchors fanning from one end. The size of the chest was clearly more for the metal tube than the powder.

"Is that going to be enough?" Morghan wondered.

Redden chuckled and stole her last slice of apple. "To blow out a hole the size of this whole city."

Redik rolled his eyes at his son and peered over the side of the hole again. "We'll start with a quarter of what I brought. Can you stand at all? We're going to have to spend one of your bullets to ignite it, and to keep from using more than necessary, you should be the one aiming."

"I'll be fine for that," she assured him, although the thought of being down to four bullets tugged at her nerves. She had already sacrificed two bullets to Redik over the years: one to show him what the gun was meant to do and the other so he could dissect it in the hopes of creating new ones. He insisted a working bullet would be ready before his death, and though he'd made steady progress over the years, last she'd heard, the primer was still giving him fits.

As Salus's military grew, she had less and less time to spend in Redik's workshop. This new powder alone meant she needed to make a point to visit him more often, at least until war scrubbed every other activity from her schedule.

∼

Last time Michael had visited Vahyir its gates had been thrown wide, but now they were closed against the threat lurking beyond. The endless rows of heads in various states of decay that hung from the walls remained a testament to years of refusing Falcroix's call for tribute, though it had apparently done nothing to stave off the requests. He landed in front of the towering gate and looked up to where the guards were posted atop it.

A guard leaned over the top of the gate and yelled down to him. "The city is closed."

Michael launched into the sky and perched on the stone edge the guard had leaned over. "I landed outside as a courtesy."

The man backed away so fast he tripped over his feet and sat down hard. The other guards on the wall pulled their swords partway from their sheaths before thinking better of it. They took a knee instead, their faces to the ground. One of them spoke, his eyes never leaving the stone beneath him. "Forgive us, Maritch, we did not recognize you."

"Forgiven." Michael hopped down to their level. "I imagine Kayla still rules here?"

The man who had apologized rose to his feet and nodded. "She does, and Kaysen has secured her place as heir."

"Already?" Of all the kingdoms in the realm, Michael tried to keep up with Vahyir's royal line the most, but he was known to let a few decades slip by unnoticed now and again. After all, Salus kept him busy. "I thought she was a child."

"Our royals start young to secure a place on the throne, Maritch. Women especially so. The city recently celebrated Kaysen's eighteenth year, and her twins were born just shy of four years ago."

So his math wasn't far off. She was still young, far too young to have children so old. Kayla hadn't become heir until well into her twenties, so late that when her brother had refused to name a single offspring of his own, the city had taken to daily prayer sessions in hopes the Creator might provide them with a set of twins before Kayne's death. When Kayla's girls were born, Vahyir sent couriers to every city worth visiting to extol the Creator's benevolence. Michael didn't mind that happy accident being attributed to him, but some of the things he was charged with doing made him ill.

Michael walked to the other side of the path that stretched across the top of the gates and gazed over the city. "Send word to your queen that I'm here and need to speak with her. I'll make it to her later this evening."

And with that he leapt from the wall and glided to the ground.

Michael planned to spend most of the day walking through the city, making sure as many people as possible got a good look at him. It felt odd to show off his wings after so long without them, especially since only a few centuries ago he'd spent most of his time wishing they were invisible. Still, the various reactions of those he passed reminded him why he had wanted them gone in the first place. As much as the awe and fear was sure to work in his favor when it came to getting what he wanted, it didn't make him any more at ease in a crowd.

It wasn't long before Michael spotted Kayla striding toward him with her personal guard in tow. Her face showed not a hint of surprise as her eyes roamed his bare chest and wings. She stopped a few paces in front of him and tipped her head forward in a quick bow. "You're looking well, Michael."

"As are you." He inclined his head in kind and tucked his wings closer to his back. "I've been told the wings suit me."

"I wasn't referring to the wings." One corner of her mouth inched up as she made another slow sweep of him with her eyes. "Though they certainly don't hurt. I haven't seen you since I was a girl, but I remember you well enough. Your eyes are brighter now, and you carry yourself like a man who knows his place in the world. Salus is what suits you. If you had presented yourself to my father like this, I have no doubt he would have pledged his sword and people to you."

"And will I be fortunate enough to have your pledge of the same?"

"That remains to be seen, as I am not my father." She dismissed the guards with a wave of her hand and gestured for Michael to follow her as she continued along the road. She clasped her hands behind her back and was silent for so long Michael wondered if he should say something. "What don't I know, Michael?"

She stopped and leaned closer to him, until he could feel her breath hot on his neck. "It is alright that I call you by name, yes?"

Michael took a small step away from her. She couldn't have meant to get so close. "I prefer it, actually."

Kayla started walking again, and he fell in step beside her. "Falcroix still sends a soldier here every month despite years of rejection and hundreds of heads cycling over our gates. The creatures come to us terrified now, as terrified as one can expect from such beasts. They know they've been sent to slaughter, yet still they come. Not two or three, not a small army to test our strength. One. From my own experiences and information I've gleaned from other rulers, Falcroix's tribute demands have remained stable for years, and they have not forced expansion."

"But then you show up," she continued. "You walk through my city in the hopes of whipping my people into a frenzy with the mere sight of you, so that if you aren't able to sway me to your cause, perhaps my people will pressure me to change my mind."

Michael opened his mouth to protest, but she silenced him with a raised finger.

"Don't deny it. One does not enter a closed city uninvited and then make a side trip to the laypeople before speaking with its ruler. You're far from oblivious, which means you've gotten much better at hiding desperation since last we met. So tell me, what news haven't I heard?"

"Falcroix has taken Arden." Michael's uneasiness multiplied several times over as they entered the royal hall, and the eyes of numerous guards fell upon him. "The Evenstars, or what is left of them, showed up in Salus last week begging for aid. Over the years they've asked time and again, but I've always denied them. I, too, thought Falcroix was content with its current stronghold. I was wrong, and they lost their home and families because of it."

Kayla didn't respond and instead led him to a hall he'd never been down before. When guards moved to follow, she stopped them with a glare and continued on to where the hall ended at a massive wooden door. An eagle with a shield grasped in its talons was carved into it. Two swords crossed behind its back and the names of Vahyir's former leaders poured forth from its beak, spiraling around the image several times until Kayla's name ended the list.

Kayla tapped her name before opening the door and walking inside. "Kaysen's name will be there soon. The Creator was with her when it came to her twins. I spent the entire pregnancy worried she would suffer a stillbirth, as I had at her age. My pair may have been born sleeping but thankfully hers were not." She closed the door behind them and sat in the only chair before gesturing to the large bed in the center of the room. "Please, sit."

Michael glanced around Kayla's bedroom hoping another chair would appear. "I'm fine standing, thank you."

"You will sit." It was less a command than a statement of fact.

Michael took a seat on the bed without further protest.

"I, like many in the realm, have no love for the Evenstars," she began. "They are long-lived like you, but they serve only themselves. However, if Falcroix has conquered Arden, it means the Legion is mobile and effective. It's anyone's guess which direction they'll turn next."

"That's our fear as well." Michael rested his hands on his knees and leaned over them. "I am nothing like the Evenstars, and I wouldn't ask this of you if it wasn't absolutely necessary."

"I may be a fool for this, but I do believe your intentions are honorable." Kayla leaned back in her chair and crossed her legs. "You know, Michael, legend has it the Creator was a winged man."

"So I've heard." He shifted his weight on the mattress, unable to get comfortable, especially since Kayla looked like a coiled snake ready to strike.

"How old are you?"

"Old, but not that old," Michael chuckled, his eyes drifting away from hers.

Kayla unfolded herself from the chair and walked across the room. She spread Michael's legs apart until hers fit between them when she stood flush against the bed. "It's rare for a man to remain attractive while lying. It's unheard of that you are more so while doing it."

Heat rose in Michael's cheeks, and he swallowed the overwhelming urge to lean forward and kiss her.

"Other kingdoms ally with each other by marriage," Kayla went on. "Their offspring a physical bridge between their differences, but that has never been our way."

"If it meant our forces uniting, I would give you a child."

Kayla laughed as her fingers traced circles on Michael's chest. "My childbearing years are at an end. It's not a child I'm after." She leaned forward, her lips whispering against his ear. "I want to feel you between my legs and know what it's like to ride a god." Her teeth clipped his earlobe, and his body bowed into hers. "Do me this honor, and my army is yours."

Michael fell back against the mattress, and his heart raced when she climbed on the bed and hovered above him. "No one can know about me," he said. "About who I am."

Kayla ran her fingers through the feathers covering Michael's wings, and she hissed when his nails bit into her thighs. "I can't keep them from wondering, but they'll never hear the truth from me."

Morghan hadn't smiled so much in years. She walked the length of the underground room again and lifted the torch to inspect the seamless way the manmade walls blended with the natural ceiling. It had taken Redik a matter of minutes to blast through the top of the cave—and half of the room next to hers—and in little more than a month, he and his sons had brought down enough stone to wall off a room easily four times the size of her living quarters. The room even came equipped with a hidden door that led to the caves. When she'd first asked for direct access, her idea had been a hole and a ladder, but this was so much better.

"Windstarr!" Redik's voice came from above her. "You down there?"

"Just admiring your work," she called back.

"As much as I enjoy being told how amazing I am, you might want to admire it later. Michael is back."

Morghan's new basement lowered significantly in importance, and she ran up the first two flights of stone steps before grabbing the rope ladder and hauling herself to the top. Bael hadn't been joking when they dug the hole; it was easily four stories deep, and while the majority of the room was complete, the stairs had yet to be finished. Eventually they would end flush against the hole in her floor, and she could wall off that section of the room in order to put a doorway leading to the stairs.

But she could trust Redik to make sure all of that was done properly. Right now she was more interested in the response from Vahyir, not to mention finding out what in God's name had taken Michael so long to return.

As she reached the top of the ladder, Redik lit into one of the coughing fits he'd been having more and more lately, despite not looking the least bit sick. She jumped onto solid ground and put a hand on his back as he finished coughing.

"I'm fine." His voice was low and raspy. He was

wheezing so loud she would have heard it from down the hall.

"Not really. This has been going on for weeks, and it's getting worse. Are you inhaling something you shouldn't?"

Redik stepped out of reach. "I bet it's that green junk the white powder gives off when I purify it. I'll get used to it."

"Wait, green junk? You mean gas?"

Redik nodded as he coughed into his hand. "Yeah, light green, almost yellow. Can't be too bad for me in the end."

Yes, it could. If he was accidentally creating chlorine gas while desiccating the powder, then it could prove deadly to more than him. "Redik, you need to stop making white until I take a look at your set up. If that gas is what I think it is, it's poisonous."

Redik grumbled an agreement and waved her off as he left the room.

"I'm serious, no white!" she called after him as she entered the hallway and shut the door behind her. When she turned in the opposite direction, the number of torches and candles in the tavern made the end of the hall glow several times brighter than the rest of it. While Michael had chosen to live near the markets in the center of the city, Morghan preferred her room where she could keep a close eye on where the most important information traded hands.

"There you are!" Michael waved her over to his table as she entered the tavern. His eyes glittered, and his smile was far too genuine considering Valerian sat across from him.

She grabbed an empty chair and spun it around before taking a seat and leaning forward over the backrest. "Is Sparkles going to be present for all our conversations from now on?"

Michael's smile faded. "Would it kill you to be civil for once? Apologize to him."

Morghan resisted the urge to belt Michael across the mouth and instead turned to the smug asshole sitting next to her. "I apologize your skin is so thin it shines when light hits it."

That sure wiped the grin off Valerian's face.

"Morghan!" Michael gasped.

She stood and pointed at Michael. "I don't know what took you so long in Vahyir, but when you want to talk about it, alone, I'll be in Redik's workshop."

Morghan hadn't made it as far as her room before footsteps hurried behind her. She stopped and turned around so fast Michael almost ran into her. "That was quick."

"I don't know why you have to be so belligerent all the time. What's wrong with you?"

"A lot." Morghan walked the last few feet to her door and opened it, ushering Michael inside. "Sorry, I killed the mood. I imagine things went well in Vahyir, because you looked so happy before I thought you'd have to be drunk or in love otherwise."

Michael stopped short when he entered her room. He pointed to the hole in the floor. "What's that?"

"A project. Don't worry, everything will be good as new before long."

Michael's face read skeptical at best, but in the end he shrugged it off before walking to her bed and taking a seat. He laid back on the pillows and crossed his legs, mud-caked boots and all, on top of her sheets.

Morghan sat in a chair across the room and rested her head in one hand. She probably wasn't going to use the bed tonight anyway, but she couldn't draw her eyes away from his boots and the mess he'd made. She waved her other hand at him. "By all means."

Michael's smile returned. "Vahyir is with us. Kayla has close to five thousand men, and she'll allow a little over half to march from the city."

"Oh, Kayne's little girl?" Morghan remembered. "I guess Kayne is dead by now."

"For nearly two decades, and Kayla is closing in on fifty." Michael turned on his side. "You used to be human, right?"

Morghan gestured to the rest of her body with her free hand. "I'm still human."

"Sure you are." Michael rolled his eyes. "I meant you were mortal at one time."

"I was. So were you. Where are we going with this?"

"I'm not sure I was." He ignored her question. "My father has wings, too. When our world went to shit, maybe I was too young to realize I didn't age."

He was probably right. "That's fair, but it has nothing to do with me."

"How did you become immortal? Alara and the Evenstars were my mistakes, and neither of them are truly immortal. Alara needs the blood of others, and the Evenstars age about a decade per century."

Knowing Valerian would eventually die was the best thing Morghan had heard in a while, but she tried not to get distracted by the happy news. She leaned back in her chair and stared into Michael's eager eyes. "Why were you in Vahyir so long?"

Michael's brow furrowed. "Don't change the subject. How did you go from being mortal to immortal?"

"Answer my question, and I'll answer yours."

Michael let out a frustrated grunt and turned onto his

back. "It took me almost a week to get there and just as long to get back. I spent the rest of the month negotiating and discussing options for attacking Falcroix."

Morghan thought about calling his bluff by asking for a few of the attack plans, but she decided to let it be. "Did you at least go check out Arden?"

"No. I didn't have time. Besides, I didn't see the point."

"The point is that we're rushing thousands of people into battle on the pretense of something I'd like to be sure actually happened." Morghan threaded her fingers together and cracked her knuckles. She'd asked him to do one thing. One. Thing. "The Evenstars came here beaten and broken, but Predlitz and Bal Mek are closer to them than we are. Why come straight here?"

"Their remaining clansmen scattered, Morghan. It makes sense Valerian, who has been hounding us for decades, would want to get to us as fast as possible."

"He's been hounding us to go to war. Now, we're jumping through our asses to do so. I still—"

"Listen," Michael interrupted her. "If it's that important to you, I'll drop by in the next few weeks, while the armies are preparing to leave. Now, I've answered your question, so hold up your end of the deal."

"I gained immortality through a blood bond with someone who was already immortal. I'm what they call a hybrid."

Michael sat up in the bed, and his eyes glowed. "Wait, I can make someone immortal with my blood?"

"One person." Morghan felt uneasy telling him any of this, but he had a right to know. "Each immortal can make one hybrid. It involves a fairly large exchange of blood, although I'm not sure if the blood flowing from mortal to immortal is all that important. As far as I know, there are only two hybrids in existence, myself included."

"Who is the other one?"

Morghan guessed answering "your father's boyfriend" wouldn't go over very well. Although, to be fair, boyfriend was the wrong word. What was Luke to her, really? Life partner? Life mate? As good as dead? Definitely the last one if nothing else. She resisted the urge to grab her throat when the sensation of it getting decidedly narrower washed over her. If she didn't leave the room and distract herself with something soon, the panic attack would win, and she'd be useless for hours. "It's not important. He's in another realm."

"With your guy?"

"No. Different realm." When her jaw started hurting, she had to concentrate an obscene amount to keep the muscles loose. "Listen, I have to go help Redik. The guy is likely going to kill himself otherwise."

"Are you okay? You're sweating."

"I'm fine." She headed for the door and turned back to Michael with her hand on the knob. "Think hard before you make decisions that can't be undone. Forever is a long time to regret something."

Michael leaned back on his elbows. "Do you regret it?"

"I have more regrets than I can count, but that isn't one of them. Then again, it wasn't my gift to squander, and I can't speak for my other half." The door swung shut behind her when she walked into the hall. Her eyes closed and a few steadying breaths later she forced her thoughts to Redik's most recent invention. Maybe he'd stumbled upon a metal chlorate. It would explain the green gas as well as why it combusted if you so much as looked at it wrong. On a more positive note, she was almost certain they were used as some of the earliest primers for modern bullets.

By the time she had moved through the bustling markets at Salus's heart and started toward the forge, all thoughts of Luke had been dutifully filed away, and she could almost convince herself Redik needed her as much as she needed him.

8

A SUCKER'S GAME

Morghan hugged her coat closer to her chest and bent her face toward the ground to shield it from the wind. It was late fall, and with the army marching so far north, the nights were already colder than Salus in the dead of winter. It had been over a month since the troops left home. Over a month since Michael had abandoned her in order to travel with Vahyir's army instead of theirs. He swore it was in everyone's best interest. That it only made sense for both armies to be protected by immortals until they met. He flew between the two every so often to make adjustments to their course so they would eventually reach what she felt was an arbitrary point a day's march east of Falcroix. His reason for leaving their army was ridiculous, and she'd told him so. Vahyir was over two thousand strong while Salus's forces were well under half that. But, as had become the norm in recent months, Michael ignored logic and did as he pleased. She had no idea who he was fucking from Vahyir, but the distraction was getting on her nerves.

"Windstarr!" Bael screamed from beside her.

"What!" she yelled back. "Christ, Bael, I can hear your voice a quarter mile away. Don't scream in my fucking ear."

"Well you haven't heard us calling you the past five times," he countered. "I thought about using your given name, but my teeth are important to me."

"Go to hell, Bael," she mumbled. Dawn was still a few hours away, and if she finished scouting the camps soon, she might have time to collapse against a tree for some rest before they started moving again. She stood up straighter, her eyes turning to Bael and the other two soldiers walking with them. "So, was your goal to make me deaf, or did you have something to tell me?"

Bael nodded ahead of them. "Well, you can see them for yourself by now."

Morghan looked up and groaned. Valerian walked toward them with Michael by his side. "Is it already time for Michael to remind me which way is north, again?" She pulled a small compass out of her pocket and tapped it. "Still pointing the right way. The magnetic field of the planet hasn't changed in the past nine days. Imagine that."

Bael put his hands in the air, as if to say he wasn't getting involved. He waved to her and turned left to finish the rounds. Lucky bastard. She bet he'd get some sleep. With Michael back, she wasn't going to be so fortunate.

As Michael and Valerian came closer, deep in conversation about whatever useless information they thought was important, Morghan imagined they might walk right past her. It was both an insulting and tempting thought. She hadn't slept in over a week, but she'd be damned if Valerian was going to whisper strategic bullshittery into Michael's ear without her knowing what idiotic plan he was pushing.

Thankfully, Michael stopped in front of her. Valerian

kept going for a few paces before turning back with an annoyed huff and trudging to Michael's side.

Michael glanced at her but kept his eyes predominantly on the ground. "Valerian says you haven't gotten over our last meeting."

Their last meeting? Michael must be talking about when he'd refused to stay and split watch with her, even when it became obvious the stick up Valerian's ass kept the man from helping with anything. "I'm so glad Valerian is an expert on my moods."

"No one is an expert on your moods, least of all you," Michael said. "But I'd appreciate it if you wouldn't slam your gun into my jaw again." He rubbed the spot where she'd hit him, as if he still felt pain.

Morghan shrugged. He'd deserved that and more. "I don't think anyone can be held accountable for their actions after over forty-eight hours without sleep. I'd been up five days straight last time you saw fit to grace us with your presence."

"And now? How long has it been since you slept?" Michael raised an eyebrow.

"She never sleeps," Valerian interjected. "My guards see her walking the camps all night, and she starts out with the troops first thing every morning."

"Well, maybe if I had help with the watch, I wouldn't be forced to stay up for days on end."

"I offered my guards," Valerian insisted. "You turned them down."

"I trust them even less than I trust you." She stepped up to Valerian. He was half a head taller than her but far from the tallest man she'd ever intimidated.

Michael moved between them and put a hand on each

of their chests before glaring at Morghan. "You don't trust anyone."

That wasn't far from the truth. Yet somehow, she kept trusting Michael, and like everyone else she'd ever trusted, he had abandoned her. "Can we have this conversation in private, please?"

"No. Valerian is waging war by our side. He can hear whatever you have to say to me."

"Fine." Morghan backed up and swatted Michael's hand from her chest. "Did you go to Arden? Is it good and burned the fuck down?"

Valerian paled, and his jaw dropped.

"Yes," Michael snapped. "Are you happy? Yes, I went, and yes, it was really destroyed."

Valerian's expression recovered before Michael whirled around on him.

"I'm sorry," Michael said. "She didn't believe you had been attacked."

"It doesn't surprise me." Valerian turned his eyes to the ground. "I told you before, her prejudices and mood swings lead to poor decisions. What makes you think the heat of battle will improve her judgment?"

Morghan lunged at Valerian and brought him down hard against the ground. In the next moment a dagger was in her hand, but she had no time to bring it anywhere close to skin before she went flying through the air. Her right shoulder slammed into a tree and her head followed. She stumbled to her feet, bright flashes of light playing across her vision as she attempted to remain standing and ended up on her knees.

Michael knelt in front of her, and she cringed when he touched her.

"Are you okay?" He sounded genuinely concerned.

"Go away," she said, keeping her head down. She couldn't look at him. He was the last person left in her life that meant anything real, and he'd chosen Valerian over her. More than that, he'd thrown her into a damn tree and nearly broken her neck.

He put a hand on her arm, and when she shied away from his touch, he pulled her closer and wrapped his arms around her. "I didn't mean to throw you. I'm a lot stronger now that my wings are back, and sometimes I forget. I thought you were going to kill him."

Maybe she was going to kill him. She wasn't even sure anymore. She'd killed people for less and when feeling a lot more in control than she currently did. Maybe it had finally gotten to the point where her insomnia overruled sanity. If she was honest with herself, even when she did have a few free hours, she was rarely able to capitalize on the opportunity to sleep. Valerian's reaction to her comment about Michael visiting Arden and the deprecating words that followed had lit a fuse that was already dangerously short.

"Morghan?" Michael held her at arm's length. "Please forgive me. I'm so sorry."

Valerian crouched next to them. "You did nothing wrong, Maritch. She provoked you, and I'm thankful you saved my life."

Michael's eyes never left Morghan. "Valerian, I need you to leave. Go to your tent, and I'll come find you later."

Valerian's jaw clenched, but he was on his feet and moving away from them soon after.

When Morghan could no longer hear his footsteps, she finally dared to look up at Michael. "Something's broken."

He moved to inspect her shoulder.

"Not there. I mean in general. With me."

Michael's shoulders slumped. "You need sleep. I know

we're immortal, but it's still a necessity. I have no idea how you function the way you do."

"Practice." She managed a lazy grin. "See, eight days without sleep, and I can still make a joke. Progress."

Michael didn't look impressed. "Can you stand?"

Morghan nodded and climbed to her feet. Her vision had cleared, but her head still felt like someone had hit it with a hammer.

"Do you even have a place to sleep?"

"Against a tree, or wherever I can find a dry spot if it's raining," she said.

Michael grumbled a few words under his breath. "Vahyir can live without me for a while. I'll stay and split watch with you for the next few days, as long as you promise to sleep. In the end, you're going to have to trust someone else to do it without us. If not Valerian's men, then some of ours."

"I know." He was right, of course. Besides the Evenstars, she had trained every last man in the camp, and other than her own insecurities, there was no real reason she needed to scout and keep watch. It kept her busy though, and that was something more than staring at the sky and fighting off thoughts of Luke and Azrael while she waited for sleep to take her. "I'll just sit under that tree over there and sleep for now."

"No." Michael steered her toward the tents where Bael had disappeared earlier. "We'll find you a tent with a blanket and something soft to use as a pillow. I'll head out with the troops this morning, and you can sleep. Take the damn weapons off and let Bael and Merrick guard you. When you wake up, the three of you should have no trouble catching us."

At that point, Morghan would have gone along with

almost anything Michael asked. She hoped he was right about sleep fixing her, but somehow she knew better.

It had taken over a week of forcing Morghan into a somewhat normal sleep pattern before Michael was comfortable enough to leave. By then, the flight between armies had lasted less than a day, which meant they would meet on the ground in a week or two. That was probably for the best, as he was certain Morghan would fall back into her old habits without his constant pestering.

The sun was sinking low in the sky by the time Michael spotted Vahyir's forces making their way through the final mountain pass between them and Falcroix. Once they were through, forests would shield them for the rest of the journey until they marched onto the barren fields surrounding the forsaken city.

Michael searched the front lines for Kayla and her guards, but they were nowhere to be found. He landed in front of the army and faced the leading officers as they rode toward him. The entire front line brought their horses to a halt and raised their left fists in the air. The men behind them stopped marching, and the call to halt flooded through the ranks, although it took several minutes for the metallic clank of armor to fade into the distance.

The officer in the center rode his horse to Michael and offered a quick bow of his head. "Is something wrong?"

Michael rubbed his hands together and shivered. He really needed a coat that would fit around his wings, or at the very least a shirt. The skies were always cold, but with the amount of time he'd spent either in the north or traveling there, it was a wonder he hadn't frozen straight through by now. "I couldn't find Kayla. Causing the entire army to stop wasn't my goal."

The officer waved a hand in dismissal. "We were about to stop and make camp anyway. Between you and me, my ass has been numb for days. Any extra time I can get off this beast is for the best."

Michael knew the feeling all too well, and he didn't miss it in the least. "And Kayla?"

The officer cocked a thumb behind him. "The queen has been ill the past few days, so we doubled her guard and sent her to the back to be safe."

"Is it bad?" Michael's wings rustled, and he nearly took off before the officer had a chance to answer.

"Difficult to tell. The winters in Vahyir train our men not to complain about anything less than a missing limb. Even in those cases, our women look at the bloody stump and roll their eyes."

That didn't make Michael feel any better about whatever illness had taken Kayla off the front lines. He thanked the man and took to the skies, speeding over the regiments until he spied Kayla riding with an impressive entourage of guards on both foot and horseback. Doubled wasn't even close to accurate. Her guard was closer to quadrupled.

Michael landed beside Kayla as her group came to a halt with the rest of the soldiers. "I heard you were sick. Need a hand down?"

Kayla glared at him and dismounted without a word. Michael caught a fleeting grimace as her feet hit the ground, but otherwise, the resolve on her face could have been carved in stone. She grabbed the reins of her horse and flipped open a saddle bag. She pulled out a thick, fur-lined coat and shoved it into Michael's arms. "If the clouds aligned, there would be snow on the ground."

That was as close to a loving "I'm worried you'll freeze to death" Michael would ever get from her while in front of her men. He closed his eyes and took a deep breath, concentrating on how he wanted his back to appear. The building pressure in his chest made it difficult to breathe, but when it passed, he was left with working lungs and a smooth back. Morghan had warned him not to shapeshift his wings away unless he was sure he could bring them back, and it had taken weeks of partially shifting them back and forth before he'd gotten up the courage to completely send them away. Now, ridding himself of them was easy, but each time he brought them out, every nerve in his back screamed in protest.

Michael shrugged into the coat and pulled it closed. He could have kissed Kayla for the warmth it provided, but she would have chastised him if he tried. The whole of Vahyir knew they were lovers before the army ever left, but their relationship had rules. Unlike Morghan, Kayla didn't think being romantically linked to him threatened her authority. In fact, it was quite the opposite, with the caveat that displays of affection in public were strictly hers to initiate. Michael had found that easier to agree with than adhere to, but Kayla was always more flustered than angry each time he forgot. That could change with a war to wage and an illness hanging over her, so he decided not to tempt fate.

They stood side by side in silence as Kayla's guards erected her tent. She was several shades paler than usual, and the hollow look of her cheeks had Michael wondering how much weight loss her armor hid. The expression on his face must have been too concerned, because her eyes narrowed when she noticed him looking at her. He cast his gaze to the ground, and his chest tightened. Had she caught some deadly illness? If so, why hadn't any of her guards suffered along with her? Kayla should have years of potential good health left, but he couldn't get that sliver of knowledge to take root in his mind. Or his heart. Instead, he took her hand in his, shocked and more than a little relieved when she squeezed it in return.

Kayla grabbed the front of his coat with her free hand and pulled him into a kiss so fierce his knees threatened to buckle. "I'm fine," she whispered against his ear once the kiss ended. "Try to look like you believe me, at least until we get inside."

Michael wasn't sure what to make of her words, but he tried his best to follow through with her request.

When the tent was finished, Kayla unstrapped the saddle bags from her horse and slung them over her shoulder. She motioned for Michael to follow her into the tent, and once inside, she turned the bags upside down and emptied them on the floor before sinking into the pile of furs that served as a makeshift bed.

"What are you doing?" Michael sat down beside her and laid a hand on her arm.

Kayla pushed his hand away and held up a finger before leaning over and vomiting into one of the bags. She wiped the back of her arm across her mouth and set the bag to the side. "I must have swallowed that ten times throughout the day's ride."

Michael stacked some of the furs into a more prominent heap and goaded Kayla into laying back onto them. He stretched out next to her and draped a larger fur over both of them before pulling her close. "How long have you been sick?"

"Far longer than you've been gone." She smiled, and Michael couldn't help but notice the dark rings under her eyes. "The past few days have been worse, so it's harder to hide. I expected you to return before now. Was there a problem?"

"I had to help Morghan with something." He leaned his forehead on her shoulder, and the cold metal against his skin reminded him she was still in her armor. "Mostly I had to keep her from killing Valerian."

"I like her more each time you bring her up." Kayla chuckled. "I'm looking forward to fighting beside her. I dreamed about it for years after the two of you visited Vahyir. It's a shame the only women soldiers in my kingdom are those who sit on the throne. There's an unfortunate lack of women to look up to for a young girl hoping to grow into a warrior queen."

"You should tell her that. It might help her warm up to you, keeping in mind she's all ice on the surface." Michael wasn't sure if Morghan would get along with Kayla or not. He could envision them being great friends or mortal enemies in equal measure but more likely the latter once he took into account Morghan learning about his romantic extracurriculars. The one thing he knew for sure, was that he didn't want Kayla fighting next to anyone if she was this ill.

"We're getting close to Falcroix," Michael went on. "What will you do if you're this sick when we get there?"

Kayla laid a hand on his cheek and smiled. "I doubt it will be a problem by then. Don't worry, I'll rally. I have a few good years left in me."

A few good years. Michael thought about burying Raelik and all the communications he'd received over the years about the passing of those he'd known. Those he'd forgotten about for a moment that stretched into decades in the blink of an eye. Decades Kayla didn't have. Being the northernmost city in the realm, Vahyir's winters were unforgiving, and Kayla was already inching up on the life expectancy of those from her kingdom. Granted, royals often lived significantly longer, but he still didn't like thinking about it.

"Do you love me?" Michael asked, knowing the question was likely to lead to either the end of their relationship or a new beginning.

The lines on Kayla's forehead deepened. "I wasn't raised to look for love, Michael. We fit together well. I care for you in a way I never did for the fathers of my children, but I wouldn't swear to it being love."

So she didn't love him? Or maybe she was saying she didn't know what love was? Nothing like complicating matters even more when trying to decide whether or not to use your one chance at a life partner. Michael kissed her forehead and smiled. His love for her would have to be enough.

"Let me make you immortal. It would heal whatever is wrong with you now, and you would rarely if ever get sick again." Michael tightened his embrace.

"What?" Kayla's eyes widened.

"I get one chance to make a partner who will live as long as I do, and I want it to be you."

Kayla sat up and untangled herself from Michael's arms. She crawled over to the saddlebags and emptied what was left in her stomach before turning back to Michael with wild eyes. "Absolutely not."

Michael frowned. His inner dialogue on the matter had revolved around whether she would take his gift and stay with him or take it and leave. He hadn't even considered she would refuse. "You want to die?"

She spit into the bag and shook her head. "Of course

not, but while my time here is limited, it is *my* time. I refuse to chain myself to anyone for eternity."

"Chained?" He sat up. "Don't be ridiculous. Morghan was mortal before someone shared their gift with her. Does it sound like she's chained to anyone? I've known her for half a century, and since we met there's been no contact between her and the man who made her immortal."

"So, you don't expect me to stay with you once I become immortal?" she wondered.

"Of course I expect you to stay with me." His hands were clamped so tightly beneath the furs the nails bit deep into his palms. "I can't make you stay with me, but I hope you would want to do so."

"Right now you say that, but what about when I decide it's time we part ways? I'm willing to risk breaking your heart once, but I would have to hate you to leave it eternally broken by taking away your only chance at a mate."

"You're just being stubborn." Michael struggled to hold back tears as the conversation moved steadily toward the end he had feared most. He never should have asked if she loved him. Never should have broached the topic at all.

"Michael, six months ago I wasn't looking for any of this." She placed a hand on his shoulder and gestured between the two of them with the other. "Men came when I asked and left when I was through with them. I thought it would be the same with you." She moved her hand to the side of his neck and brushed her thumb across the angle of his jaw. "I don't regret what we've become, but I have no idea how I'll feel after the next six months have passed. I have a kingdom to rule and a daughter to prepare for the throne. That is my world. The concept of committing to something for eternity won't even fit inside my mind."

Michael pulled back from her and kicked the furs away.

He stood and paced the room, his strides stiff. "I can't believe we're having this conversation. I offered you eternal life, and you dismissed it as if it was nothing."

Kayla's response came in a low, warning growl. "It's too much of everything."

Michael didn't care if she was angry. People were always angry with him for the stupidest reasons, and he was sick of it. His wings tore free from his back as thunder crashed overhead and a bolt of lightning ripped through the tent. It grounded in his chest and white sparks scattered from his skin like fireworks, fizzling out as they floated to the ground. The scent of ozone lingered.

Kayla scrambled to her feet. "You dare threaten me?" Her eyes were alight with fury as she pointed to the tent's entrance where a rush of guards poured through it. "Leave. Now. You can spend the rest of this journey with your own people. Vahyir will keep its word and fight beside Salus in Falcroix, but rest assured our alliance will be reassessed shortly thereafter.

"If you don't take care of yourself, you'll be dead soon anyway!" he barked, before ripping a new exit in the wall of the tent and taking to the skies.

Morghan stood in front of the line of guards that separated Salus's camps from those of Vahyir. It stretched through the trees as far as she could see in either direction. She'd have to remember to make sure they weren't surrounding Salus's army instead of creating a border, but making it past them without spilling any blood was the current priority.

When Michael had returned ranting about consequences of some nameless mistake he'd made in Kayla's presence, Morghan thought he was being dramatic. Clearly, that wasn't the case. This latest development piqued her interest and made her forget her original annoyance when Michael had asked for a favor. Why he wanted an update on Kayla's health was beyond her, especially since it looked like the queen wanted nothing to do with any of them.

The guards stared at her as she rifled through the pockets of her coat. The outer ones held the usual fare: her compass, matches, flint and tinder. The one that usually held her cigarettes was empty, so she turned to the inside pockets. These were devoted to the more esoteric: gut sutures, small satchels of various colored powders, padded bottles of chemicals, some more volatile than others, and a couple small prototype weapons from Redik. But not a single damn cigarette.

She cursed and approached the closest guard. He gave a short bow and put a hand on the hilt of his sword. The guards to either side of him turned to face her and drew their swords but did not advance.

"Do you know who I am?" Morghan asked, her eyes locking with his, although she was acutely aware of the amount of steel at the ready.

"Everyone knows who you are," the guard answered, his voice less steady than his stance. "The queen is expecting you, but she insists you be bound and disarmed while on our side of the camps."

Morghan fiddled with the hilts of her daggers as she thought over the outrageous demand. The man had given her a sliver of hope that her task would be easier than expected and then ripped it away in the next breath. "If one of you has a cigarette to spare, you can bind me with whatever you want. If you're brave enough to attempt disarming me afterwards, be my guest, but you don't have my consent for that."

The man in front of her repeated his bow before disappearing into the camps, and the wall of guards shifted, filling the hole. The men who had drawn their swords put them away, and by the time the original guard returned Morghan was halfway through her first cigarette with several more tucked in her pocket. She could get used to being frenemies with Vahyir if this was the level of hospitality she could expect.

"Follow me." The guard waved her forward. "Eight!" he yelled as she fell in step beside him, and the number of guards he'd called for created a tight circle around them as they walked.

"Where are my chains?" Morghan smirked. It was adorable how they thought a few extra men made them safer.

"Apparently, making the queen laugh means you don't need them. No one makes any sense these days."

"Well, now I feel guilty for taking the cigarettes." Morghan stuffed her hands into her coat pockets and shivered. What Redik should have made her was a portable space heater. "Not guilty enough to return them, but if you put a rope around my wrist, it might ease my conscience."

He shook his head and pulled the flap back from a large, circular tent before ushering her inside. The vaulted ceiling was massive, and the smell of well-oiled leather permeated the air. There were two large areas that had been recently patched, one in the wall and a larger one on the ceiling.

"Looks like somebody needs a new tent," Morghan quipped. "A shame. This thing screams heirloom."

"You can have Michael commission one for me in Salus and send it as the first of many apology gifts," Kayla responded, drawing Morghan's attention to the center of the tent, where she sat on a veritable throne of furs. Two of her personal guards stood to either side of her, and the walls were crowded with upwards of twenty more. Morghan didn't blame her; Kayla may have been clad in armor with a sword at her hip, but her eyes were sunken and surrounded by dark circles, her cheeks and jawline prominent in a way that led Morghan to believe whatever was hell-bent on sucking the life from her was winning.

"Michael did that?" Morghan gestured to the tent's patchwork as she moved closer to Kayla. When she came within a few steps of her, the guards at her side drew their swords and crossed them over one another, barring Morghan from going any farther. They really needed a new defensive stance. If Morghan wanted she could have disarmed both of them and snapped Kayla's neck in a matter of seconds.

"He offered me something, and I refused." Her lips pressed into a thin line. "My response was not well received."

"Shit, it was you." She couldn't believe they were a day's march from Falcroix, and the armies were at odds over a lovers' quarrel. Although, thinking back over her time in Luke's realm, she didn't have room to talk. Still, on the brink of war? Fucking ridiculous. Though it did make her analyze Kayla's illness from a few different perspectives. "I should have known."

"Excuse me?" Kayla's mouth turned down in a tight frown.

"I knew he was fucking someone around here." She pulled out another cigarette and lit it with one of the few matches she had left.

"The only females allowed to serve in our military are royal."

"I didn't know. I can't keep up with every kingdom's hypocrisy. It makes sense though. Michael has a thing for strong-willed women."

Kayla's knuckles blanched, and her tone was laced with thinly-veiled rage. "Is that so?"

"Calm down, Your Highness. I never have and never will sleep with Michael. Although, to be fair, should you even care anymore?"

"What I care about is none of your concern, but I would appreciate it if you'd tell Michael to stop sneaking into my camps. He left a letter saying you were coming—in the middle of my tent. It's frustrating when our only hope of keeping him out is to shoot him from the sky."

"Try it, and whether the archers hit their mark or not, I'll save your kingdom the suspense over when its next heir comes to power."

Kayla stood and unsheathed her sword. She pushed past her guards and pressed the tip of it against Morghan's chest. "I allowed you passage here, and I will not be threatened. I think the time has come for you to state your business and be on your way."

Morghan glanced at the sword with little interest. She drew deeply on the cigarette between her lips and exhaled a cloud of smoke in Kayla's face. "Despite whatever happened between the two of you, Michael is worried about your health. I promised him I'd take a look at you and give him a report."

"You've looked at me. Now leave."

Morghan took a step back from Kayla's blade. "You look like shit. How long has this been going on?"

Kayla lowered her sword. "I'm not comfortable discussing this with you."

"Then I'm not comfortable leaving. You can try to force me out, and you might succeed, but I can promise you every guard in this room will die in the process." Morghan tossed the remainder of her cigarette to the ground. "I can live with that. Can you?"

Kayla glared at her before turning to her guards. "Leave us."

A chorus of whispers came from the guards around the room until Kayla turned back and slammed the broad side of her blade into the chest plate of the closest guard, knocking him to the ground. "I said leave!"

They fell silent and filed out of the tent. When the two women were alone Kayla turned back to Morghan. "No matter what you bring away from this conversation, your first priority should be convincing Michael my health is no longer his concern."

Morghan had never let anyone else dictate her priorities, and she didn't plan on starting now. Kayla's first mistake had been letting her into the tent, and her second was assuming she shared Michael's concern for her well-being. "I'm going to make this line of questioning rapid-fire, because I have better shit to do than babysit Michael's ex-lovers. Are you still vomiting?"

Kayla reclined on the furs and nodded. "Several times a day. All I have to do is look at food and my body revolts, but when I skip a meal I have to force down water in order to have something to bring back up."

"Anyone else suffering from this?"

Kayla stared at the ceiling and shook her head. "The timing couldn't be worse. I need to be strong right now, and my body fails more with each passing day."

Morghan had hoped for simple yes or no answers, not the woman's life story. "Are you feeling feverish or having trouble breathing?"

"I can breathe fine, but I've been too hot or too cold for months now, long before the illness set in. It's that time."

Morghan quirked an eyebrow. "Now you decide to be vague?"

Kayla let out an annoyed huff. "I haven't bled for the better part of a year. It's normal to feel hot and cold for no reason at this point in my life."

Shit. "How long have you and Michael been together?"

"Since he came to ask for our aid, so four or five months by now. I never meant for it to be more than a single night of pleasure, but I allowed my heart to rule my mind and now look where it's taken us. There's more than one reason my family doesn't marry."

"Did you have vomiting this bad with your other pregnancies?" Morghan looked around for a chair before giving up and sitting on the ground. She was seventy-five percent sure Kayla was pregnant and one hundred percent sure things couldn't be worse.

"I am not pregnant." The fear shining in Kayla's eyes hinted that she hadn't completely convinced herself it was true. "I hadn't bled for six months before Michael and I shared a bed."

"Six months doesn't impress me." If Michael's humans were like the ones in their old realm, it didn't even count as menopause until it had been over a year. There was a good ass reason for that definition. It involved a small human unexpectedly taking up residence in a uterus. Fuck. Ninety percent sure. Morghan massaged her temples and wished someone would pistol-whip her out of this nightmare. "Just answer the question. Have you ever felt like this before?"

Kayla crossed her arms over her chest. "Only with my twins. I had four single pregnancies without issue, but I could barely stand I was so sick with both sets of twins."

Ninety-nine percent sure and possibly twins. Okay, so it could get worse after all. Morghan clung to one last ray of hope. "Is there any chance Michael isn't the father?"

Kayla looked like she was about to hyperventilate. Maybe the two of them could share a paper bag, assuming this realm even had any. "I've been sick for over two months, and I'm ashamed to say I've lost interest in sharing my bed with other men since I've been with Michael. If I am pregnant, then the child is his."

Morghan climbed to her feet and paced a short line in front of Kayla. "Okay, this is easier than we're making it out to be. You just won't fight. We can leave tonight and start for Bal Mek. It's closer than Salus. You can rest and recover there."

"The rulers of Vahyir have never let their people fight alone. I will not be the first to abandon them."

Morghan stopped pacing. "You will die if you fight like this."

"Then it will be a good death."

"No, it won't. There are no good deaths when your unborn child dies along with you."

Kayla stood and walked toward Morghan until their faces were a hairsbreadth apart. "I've already provided an heir for my throne. You can't force me to leave."

The Hell she couldn't. Morghan grabbed Kayla by the shoulder and spun her around. A dagger at her throat was enough to keep her from screaming while Morghan reached inside her coat and removed one of the padded vials. She crushed it in her hand and held it over Kayla's nose and mouth. A moment later the queen's knees buckled, and her eyes rolled as she passed out in Morghan's arms.

Morghan knelt and laid Kayla on the ground as gently as possible. The tricky part was going to be getting past the guards, both the ones who were outside the tent as well as those on the makeshift border between armies. She pulled out several pouches of black powder and ripped them open over the pile of furs, shaping the majority of it into a cone before grabbing another vial from her coat. This one had a large red X scrawled across it and when she shook it the rest of the cloth surrounding it bled into the same color as its label. She dug a small hole in the top of the mound of black powder and set the vial in the center, shoring it up against its sides. Morghan then took every pouch of blue powder she could find in her pockets and shoved them up her sleeves before hoisting Kayla over her shoulder and pulling out her last match.

Morghan struck the match against her thumbnail. She could do this. It wouldn't be pretty, but if she played her cards right, she might even get away with it. And like every smoke and mirrors plan worth having, it started with fire.

9

BLACK DIAMONDS ARE FOREVER

Under any other circumstances, Bael being speechless would have counted as a good day in Morghan's book. However, as he turned his slack-jawed face from where she sat in the corner sewing up a gash in her arm to where Kayla was tied up, gagged, and completely awake in the center of the tent, Morghan couldn't bring herself to enjoy his silence.

"You abducted the queen," Bael stammered. Good thing she hadn't celebrated the silence. "The queen. Of Vahyir."

"I'm aware." Morghan tied off her work with one hand and ripped the thread with her teeth.

"Did it occur to you that over two thousand soldiers will be looking for her?"

"It's possible they think she died in a fire. But yes, the possibility did cross my mind. The mystery will add excitement to the mix while she's under your watch."

"What?" Bael squeaked.

"I'm officially dubbing you and Merrick the queen's babysitters." Morghan stood and brushed off her pants. Residue from the blue powder was everywhere, she could even taste it coating her tongue. There was nothing like a good smoke bomb to assist with escaping from a tough spot, but she was going to insist Redik find a new formula for blue to make it more manageable after the fact.

"So, do you want her safe or hidden?" Bael muttered.

"Preferably both, but safe above all else." Morghan knelt next to Kayla and tapped the gag with her finger. "You'll have a hard time puking around this, so if you promise not to scream I'll take it off."

Kayla threw her head forward, and it connected with Morghan's nose with a loud crack. Morghan jumped to her feet and spat blood. She pinched her nose to stem the tide of red that poured over her chin.

Bael grabbed Kayla by her armor and was in the process of flinging her across the room when Morghan stepped in front of him.

"Put her down. She's not to be harmed under any circumstances."

Bael looked at Morghan as if she'd lost her mind, but he followed the order. "The woman broke your nose with her damn forehead!"

Morghan touched her nose and winced. "Master of the obvious today, Bael. She also sliced the shit out of my forearm when she woke up earlier than I expected."

Kayla broke into the conversation. "You have no right to do this! Release me this instant!" The gag had apparently slipped down to her neck when Bael yanked her off the ground.

"I have every right," Morghan seethed, shaking the blood from her hand. They were in a guard tent on the southeast edge of Salus's camps, farthest from the gates of Falcroix. With Kayla so close to Morghan's ear as she moved through the forest, it had become painfully obvious the woman had too many heartbeats. "That's Michael's blood you're carrying. My blood. And I will not stand by while you recklessly throw yourself on a sword in the name of honor. Give it five or six months and I'll hold the sword for you. Until then, you belong to me."

"Your blood?" Kayla's brow furrowed. "That's impossible. Do you even realize what Michael is?"

"Yes, my only living descendant." Morghan didn't give a shit about the shock in Kayla or Bael's eyes. They were a stone's throw from a city they shouldn't be attacking, with an outnumbered group of soldiers that didn't represent a united front, and now she had to manage this clusterfuck on top of it all. "You will sit your ass right here until I deem it safe to evacuate. Are we clear?"

Kayla frowned. "Michael never said anything about the two of you being related."

"It's complicated." Morghan's face itched where the blood was drying. She had to get cleaned up before Michael wondered what was taking her so long. Or worse, before Vahyir's soldiers came to him regarding Kayla. "And if I hear even a whisper about it once I leave this tent, heads will roll."

"He doesn't know, does he?" Kayla leaned against the pole in the center of the tent. "You're his second-in-command. You shouldn't be keeping secrets from him."

Bael's laughter rolled through the tent until Morghan silenced him with a warning glare.

She turned to Kayla once Bael had himself under control. "I play my cards close and do what needs to be done."

"Does anyone else even have any cards?" Kayla sneered.

They thought they did, which was all that mattered.

Morghan could have kissed Merrick when he walked

into the tent a moment later. He stared at the three of them through a curtain of blond hair but didn't say a word as he walked across the tent and handed Morghan the travel pack he'd retrieved for her. Merrick waved his hands in protest when she opened her mouth to explain. "I don't even want to know. Just tell me who I should and shouldn't be sticking the pointy end of my sword into tonight, and let's leave it at that."

"Anyone who tries to hurt the queen." Morghan shouldered the pack and headed out of the tent. "I shouldn't be long. I want to be out of here before dawn."

Merrick beamed. "My favorite kind of mission, the one where I don't have to die a horrible death at the hands of monsters."

Morghan rolled her eyes and walked out of the tent, leaving Bael to fill in any blanks Merrick might care to know. The two men couldn't have been more different, but that didn't keep them from complementing one another well in and out of combat. As Morghan cleaned her face and changed into a fresh set of clothes, she felt guilty and more than a little selfish for stealing them away from the battle. She tried not to play favorites among the soldiers, but Bael and Merrick had become the closest thing to a personal guard she allowed.

Michael was sitting by the fire when Morghan made it to the central camp. He looked up when she approached, but there was no smile on his face. "Kayla is missing. A contingency of soldiers from Vahyir just left, and they were looking for you. I don't think they believed me when I told them I hadn't seen you since this morning."

Morghan sat next to him and stared into the flames. "Doesn't matter. It was the truth."

"You were supposed to look at her and give me a

report, Morghan. I'm not sure how you created more chaos than I did. They're screaming abduction or worse —murder."

"Don't be ridiculous. I went and saw her like you asked. She looked like shit, we talked a little, and I left. Her guards weren't even in the tent with us most of the time. How would they know anything?"

"They know you were there with her. Now, the tent is in ashes, and Kayla is missing." Michael put a hand on her arm and squeezed it just hard enough to be uncomfortable. The warning look in his eyes didn't quite match his words. "I'm not naïve enough to believe you. Please tell me you didn't kill her."

"She's safe." Morghan touched her aching nose. "Stubborn but safe."

Morghan heard the soldiers sneaking out of the trees behind her, but Michael's hand on her arm held her in place until cold steel pressed into her back and against the side of her neck.

Coming back had been a mistake. She had wanted to alert Michael he'd be waging war without her, and she'd meant to let him know only what was necessary to insure he was on board with getting Kayla healthy again, even if abduction was the only way to do so. She should have had Bael and Merrick ride ahead a few miles to insure the way south was clear and been done with it; they could have been well on their way to Bal Mek by now.

Michael leaned in close. "Try not to kill them," he whispered. He stood up and smiled at the soldiers before punching the nearest one in the face.

A trail of blood warmed the side of Morghan's neck as the blade against it slid to the ground with its owner, but she could have come out a lot worse. She dove forward to escape the rest of the swords at her back as a second soldier hit the ground beside her.

She stood and drew her sword, turning back to the fight where Michael was engaged with six other men wearing Kayla's crest. Several of Salus's soldiers stood to the side, their eyes darting from Michael to Morghan and back, as someone had forbidden them from fighting. Probably Michael.

Morghan decided the best way to honor Michael's request and be efficient was to pick them off one by one with minor injuries. But before she could charge into the fray, a horn sounded far to the north. It may have been beyond the reaches of Salus's army, but the sound was universally known: a warning call to battle.

The soldiers from Vahyir backed away from Michael and lowered their weapons, turning to one another in confusion. Michael glanced back at Morghan, his chest heaving. "Maybe it was a mistake."

A moment later the sound repeated, this time to the east, and Morghan couldn't even finish her curse before another blasted from the south. "For fuck's sake!" she screamed. "Has anyone scouted at all today?" Not that it mattered anymore.

Michael threw his coat to the ground and his wings bloomed from his back. "Falcroix has been quiet all day."

"We have three other borders!" Morghan sheathed her sword, her mind running over a thousand possible outcomes, all of which ended in various levels of them being fucked. "Why bother marching an army from your stronghold if you can force your enemy to retreat to your front door?"

She bolted to the nearest horse and swung herself onto it before turning back to Michael and pointing to the sky.

"I'm not sure you'll be able to see anything between the trees and the sliver of moon hanging up there, but check if there's an opening for retreat that doesn't lead straight to Falcroix."

"And if there's nothing?" The desperation shining in Michael's eyes told her their assessments were equally grim.

"Falcroix doesn't expect this attack to last long. Push north with Vahyir. Just keep going and whatever follows you will eventually give up, starve, or freeze to death." Morghan turned to the soldiers they had been fighting. "Work for you, eagle boys? Let's pretend to like each other for a while. I know you aren't the retreating type, but go make sure your people are moving north all the same."

Morghan turned the horse south and gunned it. As she rode past a bewildered Valerian she let her foot slip the stirrup and gave him a swift kick to the chest, sending him sprawling. It was childish and uncalled for but provided a small amount of joy in an expanding sea of despair.

The southern call to battle blared several more times before Morghan reached what was left of the tent where she had hidden Kayla. The canvas was tattered and stained with a mix of crimson and grey. Dismembered Legion bodies lay where they had fallen in an expansive arc surrounding it. While the battle had shifted locations, two orcs hovered over the wreckage, intent on whatever was on the ground.

One looked up as Morghan's horse approached. Its mouth was stained red and what was left of a severed limb was held loosely in one hand. It dropped the body part and pushed its companion to the ground before taking off through the trees. Morghan passed the fallen orc and jumped from her horse onto the back of the one fleeing. They rolled to the ground together, and when they finally came to a stop, Morghan was on top, her dagger buried in the center of the monster's neck. She twisted the hilt and grey droplets sprayed from the wound as the expanding blades severed the head from its body. She wasn't sure how much it took to put Alara's creations down and keep them there, but she doubted there'd be much fight left in them without a head.

Morghan stood and strode back toward the one who had fallen to the ground at the tent. It had regained its footing, and for some reason, it thought backing away while watching its attacker was the best course of action. Morghan pressed a button on the side of her dagger and three blades became one. She flipped it over in her hand and sent it flying end over end to bury hilt-deep in her target's chest. As the orc fell to its knees Morghan pulled her katana and sliced through its neck with a single fluid stroke. She retrieved her dagger and trudged back to the remnants of the tent and Bael's half-eaten corpse.

She closed her eyes and tightened her grip on the hilt of her sword. She knelt beside him and forced her hand beneath his breastplate. His body was still warm, and she felt around the sweat and blood-drenched undershirt until her fingers ran over a hard circle of metal near his heart. She forced her finger through the ring and tore it from the fabric it had been sewn into. Bael's wife would be having their second child any time now. He'd talked about it as much as Merrick had endlessly teased him for sewing his wedding ring into his shirt for safe keeping.

Morghan shoved the ring deep into one of her inside pockets and went about sifting through the rest of the bodies. By the look of it, Bael had stood alone in defense, at least near the end, but she had to make sure. As she became more convinced Kayla and Merrick had escaped, the repeated calls to battle she'd heard while riding pushed to the forefront of her mind. It was rare to have the same call sounded in such short succession, but maybe this had been less of a warning and more of a guide.

Morghan mounted her horse and headed northeast, toward the most recent call. She rode at a speed that allowed her to sweep the trees with her gaze and cut down the few Legion stragglers without being forced to dismount.

The sound of ringing steel mixed with the screams of the dying warned Morghan she'd caught up with the battle long before the first glint of armor shone through the trees. She pushed the horse into a sprint and stood up in the stirrups, scanning what she could see of the battle. The gleaming scales of Kayla's armor stood out among the breastplates and chainmail of the other soldiers. Morghan had enough time to spot Merrick fighting at Kayla's back before a blade caught her horse's front legs and she was thrown forward. She flew over several heads before crashing into the back of one orc and rolling to a stop at the feet of another.

Morghan's katana landed a few feet away. She reached into her coat and cursed when she remembered all her blue powder was gone. The orc above her recovered from his shock enough to realize they weren't on the same side, but instead of running her through, he grabbed a dented horn from a strap around his chest and sounded a call identical to the ones she'd heard since her scuffle with the Vahyiran soldiers. The few orcs she could see from her disadvantaged viewpoint stared down at her and echoed their comrade's action with similar instruments. How nice that Alara had used Galmedea's metalworking prowess to create a marching orchestra.

Morghan jumped to her feet and wrapped a hand

around the horn of the closest orc before shoving it down its throat so far the mouthpiece tore through the skin at the back of its neck. She flung the orc's body into the others who were trying a death by splitting headache approach.

Her head spun as she worked through how echoing calls to battle would benefit the Legion. When she bent to pick up her katana, an arrow sliced through her left shoulder, and she fell to her knees. She broke the arrow in half and pulled it out, the S etched into the arrowhead shining red as her blood fed into it.

"Really?" She flung the arrow to the ground and swapped her sword to her right hand as she stood. Maybe, at some point she would be injured by someone or something that wasn't supposed to be on the same side as her.

She finished off the orcs surrounding her and ignored the pain in her shoulder as she pulled herself into the low-lying branches of a tree. Kayla was still standing with a few soldiers from Salus fighting by her side, though they were overwhelmed, and Merrick was nowhere to be seen.

Morghan jumped from the tree and cut her way through the enemies between her and Kayla. While the majority of the Legion's forces attacked when they saw her, several others stepped away and wasted the last moments of their lives sounding a fruitless alert. She fell to one knee as she finished with a particularly strong enemy, or maybe she was just exhausted. She wasn't as fast or effective with her right hand, but she doubted her left shoulder was strong enough to parry.

"I'm thankful you were able to save me from the stress of battle." Kayla's venom-laced words came from above Morghan. She drove a heel into Morghan's back, sending her into the protective circle behind her as she brought her sword around in an arc, splitting her newest adversary's body in two.

Morghan fell behind Kayla and into Merrick. She pushed away from him and struggled to her feet. His eyes were wide and unseeing above a neck laid open to the gleaming white rings of his trachea. His golden locks floated behind his head in a muddy pool of blood.

"We have to get out of here," Morghan screamed as she squeezed between Kayla and the soldier to her left. "We can head back the way I came. It's deserted."

"Away from battle? Do you care nothing for the men you abandon to die?" Kayla winced and placed her left hand over her abdomen before raising her sword and parrying an attack as if nothing had changed. "I never envisioned fighting with you would involve running while others died in our stead."

"Some days you run." Morghan readied herself for the next challenger, but the line of attacking orcs backed away and lowered their weapons as several horns sounded in chorus.

Kayla's sword remained at the ready, but her brow furrowed. "They're winning. Why are they giving up?"

Morghan stepped forward and moved in front of Kayla as the orcs parted to create a clear path for two glittering black figures riding toward them atop horses the color of midnight. "Not giving up." Morghan turned to the soldiers behind her. "Take the queen and go. I've got this."

"What are they?" one of them gasped, his eyes wide.

"Stand there long enough and you're sure to find out," Morghan snapped. "I said go!"

Kayla glanced back at Morghan as she allowed herself to be led away by several soldiers. Morghan gave her an approving nod before turning to the few remaining soldiers at her back. "I meant all of you. Protect the queen."

"We can't leave you alone," one of them protested.

Morghan cuffed him on the ear and pointed toward Kayla with her sword. "That's an order."

She turned back to the Legion's forces and squared her shoulders before starting down the makeshift path the orcs had created. Morghan looked straight ahead as she walked toward the figures on horseback, but she was acutely aware of the orcs on either side of the path as they closed in behind her, blocking any hope of retreat.

The creatures on horseback came to a halt in front of her. Darkness swallowed their eyes and fangs peeked out from behind punchable smirks that were a mirror of one she knew well.

Valerian's sons loomed above her. They glittered like black diamonds in the scant moonlight, the paleness of their skin erased by the dark blood coursing through their veins.

Morghan turned in a slow circle, taking in the mass of enemies surrounding her before facing what was left of the Evenstar princes. "Varin and Vallos, right? I'm going to be honest, I could never tell the difference between you two." She pulled a dagger from her belt and raised the blades in either hand. "So, what are we doing here? Fighting? Waiting for suspenseful background music? You can't tell me a battle call is the only thing you people have learned to play in half century, because that'd be a damn shame."

"Vallos is the short one." Varin grinned. The darkness in his eyes shimmered as he faced the direction Kayla and the soldier's had gone. "He'll be the one draining you, while I tie up some loose ends."

Varin dug his heels into the side of his horse, and it shot forward, tearing through the line of orcs and trampling several in the process. Morghan lunged for him as he passed, but Vallos took her down from behind, slamming into her back and sending her face-first into the muck. He kept his knee in her back and wrapped a hand around each of Morghan's, twisting them until her grip on the blades loosened and her wrists screamed.

Morghan threw her head back and saw stars as it connected with Vallos's, but it was enough for her to pull free and flip onto her back. Her fist connected with his jaw, and he fell to the side. She sat up and grabbed a dagger from her belt, driving the blade through the back of his neck. Vallos made a meager attempt to rise but collapsed without ever getting his chest off the ground.

Morghan turned back to pursue Varin, and her breath caught at the sight of him engaging with Kayla and her dwindling group defenders. She moved to follow Varin through the path he'd created in the line of orcs, but it was as if the act flipped a switch and turned the horde back on. They converged on her, forcing her back until she tripped over Vallos and spilled onto the ground.

She rose to her knees, enemies attacking as fast as she could put blades to flesh, and it was then she spied Valerian out of the corner of her eye. He rode toward them with a group of his men charging behind on foot, and for the first time in her life, she was thrilled to see him.

Her view didn't last long as she was overwhelmed and forced back to the ground. Clawing her way up through the orcs was no easy feat, and by the time she thrust her hand past the last writhing body, every inch of her sang with pain.

A hand grasped hers and hauled her up until she could see a smattering of stars through the trees. Valerian smiled down from his horse and pulled her up until their faces nearly touched.

"Let's find out how immortal you really are," he rasped in her ear, before thrusting her back the way she'd come and ripping his hand from hers.

The triumphant grin on Valerian's face was the last thing Morghan saw before she was pulled down into the pile of enemies and her world went dark.

Alara braced herself over the balcony outside her throne room. The gates in the lowest tier of the city pulled closed behind the cadre of soldiers that no doubt had her prize in tow. It took every bit of restraint she could muster to keep from running down to meet them.

It had been two days since a messenger delivered news that the immortal bitch who had replaced her at Michael's side was captured. Alara's jaw throbbed from the perpetual smile that had taken up residence on her face since then. She couldn't have hoped for a better outcome. Capturing Michael had been her original goal, but Valerian insisted it would have come with so many more complications than this. Neither of them really understood the extent of Michael's power, and beyond that, he would be missed. The woman supposedly lacked wings and relied on weapons and alchemy to make up for a dearth of physical strength. Keeping her subdued would be infinitely easier but with the same benefit of an endless, potent fount of blood. Valerian assured her the woman was unpredictable enough that he could convince Michael she'd abandoned them.

Alara walked into the throne room and crossed to a full-length mirror tucked against the back wall. She adjusted the scarlet cloak on her shoulders and made sure the clasp of golden vines was centered at the base of her neck. The eyes staring back at her were not her own—the irises and much of the white sclera suffused with an insatiable darkness. Thin tongues of black flickered out toward the very edge of her eyes. Her lesser senses were all but gone, and she needed to feed by nightfall or risk her sanity.

Soon.

Soon, she would never have to worry about losing herself to the darkness again. She could look in the mirror without fear, knowing the soft brown of her eyes would be smiling back at her.

This boon couldn't have come with more perfect timing. She had sucked the last mortals of the lower tier dry years ago, and the tributes had slowed to a trickle as Salus and Vahyir's persistent refusal to contribute emboldened other cities to do the same. A self-sustaining food source would make her life so much easier. Maybe, she could concentrate less on toeing the line between sanity and starvation and more on expanding her borders and feeding her ravenous horde.

She hurried to the throne and spread the cloak out behind her as she sat. She crossed her legs, uncrossed them, and pyramided her fingers in front of her, trying to find a posture to exude authority and fear in equal measure. The back of her head thumped against her throne, and she let out a frustrated sigh. One of the perks of commanding a mindless horde was she didn't have to worry about such useless formalities. There would be only one chance at a first impression, although she couldn't decide if she would rather the woman be unconscious or not during their first meeting. It would make things infinitely easier if she was unconscious, but deep down Alara wanted to meet the woman before she hollowed her out with an eternity of pain and suffering. She enjoyed the feel of her victims struggling beneath her as they realized the futility of it all. There was nothing so satisfying as watching the flame of hope die in the eyes of the forsaken.

The double doors at the far end of the hall opened, and Alara leaned forward, her hands gripping the armrests as all thoughts of decorum faded. Her excitement turned to concern when Varin stalked into the room with a large group of her minions trailing behind him. From her vantage point on the dais, the clusters of monsters at his back formed the points of a star, with Varin completing the fifth point at the front. A heavy chain wrapped around his left hand and was held taut over his left shoulder, while his brother lay like so much meat over his right. Her minions strained to keep their own thick, metal chains taut, staggering every few steps. Alara's eyes followed the chains to where they converged in the center. She was sure there was a person somewhere beneath all the metal, held parallel to and easily four feet above the ground, but the metal links were wrapped so many times over that Alara couldn't tell where chains stopped and flesh began. If the chain Varin held hadn't wrapped around the woman's neck and spared her head, Alara wouldn't have known which side of her was which.

Varin stopped at the base of the dais and knelt, dropping Vallos to the ground and giving the chain a hard yank before offering the end of it to her. "Your trophy, my lady."

Alara ran a finger over the chain but didn't take it. "Is this really necessary? These chains are strong enough to lift drawbridges. Are you so weak that you need half the city's worth to subdue a single woman?"

One side of Alara's mouth inched up when Varin's gaze hardened. "She's difficult to contain and remains armed. There's a sword we couldn't take from her. After the first soldier burst into flames, I forced another to try with the same result. We lost scores subduing her." He gestured to where his brother lay on the floor, his breathing so shallow it would have been easy to mistake him for dead. "She even took down Vallos, and despite drinking from several mortals, he hasn't recovered."

"She has bones the same as you and me, Varin. Bones can be broken." Alara walked past him and made a slow circle around the woman who needed a shipyard's worth of iron to keep her from escaping. If this was what it took to hold her, perhaps Valerian was right about Michael being too much.

"I broke both her legs the first time she attempted escape," Varin replied through clenched teeth.

"First?" Alara turned back to him and raised an eyebrow.

"We had her tied to a horse afterwards, but she slipped the ropes and fell to the ground. She took the legs out from under five of us before I realized what happened. Even then, the explosive metal stick she carried killed three more and my side was left burning where one of the projectiles went straight through me. I sent the troops for chains after that, which is why we were delayed."

Alara turned back to her captive and tsked. "So much effort for nothing. Morghan, isn't it? You're awfully quiet for such an unruly captive. Did it take cutting out your tongue to crush your spirit?"

Morghan spat in Alara's face and turned her eyes back to the ceiling.

Varin pulled his chain, and Morghan gagged as it tightened around her neck. "Trust me," he grumbled, "She can talk. I thought you would want to receive her whole, otherwise her tongue would have gone before her legs."

Alara wiped Morghan's saliva from her cheek and pointed to the ground. "Drop her. Remove the chains."

Her minions released their lengths of chain, and Morghan hit the floor with a groan. Varin held fast to his and shook his head. "I wouldn't."

Alara snatched the chain and threw it to the ground. "I can neither see her through chains, nor can I pick a body part from which to feed."

Alara's minions rolled Morghan from side to side as they removed layer after layer of chain until Morghan's blood-drenched clothes showed through. Alara's eye caught the gleaming white hilt of the sword at her hip. It was similar to the one Michael carried, but the initial embossed on hers was upside-down. Morghan's right hand gripped the hilt, but her shoulder was dislocated, and jagged edges of bone poked through the flesh below her elbow.

Alara stepped down hard on the shattered forearm, and Morghan's fingers loosened as her screams echoed through the hall.

"Knife!" Alara put out her hand, and three daggers were offered hilt first. She plucked one and knelt beside Morghan before grabbing the sword by the sheath and slicing through the leather belt securing it to Morghan's side. She had retrieved Michael's sword for him enough times to know how to skirt the rules of the deadly weapons. Even knowing the havoc it could wreak on her body, holding it brought the compulsion to wrap her hand around the hilt. Her right hand hovered over it, and it moved ever closer until golden sparks snapped to life around the hilt and broke whatever spell she was under. She threw the sword to the ground as the sparks ignited and a flame bloomed dangerously close to flesh. She made a mental note to lock the relic away in her deepest vault and forget it.

"Now, she's unarmed." Alara turned to Varin. "Bring your brother here. I'll allow him to drink first for the sake of his injuries." And because she wanted to make sure Morghan's blood wasn't tainted by the same power as her sword.

Varin carried his brother to Alara's side. "Where?"

Alara drew the dagger over the inseam of Morghan's right leg and ripped the fabric to expose her thigh. It was swollen and bruised where Varin had snapped the bone. She tapped Morghan's inner thigh with the dagger. "There's a strong blood line here. I can hold her down while you help him latch to it."

"Get the fuck off me!" Morghan balked, but Alara had no trouble crushing Morghan's chest to the floor with her knee while pinning her arms at her sides.

Varin held down her legs while what little conscious-ness Vallos had left allowed him to latch and draw deeply from her thigh.

Morghan gasped and several more colorful words flew through the air. As time passed, her words slurred until she fell silent, and what little pushback Alara had fought against vanished.

Alara smiled down at Morghan, whose eyes were glazed over and half-closed. The veins of her neck had flattened to nothing and what few breaths she took came as erratic gasps.

"That's enough." Alara ripped Vallos off her prize.

He rolled a few times before coming to a stop and slowly rising to his knees. A shudder ran the length of his body. He looked up at Alara in time for her to see the darkness in his eyes disappear into his pupils, leaving behind the glittering grey her gift had obliterated. None of her creations lost their darkness when they fed, be it on blood or flesh. That trait had always been reserved for her alone.

Vallos licked his lips and stood, rubbing a hand against the back of his neck where the skin was already knitting together over his healing wound. His mouth hung open as he closed his eyes and moaned. "I didn't know it was possible to feel this alive. There's so much more to me now."

Alara's eyes widened when the dark beauty of his skin began to fade. It started at his neck and spread from there, until he stood before her as pure as the day she'd first laid eyes on him. She turned back to Morghan. This woman could heal her. Her blood could provide another chance at life. A normal life.

The temptation overruled Alara's better judgement, and despite Morghan's depleted state, she fell on her, ravaging her neck. She paid no mind to the precious liquid oozing from the gash, and when her teeth sank into Morghan's pulse she drank deep, her veins filling with liquid fire.

Alara pulled back, and every last nerve hummed with power as a kaleidoscope of colors tumbled through her vision and the floor rocked beneath her. She fell forward across Morghan's chest, and a high-pitched giggle met her ears. It took a moment to realize it was coming from her. The woman beneath her was still as death and as pale as the hilt of her accursed sword.

But it was a lie. Morghan may have worn the shroud of death, but her heart beat against Alara's palm with such ferocity it might have burst through her chest and taken flight.

Alara hissed when a hand clamped onto her shoulder, and she whirled around with a flurry of swipes before realizing it was Varin. He dodged her blows and waved his hands so wildly that Alara couldn't help but fall into another fit of giggles. But once she regained her composure, Varin's gestures weren't humorous at all.

Vallos knelt on the floor across the room. Gone from his eyes was the twinkling grey he had so recently reclaimed, and in its place was a fiery red burning through his pupils and stretching to the outer reaches of his eyes. His hands clawed at his neck, and a thick pink froth bubbled past his lips.

Alara didn't have much time to wonder what was happening to him before pain spiked through her chest. She rose and stumbled backward into Varin. Her hands shook, and when she looked down at them the smooth, youthful beauty was gone. In its place were thin, gnarled bones with loose skin and dark blotches spreading up her arms like a rash.

She dared not move to the mirror, and it took all her willpower to put a hand to her face. Alara screamed when limp skin met her fingertips, and when she stepped forward, her leg snapped under the weight of her body. Her shoulder cracked against the stone floor, and she rolled a short distance until she came up against Vallos's body. His eyes were wide and blank, their color drained, leaving them pale and white. Thick pink froth filled his nose and mouth and dripped to the ground beneath his corpse.

Alara sobbed as the skin on her hands aged until it cracked. She shouldn't have been so foolish. Why hadn't she waited for the blood to work through its magic on Vallos first? Now, she would have no one but herself to blame when she withered away to nothing and fell to ash on the floor. And who would rule her kingdom when she was gone? The thought had never crossed her mind. Why would someone with an infinite lifespan contemplate the end? It was the last coherent thought she had before pain tore through her and she tasted blood in the back of her throat as her surroundings faded.

~

Morghan was certain she'd died and gone back to her old existential hell. It was the only way to explain the amount of pain ricocheting through every inch of her. Even swallowing what little saliva she had was like a thousand knives stabbing their way down her throat. She tried to open her eyes, but the lids were glued shut. Eventually they peeled back, offering a first glance of her new home. She hung suspended in the air in the center of Alara's throne room. The chains holding her bit into wrists and ankles, forcing her arms and legs behind her at awkward angles and leaving her in a perpetual state of falling.

Morghan traced the chains around the pulley system mounted to the walls and ultimately to the floor where their free ends wrapped around large wooden spools attached to cranks similar to those used to raise and lower a drawbridge. That meant Alara planned on taking her down sooner or later. She didn't want to think about what they'd be taking her down to do and was certain in the grand scheme of things that being hung from the ceiling like a living chandelier was the lesser of two evils.

Alara's voice floated up to her. "Look, dear. She's finally decided to wake up."

Varin slumped in one of the two thrones on the dais, and the hatred burning in his eyes made Morghan happy she wasn't on the ground. Alara lay curled in his lap. She stretched and slid off him before walking to the cranks and forcing one of them half a turn.

Morghan bit down hard on the inside of her cheek as her arms wrenched farther behind her. The tendons in her shoulders strained to accommodate the unnatural position and failed, causing her body to bow forward when they tore free from bone.

"My apologies." Alara smirked. "I always forget which way is which." She grabbed both cranks and flung them in the opposite direction, sending Morghan into free fall.

Morghan wasn't sure how many bones cracked when she landed on the stone floor at the base of the dais, but she was willing to bet it was somewhere in the neighborhood of two hundred and six. She attempted to roll over, but Alara snatched her up by the hair and forced her onto her knees.

"You will stay," Alara commanded. She released Morghan's hair and went about wrapping her body in chains, pinning her arms to her sides in the process.

"Your hospitality is terrible," Morghan chuckled as blood seeped over her cracked lips.

Alara finished securing the chains and stood in front of Morghan. "Vallos is dead because of you, and I was very near the same. By some miracle, whatever poison your blood is laced with brings me to the brink of death before rebuilding me stronger than ever."

"Sadly, I can't take credit for that." Morghan spat a few fragments of teeth at Alara's feet. "Poisonous blood comes with the whole immortal hybrid package, or so I've heard." At least now she knew it was true. She looked at Varin. "No hard feelings. I hope Sparkles Jr finds a nice toasty spot in the afterlife to sit and rot."

Varin shot from the throne, and Morghan hoped to regain the luxury of being out cold, but Alara stopped him before he made it off the dais.

"Time. Give it time," she cooed. "Why don't you retrieve the gift we saved for our guest?"

Varin readjusted his armor and glared at Morghan for a long moment before stalking out the door. Alara sat on the dais, a languid smile holding steady on her face until Varin returned with Kayla in tow. He brought her to a halt a few feet in front of Morghan.

Kayla's thin linen shirt accentuated both her wasting frame and the growing bulge of her abdomen.

The pain thundering through Morghan's body was nothing compared to the panic rising in her chest. Morghan had thought her dead, and now she wished it was true.

"You were out so long." Alara smiled at Morghan. "Close to three months. Imagine our excitement, when we realized the queen was expecting."

Alara placed one hand on Kayla's shoulder and the other on her rounded belly. Morghan really hoped Kayla would vomit on her. Or slit her throat. Maybe she had a blade hidden somewhere in her clothing, or maybe her fingernails were really long and sharp by now.

It could happen.

"On your knees, your highness," Alara purred.

Kayla spit in Alara's face and made no move to follow the command.

Varin grabbed Kayla and forced her to her knees before yanking her hair hard enough to make her face the ceiling.

Alara brought a wrist to her mouth and bit deep before turning back to Morghan with a wicked grin. "I've never turned anyone carrying a child. We can discover what happens together."

"No!" Morghan screamed. She fought against the chains to no avail as Varin held Kayla in place while Alara force fed her the blood pumping from her wrist.

When Alara was satisfied with the amount Kayla had consumed, they released her, and she fell to the ground.

Kayla pulled herself across the floor toward Morghan, and a glint of steel slipped through the long sleeve of Kayla's shirt. A quick glance at Varin confirmed there was an empty loop in his belt.

Kayla glanced up at Morghan. Her pupils shimmering as the first strands of black stretched out from them to obliterate the dark brown of her irises. "I'm so sorry," she whispered as she struggled to her knees. "She can't have them."

Kayla's fingers wrapped around the hilt of the dagger when it fell from her sleeve. Tears slipped over her cheeks as the darkness continued its steady march through her eyes. "A good death."

Kayla thrust the dagger through her own heart, and as she fell to the ground a final time with Alara howling in the background, Morghan felt nothing at all.

Alara ran to Kayla's body and flipped her over, screaming at the ceiling as Kayla's dead brown eyes stared up from the floor. She grabbed the dagger and kicked the corpse out of her way as she knelt in front of Morghan. "You! You did this!"

Morghan didn't answer. There was nothing to say. In so many ways, Alara was right. Morghan may not have held the dagger, but a string of her poor choices had led them to this crossroads. And in a way, she was relieved Kayla had stepped up to the task, saving her a few sins and immeasurable regret when she would have been forced to do away with all of them herself.

"Did you hear me?" Alara hit Morghan across the face with the broadside of the dagger, but Morghan only stared at the ground, blood dripping from the fresh wound on her face. Alara clenched the hilt of the dagger and pressed the tip into Morghan's chest just enough to nick the skin. "I'll hack you to pieces and enjoy the music of your endless screams as you regrow every last bit so I might do it all over again."

Morghan should have been terrified, but there was no room left in her for fear. No room for remorse. No room for anything but the guilt expanding to fill every fiber of her being. She brought her gaze up to Alara. "I'm not afraid of you."

Alara bared her fangs and brought the dagger down hard across Morghan's throat. A broad, crimson waterfall poured over Morghan's shirt, and she fell to the side as she choked on her own blood. Alara yanked her up by the hair. "You will be. I will break you, even if it takes eternity."

She dipped her finger into the gushing furrow at Morghan's throat and sucked it clean before caressing a hand down Morghan's cheek. "We have so much time, you and I, because no one is coming for you. No one even knows you're here."

THE SLEEPING GIANT'S TERRIBLE
RESOLVE

"You're being ridiculous," Azrael said, as he sat at the edge of Lucifer's bed. "One look, that's all I'm asking."

Lucifer sat at the head of the bed, his legs stretched out and crossed at the ankles. He leaned back against the bars of the headboard, and his eyes closed. "No."

Azrael stalked to the other side of the room before turning back. Not only had Lucifer forbidden him from watching Morghan for the better part of three years, but he had also started guarding his thoughts so fiercely Azrael didn't dare attempt to tear down his mental defenses. He should have, but he wasn't sure if he was more afraid of Lucifer's retaliation or what information he'd find there. What he was sure of, was that ever since Morghan had marched to Falcroix with Salus's army, Lucifer had fluctuated between absolute catatonia and fits of blind rage, with only rare lucid moments such as this one. "I can't make this easier on you if you won't show me what's happening."

"There is no making this easier. You can't fix everything with words, Azrael. I appreciate your efforts to keep me from doing stupid shit for the past several decades." Luke opened his eyes and frowned. "I'm trying to return the favor."

After millions of years sharing a realm with Lucifer, it was still hard to tell how much of his moods were realistic responses versus melodramatic ones. Especially when Morghan was involved. "At the moment, I'm certain I can make responsible decisions better than you."

Lucifer closed his eyes again. "Go away. I've said no a million times. A million and one won't be any different."

Azrael stormed out of the room before turning his back to the wall and leaning against it. He dropped the sight shield from his sword and wrapped a hand around the hilt. His body relaxed against the wall as a calming warmth spread through him. When his mind cleared, he caressed his thumb over the top of the hilt before letting go and shielding the sword from view once more.

This madness had gone on long enough. Morghan obviously wasn't going to die from whatever was happening in Michael's realm, otherwise Lucifer wouldn't have been moping in bed. But there were so many things worse than death. Lucifer may have cut him off from watching Morghan, but he wasn't the only person with the power to do so.

The thought caused Azrael's chest to cramp, and he almost dropped the sight shield on his sword again before thinking better of it. The sword was a crutch. A weakness cloaked in strength.

Azrael jumped at the sound of shattering glass. The number of things Lucifer had broken in the last three years could fill one of his collector rooms to bursting. Azrael knew Lucifer could get lost for an eternity fluctuating between blind rage and soul-crushing despair. He'd wandered the path a few times himself, and it was a half-life he wished on no-one, least of all Lucifer.

Azrael's hands fidgeted at his sides until he realized what he was doing and shoved them into his pockets. He closed his eyes, and when he opened them again, he was greeted by the images papering the walls in Nikoli's control room. His old room.

It was so easy to shift here. Like breathing. The power pulsing through the room and emanating from every image should have made it near impossible, but somehow this space would always belong to him. And Lucifer.

Azrael walked to the console where Winstin sat blatantly ignoring him.

Winstin cut his eyes to the side. "I was hoping you'd walk the other way. The door is over there." He cocked a thumb behind him.

Azrael slid into the chair next to his. "I know."

Winstin moved his chair farther away from Azrael and refused to look at him. "What are you doing here?"

"Something stupid." Azrael forced a smile. "Now, show me Morghan."

Winstin's expression soured. "You don't want to see her. Trust me. Even I can't stomach what they do to her most of the time."

"Who?" Azrael waved away his own question. "Just show me."

Winstin turned back to the keyboard and pressed a button. One of the images on the wall flew to the console and hovered above it. He punched in an impossibly long line of keys, and the image flickered like a dying flame. When it flared back to life, Alara strode down one of the halls of Falcroix, but Morghan was nowhere to be seen.

"I asked for Morghan, not her," Azrael insisted. "Stop stalling."

"It's not that easy." Winstin punched a new line of keys and the image changed to where a dark figure sat on the throne next to Alara's. He could have been Valerian's twin, if Valerian's skin had glittered like onyx instead of diamonds.

"This machine can't directly view Morghan," Winstin elaborated while he spun the image until Morghan came into view. "I can bring her up, but the image is so blurry and disjointed I wouldn't even swear to it being her most of the time. If I ever want to see her, which lately I don't, I have to find someone near her."

Azrael filed away Winstin's words for later, but at the moment he was too overwhelmed by the image before him to comprehend much else. Morghan hung suspended from thick chains wrapped in barbed wire. The deep gashes in her flesh were at odds with the sluggish pace her blood oozed from them. Dark circles the width of a finger had taken up residence around unblinking eyes, and her cheekbones were jagged edges rising from skin that lay drawn and sallow over her jaw. "How long has she been like this?"

"Ever since they captured her and brought her to their putrid city." Winstin shook his head. "It's going on three years. I don't understand why Michael doesn't even look for her. After all she's done for him."

Azrael raised an eyebrow. "For someone who has a difficult time watching, you know an awful lot about what's going on in her life."

Winstin glared at the wall. "For someone who lives with a being who can show you this himself, with audio no less, you sure are spending a stupid amount of time skulking around where you don't belong."

"I belong where I want to belong." Azrael looked at Morghan, and his heart sank. "Is she conscious through all this?"

"Most of the time, yes. I think they want her aware when they take her down for Alara to feed. Or, you know, worse."

Azrael didn't know, and for once he didn't want to, although he was sure Lucifer was aware of everything Morghan had endured over the last three years. Lucifer's response to Morghan's current situation didn't seem quite so over-the-top anymore.

Azrael sighed. "Can you watch me?"

Winstin cut his eyes to the side. "I'm looking at you right now."

"I mean on there." Azrael gestured to the image of Morghan.

Winstin's expression sobered. "It's not allowed."

"Shocking." Azrael rolled his eyes. "Show me, anyway."

Winstin looked at him as if he'd lost his mind. "No. The Master's power flows through this system, and if I attempt to watch you, he'll be here to mete out punishment in a matter of minutes. You don't know how he is. No one is even allowed to speak your name without permission."

"I know exactly how Nikoli is. Unfortunately, I also need to speak with him. Now, work whatever magic you need to with those keys to put my image on the screen."

"Everyone knows where he is." Winstin angrily punched the keys. "Why can't you just go there?"

"I prefer he come to me," Azrael said, and as a man about to sign away his freedom, it was the minor aggressions he would come to rely on in order to stay sane.

"Fucking psychopath immortals," Winstin mumbled as he finished the final keystroke. The image on the console flickered and died. When it came back moments later, it was a pale blue rectangle and nothing more. One by one the images papering the walls blanked and returned as the same, until the entire room was bathed in an eerie blue glow.

Azrael stood and faced the door. It wasn't long until Nikoli's aura barreled toward the room. The tide of anger riding along with it was all-consuming, and Azrael wondered if Nikoli had spent any energy beyond it to notice his realm had been breached.

He got his answer as Nikoli burst through the door and staggered to a halt when his eyes met Azrael.

"Nikoli." Azrael inclined his head toward him and settled his hands in his pockets as fear crept up his spine.

Nikoli recovered his composure so fast it might have never been gone. He took a few steps closer and afforded Azrael a similar nod. "Azrael. Dare I ask to what I owe this blatant intrusion? The updated terms of our agreement in no way allow you free rein in my realm. It's infuriating that neither you nor Lucifer understand the meaning of the word banished."

Azrael closed the space between them and leaned closer. "You came in this room furious, but your heart is beating faster now than when you arrived. Be honest. You missed me."

Nikoli took a hasty step back. He snapped his fingers and pointed to Winstin. "You. Out."

Winstin shot from his chair so fast it was still spinning when the doors swung shut behind him.

"Why are you here, Azrael?"

"I need to go to Michael's realm."

"Then go," Nikoli sneered. "You don't need my help to shift yourself there."

"True, but I do need your permission to safeguard against the repercussions of doing so."

Nikoli's laugh echoed off the walls, and by the time it died down, the light shining in his eyes chilled the room. "My permission? What makes you think I would grant such a thing? No, Azrael. You can go to my son's realm and save your little succubus, but you do so at your own peril."

"I didn't expect you would simply grant it, but I'm willing to bargain if you are."

Nikoli raised an eyebrow, and the room warmed. "Go on."

"I need your word that you will punish no one—harm no one—for my journey to Michael's realm and whatever it is I do there. Once I leave, I want Morghan left alone until she is fully healed. On this, there is no negotiation."

Nikoli leaned against the console closest to him. "I expected this to come from Lucifer, not you. I wake every morning wondering if the day has finally come when he'll drag you into my chambers and throw you at my feet in the hopes of exchanging you for time with his woman."

"Sorry to disappoint you," Azrael said. Nikoli wasn't the only one who had wondered about that particular scenario, but it had been years since Azrael entertained the thought. Instead of reverting back to their old, sniping ways once Morghan left, Lucifer had become more open with his emotions. Until Morghan's capture, they had spent most of their time watching her together. It wasn't ideal, and Lucifer's time outside of watching her was spent in a resigned melancholy, but it was better than the anger and hatred Azrael expected.

"I know disappointment well enough, and this is not it." Nikoli made a show of blithely examining his fingernails. "But what you're asking for has potentially devastating consequences. Complete freedom? What could you possibly offer in return?"

"Me," Azrael responded, struggling to keep his expression neutral. "For every day I spend there, I will give you the equivalent."

"Willingly?" Nikoli wondered.

"Day for day. Willing. Only you."

"Only me?" Nikoli smirked. "I come as a pair now, Azrael. I have a life mate, as you've so fondly reminded me in the past."

Azrael swallowed the acid surging up his throat. He could draw this line in the sand and risk losing the deal or let it slide and lose the upper hand. Nikoli didn't seem particularly attached to his hybrid, but that didn't mean much. Nikoli ran hot and cold with everyone and every thing he had ever created. Azrael glanced at one of the blue screens and thought about Morghan strung up like a morbid decoration in Falcroix and Lucifer losing any semblance of sanity back home. "If you insist on Krishna as well, it can be arranged."

Nikoli's smirk spread into a broad grin. He stepped up to Azrael and took hold of his chin. "As if I would share you. But your desperation is entertaining." Nikoli's eyes glittered. "Krishna will be livid."

"You don't seem bothered by it."

"Please. He may be the most loyal person in my service, but it doesn't make him any less annoying. And lucky it is for you the situation stands as such." He held up a finger. "One week. I accept your offer, but do not test the limits of my generosity."

"Fair enough," Azrael said.

Nikoli hauled Azrael forward by the collar of his jacket until their chests pressed against one another. "A parting kiss," he whispered against Azrael's ear before pulling back and covering Azrael's mouth with his.

Azrael's body stiffened, and he refused to engage.

Nikoli backed out of the kiss, disappointment plaguing his features as he let go of Azrael, who casually tugged on his jacket to smooth it out as if nothing had happened. "Not quite as willing as I hoped. If you try to get away with that once you return, I'll bring Lucifer's little harlot back here and make you watch while I do things to her even Michael's bloodsucker would find unconscionable."

Azrael shot him a withering look. He grabbed the front of Nikoli's robes and crushed their bodies against one another. Azrael cut the leash on his power, and it diffused through the room, making the air heavy and difficult to breathe. Picking an emotion to project wasn't a problem; lust always surged through first, even when he made a conscious effort for it to be something else. Azrael took a steadying breath and struggled to maintain his composure. Projecting his emotions this way was a double-edged sword, and he had as much chance of falling victim to them as the person he enthralled. "I know my part," Azrael said through clenched teeth before leaning forward and ravaging Nikoli's mouth.

At length, Azrael ended the kiss, and Nikoli sank to his knees in a daze. Azrael frowned down at him, reeling in his power and locking it away where it belonged. "Satisfied?"

"With you, always and never," Nikoli replied, his voice husky. "One week."

"I heard you well enough the first time." Azrael walked out of the control room without another word. It had been ages since he'd let his emotions run free, not since before he'd become a ranking immortal. He'd dedicated his life to keeping them locked away as tightly as possible. And what had he gained from it? A cold, lonely existence that culminated in opening up for Nikoli, of all people. It was a cruel joke. He leaned against the wall and closed his eyes, breathing deep and willing himself away from the dimension he so greatly despised.

Thunder roared from the dark clouds blanketing the skies above Falcroix. The ground was painted black, long bare of any sign of life, and Azrael's shoes sank into the viscous earth as he made his way to the city walls.

Alara's monstrosities were clearly uninterested in the upkeep of their mistress's territory. Bodies, human and orc alike, littered the well-beaten path. In still greater numbers, they lay shorn up along the sides in haphazard piles of broken bone and flesh: torn open, half eaten, and rotting. The air hung heavy with the smell of decay and the loud buzzing of flies as they hopped from limb to limb, gorging on their fetid treasures.

Azrael came to the end of the path and crossed a rotting drawbridge that was forever wedged at an odd angle between the banks of a mud-colored moat. The walls of the lower tiers of the city were lacquered with dark green, stagnant foliage, and the smell of decomposing flesh and excrement filled the air. He contemplated shifting into one of the top tiers, but the thought of materializing in an area with an unknown number of enemies was less than appealing.

A dozen orcs milled around the entrance. Of those, four appeared to be dedicated guards for a city Azrael imagined no one dared enter without being dragged there. Except him.

The guards turned to one another in confusion when Azrael approached, eventually deciding to draw their weapons and rush him.

"Stop." Azrael put up a hand to give a visual signal.

The four orcs stopped short, and their weapons dropped to their sides as Azrael continued to hand out orders. "Take me to Alara."

He slipped his hands into his pockets and let out a relieved sigh when they turned and beckoned him to follow. He sank deeper into their minds until they became one with his, and his vision split to share not only their thoughts but their view of the world. They pushed through the unending mass of bodies crowding the lower tiers without issue; however, the population of the top tiers was nothing compared to those below, and as they mounted the steps to the final tier a wary guard blocked their path.

Azrael reached into the guard's mind and attempted to merge it with his own as he had done with the other four. Unfortunately, as the guard's perspective became more crisp, those of the others faded, until the view he had through their eyes flickered to black in the corners of his vision. What a perfect time to learn his limitations with regards to Alara's minions. Exerting control over new beings was always an experience.

Azrael took a few hasty steps back when the four guards who had so recently been his willing escorts turned on him, weapons raised. As their minds recovered, there would be a span of time during which he was unable to thrall them again, and seeing as it varied from person to person and species to species, it was impossible to guess how long that would be. Within the angelic host alone it could take from a matter of minutes to hours—long enough that once he'd been pushed out, it was necessary to explore other avenues of self-preservation.

He sent a silent command for the fifth guard to protect him, and one of the original four fell forward, a sword protruding from his chest. The upper tier guard quickly dispatched the remaining three, and despite the imminent danger, all Azrael could think about was whether these counted as his kills or those of the monster slaying them. Probably a bit of both, but despite Azrael's long life, he had never ended one. He would do what was necessary to save Morghan, but taking lives was a slippery slope. He imagined the more one killed, the more nonchalant they became about doing so, and the last thing anyone the four realms over needed was for someone like him to be indifferent to murder.

When his new charge finished with the last of his previous escorts plus the few others who had joined the fight, Azrael ordered him to grab his arm and lead him to Alara as he would a prisoner. The façade worked well, and by the time he crossed the throne room's threshold, he had three guards by his side.

Alara's scarlet cloak was draped over the back of her throne, but she was not in the room. The tall, dark man, Varin, occupied the throne beside Alara's. He scrunched his face at Azrael's entourage and jumped down from the dais.

"What's this? Your mistress is not here to accept a tribute." Varin came up short when he was close enough to get a better look at Azrael. "What in the Creator's name are you?"

"Something far more ancient than your creator," Azrael said. He glanced up as they walked beneath Morghan. Seeing her in person was so much worse than on the screens in Nikoli's realm. He turned his eyes away and focused on Varin, rifling through his thoughts and bringing up every memory of the vile things they had done to her. Of what he had done to her.

Thus ended any illusion he may have had about leaving Falcroix without taking a life.

The tension bled from Azrael's muscles, and he pulled his arm away from the orc that was pretending to drag him toward the dais. He sent the guards to lower Morghan, and when Varin moved to stop them, Azrael lifted him from the ground with a thought. Varin crashed into his throne so forcefully the crack of bone echoed through the room.

Azrael mounted the steps to the thrones and approached the broken man, who was squirming in his seat as if he might be able to press himself through the back of it. His legs weren't moving, so it was likely his spine had made up at least part of the shattered bone. Varin stopped moving as Azrael took a seat in the throne beside him.

"By all means, keep struggling." Azrael crossed one leg over the other and patted Varin's shoulder. "It won't help, but entertainment has been in short supply for decades."

Azrael turned back to Morghan as the orcs laid her on the ground and removed the chains. "I hope you enjoyed these last few years. Maybe you can cling to whatever sick satisfaction they gave you while I burn away every thought you've ever had. When I'm done with you, only the most primitive part of your brain will be left to keep your heart beating."

He leaned over and grabbed Varin by the hair, forcing his face toward him. "By then, I'm sure the guards will be hungry."

He slid into Varin's mind and snapped the connections linking his conscious thoughts. The happy memories went first, one by one until only fear remained. Azrael let Varin drown in despair for a while before sinking deeper and ripping through his subconscious. As Varin's once animated features faded to a blank, slack-jawed stare, Azrael released him, and the remaining shell slid further down in its throne.

The haze of anger Azrael had been operating under

clung to him like a second skin. He leaned back in Alara's throne and closed his eyes. This was something he could get used to. He grabbed her cloak from the back of the throne and ran his fingers over the velvet fabric. She would be next. He would lie in wait and end her reign in an instant. Well, a series of instants. A series much longer than what he had done to Varin, and with significantly more screaming.

A short, coarse burst of coughs broke into his thoughts. Morghan.

She lay shivering on the cold stone floor, the three guards standing over her awaiting orders. And just like that, his anger was whisked away by concern. Azrael glanced at Varin's unseeing eyes and cringed. He needed to leave with Morghan now, before Alara returned. The goal of this trip was to rescue Morghan, not to test the limits of his own thinly veiled depravity.

Azrael left the throne and knelt at Morghan's side. He wrapped her in Alara's cloak, which was an improvement over the stained, threadbare clothes hanging on her wasted frame. He cradled her against his chest and released his hold on the guards as he shifted away from Falcroix.

Morghan's eyes fluttered open, and she cringed at the deep ache weighing on her body. She blinked a few times, puzzled by the foreign surroundings. This didn't feel like a dream, but with the expansive blanket of green grass with patches of red, yellow, and brown spread here and there. How could it not be?

"This is nice," she said in a harsh whisper, her throat on fire. "I was due for a good dream years ago."

"It's not a dream," a familiar voice said from behind her. "You've seen the last of Falcroix."

"Azrael!" Morghan rolled onto her back so she could get a good look at him, which the pain screaming through her body marked as a grave error. She struggled to focus on him, her eyes still heavy.

Azrael crouched beside a swiftly flowing brook. He was nude from the waist up, but still more shocking was the difference in his physical appearance. Both sides of his face were the same color, and only a light scar remained where the break in his skin should have been.

"You've never been fixed before in my dreams."

"Again, not a dream." He glanced down at his right hand and turned it over as if observing the difference for the first time. "I don't like hiding, but I wouldn't want to give any poor, unsuspecting human nightmares."

Morghan laughed and regretted it. She groaned as pain throbbed through areas of her body she hadn't known existed until her time in Falcroix. She tried to move again and found herself too weak to do more than tighten her fingers around the garment tucked around her chest. She looked down and smiled: Azrael's jacket. His shirt peeked out from beneath it, and scarlet fabric was wrapped several times over around her waist as a long skirt. "Did you steal Alara's cloak?" She cleared her throat. "I guess the better question is: Did you undress me and then wrap me in Alara's cloak?"

Azrael froze for a moment before pinning her with a frustrated glare. "There wasn't much time for wardrobe hunting, and someone had to get you clean. You weren't quite up to the task."

"Were you?" Morghan flinched when she tried to move

again. "I'm more sore now than I was at the end of my last trip to the throne room floor."

"You've been free less than a day." Azrael turned back to the water. "While you were unconscious I had to break a number of your ribs and your legs to help the bones heal in the correct position. Once you're able to eat a decent meal and aren't half-naked in a late autumn breeze, I suspect you'll heal faster."

"I'm particularly interested in the not half-naked outside part," Morghan mumbled. "Where are we?"

"I'm not sure. I meant to shift us to Vahyir, but I don't know the geography of this realm well. I knew Falcroix because we spent so much time watching it when Michael lived in Galmedea. I think I ended up near the wrong city. Vahyir would be a lot colder this time of the year."

Morghan burrowed her face deeper into Azrael's jacket. "Take a look in my head. I have a really nice map tucked away in there."

"You didn't handle the last shift well, and I'm not comfortable letting you shift again right now. We need to find a town so you can heal. My time here is short, and I need you to be able to fend for yourself within the next six days."

"Six days?" Morghan's chest tightened. She'd just gotten Azrael back. There was no way she was letting him go so soon. "You just broke my fucking legs!"

"You broke your leg when Michael uncased his wings at the waterfall. You were bearing weight in five days."

"I was healthy then. Who knows how long this will take to heal? Please stay, Azrael. It's so lonely here. I miss the two of you."

"If it was up to me, I'd never leave. Nikoli released me from our contracts for a week. No extensions."

"He gave you permission to come here and spend time with me? Without rules?" That made little to no sense. Nikoli hated any and all interactions between her and Azrael. The idea of him approving a free-for-all week with her was preposterous. Not that she was in any shape for scandalous activity. "What'd you offer up as collateral, your fucking soul?"

Azrael shrugged. "It's only a week."

Morghan had the feeling he wasn't talking about his trip to Michael's realm anymore. "Damn it, Azrael."

"No one asked me to do this. I'm here because it's necessary." When he finally turned to face her, his eyes were two golden flames. "You choose your path, and I choose mine. You need to control others, whereas I need to control myself. The basic need is the same."

"My current basic need is to slap some sense into your ass, but you're right. You make your own decisions, and even if I don't like them, I appreciate the rescue. I'll settle the score with Nikoli later."

Azrael's eyes dimmed. "He would destroy you. Even at your best."

"Maybe," she conceded, grinning so wide she flinched against the effort. "But I'm not accustomed to dying alone."

"I'm refuse to laugh at a joke about death when you look so close to the part." He reached into the pocket of his slacks and came out with a metal flask. "Have a swallow or two of this. We need to get you inside and on the road to healing as soon as possible. This will keep you comfortable during the trip." He opened the flask and put it to her lips.

Morghan turned her head away. "What's in it?"

"Mostly water. Swallow."

"That's not a real answer." She put her lips to the flask and took a few hesitant sips. It burned down her throat, and settled as a warm ball in her stomach before radiating through the rest of her body. The pain rolled away, and for a few moments she entertained the idea of sitting. Azrael placed a hand on her shoulder and shook his head. She looked up at him with a tight frown, the metallic taste coating the inside of her mouth. "Whose blood?"

"Mine. I'm sure Lucifer would have offered his, but the trip was a little too spontaneous."

"Wait, Luke doesn't know you're here?"

"I highly doubt that's true anymore."

"Azrael, he's going to be pissed!" She sat up, and her world spun. "Shit!"

Azrael caught her and urged her to use him for support. "He'll be fine. You need to slow down. You've been strung up, tortured, and drained of blood countless times over the last three years."

"Yeah, I remember, but at least I was in a healing period." She leaned her head against Azrael's shoulder. "Apparently you can't torture immortals every day of the year and expect them to regenerate enough blood to keep an asshole vampire queen satisfied. Speaking of which, how long am I going to have to drink this stuff?"

Azrael gathered her against his chest and set off through the trees. "Until you're healed. I brought two flasks, and before I leave I'll refill both. You can mix it afterwards on your own. It doesn't have to be water. In fact, it doesn't have to be mixed at all, but if you take it straight, then I suggest you do it in very small amounts and while sitting down."

"I'm not like Alara. Drinking your blood shouldn't do anything to me." And yet she couldn't deny the effect of the small, diluted amount. Her body felt lighter, her breathing easier, and the pain, while by no means gone, had subsided to a pulsing throb.

"The blood of immortals is a powerful thing, whether you need it to survive or not. Where you're concerned, mine is a poor substitute for Lucifer's, but the energy is there; your body only has to absorb it."

"I guess injecting it is out of the question? Although I'm already Luke's hybrid, so I doubt I'd take away your ability to make one."

"I don't need a hybrid. The only people I want to spend eternity with are more immortal than I could ever make them. Still, I strongly suggest you drink, not inject. The power will hit you harder in your veins, and I'm uncertain how your body would react."

She mumbled a few half-hearted curses and settled against his chest, deciding to take advantage of the warmth of his embrace to grab some much needed rest. "If you change your mind and decide to shift us somewhere, take me wherever Michael isn't. He would go crazy if he saw me like this." She sighed, and her eyes closed as she drifted toward a peaceful sleep, something she'd been denied for the better part of a century.

INHIBITIONS ARE OVERRATED

Morghan's thoughts remained fuzzy as she climbed toward consciousness. She tried to blink away the haze, confused when a light mist remained. The cool caress of it against her cheeks threatened to lull her back to sleep, but she forced her eyes open and climbed to her feet. A low-lying fog swirled lazily about her ankles. The clothes she wore were foreign—a dark green shirt hugged her chest and hide leggings dyed grey trailed down to her bare feet. Everything about this place was new yet familiar. Comforting. Home.

She stretched her arms above her head, arching her back until her muscles sighed.

"Do you have any pain?" Azrael's voice jolted her from the languid stretch.

She turned toward his voice, and her mouth hung open. He leaned against the gleaming white wall across the room from her, and over the pale skin of his human form he wore a loose linen shirt with laces intertwined over his chest. His thumbs caught in the pockets of tan leggings the same make as the ones she wore, and dark brown boots folded down at his calves.

"Morghan?"

She glanced at his face for the briefest moment before going back to her study of his body.

"Pain?" he asked more forcefully.

"Pain?" she echoed. "No, I don't feel any pain." She sucked in a long breath between her teeth. "For the love of God, Azrael, can you turn yourself off? I can't get a non-sexual thought in edgewise."

His laugh rolled across the space between them, and she sank to her knees as her breathing quickened. Azrael pushed off the wall with his foot and sauntered toward her until he stood within arm's reach. "Is this how you always react to me in your dreams?"

She shook her head and concentrated on keeping her hands to herself instead of dragging him to the floor along with her. "This is not my dream."

His smile crept wider. "Are you sure?"

"This place is alive with power, and it's not mine." She closed her eyes and counted to ten before continuing. Sex should have been the furthest thing from her mind. For several decades it had been, and in the last few years she'd loathed even the idea of being touched, but she was different here. She wasn't sure if the power permeating this place had pieced her together or simply pared down her psychological baggage. Or perhaps the latter was necessary to achieve the former. "Why are we here? Besides the obvious."

"We can talk freely here. And while your body recuperates, I thought it best to keep your mind from wandering to the less pleasant. Of course, I won't lie. The obvious, as you put it, has crossed my mind several times."

"I've offered you my body before, Azrael. Am I only good enough for a mind fuck?" Morghan frowned. "Do I not do it for you on the physical plane of existence?"

"That is horribly unfair. Between Lucifer and Nikoli there are any number of reasons I refused. It wasn't easy, and let's not pretend I was the only one refusing advances. Over the years, there have been several people who have possessed my body, but you and Lucifer are the only ones I've ever brought to this place." He gestured to their surroundings. "You're right; my power has a life of its own here. Everyone needs a sanctuary, and this is mine. This is where I retreat when sanity is in short supply. I've made it as empty as possible in an attempt to remain neutral." A devastating grin flashed across his face "But some of my emotions do strain their leash."

He crouched in front of her and took her hands in his. "This is my canvas. I can give you anything here. Tell me what you want, and it's yours."

Her eyes trailed down his chest, the loosely threaded laces allowing for a generous view of bare skin. "I want you to take off that ridiculous costume."

He glanced down at himself and shrugged as he started unlacing the front of his shirt. Morghan placed a hand over his. "No, I'll handle the clothes." Her smile broadened as his brow furrowed. She leaned forward and laid a hand on his cheek, pressing her forehead to his. "You could never give me nightmares, Azrael."

Their lips touched, and a spark jolted through her. When she opened her eyes, Azrael's human façade was gone.

Azrael pulled her against him. "To think I almost forgot one of the main reasons I'm such a fool for you."

She tugged at his shirt as they kissed, determined to rid

him of it but unable to work the laces free while they were crushed against one another. Her hands stilled when something caressed her inner thigh. She drew in a sharp breath and glanced down in confusion, as she remained fully clothed. She looked at Azrael, and the smile on his face grew wider when she gasped as the phantom touch slid across her skin, slipping inside her.

"One of the beauties of my craft." He lowered her to the floor and hovered over her. "You wanted to undress me?"

She nodded, unable to catch her breath as his rhythmic caresses moved within her. Her back arched, and she grabbed his shirt. The cloth shred like tissue paper beneath her hands, and it was his turn to gasp when she brought both hands down to his pants and gave them the same treatment. She pushed him away and rose to her feet, smiling down at where Azrael knelt naked before her.

"Stand up," she ordered, and he complied without a word. She leaned in and pressed a light kiss to his lips. She moved to his neck, kissing her way down his chest, and sinking to her knees as she dipped below his waist.

Azrael gripped her shoulder as she took him into her mouth. His head lolled back and his hips jerked as she coaxed him in and out of her.

Morghan struggled to concentrate as a change came over the feeling within her. The firmness of Azrael's fingers melted away and she felt the warmth of his breath quickening against her skin. The wetness of his tongue painted her inner thigh before delving into her and spinning tight circles that threatened to shatter her sanity. She pulled back, not trusting herself to maintain such a delicate hold on him as every muscle tightened.

He knelt in front of her, taking her face in his hands and kissing her deeply, his mouth ravishing her twice over as her body trembled. She cried out and fell against him, burying her face in his neck. He ran a finger down her back and the fabric of her shirt split at his touch. He smiled as he brought his hands down to her thighs, and her pants disintegrated beneath them, leaving bare skin in their wake. He let loose of her long enough to peel the shirt away from the front of her body, before pulling her against him once more. She moaned into his neck, wrapping her legs around his waist as she pushed their bodies closer, urging him inside her.

Azrael pressed his forehead into her chest. He kissed her between the breasts and rose to his feet, holding her close so he remained within her as he walked to the wall.

The chill of the wall at Morghan's back soothed her sweating skin as Azrael rocked within her. Her head fell back, and she closed her eyes. His hands held tight to her waist, but she was lost as to where his actual mouth was at work and could not care less as she felt it teasing her breasts, nipping at her neck, and encircling her navel in a synchronized rush. Her eyes rolled as she was flung over the edge, and by the time she'd landed on solid ground Azrael's pace had quickened. The phantoms assaulting her faded, and he pressed his face into the side of her neck, moaning as he came closer to climax.

A loud bang drew Morghan's attention away, and pain surged through her body. Her vision clouded, and though she could still feel Azrael moving inside her, the room darkened and spun.

"No," Azrael pleaded. His voice was so far away.

She swam back through the darkness, but the noise repeated, and the pain was too much to ignore. Her eyes opened, and she struggled for air as she stared up at an unfamiliar ceiling, the pain a living thing as it clawed at her from the inside. When the noise came a third time, it was a knock on the door of whatever room she was laying in.

Azrael opened his eyes and glared at the door. "Go away!"

"Where are we?" Morghan asked, not daring to move. Even with a thick quilt wrapped around her, the cold seeped through her skin. She didn't want to know what it felt like outside the quilt.

"Malon." Azrael sat beside her on the bed. He wore the same clothes as in their dream, but the physical versions remained intact. "It wasn't far from where we originally shifted, and it looked reputable enough. "

"Malon is a huge brothel." Morghan laughed and regretted it as the pain intensified. "Totally reputable."

"I've lived in worse places, though I did have to turn down an escort several times before convincing the surly woman at the bar to loan us a room." Azrael's eyes glowed as he caressed a hand down her arm, and Morghan's pain faded to a dull throb. "Better?"

"Better," Morghan sighed. "I didn't want to wake up, Azrael. I'm sorry."

"Don't be." He bent forward and kissed her forehead. "Bad timing is no one's fault."

She shivered from the chill that seeped through the blankets. "Why in the world is it so cold here? This place is usually warmer than Salus."

Azrael loosened the quilt from around her and slipped beneath it, wrapping his arms about her waist from behind. "The main hall was overwhelming. Visually. Psionically. Between those distractions and floating your body above me under the cover of a sight shield, my gift of persuasion was lacking."

"What does that even mean?" Morghan wondered,

though she appreciated him not allowing others in the realm to see her current state.

"It means I talked us into a free room, but it's small, and directly next to a room filled with ice I imagine they use as a freezer."

Morghan laughed until it turned into a hissed inhale as pain shot through her once more.

Azrael pulled her closer, and the pain subsided as his breath tickled along the back of her neck.

"I'm sorry, Azrael." She threaded the fingers of one hand through those of the hand he had draped over her abdomen. "My body is a little too broken for anything useful right now. Definitely too fucked up for anything fun."

"I know," he said. "Being here is enough."

For him, maybe.

She should have been thinking about Luke. Should have been ashamed on any number of levels, but she'd have plenty of time to sit alone with her thoughts and be ashamed once Azrael left. Besides, Luke had known what she was going through in Falcroix. If he hadn't, Azrael would never have found out. And still, Luke hadn't come for her. It made her wonder what, if anything, would be a strong enough incentive for him to defy Nikoli for her.

Morghan swallowed the lump in her throat. "I'm bound to need a lot of sleep if I'm going to heal this broke ass body over the next week."

I'm counting on it. Azrael's voice whispered through her mind, his breath hot against her ear.

She smiled into the pillow, thankful for the added warmth of his body against hers. "Can you do me a favor?"

"Anything."

"Our door needs a sign on the other side of it," Morghan

said, squeezing his hand. "I think 'knock on pain of death' should work just fine."

If Azrael could have stopped time, he would have. While he was relieved Morghan's pain was no longer constant, and that her food stayed down more often than not, he mourned the days as they passed and woke with a crushing weight in his chest on his final day of freedom.

They stood in silence as they waited for a horse. While he had used his powers to talk them into a basement room in the beginning, such underhanded tactics were no longer necessary. Once Morghan had deemed herself well enough for a public appearance, every amenity in Malon had opened to them, though Morghan insisted on taking only the bare necessities. Despite her stories of old clashes with the previous ruler of Malon, the current matriarch didn't seem to hold it against her.

Morghan thanked a stable girl as she took the reins of a grey horse. She hoisted herself into the saddle and held her hand down to Azrael. He didn't take it.

"I can't believe you've never ridden a horse." She grasped his forearm and hauled him up behind her. "How old are you again?"

"We're not even riding a horse to Vahyir," he mumbled, ignoring her question and grabbing her around the waist as the horse trotted away from the city. "This is pointless."

Morghan gasped and pulled at his hands. "I'm still not a hundred percent. Think you could try not to crush all my organs? And I know we're not riding to Vahyir. Give me a few minutes to enjoy this in a place without sub-zero temperatures. I've been cooped up for a while."

Azrael grumbled a half-hearted apology and loosened his grip. As the horse sped up, he let go and clutched the saddle instead. "This is an experience I could have lived a few more million years without."

She grinned and stood up in the stirrups. Panic rose in the back of his throat, and it wasn't because she had closed her eyes as the wind played across her face—although that was clearly reckless as well. "You just started putting weight on your legs yesterday," Azrael shouted as he bounced atop the horse's flanks. "This strikes me as a bad idea."

She glanced back at him and frowned as she sank into the saddle and slowed the horse to a trot.

"I'm not optimistic enough to think you're finished," Azrael said. "Why are we stopping?"

"You're right." The joy bled from her eyes, and as much as he hated watching them dim, the reminder was a necessary evil. "My legs ache, and I shouldn't be testing them like this so close to when you have to leave."

Morghan reached back and grasped his hand. "Not to mention you looked like you were about to piss yourself when I stood up and gunned him. It's okay though. I had my fun. You can shift us to Vahyir now, and while I know it's important to shift away from people in this realm, be careful where you put us. I'd rather not land in the Galean Sea. It's freezing even more than usual this time of year."

"Are you insinuating my navigation skills are poor?" Azrael smiled in spite of himself.

"Let's get this over with." Morghan placed a hand on his thigh and squinted her eyes shut. The poor woman. Lucifer's terrible concentration while shifting had clearly left a lasting effect.

Azrael closed his eyes and turned all his concentration toward shifting to Vahyir. The last thing he wanted was to cause Morghan more pain with a poor shift, because while his shifting skills were superior to Lucifer's, his nerves weren't at their best, and they were more tightly wound with every passing moment.

Azrael opened his eyes and frowned; something wasn't quite right. His eyes widened as he hit the ground with a hard thud. He sat up and rubbed his lower back. Between riding that beast of a horse and hitting the ground, it was a wonder he didn't have an array of broken bones.

"Forget something?" Morghan raised an eyebrow, glancing at the saddle laying between them in the snow. "Weren't you touching the horse?"

"It would seem not." Azrael stood and dusted the snow from his pants. "I hadn't given it much thought since we were sitting on top of it, but I guess both of us were only touching the saddle, which was apparently too thick of a barrier to grab something as large as a horse."

A grin spread across Morghan's face until she burst into laughter.

"Well, we aren't in the water," he pointed out. "And I'm guessing the enormous wall is the border of Vahyir? Another mile or so and we would have been not only horse-less, but wet and half-frozen as well."

Morghan wiped a hand beneath each eye and nodded. She stood and turned toward the city. "Yeah, that's the place. I admit, other than only two-thirds of us making it here, you did a pretty good job given the memory of this place wasn't yours."

Azrael rose to his feet and nodded toward the saddle. "Slightly more than two-thirds."

"Smartass." She picked up the saddle and slung it over her shoulder. "C'mon, enough of this craziness. Let's head into town before my ass literally freezes off." She started for

Vahyir, stopping after only a few steps when Azrael didn't follow. She turned back, and her good humor vanished. "You're not coming, are you?"

"I planned on seeing you to Vahyir, and I have." He didn't want to leave. Technically, he had a few more hours, but with Morghan's body on the mend, every moment alone with her was a dangerous temptation. Nikoli's rules may have been on hiatus, but he would have found a way to make Azrael pay. To make Morghan pay. And then there was Lucifer to think about, not to mention the disturbing possibility of him abandoning Morghan after impregnating her. Not only would Morghan have to face pregnancy alone, but the child would be born months after Azrael's truce with Nikoli ended. Even if Nikoli was feeling generous enough to let a child live, he would never allow Azrael or Lucifer to take part in raising it. Assuming Lucifer wanted anything to do with him or Morghan after such a betrayal.

"Azrael?" Morghan laid a hand on his chest, her touch rousing him from his increasingly dark thoughts. But it didn't change the truth behind them. Morghan gained nothing from him staying a few hours longer. Nothing beneficial at least.

Azrael brought a hand up to her face and caressed her cheek with his thumb. "You have no idea how relieved I am that you're recovering so quickly." He reached in his pocket and pulled out the flasks Morghan had been drinking from for the past week. "Both are full, as promised. If you keep improving at your current rate, I doubt you'll need all of it, or even all of one."

"I'll be good and take care of myself," Morghan assured him as she stuffed a flask into each of her front pockets. "I promise."

"I'll hold you to that." He leaned forward until their lips met. Despite numerous trysts while asleep, they hadn't shared a single kiss while awake. Until now.

Morghan dropped the saddle and wrapped her arms around him, pulling him deeper into the kiss as if trying to hold him with it indefinitely. He would have loved nothing more.

"Come to Vahyir," she whispered as their lips parted. "Just for a little while. My body's not as frail as it was a week ago."

He stilled in her arms, and his heart ached as he pulled away from her. He took a few steps back and shook his head. "I can't. I'm sorry."

She hugged her arms across her chest and stared into the distance. He would have offered his jacket for warmth, but if her chill was anything like the one settling over him, then no amount of warm clothing would keep it at bay.

"I guess this is it then." She sniffed and wiped her sleeve across her face, but it did nothing to hide the tears freezing against her cheeks. "Tell Luke I love him. He might not believe it after this."

"I will." Lucifer was going to hate him for several legitimate reasons after this trip, but Azrael doubted Lucifer had it in him to hate Morghan. "He will."

"I love you, too." She forced a smile, her heart hammering so loud Azrael could barely think past the sound.

"I know." Azrael turned his eyes to the ground, and tears burned at their edges as he shifted to Nikoli's realm. His brow furrowed at the shadow stretching in front of him. The body might have been his, but the wings spread wide behind the shadowy silhouette were not. He turned to find Lucifer perched atop the wall in his angelic form. Lucifer's intentions whispered through his mind a moment before he sprang from the wall and brought a handful of claws across the left side of Azrael's face.

"Damn it, Azrael." Lucifer shook blood from his hand. "Why didn't you move?"

Azrael brought a hand to his cheek, and it came away red. "You wanted to hurt me, so I let you."

Lucifer's lip curled atop his elongated teeth. "You hurt me first. Was it not enough to go save her without telling me? You had to seduce her, too?"

"I kissed her, Lucifer. I'm sure you watched the entire time once you realized where I'd gone. It was only a kiss."

"Don't lie to me! I know what you can do." He took a step closer to Azrael, and his voice cracked. "I know what you did."

Azrael turned away from Lucifer when footsteps echoed down the hall. Nikoli walked toward them with a small contingency of angels at his back.

"Go home," Azrael said. "Right now I have other tasks to handle. We can continue this a week from now when I return."

Lucifer glanced down the hall. "A week? Why are you—"

"Go!" Azrael seethed, relieved when Lucifer flashed a mouthful of jagged teeth and disappeared. He turned toward Nikoli and struggled to keep his body from shaking.

Nikoli greeted Azrael with open arms, his eyes shining with excitement as he embraced him. "An entire week of freedom without degenerating into sexual congress—a miracle so grand I may be willing to overlook Lucifer intruding on my realm to communicate with you on my time." Nikoli frowned at the bloody mess that was Azrael's face. "I'll even consider not punishing him for harming you if you would do me an extra favor while here."

"And what is that?" Azrael was in no mood for bargaining. His face throbbed, but his soul was bleeding more than any wound Lucifer could have scored.

Nikoli smiled. "I had no idea you could shape-shift so well. You have to show me the masterpiece you sport for the humans. It's brilliant. Everything I'd always hoped for you."

"Fine. Leave Lucifer alone, and you can spend the week pretending I'm perfect."

"Don't be absurd, Azrael. I know you're not perfect." Nikoli threw an arm over his shoulders as he walked them toward his quarters. The other angels spread to either side as they passed. "You're simply the best I could get for the price I was willing to pay."

THAT CAN'T BE HEALTHY

Michael gazed over the vacant docks of Vahyir. It was only late autumn, but the freezing temperatures along the coast of the Galean Sea had been unrelenting for weeks. Only a small percentage of the ships bearing winter stores had made it to port before thick sheets of ice took hold of the water. Supplies were already running low, and if the weather failed to break in the next few weeks, it would be close to four months before anything could be brought by ship. The closest city was over a week's ride in fair weather, and what it could offer had no hope of sustaining Vahyir's expansive northern kingdom.

Michael kicked a chunk of ice down the dock and sighed as it skid across the frozen waters below. The last three years had been painful. While Falcroix continued to flourish, making most roads unsafe for travel, the number of men willing to risk their lives as opposed to paying the increasingly hefty tribute costs dwindled by the day.

The catastrophe of three years ago was far from forgotten, seeing as it was impossible to find a family between

Salus and Vahyir that hadn't suffered a loss. The only positive thing to come from the ordeal was that every last person
who had known about Kayla's abduction had died in battle.
Which brought its own dose of shame.

Still, Michael was tired of catering to a people who
would just as soon string him up if someone came along
with a large enough pouch of gold or an honest-sounding
proposal of good fortune. He wanted to return to Salus. At
least there he was accepted as more than a fickle religious
icon; not to mention he missed indoor plumbing. Dousing
himself with lukewarm water in a place which rarely rose
above freezing had gotten old fast, but he stayed anyway.
Because this was where Morghan had told him to go.

It wasn't as if he'd completely forsaken Salus. He'd
flown back and forth a few times to make sure the city was
managing without them, and to see if Morghan had
returned there instead. He wasn't sure why he clung to
Morghan's last words, but he had some ridiculous hope
she'd show up in Vahyir one day and everything would go
back to the way it had been before Falcroix.

But even without his hopes regarding Morghan, of all
the places he could think to go, this was where he was
needed most. Illness and starvation ran rampant in the
streets of the once great kingdom. Kayla was assumed dead
when she hadn't returned from Falcroix, making Kaysen the
new queen at eighteen. She wasn't a bad queen per se, but
her skill at leading was nonexistent compared to her mother
and grandfather. Michael could empathize. Salus had inner
workings he hadn't known existed before Morghan's disap-
pearance, and when Raelyn's family had turned to him for
guidance, he'd panicked and fled back to Vahyir.

Michael sighed and sat down on the icy dock. He lay
back and stared into the muted grey sky; it would snow

again before the day was out. He winced when the dock shook, splinters of ice jabbing into his neck as the thin top layer shattered. He tilted his head back, getting an upside-down view of a thickly bundled boy running toward him. He closed his eyes and forced himself to sit, wondering what task he was needed for this time.

"Maritch!" The boy tried to slow down, but he lost his footing. He yelped and closed his eyes as he went sliding across the dock on his knees.

Michael hooked an arm around the boy's chest and set him on his feet.

The boy opened his eyes and beamed.

"You had something to tell me?" Michael dusted the ice from the child's legs before standing and brushing off his own clothing.

"The General is back!" The boy's smile broadened. He rubbed his gloved hands together and stomped his feet as the wind whipped around them. Snowflakes floated from the sky. "She's up at Pryer's." He gestured away from the docks, though the tavern he named was easily half an hour's trek through the city. "Doesn't have much in the way of warm clothes though, so I offered to come get you."

"Morghan?" The icy fingers around Michael's heart loosened the slightest bit, allowing a sliver of hope to beat beneath them. Finally, he wouldn't have to face these people alone. He would take her caustic attitude over their fearful chatter any day.

"Is that her name?" The boy hurried to keep pace as Michael started for the tavern. "All the stories say she has an endless supply of weapons and magic, but she doesn't have any weapons now. Maybe she was too sick to carry them through the snow."

Michael all but ignored him. Morghan, sick? Laughable.

The boy must have caught her during one of her more morbid moods. And without weapons? That was even harder to grasp. She'd been missing for three years, but the woman slept with an arsenal strapped to her body; it was unlikely she would show up unarmed. Then again, he knew nothing of what she had been doing the past few years. The thought gave pause to his excitement.

"Maritch?" The boy's timid voice broke into Michael's thoughts.

Michael looked down at the expectant face and flinched. He didn't want to know what miracle the boy expected him to perform for the message service.

"My mother died last winter," the boy continued. "My sister has been blind since before I was born, and my father is tired of dealing with her. I do odd jobs and carry mail to keep food on the table."

Michael fought back a groan. "I can't heal the blind."

"I don't want you to heal her. She does fine without her eyes. But I would appreciate anything you could do to stop my father from hurting her. He's always making her cry at night, and he threatens to sell her off to Malon." The boy wiped his sleeve over his face as if brushing away the snow, but Michael had used such tactics too often to be fooled.

"I'm sorry. I can't help with your father." He looked away in shame and put on enough speed that the boy had no chance of keeping pace. His chest burned with the need to do as the boy asked, which was why the answer had to be no. He'd made enough mistakes when it came to such things, and the world didn't need another Alara.

Michael's thoughts hadn't become any less dark and tumultuous by the time he reached the tavern. Which might have been why he didn't see the door swinging toward him until it was too late.

The door slammed into him, and he stumbled back, landing hard on his ass as a crackle of pain spread across his face. He cupped his hands over his nose and cursed as blood oozed between his fingers.

"Now we're even." Morghan's voice came from above him. Her hand stretched toward him in an offer at odds with her words.

Maybe his distraction hadn't caused the accident after all. Maybe it wasn't an accident.

"Even?" Michael pushed her hand away. He spit blood in the snow and glared at her, but the anger bled from him as he gave her a once over. Her skin was sallow, and the woman was one step shy of skeletal. "You look like shit."

"Always the charmer," she chuckled. She ran a finger over the hollow of her cheek and grimaced.

"You look like you haven't eaten in weeks." He climbed to his feet and removed his thick, fur-lined coat. His bloody nose was a forgotten detail as he draped the coat over her shoulders. "It's no wonder, the way you treat yourself. There's over a foot of snow on the ground, and those clothes wouldn't suit this place in summer. Come on, let's head to the place I'm keeping. We can get warm and talk."

"I could go for a talk." She trudged behind him as he headed away from the main streets of the city.

What it looked like she could go for was a warm bed, a meal, and about a month's rest. He turned around and swept her into his arms before she could make so much as a sound in protest.

"Put me down!" She twisted this way and that, but he used his coat as a restraining device and held her tighter against his chest. After a few more tries at dislodging herself, Morghan sighed and gave up.

"You're an asshole," she mumbled.

"I learned from the best," he said as the small cabin he kept near the outskirts of town came into view. He set Morghan on her feet so he could disarm the lock. She wavered for a moment before standing firm and sending a snarl his way. Presumably for the concerned look he'd thrown her when she almost fell.

"Why don't you rest on the bed while I get the fire going?" he suggested, ushering her into the room and toward a small bed situated in the back corner, not far from the empty hearth. "I'll heat some broth so you can get some food in you."

"Broth?" Morghan dropped onto the bed, Michael's coat hugged tight to her wasted frame. "In the past week, I've had enough broths and soups to drown a small army. Don't you have any meat?"

"I doubt you could handle meat. Maybe a thin stew at best."

"I've been eating stews for the past couple days. And fair warning about your look of disapproval: the last man who tried to convince me I needed more soup ended up wearing it."

"You've had a man tending you?" Michael wasn't sure how he should feel about that. Disappointed? Jealous? Neither of those struck him as reasonable reactions. Morghan was a friend. Nothing more. And after abandoning him for so long, he wasn't sure friend even applied to her anymore. He knelt by the hearth and built up a fire.

"I have a man tending me now, don't I?" she said. "And believe it or not, I do know other men besides you. None of you would win timed competitions for heroic rescues, but that's one area where the 'better late than never' cliché definitely comes into play."

"I wasn't aware you needed rescuing." Michael sat on

the floor and dared to look at Morghan while the fire crackled beside him. Sooner or later, he would get used to the gaunt features, or perhaps she'd fill out to her former self fast enough he wouldn't be forced to do so. "Maybe if you had come to Vahyir after the battle instead of wandering off and abandoning the troops to fend for themselves, I would have been a little better informed."

Morghan shivered, hugging the coat closer and huddling in on herself. Good. She had reason to be ashamed.

"So how is our dear friend, Valerian?" she said at length. "I take it he's still allied with you?"

"Barely. The loss of life at Falcroix was devastating. Valerian's embellishments of the loss as a result of your incompetence only gained credibility when you never returned, and because you lost credibility, so did I. Morghan, I have never been a great leader of men. I've been at a complete loss without you by my side. These people are ravenous. They can smell weakness on a man from miles away."

"All people are ravenous." Morghan glared at him without raising her head. "They all smell weakness, and you don't have to be a great leader of men to steer them along a chosen course. Only a great intimidator. If you act like you own them, at least some of them will wonder if it's true. If you act like their friend, they'll run you into the ground before you can blink. Respect is earned, but power is taken. No one ever gained control by acting like it wasn't already theirs."

"You're probably right," Michael said. Most of his life experiences fell in line with her bleak view of humanity. "Doesn't mean I have to like it."

"You shouldn't. Some people don't have it in them to be

so cruel, and there's nothing wrong with that. But I'm back now. I'll be your cruelty." She winced and slumped against the wall, her eyes drifting shut. "But I need to look less like a poorly put together pile of bones, or no one will take me seriously. And weapons..." she trailed off, jerking between sleep and wakefulness. "I need weapons."

"I was wondering where all your weapons went." Michael sat on the edge of the bed and helped her stretch out on top of it as opposed to falling asleep crunched in an uncomfortable knot of limbs. He tucked his coat around her for added warmth. "Where's your ranking sword?"

But she only shook her head as she sank into the mattress. When her eyes closed a second time, Michael didn't bother waking her. It was clear she needed the rest. Needed to recover. From what he wasn't certain, and he wasn't sure he wanted to know.

Morghan opened her eyes, or at least she thought she had. She held her hand in front of her face and saw nothing, but someone was calling her name.

Azrael.

She moved through the darkness and was met with more of the same. Rain came down in sheets. Black on black. There was no light in this place and a dearth of sensation in general, with only the pounding of heavy drops against her skin. She turned around, and her feet sloshed in what she hoped was standing water.

A dim point of light appeared in the distance, and she took off running toward it. "Azrael!"

The light flickered as she ran, and then Azrael stood before her, his body a glowing beacon in the dark.

Morghan threw her arms around him and buried her face in his neck. She'd thought once he left their minds would no longer be able to meet. When she pulled back and saw the confusion on his face, it was clear she wasn't the only one.

"How did you get here?" His eyes searched the darkness, as if he expected something dangerous had come with her.

"You called me. I fell asleep and heard you calling me. Everything was so dark. All I had was your voice."

"I'm sorry." His turned his face to the sky. At least, Morghan imagined up was the sky. "I was thinking of you. I didn't know you could get here on your own. You have to leave. Now."

"But I just got here," she protested, trying to pull him closer. She frowned when he backed away, their hands held loosely between them. "What's wrong with you? And why is it so different here?"

"The darkness and the rain are calming. I told you before, this is where I come when sanity is in short supply. I come here to break myself and regain my composure one hard-fought piece at a time. It's not safe for you when I'm like this."

"I'm not afraid of you." Morghan squeezed his hands. "Besides, you've already been gone the better part of a day, and you don't look very dangerous."

"This." He dropped her hands and gestured to himself. "Hasn't gone anywhere yet. Once the real-world part of me becomes too overwhelmed to continue the outward façade, it will return here, where a calmer, more collected side is ready to take its place." He tapped two fingers against his chest. "You can't be here when the other half returns. It will want you, and it will trap you here. Knowing I've hurt you is the last thing I need right now."

"If I stay, it won't be you who hurts me."

"It will be me," Azrael insisted. "But it won't be sane. Please leave. I'm begging you. Don't make me live with the knowledge of what sick things I might do to you, even if it's only in my mind."

She took a step closer to him, and when he didn't pull away, she pressed her lips to his. "We both know I'm not going anywhere."

"You make my soul tired." He ran a hand through the heavy, wet locks of her hair. "If you're staying, then you'll need this."

She stepped back as the weight of her clothes multiplied several times over. She glanced down at her old attire and ran a hand along the edge of her coat. She pulled it aside, knowing even before they became visible that her daggers and sword were back in their usual homes about her waist and at her side. Her smile bled out as she realized the implications of such a gesture. "I'm not using these on you."

"If it comes to it, you will do exactly that." Azrael grabbed her shoulders, and his eyes flared. "Not if. When. Blind rage will be all that's left of me, and you know well enough what anger craves."

"Blood." Morghan frowned. "Release."

"And you could supply me with both. In ways you could never imagine."

She opened her mouth to protest, but the ground lurched beneath them, and she collapsed to her knees. She glanced up and cringed at the brightness above her. It shattered the dark, as if the sun had exploded into being and was hurtling toward them with no regard for what stood in its path. She shaded her eyes with a hand as she turned them to Azrael. He stood with his hands resting in the pockets of his pants, a mask of resolve muting any expression, as he stared into the sky.

The light screamed toward them and landed with an earth-shattering crack as water sprayed up in all directions. A disturbingly realistic replica of Azrael crouched in the circle of wrecked earth, one hand thrown up and back, the other embedded where the ground had crumbled on impact. He looked up and grinned at his twin before turning his face to the sky and letting out a roar which shook the very foundations of the realm they occupied. The once clear droplets splashed crimson against his upturned palms, and he licked the heavy liquid from his hand as the water at their feet suffused with red.

Azrael grabbed Morghan off the ground and set her on her feet. Fear burned in his eyes, and crimson rivulets slid over his face as he pressed a hard kiss to her lips. He pushed her away. "Run!"

She stumbled back a few steps and stood rooted in shock as the brightly glowing version of Azrael strode toward them, grabbing his lesser brother and flinging him into the sky. Azrael's dim light faded into the darkening abyss overhead, and Morghan had no time to mourn his loss before a low growl forced her to face the animalistic version left behind.

Power rolled from him in waves thick enough to choke the air, and he burned so brightly he was painful to look at. Morghan's eyes adjusted as he circled her, his usual feline grace making the way he stalked her still more unsettling.

Running was the farthest thing from Morghan's mind. Azrael was sizing her up, deciding what part she would play in his sadistic game. She couldn't afford to show weakness, because if it was a choice between mate and prey, she'd much prefer the former.

She made a slow turn in order to keep him in view. Her lip curled into a snarl, and she growled a warning similar to his before pulling her coat back far enough to flash a hint of steel.

Azrael stopped and tilted his head. He closed the gap between them with lightning speed, a wicked grin crossing his face when Morghan was unable to suppress a small gasp. He grabbed her around the waist and forced their bodies together. He bent forward and lapped at the red streams that drizzled down her neck, drawing his tongue up the side of her chin before covering her lips with his and forcing the metallic taste inside her mouth.

Power burned through her as white hot daggers of pain raked along her insides. The flood of energy was too much, too fast. It took all the concentration she could muster to pull her thoughts away from the kiss, away from the pain, long enough to grab him by the shirt and shove him across the void.

"Fuck that!" she screamed as she reached for her gun. How much raw power did Azrael have, anyway? That a fragment of him could spare the energy to rip another ranking immortal apart from the inside? She might have let the scene play out in a dream, but Azrael's subconscious was so much more than that. And she wasn't about to pretend she knew where the real world ended and this one began.

The movement of her hand gave him pause, and he turned away from her. Seriously, did he think she was stupid? There was no way in hell he was giving up. She expected him to pounce at any moment. What she didn't expect, was for the void to shudder around her.

Shards of black stone shot up from the ground, forcing her back as one grazed her thigh and took a shred of her pants along with it. The world dropped from under her, and she grabbed at the jagged stone, digging deep furrows across her palms as she clung to it. She gaped as the newborn mountain rose higher, countless razor-sharp, haphazard shards of rock crashing together at its base.

Azrael stood at the summit, his arms spread to either side as he stared into the darkness overhead. He turned and crouched near the edge, smirking down at where Morghan clung to the rocks at his feet. He reached down and took her by the hands, but instead of hauling her up beside him, he ripped her away from the mountain and flung her into the abyss. He dove after her and grabbed her around the waist, crushing her against him as they plummeted toward a gathering sea of red.

Her coat billowed behind them as they fell, and she gasped when her back lit with pain. She twisted her face around and watched her coat split in two, shedding feathers as black as their surroundings as it morphed into wings.

Well, if Azrael was going to give her wings, she might as well use them. She spread them wide, hoping to stop their fall, but who was she kidding? She had no idea how to fly.

Azrael's hold on her slipped, and she looked down into his shocked expression as he fell away from her. Maybe the wings hadn't been his idea, after all.

His body stabbed deep beneath the crimson waves and sent up a gout of glistening red. Morghan cringed as she punched into the viscous fluid behind him, coming up sputtering and blinking a red film from her eyes. She searched for where Azrael surfaced, instead finding the latest adjustment to the dismal state of their world. A thin strand of beach stretched out in the distance between the mountain they'd fallen from and a far off point that glittered beneath a waxing moon. But that nightmare was going to have to wait.

She cursed under her breath when another sweep of her surroundings yielded no sign of Azrael. He should have surfaced already, and while he may have been dangerous and completely out of his mind, she didn't want him hurt.

The light emanating from Azrael illuminated the scene below. He was so far down already, and his eyes closed as he sank deeper. The depths of the bloody sea teemed with a school of ravenous fish, and their long silver bodies darted through the carnage as they ripped Azrael's his flesh with the razor-sharp teeth that jutted from their long, pointed snouts. Pale blue eyes sank deep into their slender figures and gleamed hungrily as they made one pass at him before doubling back, ready for another turn at their destructive sport.

Morghan dove toward Azrael and grabbed one of the lurid fish by the tail with both hands as it passed. It turned on her, teeth gnashing. She swiped a dagger from her belt and slashed through the fish's gut, kicking away as hundreds of brightly colored orbs gushed from the wound and floated toward the surface.

Azrael continued to sink, and although he burned bright enough to light up their bloody surroundings, he was nowhere near as radiant as he once was. She slammed the dagger into her belt and continued toward him, cursing her wings as they hindered her progress no matter how tightly she held them against her back. She flew into a fit of rage, twisting her arms around and grabbing the wings at their base before ripping them away from her body.

Pain clouded her vision, and she struggled to move past it. How could imaginary wings produce such extraordinary pain? After three years languishing in Falcroix, Morghan was well-versed at ignoring pain, and above the howl in her back, her burning lungs never fazed her as she dove deeper.

Azrael's eyes opened when she wrapped an arm around him. She glimpsed a moment of recognition before his pupils dilated, and he disappeared behind a curtain of rage. He grabbed her around the waist, and their bodies propelled upward.

When they broke the surface, the tightness in Morghan's chest eased as air filled her lungs, but her body arced when they slammed into the shore. Sand dug into the fresh wounds at her back, and she screamed until they came to a stop not far up the beach. She didn't protest when Azrael rolled off of her. He stood, paying her little attention as he walked down the shore toward the glittering edge of beach she'd spied earlier. She struggled to her feet and followed, keeping a short distance between them. The intensity with which he burned had diminished, but she doubted he was safe to approach. A tired smile spread across her face as the deep gashes covering his body began to heal, leaving only the blood-soaked ruin of clothes as evidence of the previous nightmare. At least he was healing. She touched her back and flinched. Her—not so much.

Morghan came up short when Azrael's destination came into focus. Hanging vines sparkled from an enormous canopy as they created a semi-solid curtain that stretched toward the ground. Apples dotted its glittering mass, and even the gate was included in his replica of Eden, its hinges broken and gleaming in the scant moonlight. But something was wrong, and as her gaze trailed from the gate to the carpet of grass below, she realized what this garden lacked. The true garden was a menagerie teeming with life, and despite being created by the coldest bastard in the universe, its warmth stretched well beyond its outer edge. This garden gleamed cold and foreboding, devoid of even a false sense of welcome. It made no attempt to lure the onlooker with soft edges or tempting scents, but was instead a wealth of hard lines glinting in the night as if the slightest touch would rend flesh and bone.

Azrael left the beach, and the grass shattered beneath his bare feet. He moved forward.

Morghan cursed under her breath as he came to the gate and it, too, splintered at his touch. She couldn't stand by and watch him do this to himself, but she wasn't keen on putting herself through the same torture.

"Azrael!" she screamed, relieved when he stopped and flashed teeth in her direction. "I'm not following you in there." She rested her hands on her hips. "This is getting fucking ridiculous. I've been flung off a mountain, swam through a sea of blood, fought off fish chock full of souls, and was most recently rocketed onto a beach where I developed road rash across my already injured back. An injury, I might add, which resulted from ripping off wings I should have never fucking had." She paused and took a deep breath before setting her jaw. "I'm sorry, dear, but I have to draw the line somewhere, and a Biblical garden made of explosive glass is it for me."

He turned away in disinterest and continued toward the wall of green.

"Fine!" She ripped off what was left of her blood-soaked shirt, and Azrael turned back at the sound. He took a few hesitant steps toward the beach, his eyes dancing with light.

"You want me?" She grabbed a dagger from her belt before loosening it and letting it fall to the ground. She dragged the dagger in a shallow line above her breasts, a thin waterfall of blood slipping over her bare chest.

Azrael stepped back onto the sand.

"Come get me," she rasped. She speared the dagger into the sand and bolted along the shoreline.

Azrael's footfalls pounded behind her. This was a race made to be lost. Not only could he easily outrun her, but he could flash in front of her whenever he liked. But chases weren't as exciting when they were rigged, and they both knew there was nowhere to run. Where would she go? It was a choice between an unscalable mountain, a sea of blood filled with ravenous fish, or a garden of razor-sharp glass. Given the options, Morghan viewed sex with an entity powerful enough to annihilate her from the inside out as borderline sane.

She was halfway to the mountain when he snagged her around the waist, and they tumbled into the sand. He flipped her onto her back and knelt above her, his pupils expanding and contracting as the tattered remnants of his clothes disappeared.

"That was some wicked foreplay." Morghan closed her eyes as he bent to lap the blood from her chest, and as he did so, he pressed her body hard against the ground.

The sand more than anything would drive her mad. She turned her thoughts inward, determined to move away from the sensation of it grinding into her wounds. She smiled when her favorite dreamscape flashed through her mind: the river bubbling through the foothills surrounding Luke's labyrinth, crisp, fragrant grass stretching along its bank. Azrael was always there—sitting cross-legged by the water or gazing into the spread of stars overhead as he lay by her side. Against her chest, she clutched the red and white roses he always brought with him, and by some miracle, their heavy thorns never drew a drop of blood.

Something warm and wet slid across Morghan's cheek, and she opened her eyes, her brow furrowing. Azrael hovered above her, tears streaming from his eyes and splashing against her face and neck. The light surrounding him had vanished, and the beach had gone with it. Freshly-turned soil cradled her back, and she smiled when the melodic sound of flowing water met her ears. Somehow they had made it into her dream, and by the look on Azrael's face, it hadn't been his doing. She brushed the backs of her fingers across his cheek, ignoring the multitude of roses that fell away from her arm as she moved it. Her mouth turned down in a tight frown as his brooding eyes filled with terror and he sat back on his heels to escape her touch.

"I don't understand," she said. "What's wrong?"

Azrael's eyes turned to the sloping hill behind her, and a low whine escaped his throat. He remained in the position as if frozen in time until Morghan slipped her hands into his and coaxed him to lay down on top of her. He sank into the roses and winced as the thorns tore his skin.

"Get up," she insisted, as he lay his head on her chest. "They're hurting you."

She tried to push him away, but he clamped his arms around her waist and would not be moved. When his eyes turned up to hers, pain wasn't even an afterthought behind the fear drowning them. He sighed against her chest and traced circles around her navel with the sand that clung to her skin.

She gazed up at the moon and stroked a hand through his hair. Somehow, she had come out of this insanity with limbs intact and her pants still buttoned around her waist. She kissed the top of Azrael's head. Would he even remember any of it? She thought back to their conversation before this half of him appeared. Yes, he would remember. From the vacant expression that had passed as a shadow across his face, she guessed he remembered everything. It was unfathomable how he dealt with such torture once, let alone on a regular basis. It made sense that his time with Nikoli would trigger his survival mechanisms, but what about his time with her? With Luke? Alone? At what level of stress did he resort to this? She wanted to believe it was rare, but she doubted that was true.

A gasp caught in her throat as their surroundings flickered and died, leaving nothing save the dark void where she had first met Azrael. She shielded her eyes against a familiar blinding light when it appeared above them.

"No." A denial of something she had no hope of stopping. "You can't have him like this."

The cries of another broke into her mind, and the choice became one between child and lover. Morghan hugged Azrael and ran her fingers through his hair one last time. If she didn't leave soon, while Azrael's mind was calm, it was unlikely she would have another chance until the part of him hurtling toward them burned itself out. So, she prayed for some shred of mercy, before closing her eyes and launching toward consciousness.

Michael had seen a lot of blood in his lifetime, but the amount painting the walls of his cabin was obscene. And the feathers! Black feathers carpeted the floor, and the walls were a collage of feathers, blood and bone fragments. Had a murder of crows exploded in his home while he was away? He'd only been gone for a few hours. After all, someone had to find Morghan clothes fit for the snow, and he'd gathered a few staples to make her a heartier trial meal as well.

Michael knelt at the bedside, his voice trembling as he

tried and failed to hold back sobs. "I'm so sorry. I didn't think anyone even knew you were here."

Morghan's eyes flew open, and she glanced around the room. Her body shook as she attempted to rise, a bumpy, awkward outline pressing into Michael's coat, which was still partially draped over her.

"How do I manage to reduce every man in my life to tears?" Morghan's voice was a deep rumble, and it cracked on the final word as she sucked in a sharp breath and collapsed onto the mattress.

"You're awake!" Michael wiped at his eyes. He wasn't sure if that was good or not given the state of her. "Who did this to you? Shit, how could I let this happen?"

The bed squelched beneath Morghan's palm when she tried to rise again, and blood gushed over her hand when her weight shifted. "What the fuck is this?"

Michael's coat slipped off her torso as she rose, and the thin shirt she wore was shredded, exposing her shattered back. Black feathers clung to the blood painting it, and bloody stumps of bone protruded from open wounds to either side of her spine.

"Your back." Michael's voice was no louder than a whisper. "I didn't know you had wings, too."

"Wings?" Morghan screamed and sank back onto the pillow, her eyes barely open " Fuck. My back. I don't have fucking wings."

Morghan craned her neck to look at her back and let out a long string of curses punctuated by bloodcurdling screams. The short stumps of bone extending from her back had begun to form the first joint in each wing.

"They're regenerating," Michael whispered. He had more experience regenerating body parts than he liked to admit, but never with his wings. They were the most sensitive part of his body, and even in his darkest moments, he had never built up the nerve to sever them. If the amount of pain to regenerate them at all correlated with the pleasure they brought, he doubted he would have come out sane on the other side. It was hard to believe anyone would.

"Stop it," Morghan gasped. Her arm waved behind her in erratic arcs. "Make it stop."

"They have to heal." Michael laid a hand on her cheek. "I'm so sorry. It's going to take a while."

"No." Morghan groaned, laying a hand atop his. "I don't want them. Cut them off."

"I'm not going to cut off your wings!"

"Your sword, Michael," Morghan begged. She gripped his hand hard enough to shatter any mortal bone, and her jaw flexed. "Flush against my back. They won't grow again. My skin will cover the defects. Eventually."

"I'm not using my ranking sword on you, Morghan. You could bleed to death."

"I can't do this, Michael." Tears streamed down her face as she dug into her pockets and came out with two shining silver flasks. She opened one and tilted it up to her mouth, gulping whatever liquor was in it.

Her back arched until Michael thought it might snap, and her fists plunged into the mattress, ripping through it.

"OFF!" Morghan screamed, the vessels along her neck standing out against her skin as she tore her hands from the mattress, scattering white and red feathers along with the black. She stood on the remnants of the bed and pressed the front of her body to the wall, her fingers carving bloody lines in the wooden planks. Michael had no idea where she'd found such strength after being barely able to lift her head moments earlier. "Do it, Michael. Help me. Don't make me rip them off again."

"You did this?" Michael wondered how that was possible, but his entire day had been a little impossible. And who was he to judge? After all, he'd also sprouted wings in a short period of time. A time when he would have given anything to no longer have them. No one should be forced into something like that.

He climbed onto the bed and stepped to the side of her. "I've never used this sword against someone like us." His voice trembled as he held out the sword and pressed the broad edge flush to her back. "You're certain this is what you want?"

"I'll be fine," she said. "Trust me. Just sew the wounds up afterwards. If the bleeding won't stop..." She trailed off, her body swaying against the wall as if she were about to fall back to the mattress.

"The flasks," she continued, nodding toward the blood-smeared containers at her feet. "Pour them over the wounds if they aren't healing."

Michael tightened his grip on his sword and put as much power into the downward stroke as he dared.

There was little resistance as the blade sliced through the bone at her back, and a muffled grunt was the only evidence she'd felt anything at all. Morghan thudded onto the mattress face first, and she didn't get up.

The sword had done its job. Michael could no longer see any part of Morghan's wings peeking out from the wounds at her back, but the amount of blood gushing from them wasn't slowing. He cursed when he realized what he'd forgotten in his haste.

Just sew the wounds up afterwards.

"Shit!" He glanced around the room in a panic. Where in God's name was he going to find a needle and thread before she bled out? His eyes darted to the flasks on the bed.

Morghan had been adamant that whatever was in them would help her wounds heal once he'd sewn the skin together. Maybe it could help even without the stitches. He opened both flasks and emptied the contents over the open wounds.

The thick crimson liquid mingled with Morghan's blood, and a sweet-smelling steam rose from the wounds as they shallowed and the skin knit together in a matter of seconds.

Michael had no idea why Morghan was carrying around flasks of blood. And whose blood could possibly heal a wound? Let alone ones so grave so fast.

Michael wiped the blood from Morghan's back with the sleeve of his shirt to see how much of the wounds remained. Maybe now that they weren't so serious, he could run into the city proper for a needle and thread.

His mouth hung open as he cleaned the last of the blood from her back. Michael stood and wondered at its near-perfect appearance. A thin black scar remained to either side of her spine, but no one would have guessed her wings ever existed.

Nikoli glared at the reflection the mirror spat back at him. He ran his hand over the gashes scattered across his chest, fresh as the moment they had been made. He pressed a finger along the length of a particularly nasty set of wounds which ran from neck to navel, and blood oozed onto his hand.

His eyes narrowed as the blood dripped across his bare chest, and he glanced at the bed behind him, where Azrael lay in a restless sleep. It was the first time Nikoli had allowed him any rest since he arrived, and it had nothing to do with a sudden attack of generosity.

Nikoli hadn't expected this level of violence. It wasn't unheard of, but he was accustomed to dealing out pain these days. The fact he had allowed Azrael to assert dominance, that he'd enjoyed being bled, even kept the wounds open so he might look at them afterwards—that was the real problem.

The sheets rustled, and Nikoli took a wary step toward the bed as Azrael's body arched. Azrael's eyes flew open on a scream, and a crimson stain spread beneath him, soaking the linens at his back.

"Azrael?"

The only response was another mind-shattering scream as Azrael brought his hands to his face and rolled off the bed.

Nikoli hurried to the side of the bed where Azrael had fallen. He lay on his stomach, his back was a mass of blood and broken skin, and an invisible hand painted lines of gore deep into his flesh. The outline of wings spread across Azrael's back, from the tops of his shoulders to well below the small of his back. Once the gory outline was finished, the pattern moved inward, creating the intricate detail of individual feathers until the whole of his back was layered with them.

Nikoli narrowed his eyes at Azrael as his body went limp. Power burned down his arm as he called on Michael's soul, and moments later he had his image on the wall in front of him.

Lilith lay in a bloody wreck of a room. Black feathers and bone chips interwove with the crimson stains spreading across the floor and dripping down the walls. Michael stood over his nemesis's prone body, crimson waterfalls pouring from the flasks he held above her.

Nikoli knew those flasks. He hadn't missed a moment of Azrael's trip to his son's realm.

"What manner of treachery do we have here?" Nikoli stepped closer to the moving image, and his anger flared as the wounds on her back sealed in a matter of moments. Nikoli knelt beside Azrael and wrenched his head back by the hair. He ran his free hand along Azrael's back, the excess blood sluicing down Azrael's sides as his body shuddered. "It seems God will have his pound of flesh no matter what realm your other half is in."

Azrael's eyes opened, but his words were strained and quiet. "Nikoli, please."

"You dare beg for mercy, when your deception is lain bare at my feet?" Nikoli turned his attention toward the sword hanging above his bed. He lifted his arm, and it flew to his call, the hilt warm against his palm.

Azrael groaned. "I don't know what you're talking about."

Nikoli bent over his sword until his lips brushed Azrael's ear. "Aren't you supposed to know everything? So much potential. Shame you're not living up to it lately." He slammed the hilt of his sword into the base of Azrael's skull, and a satisfied smirk spread across his face when Azrael's body went still beneath him.

"You always were missing out on the best of it, Azrael. No other area is quite so sensitive as the wings." Nikoli ran a finger along the depressed outline of Azrael's right wing, and he smiled when Azrael's eyes flew open on a strangled gasp. "It's tragic that you insist on being so uncooperative. I could have shown you ecstasy beyond imagination." Nikoli ran his tongue along the ridge his finger had traced, and his grin stretched wider as Azrael jerked beneath him, several curt, surprisingly vulgar phrases flying through the air.

"Now, Azrael, there's no reason to sacrifice your civility." Nikoli gave a disappointed tsk. "Perhaps you will be more receptive to pain." He floated a hand halfway down Azrael's back before pressing his fingers deep into the flesh and slicing the skin with the nail of his thumb. Nikoli's pulse quickened as his thumb sank deeper and Azrael's screams exploded through the room. He backed off the pressure and smiled. "Can you stand?"

Azrael made a move to push himself up from the floor, but as he did so, Nikoli increased the pressure against his back, and he collapsed.

"No." Azrael said between gasping breaths. "I can't stand."

"Pity. You're sworn to follow my commands for the next several days, and I want you standing. I would hate to see you break the terms of our agreement."

Azrael attempted to rise again, but the result was no different. Sweat beaded on his forehead as he tried a third time, and he made it to his knees before Nikoli forced him to the ground again with his thumb.

"I'm begging you—"

Nikoli punched his remaining four fingers through Azrael's skin before he could say anything else.

"Lucky for you, I'm feeling generous." Nikoli closed his eyes and sighed into the screams echoing around the room. He wrenched his hand from Azrael's back and wiped it clean on the ruined bed linens. "We will keep our bargain, but your seven days will begin again when you are well enough to follow my orders without fail. Agreed?"

Azrael turned his face to the floor but didn't answer.

"I would let you leave now, but there's the matter of

Lilith—" Nikoli began, but Azrael allowed him no time to finish.

"Agreed." Azrael rolled onto his side, and amber fire blazed in his eyes. "I'm yours for however long you wish it. We both know that. Let's not add insult to injury by pretending otherwise."

"No injury is complete without the proper insult, my love—a lesson I will gladly teach you as often as necessary."

13

LOST AND FOUND

Luke stood atop the hill at the labyrinth's edge, dark clouds rumbling overhead. The driving rain had long since soaked through his clothes. The river wound lazily below, and Eden sprawled in the distance on his right.

He blinked to clear the drops of rain from his eyelashes and ran a hand through his hair, plastering it against the back of his neck. It hadn't been this long in ages. He should probably cut it, or at least shape shift it into looking like it was cut, but he hadn't felt like doing much of anything since his run-in with Azrael in Nikoli's realm. One day, maybe he'd learn how to make choices he didn't immediately regret. At the time, he hadn't known what Azrael had bargained with to buy Morghan's freedom.

He knew now.

Continuing to spy on Azrael for his first few hours with Nikoli was yet another decision he regretted, and not because of the three-day migraine Azrael had afflicted him with once the intrusion was recognized. God, where was he? There was no way Azrael would have agreed to over three months of that for a week with Morghan. When they were in Nikoli's realm, he had said a week.

The hair on Luke's arms stood on end as power crackled through the air, and his wings rustled behind him. He turned toward the labyrinth, narrowing his eyes at the pillar of blue light slicing through the clouds.

The shifting chamber was active.

Luke launched skyward and sped toward the whirring focus of power. He was in no mood for one of Nikoli's slights; this unannounced intruder would die. It was the least he could do to avenge Azrael's torture.

The stone wall of the labyrinth was cool and slick with rain where he landed, despite the flames dancing near his fingertips. He stood and took a step off the wall, falling through the flames and alighting on the floor beneath. A cyclone of fire trailed down behind him as he walked, steam rising from his clothes.

Azrael's familiar figure stood wreathed in the shifting chamber's eerie glow. His head rested against the back wall, his eyes closed. Luke's boots squeaked to a halt, and Azrael opened his eyes. He pushed off the wall and stepped forward, the light fading as he crossed from marble to stone.

"Why are you using the shifting chamber?" Luke demanded. "When it activated, I thought for sure I would be roasting one of the other angels before shipping them back to Nikoli in pieces."

"Are you going to roast me?" Azrael flashed a smile that was all teeth.

"Seriously—"

"I felt like it," Azrael cut him off, his smile fading as quickly as it had come.

There was more to it than that, but Luke decided not to press for an answer. "Are you okay?"

"Is that a joke?" Azrael's eyes hardened, and he attempted to push past Luke, apparently finished with the conversation before it began.

"Wait, I'm sorry." Luke grabbed Azrael's shoulder as he passed.

Luke didn't see the wall explode behind him, but the sound was deafening. Fragments of stone rushed past him as he was thrown backward through what had been one of the labyrinth's outer walls only moments before. He slid to a halt in the grass and jumped to his feet, his wings spread wide behind him. He half expected to see Nikoli when he looked up, but deep down, he knew that wasn't the case.

Azrael's eyes were amber beacons shining through the night as he crossed the new threshold and took slow, measured steps toward Luke. The rain did not touch him, as if it, unlike Luke, knew better.

Luke wiped a hand across his eyes and saw red. Odd, since despite taking an unexpected trip through the labyrinth's new front door, he wasn't in pain. He looked down at his hand as the rain mixed with blood.

"It's not yours." Azrael answered the question Luke hadn't asked. His longsword hung at his side, and amber sparks flitted across his chest.

"I really am sorry." Luke didn't know what else to say. There was no way to fix this. No way to take back the past few months and unbreak whatever Nikoli had shattered.

"Why?"

"What?" Luke's shoulders slumped.

"Fine, what?" Azrael pressed, shoving one hand in the pocket of his slacks and waving the other toward Luke. "I don't accept blanket apologies. Tell me, exactly, for what are you sorry?"

"Azrael, please—"

"Enough!" Azrael snapped.

Luke opened his mouth to respond, but he couldn't make a sound. He concentrated on his breathing and tried to blank his mind, but his vocal cords refused to function.

Azrael walked toward him until they were little more than arm's length from one another. "I haven't seen you in months, and you're just generally sorry? Is it for being childish about me saving Morghan without telling you? For accusing me of seducing her? Attacking me when I was most vulnerable? Or maybe, you feel the need to apologize for the poorly-timed voyeurism?"

Luke stopped trying to speak. Not like it made a difference. He did, however, dare to hope the rain masked his tears. They'd been alive for millions of years, so many Luke had lost count and made up a number, and never before had Azrael so much as attempted to control him.

Azrael rolled his shoulders and winced. He turned his neck to the side until it cracked, and the gesture was so inherently Nikoli's that Luke tried to take a step back out of habit. It was then he realized his vocal cords weren't the only thing frozen in place.

It's all of that, Luke thought. *Anything you can think of. I'm likely sorry for all of it in one way or another. Same as you.*

"You're wrong." Azrael held Lucifer's gaze. "I've been apologizing to you for the better part of my life without a sliver of hope for forgiveness. I'm so sick of it. I'm not sorry I went to Michael's realm, or even that I ended up trapped in Nikoli's. And I'm certainly not sorry I spent the majority of my time locked in a dreamscape with Morghan, playing out an array of sexual fantasies I've spent the last several million years repressing."

Even though Luke had expected as much, hearing it

aloud tore a fresh wound in his heart. Still, he didn't have the energy to be mad anymore. He only wanted this to be over, for Azrael to go back to being, well, Azrael.

Let me go, Azrael. Just let me go, and we'll forget all of this ever happened. We'll start over. I promise.

"Are you afraid of me?" Azrael closed the gap between them without taking a step. His feet hovered several inches above the ground, putting them at eye level with one another. "You may answer."

"What did he do to you?" Luke's words were barely a whisper as his eyes searched Azrael's. He regretted asking as soon as the words passed his lips. In no way did he want to know.

"Enough to drive me to the edge of sanity." Azrael's feet lowered to the ground. "The usual."

"I think he may have overshot this time."

"Let's hope not." Azrael's hold on Luke released so fast he crumpled to the ground. "Were you not even trying to stand?"

Luke rose to his feet. "I thought maybe if I relaxed everything, I could slip away."

"There is no slipping away from what I can do to you." Azrael shivered and looked up at the sky, as if he'd just realized it was raining. "We should go inside. It's freezing out here."

"It's summer." Luke frowned.

Azrael stared at him for a long moment before turning toward the labyrinth.

"Your back!" Luke gaped. The backside of Azrael's jacket clung to his skin, every inch of it stained crimson. Luke glanced down at his hand, but the blood from earlier had long since washed away with the rain.

"It's nothing." Azrael left the rain behind as he stepped beneath the flames.

"Bullshit! Why haven't you healed? Let me see your back."

"Why, so you can rub salt in the wounds?" He kept walking toward the main hall.

"Don't be ridiculous."

"I won't bleed to death from it, if that's what concerns you. I'll be alive plenty long enough to steal Morghan from you and repeat history."

Luke's eyes burned through their human facade, and a wall of fire poured down from the ceiling in front of Azrael.

The bastard walked right through it without missing a step.

Luke followed, and as he passed through the fire it disappeared. He caught up with Azrael as he entered his room. "Why do you keep baiting me? I'm trying to help you!"

"I don't want your help. Go away."

"No." Luke's teeth grated against one another. "You're lying. I don't know why, but you're trying damn hard to push me away. Too hard. Show me your back."

"I've spent enough of my life undressing on command, Lucifer. The answer remains no."

How was he supposed to respond to that? "I thought we were past all this sniping. We've gotten along for centuries. You know I didn't mean it like that."

Azrael turned away from Luke as he began unbuttoning his jacket. "There are only two people in this entire dimension, and I still can't get any peace." His jacket fell to the floor. "If I show you, will you leave me alone?"

"That depends on what's under there."

"So, no then," Azrael grumbled as he finished unbuttoning his shirt. "Well, the least you can do is come over here and be useful." He gestured to his back where the shirt clung to him. "Rip it off quick."

Luke hadn't thought about the logistics of it when he'd asked. He helped Azrael shrug his arms out of the shirt before balling the loose fabric in his hands.

Azrael held up a hand to stop him. "Try to ignore the scream," he warned. He took a deep breath and nodded.

Luke didn't find Azrael's scream nearly as disturbing as the sound of his flesh tearing away with the fabric. Azrael sank to his knees beside the bed and pressed his face into the mattress. Fresh blood welled up from the deep gashes that crisscrossed his back and continued below the waistline of his slacks. It took Luke a few seconds to pull his attention away from the individual wounds long enough to recognize the overarching pattern.

"That fucking—I'm going to kill him!"

"No, you're not." Azrael rose to his feet and turned to face Luke. "If you care for me at all, you'll leave it alone."

"He carved wings into your back! Was that done with his sword?"

"Traced. And no, not with his sword."

"What do you mean traced?"

"Something strange happened with Morghan after I left Michael's realm. She somehow got into my head from a dimension away. Nothing less than complete insanity ensued, and I woke up with wings being etched into my back. Nikoli had no trouble exploiting the weakness by making the last few months an exercise in how much pain he could extract from the new additions." Azrael sat down on the edge of the bed. "Can I be alone, now?"

"What?" Luke wasn't sure he'd heard that right. Any of it, really. He was having a hard time wrapping his mind around wings being etched into Azrael's back by no one in particular. "Alone? No! We need to take care of your back. It should be healing."

Azrael hung his head. "The healing is excruciating. It hurts worse than the wounds. I've been keeping them open."

"No shit." If there was one part of this Luke did understand, it was the pain associated with healing wings. "Doesn't change the fact they need to heal. Lie down." He goaded Azrael into swinging his legs onto the bed. "On your stomach. Let me get a better look at the wounds."

Azrael looked skeptical. "It's not necessary."

"Yes, it is." Luke pushed him down into a prone position.

"Let me up." Azrael's body tensed beneath Luke's hand. "I can't stay like this."

Luke crouched next to the bed and brushed Azrael's hair away from his eyes.

"I'm not holding you down," he soothed. "You can move if you want, but this is the best position to heal your back. I'm going to leave for a second to get some towels and water." He stood to leave, but Azrael grabbed his wrist. The fear shining behind his eyes had Luke playing over the wide array of things he would like to do to end Nikoli's life. "I'll be right back. I promise."

When Luke returned a few minutes later, he was surprised to see Azrael hadn't moved. After warming the metal bowl of water over his hand, he soaked a small cloth and squeezed out the excess water before draping it over the top half of Azrael's back.

Azrael tensed for a moment before his muscles relaxed. "You don't have to do this. I would eventually let it heal."

Luke chose to ignore his comment. "I'm not going to

unbutton your slacks. The wounds clearly go farther down, but I don't know how much farther."

"Barely. Leave it."

Luke covered the bottom half of Azrael's back with a second towel. "Even without holding the wounds open, you're in bad enough shape to take several days to heal."

"I know."

Luke nodded, mostly to himself. "You're stuck with me until then. I'm not leaving you alone like this."

Azrael groaned and buried his face in his pillow, but he didn't protest.

Luke walked to the other side of the bed. He leaned against it, one hand pressing into the mattress. "So, where do you want me to crash? Floor or bed?"

"Don't ask stupid questions." Azrael's voice was muffled by the pillow.

It wasn't a stupid question. Luke snatched another pillow from the bed and tossed it onto the floor.

"Oh for—the bed. You can sleep in the bed."

"Great!" Luke tossed the pillow back onto the bed and sat down on the edge as he pulled off his boots. "I haven't had to sleep on the floor since before Morghan left. Stone is hell on the back."

Azrael rolled his eyes and laid his head back on the pillow as Luke swung his legs onto the bed.

"Go to sleep, Azrael." Luke turned on his side so they would be eye to eye. "It'll be easier to heal while you sleep. You'll wake up every now and then from the pain, but it's your best bet for making this tolerable."

"I sleep on my back." Azrael frowned.

"Well, not right now you don't." Luke chuckled before thinking better of it.

"I mean, I can only sleep on my back. I can't sleep like this."

"Sure you can," Luke insisted. "How have you been sleeping for the past three months?"

Azrael didn't answer.

"When was the last time you slept, Azrael? And I swear if you say when you were in Michael's realm, I am going to lose it."

"Beyond the first few days? I passed out a time or two from the pain," Azrael said. He continued before Luke had a chance to respond. "I would love nothing more than to sleep, Lucifer. I just can't."

Luke wavered between screaming and setting every last thing in the room on fire, but in the end he took Azrael's hand, winding their fingers together. "I'm not going anywhere. I'll be right here, and I will rip whoever comes into this room limb from limb before I let them near you. Trust me. You can sleep."

"Why are you doing this?"

"You would do the same for me. You have, several times."

"You don't owe me anything."

"Oh, I know." He looked into Azrael's bloodshot eyes and squeezed his hand. "I love you, you idiot. You don't make it easy, but I've always loved you." Luke averted his eyes and stared up at the flames when Azrael turned his face back into the pillow. He wasn't sure what kind of reaction he had expected, especially with the impeccable timing of professing his undying love to someone who was injured, terrified, and hadn't slept in a quarter year.

Azrael squeezed his hand, pulling him away from his thoughts. Was he crying?

"Other than very, very late, your timing is fine," Azrael

choked out, but his eyes lit up with the first real smile Luke had seen in ages. "And I am not an idiot."

"Have you seen your back?"

"Transiently an idiot."

They both laughed, although Azrael's was cut short by a pained grimace.

"Please try to sleep." Luke brushed the tears from Azrael's cheek before leaning in and gently pressing their lips together.

Azrael moaned, and his power swept through the room, taking Luke's breath away. It took all his willpower to swim through the haze of emotions directing him to do things to Azrael which would do far more harm than good to him in his current state.

"Turn it off." Luke swallowed hard, his lips only a hairsbreadth from Azrael's. "Take the time to heal. It's been this long. What's a few more days?"

He gave Azrael one last peck on the cheek before pulling away.

The heaviness in the room faded, and Luke lay listening to Azrael's breathing as it became slower and more measured. He hadn't realized how tightly Azrael had been holding onto him until his hand relaxed as he fell into a deeper sleep.

Luke glanced around the room and up to the flames before adding an extra layer of power to the ceiling and walls. If anyone short of Nikoli tried to enter without his permission, it was doubtful they'd live long enough to regret it.

~

Morghan sat hidden away in the back corner of a tavern, picking at the food on her plate. It had been months since her escape from Falcroix, and she was starting to feel more like herself, although her stomach had never quite caught up with the healing process.

"What are you eating?" Damn it, Michael had found her.

She stabbed her fork at the plate of meat and raised it up for inspection. "Steak. It comes from cows."

"Funny." Michael grabbed the fork and plate away from her before shoveling most of the remaining food into his mouth.

"Hey!" Morghan stood and grabbed for the plate, which Michael deftly moved out of reach. "That's probably from the last damn cow in the whole kingdom!"

"I'm saving you a trip outside to retch up this stuff in the snow," he said matter-of-factly.

"I already ate half of it, and I feel fine."

"Give it another ten minutes."

To her credit, it took fifteen.

A side effect of vomiting half of what she ate on any given day was getting to know the drunks of Vahyir better than she'd hoped. The only upside was Michael no longer came outside with her to gloat about being right. She leaned her forehead against the cold, stone wall of the tavern and tried not to breathe in the stench of vomit and urine assaulting her from every side. She pushed away from the wall, her breath somersaulting through the air as she decided whether or not she was fit to leave.

"Fuckin' Dayl's boy." Gray, a regular, found an open area of wall and spat in the snow. "About split my head wide open yelling about needing some healer. Sun's barely up. Ain't no healer around here even awake."

"Where I'm from, healers don't sleep," Morghan chuckled. She still didn't sleep much, although she'd kept her word and at least laid down every night to give it an honest try. Murmurs and a few disinterested glances were all Morghan received in return. Most of the wall crew never spoke to her, maybe because they were scared of her. Probably.

She rubbed her hands together before shoving them into her pockets and walking out of the alley. New snow crunched under her boots. There was always new snow. It kept the gravedigger's cart piled high each morning. The main city, expansive as it was, had little left in the way of food, and most of the population had long ago run out of kindling. Every morning those who were able trekked to the forest's edge to fell trees and salvage what they could before dusk, but days were short, and being outside of the city walls when the sun set was a surefire way to freeze to death or worse.

Morghan had helped hunt and retrieve firewood only once. It was then she realized what Michael had kept from her while she was shut away in his cabin re-learning to be human; as far as the citizens of Vahyir were concerned, not only had she abandoned them in their time of need, but her reappearance had heralded the worst winter in known history. She might as well have been throwing all those bodies on the cart herself.

"Superstitious assholes," she mumbled. A high-pitched yell from up the path grabbed her attention.

"You're supposed to help people!" A boy who couldn't have been more than ten stood outside an herb shop, no doubt screaming at the "healer" who owned it. "I'll work off the debt, I swear it. She needs help now!" A hand reached across the threshold and pushed him hard enough he tripped and sat down in the snow. The door slammed.

Morghan did an about face, and the new line of daggers around her belt clanged against one another. She took a few steps back toward the tavern before the boy's sobs floated by on the wind. "Fuckin' Dayl's boy," she muttered as she trudged to where the boy sat sobbing in the snow. She offered him a hand up, but he looked at it as if she'd thrust a poisonous snake in his face.

"I need a healer." He sniffed.

"Looks like I'm the best you're going to get." Morghan hauled him up by the back of his coat and set him on his feet. "How can I help?"

"I don't need anyone killed," he stammered, taking a step back.

She could have been halfway back to Michael's place by now instead of calf-deep in slush being lectured on her station in life by a boy so young he still sang soprano. "Listen, kid, you can show me what you need help with, or I can go on my way and leave you to beg people for charity you'll never get."

The boy thought for a long moment before he took off through the snow and beckoned her to follow with a wave of his hand. He stopped in front of a dilapidated shack pinned between two larger buildings and put a gloved hand on the door before turning to face her. "I don't have any money."

"Good thing I didn't ask for any." Morghan stepped through the door, and somehow the filthy, one-room hovel looked even worse on the inside.

Morghan hurried to the pallet of blankets where a young girl not much older than the boy lay writhing in a growing pool of blood. She knelt and gave her a once over. Sweat beaded on the girl's forehead, but the blood was coming from below, closer to her thighs. Her rounded abdomen poked up through the tattered blankets.

"How far along is she?" Morghan demanded, rolling her eyes when the boy only stared in horror. "Boy! Damn it, kid. What's your name?"

"Dravyn," he sputtered, kneeling on the other side of the girl. "This is my sister, Dayla. What do you mean far along?"

Well, that was a dead end. She turned her attention to the girl, who had yet to give them even a wayward glance. "Dayla, my name is Morghan. I think you're in labor. How long have you known you're pregnant?"

Dayla made no move to acknowledge Morghan and only flung her head from side to side as she panted and screamed. This route wasn't any better than asking the boy.

"She can't see," Dravyn offered, as if it might explain why she was screaming in pain and in danger of bleeding to death.

"I have to lift up your dress." Morghan tried to strike a soothing tone. Dayla may not have been responding, but there was no reason to think she was completely oblivious to what was happening to her.

Lifting the dress was all it took for Morghan to tell just how far along Dayla was. A dusky foot peeked out from between blood-slicked thighs, and by the look of the skin creases on the sole, she was close to full term.

"Fuck!" Morghan slapped her hand against the dirt floor and turned to Dravyn. "I need clean water, a knife, needle and thread." And a shitload of luck.

The boy shook his head. "We don't have any of that."

Of course they didn't.

She shrugged out of her coat and tossed it to the side. Her daggers went next, but she thought better of it and pulled one from the belt before dumping the rest of them on the lopsided table. The belt slid off it and landed across what looked to be the only chair the family owned.

"Don't sit on those." She waved toward the chair and returned to Dayla, spreading the girl's legs and kneeling between them. "Get her something to bite down on. This is going to get worse before it gets better."

"What are you doing with that dagger?" Dravyn's face paled. "Don't cut the baby out; the feet are already coming. Just pull!"

"Can you please leave the baby delivery to me and get your sister a piece of leather, or wood, or, I don't care, maybe your arm to shove between her teeth? I'm about to slice open a particularly sensitive area to give this kid more room to be born backward."

Dravyn stared at her but made no move to follow her command.

That was it. She couldn't do everything by herself, and if she waited much longer, there wouldn't be much point in doing anything at all. She flipped the dagger around in her hand and made a clean, vertical incision through the perineum. Dayla's legs thrashed and Morghan took a knee to the jaw before throwing her weight against the girl's left leg to hold it in place. "Grab her other leg and hold it out to the side with her knee bent." Morghan barked the order, and this time Dravyn obeyed.

"What I wouldn't give for a pair of sevens." She sighed at Dravyn's confused stare. "Gloves, I want some fucking gloves."

She felt her way up the baby's torso, part of which had started to come through, but the shoulders were stuck. She turned the body, and with gentle pressure delivered the first shoulder before rotating the baby further to deliver the second.

The door burst open behind her, and though she didn't think it possible, the room grew colder.

"What's all this?" a gruff voice called from the doorway. Dayl, one of the most useless people she'd had the displeasure of meeting, had perfect timing.

Morghan ignored him and glanced up at Dravyn, who, while still holding his sister's leg, had turned terrified eyes on his father.

"Dravyn, look at me." He did as she asked. "I need you to put pressure low on her belly, not far above where my arms are sticking out."

"Don't you tell my boy what to do, demon!" Dayl bellowed. "Get out of my house!"

Morghan glanced behind her as she got a better hold on the baby, snaking her hand up until she could place a finger to either side of its nose. "I'm a little busy here trying to save your pregnant preteen daughter and her partially born son. I'll leave as soon as I'm satisfied they're either stable or dead." She turned back to Dravyn, "Anytime now on that pelvic pressure, kid."

Dravyn moved to follow her command, but before he was able to do so Dayl grabbed him by the neck and flung him into the nearest wall. She heard the familiar sound of one of her daggers being unsheathed from her belt and groaned at the thought of having to decide between saving Dravyn and delivering the baby without a broken neck.

When Dayl wrenched her head back by the hair and cold steel pressed to her throat, she couldn't help but grin. This decision was much easier.

"No, stop!" Dravyn cried from the wall. He launched at his father, but Dayl gave him a swift kick to the side of his knee, and Dravyn collapsed, rocking back and forth while cradling his leg.

"Let go of the babe, or I'll slit you ear to ear," Dayl snarled. "We don't need help from the likes of you."

"Listen, I'm currently elbow deep in blood, shit, and vagina. Let go of me, drop the dagger, and leave the way you came. We'll write this off as a stupid, drunken mistake." He was already a dead man, but him knowing as much wouldn't do her any favors. It would be a lot harder to save anyone if she was choking on her own blood.

"I don't think you understand. You're about to die."

"I lost count how many times my throat was slashed over the past three years," she said, a thin trickle of blood sliding down her neck. "I don't die easy. You, however, that's a different story."

Still holding the baby with one hand, she reached up with the other and grabbed the dagger by the blade, wrenching it from Dayl's grasp before turning it on him and burying it below his right diaphragm. She pushed away the thought of the deep, bleeding furrows carved in her palm and went back to the task at hand as Dayl fell to the floor screaming.

"If you want to live longer, leave that dagger in." She twisted around, used her knee to exert pelvic pressure, and finally pulled the child free from his mother.

Aside from Dayl's screams and his daughter's moans, the room was silent. The child lay blue and limp in Morghan's blood and meconium streaked arms, but he had a paradoxically strong pulse. She breathed out as hard as she could before sealing her lips over the baby's and breathing deep. Mucous, amniotic fluid, and other things she'd prefer not think about rushed into her mouth faster than expected, since she wasn't sure the makeshift suctioning move would work at all. She coughed up the foul mixture and smiled when a weak cry met her ears. Her coat worked well for drying off the child and even better as a warmer. She sliced through the cord and finished tucking the baby into the thick folds of fabric before turning back to his mother.

It took Morghan a moment to realize Dayla was no longer breathing. She stepped over Dravyn and felt along her neck for a pulse. Nothing. Morghan rolled her eyes to the ceiling. She positioned herself over Dayla's chest and was about to start compressions when the mottled appearance of the girl's left arm caught her eye. Morghan ripped away the sleeve and cursed when she saw purple dots of various sizes running the entirety of her arm. Glancing down to Dayla's legs, she noted similar marks that hadn't been there when she'd first entered the room. She rocked back on her heels and hung her head: that was that, a sure sign her blood had stopped clotting properly. She knew a lost cause when she saw it, and so she reached down and closed Dayla's eyes. Morghan's chest tightened as she stood, and she had to concentrate to keep her breathing slow and steady. Everything was moving too fast and too slow at the same time. It had been ages since she had a patient to lose, but apparently the hollow, detached feeling never changed, even if you'd slain hundreds on purpose in the meantime.

"My daughter." Dayl's raspy voice broke into Morghan's thoughts. Dark blood oozed around the dagger, saturating his shirt. "You killed my daughter."

"No." Morghan glared at Dayl, and a rush of warmth swept through her, a sure sign her eyes were alight. She stalked toward him, grabbing another dagger from her belt as she passed the table. "But I'm damn sure going to kill you."

She ripped his head backward by the hair and shoved

the dagger down his throat until the hilt hit his gaping mouth. She cinched her belt around her waist and retrieved her daggers to refill the loops.

The infant squirmed when she gathered him in her coat and held him close to her chest. It was going to take a miracle to keep him warm long enough to make it to Michael's cabin. She shivered thinking about how a thin shirt and deerskin leggings would be the only things between her and the snow once they left the shack.

Morghan nudged Dravyn with the toe of her boot. "Kid, you can open your eyes. It's over."

Dravyn peeked out from under his arm, tears staining his cheeks.

"Do you think you can walk?" she asked.

Dravyn nodded. He stood and took a step, wincing when he put pressure on his injured leg. "I'm okay." He frowned down at his sister's body, and fresh tears fell from his eyes. "She's really dead?"

Morghan nodded. "I promise it wasn't on purpose. Childbirth is dangerous business."

"I know it wasn't you." Dravyn glanced at his father's body, and his jaw tightened as he wiped away his tears with the back of his hand. "It's his fault. All of it. If it wasn't for him, she wouldn't even have been pregnant."

Somehow, Morghan wasn't surprised.

"Come with me, kid. There's nothing here for you anymore."

"Where are you taking us?" Dravyn hobbled behind her as they stepped into the biting wind.

"Over the hills and far away."

～

"No, absolutely not!" Michael couldn't believe what Morghan was proposing. He still hadn't wrapped his mind around her barging into his home with a child and a newborn. Now, she wanted to keep them and take them back to Salus? "You can't just randomly claim children!"

"I'm not," Morghan insisted. Dravyn stood a few paces behind her, attempting to soothe an infant whose wails were loud enough to wake the dead. "They're orphans."

Michael pointed to the older boy. "That one brought me news of your return not three months ago, and he wasn't an orphan then."

"He's newly orphaned."

Michael knew better than to ask how that came to pass. "So you're adopting them?"

"In a way."

Michael paced in front of the hearth. "No offense, Morghan, but you don't seem like the mothering type."

"The irony. It's killing me."

What was she talking about?

"And I'm recruiting, not adopting," Morghan continued, her tone less than friendly. "I've been toying with the idea of training a dedicated group of assassins for a while. I think if I have a group of my own, Salus's army has a better chance of coming across as yours. And don't worry. Dravyn has been taking care of himself and his sister for the better part of a year. He'll have little need for my inadequate mothering skills, and the baby is his responsibility, not mine."

Dravyn inched closer to Morghan and tugged on the sleeve of her shirt. "Morghan?"

Had the boy used her given name? Michael could count on one hand those who referred to her as such, and most of them he'd only heard about in passing.

"Can you not see I'm busy bargaining for your livelihood, kid?"

"I think the baby really needs something to eat. He won't calm down."

Michael settled his hands on his hips. "This is exactly what I'm talking about. The ten-year-old can't take full responsibility for an infant. He doesn't even know how to feed it."

"I'll be eleven next month," Dravyn protested. "And I know how to feed a baby, but I don't have any food or money."

"Oh, eleven next month? Well, that makes all the difference." Michael nodded at Morghan, who appeared unfazed by his sarcasm.

She walked to the icebox and picked out a carafe of goat's milk. She sniffed it, shrugged, and headed back to Dravyn. "Dip your finger in there, and let him suck on it. We'll find a better solution later."

Michael sat on the edge of the fireplace and rubbed his temples. He tensed when Morghan sat beside him.

"Listen, I know this isn't ideal." She draped an arm over his shoulders.

"Or practical," Michael said. "That baby looks about five minutes old."

"Maybe half an hour."

"What? I was joking."

"I'm not. I delivered him myself, but I couldn't save his mother." There was real regret in her tone, something he'd rarely heard from her.

"How the Hell do you know how to deliver a baby?"

"Because I remember at least a few things from my mortal life, during which I was a physician. Although to be fair, in over a decade of training and practice, I've come across a scenario like that only once. But it sticks with you when a newborn dies in your arms."

"I thought you were an assassin?"

"I'm a multifaceted, complex individual, Michael. Like a Rubik's cube that stabs you if you can't figure it out fast enough."

Michael had no idea what a Rubik's cube was. He stood and walked halfway across the room before turning back. "What kind of doctor were you? Why haven't you ever told me this before?"

"We rarely talk about our mortal lives, and not that it matters, but I was a trauma surgeon. Well, sort of. I got fired a few months before completing my fellowship. Totally not my fault, by the way."

Michael had the sneaking suspicion it probably was her fault. He shook off his confusion and concentrated on the important part: she was a damn surgeon. "It does matter! You could have been tending the wounded during battle instead of fighting. Don't you think it's a little irresponsible to let your troops die around you when you could have saved them?"

Morghan stood, and all the humor drained from her eyes. "It was a long time ago, Michael, and even then I spent half of my day fighting to keep people out of a grave and the other half shoving people into one. I was a surgeon, not a fucking magician. I can't fix the kind of broke you find on the battlefields here, especially not alone and without advanced technology. I mean for fuck's sake, in my mortal life I helped develop a nanobot that could be programmed to regenerate neurons, but here I can't even see shit in the dark without lighting something on fire."

Michael couldn't even look at her. "You disappoint me."

"Not half as much as you've disappointed me," she shot

back before glancing at the children. "Stay here. I'll be back with food for both of you."

She opened the door and turned back, the afternoon sun framing her in the doorway. "And to keep you up to speed, Michael, I was a mother once. Around ten generations later, your entitled ass came along."

Michael gaped at the door after she slammed it.

Dravyn's eyes widened. "Wait, she's your grandmother?"

"What? No." Michael shook his head. "That's not possible."

Michael grabbed his coat and rushed out the door. Morghan hadn't made it very far, and she'd left before donning anything remotely resembling winter gear. Michael shrugged out of his coat and held it out to her as he reached her side.

She wrapped her arms against her chest and shook her head. "Keep it."

Michael dropped the coat around her shoulders and pulled her to a halt. "You need to take better care of yourself. If you weren't a ranking immortal, you would have died a hundred times over by now."

"A thousand." She refused to make eye contact.

"Is it true? What you said back there?"

She pulled the coat closer and nodded.

"I don't know how to process that. Not after all these years."

"I'm your friend." She finally looked at him. "We just happen to be distantly related."

"Directly related."

"You were born over two hundred years after I died, Michael. We share less than one one-hundredth of our genes. You'd be hard pressed to find a pair of mortals in all of Vahyir who share less."

"I didn't know you died. I didn't know people could come back from the dead." Apparently, he didn't know much. Nothing made sense. Did he know anything about her at all? The truth was, he didn't know much from before she showed up in his life and refused to leave.

"Neither did I. Your father was tricked into starting my heart again."

Michael's thoughts spun out of control. "You know my father?"

"We've met." She traced the scar on her left cheek and pointed to the jagged scar along the underside of her chin. "Let's just say he wasn't thrilled with his mistake."

"We've been friends for the better part of a century. We've fought and bled together, planned and built an entire city together. Why now? Why the multifaceted confession on today of all days?" His life had been confusing enough up to this point. The last thing he needed was more secrets and lies from what amounted to his only real friend.

"It was my mistake. I didn't plan on ever telling you, but I'm still not back to normal. The past couple hours have been a little too full of memories from a different life." She looked up at him and shook her head. "I don't belong here, Michael. I don't belong anywhere anymore."

He knew the feeling. Most days, he busied himself enough to feel a sense of purpose; however, there were so many times the memories of the past came without warning, and the sense of loss cut so deep he would have preferred a physical wound.

"You belong here as much as I do." Michael wrapped his arms around her and rested his chin atop of her head.

"Why don't you head back inside? I'll get food for the boy and the baby."

Morghan pulled away enough to give him a skeptical look. "So you're accepting them now?"

Michael's breath came out as a large white puff of air. "Just please don't call them assassins."

"Spies?" Morghan smirked. "Lethal little spies? Nah, doesn't have a good ring to it."

Michael groaned. "Seriously, Morghan."

"Ok, trackers then."

"Do you even know how to track anything?"

"I'm really good at tracking people I want to assassinate."

Michael laughed before he could stop himself. "Be judicious, please, whatever you do."

"Fine, I'll call them Seiyaku. No one will even know what it means, and let's be honest, every group of lethal little tracker spy assassins needs an air of mystery."

He tried not to smile and failed. She was right. Despite the glut of information she'd dropped on him, they were still friends.

Luke stood behind Azrael, a hand on each shoulder as he inspected the intricate lines that wove together to create the feathers on Azrael's back. Despite being healed, each line remained ever-so-slightly depressed, and while the wing on the left side of his body healed black, the right remained crimson against the darkness of his skin. Luke's hands drifted down to brush over several of the markings.

Azrael sucked in a sharp breath. "Lucifer!"

Luke took a step back and shoved his hands in his pockets. "Sorry! It still hurts?"

Azrael sat on the edge of the bed and shook his head. "No, it doesn't hurt. Does it look bad?"

"It looks amazing, like someone spent a lifetime detailing each individual feather."

"I'm sure that would have hurt less." Azrael glanced over his shoulder before turning back to Luke. "At least the pain is gone."

Silence stretched between them, not to mention the question of what came next. Luke gazed up at the night sky, the flames long abandoned due to the summer heat. Azrael was healed. He didn't need Luke to watch over him anymore. It had been over a week since Azrael returned home, and in that time neither had brought up the intimate moments of the first night.

Luke sat beside Azrael and leaned onto his knees. His heart thundered in his ears.

"It's okay." Azrael laid a hand on his shoulder. "You can go."

"I don't think I want to go." Luke glanced at Azrael. Why did he look so sad?

"Come back when you're sure." Azrael squeezed his shoulder. "You have to consider Morghan and Nikoli. I doubt I'd survive being your mistake a third time."

Morghan. Luke ran a hand over his face. He probably should be thinking about her more. He spent the majority of his waking hours obsessing over her every move. He'd still watched her, even while Azrael healed, but there was a disconnect. It had been nearly a century since he'd touched or spoken with her, and it wasn't like there was a future date to look forward to her return. If Nikoli had his way, he would never see her in person again.

"You will," Azrael chimed into his thoughts. "Whether we are together or not, you'll meet again."

Luke glowered at Azrael. "You reading my mind isn't helping things."

"Then stop broadcasting your thoughts at a scream," he shot back. "Besides, if we're being honest about this, Nikoli is the problem, not Morghan."

Azrael was right, but Luke was sick of tiptoeing around that self-righteous jackass. All he did was punctuate interminable stretches of nervous misery with more profound horrors. It didn't matter how many of his rules they followed, in the end he always found a justification for torturing them anyway. Luke's gaze fell to his hands, and he let the human façade slip. He flexed the dark, clawed fingers. What was left for Nikoli to do this time? Kill him? That might not be so bad.

No, they all knew Morghan was the easiest target. She would be the one to pay for whatever he decided. He didn't want to think about that, about any of this.

"Why now?" Luke glanced at Azrael. "A week ago you were more than willing to do this without a word of soul-scarching."

"I think we can agree I wasn't in the best frame of mind." Azrael stared at the ground. "And you said you loved me. You kissed me." He sighed and turned his eyes back to Luke. "There isn't a shadow left of the man I was when Nikoli created me, but I have loved you from my first breath. It's the only constant I've ever known."

They could deal with Nikoli later.

Luke reached for Azrael and stopped before the clawed hand touched his shoulder. The claws receded, and pale, smooth skin knitted over top the charred flesh.

"I don't care what you look like, Lucifer. I never have."

"I do." Luke straddled Azrael's lap and put a hand to either side of his face. "We're stronger together, and I'm so tired of missing you."

The kiss he offered Azrael was nothing like the timid caress of lips the week before, and a blur of touches and whispered promises later he was laying on his back, stripped of every bit of clothing, not to mention any thought of consequences.

Azrael froze above him, his eyes shining against the backdrop of stars. "Nikoli," he whispered, and fear flashed across his face. Azrael took a few long, deep breaths and his eyes grew brighter. He sat back on his heels. "He's watching. Give me a minute, and I can push him out."

"No." Luke didn't want Azrael dedicating a sliver of attention to Nikoli. He pulled Azrael back down to him, and the tension melted from Azrael's body as their lips met. Luke wrapped one arm around him and let the other hand slip its human form as he pointed a middle finger at the sky. "Let him watch."

14

TRUTH AND CONSEQUENCES

KRISHNA'S HAND trembled on the hilt of his sword as he sat huddled against the wall, his gaze fixed on the sky. No more did the sun, framed by lazily moving white clouds, hang above him. The illusion had shattered hours ago, yet his gaze kept returning to the dark, swirling maelstrom above him. It stretched out forever, spinning around a central point over Nikoli's chambers. Flecks of light dotted its expanse, carried along with the clouds' momentum.

He turned his eyes from the spectacle above him to the equally horrifying state of the hall. To his left, blood spattered the walls, snaking past melting frost and ice. Hellions and angels alike lay strewn across the floor. Uriel's body twitched, a spike of ice rising from his chest. One of his wings had been ripped free from his back, and the pool of blood he lay in had already begun to congeal.

In the other direction, Nikoli braced himself against the wall with his left hand. Nikoli's head bowed toward the ground, his breathing heavy and uneven. Blood trailed down his blade, collecting in a puddle at his bare feet. Like the maelstrom of souls above Krishna, the prismatic wings stretching from Nikoli's back drew his eyes like a magnet. Krishna would have staked his life on the assumption his master didn't have wings. Now, as he looked past the wings to the thick scars wrapping around Nikoli's torso like so much rope, he wondered if he knew anything about the man at all.

"Master?" Krishna's voice cracked.

Nikoli turned toward Krishna, a frosted handprint glimmering on the wall where his hand had lain. He walked to Krishna and knelt in front of him. The face staring back at him was decades younger than the one he knew so well.

"Are you hurt?" Nikoli laid a gentle hand against the side of Krishna's neck.

Krishna shook his head, and when Nikoli crushed him in a tight embrace, he wasn't sure if he should be relieved or terrified.

Nikoli stood and pulled Krishna up with him. He glanced down the hall and cringed. "How many did I kill?"

Did Nikoli not remember the chaos he'd unleashed only moments before? If not, that was the most terrifying thing about all of this.

"Easily a hundred Hellions." Krishna gestured toward Uriel. "Two angels. Phanuel ordered the Host to the sky when your wings emerged. Uriel was the slowest. You gave chase and ripped his wing off midair. Zaphiel came back to help. There are pieces of him mixed in with the rest."

Nikoli turned his face to the sky. "You didn't run?"

Krishna shook his head. He knew his place, and it didn't involve running away from Nikoli, no matter how loud his instincts screamed for him to do so.

Nikoli sheathed his sword and turned his eyes back to Krishna. "If something like this ever happens again, hide if you can, but don't run. Never run."

"Yes, Master." Krishna bowed his head and dared to stare at Nikoli's scars through the curtain of his hair. They had to be almost as ancient as Nikoli, seeing as no blade could make such a mark, certainly not a ranking sword. The compulsion to run his fingers across them was strong, but not as strong as the one to end the life of whoever had put them there. The real tragedy being that the culprit was certainly long dead.

Nikoli took a step back and glared at Krishna. His wings fluttered behind him before disappearing into his back. A ripple of energy ran over Nikoli's skin, and the scars melted away as his youthful features were replaced by the usual skin creases accentuating his eyes and forehead.

"Gather whatever Hellions are salvageable," Nikoli ordered. "The call is already out to Phanuel. When the angels return, we're leaving."

"Leaving?" Krishna wondered. "For where?"

"My son's realm." A chilling grin spread across Nikoli's face. "We have a kingdom to usurp."

Winstin dragged himself into the shifting chamber with his one good arm. His right arm dangled uselessly at his side, torn from the socket with so much force that most of his flesh had separated along with it. Aside from his arm, his back was a riot of pain. His legs followed few commands and supported his weight for no more than seconds at a time. He struggled to reach the keypad and squinted the eye Nikoli hadn't ripped out. A million codes flowed through his mind, and he struggled to remember the one he needed now. The one he thought would never be necessary.

When his mind lit upon it, he punched the keys and

prayed the chamber was still functional. The intensity of the light surrounding him increased until he could see nothing beyond it. His chest lurched, and when the light dimmed, he tumbled out of the chamber and onto the stone floor beyond.

His limited gaze strayed from the flames billowing overhead to the gaping hole in the wall. Maybe, he should have stayed in Nikoli's realm. Eventually, he would have adapted to his new state of disrepair. Several of the other Hellions had done just that since Morghan was banished and Lucifer stopped repairing them. Winstin had almost convinced himself going back was the best course of action, when Lucifer tore through the ceiling of flames and landed in a crouch before him. Winstin pressed himself against the wall when Lucifer looked up. He may have been predominantly in human form, but the eyes he trained on Winstin were blood red.

Lucifer stood, and the anger in his expression faded into confusion. He pointed to the shifting chamber. "Drag your ass back in there and leave. The repair shop closed decades ago, and I don't give a fuck what you run in Nikoli's realm."

Winstin was more than happy to oblige, and he was about to tell him as much when Azrael flashed into existence at Lucifer's side. He pulled a shirt over his bare shoulders and secured the first few buttons as he leaned against what was left of the wall.

"Give him a minute to collect his thoughts, Lucifer." Azrael smiled. "It's so much easier to strip him of them when they're all in one place."

Winstin scrambled toward the shifting chamber and tumbled to his side in the process. When Azrael took a step toward him, Winstin closed his eye and shielded his face with his good arm. "Wait! I came to help!"

Nothing happened, and he dared to peek around his hand. Azrael hadn't moved beyond his first step, but Lucifer towered above him, ready to snatch him from the ground and throw him into the shifting chamber.

"How could you possibly help us?" Lucifer asked.

"Moreover, why should we trust you?" Azrael raised an eyebrow.

"How do you think I ended up like this? Does these look like normal wear and tear injuries?"

"Well, I was about to find out." Azrael shrugged as he walked to Lucifer's side.

"You could have just asked!" Winstin bit off. These two were more exasperating in half a minute than Morghan had been in half a million years. No wonder they all got on so well. "The Master destroyed dozens of my kind in a fit of rage. I was luckier than most. He even went after the angels. It was a bloodbath."

Azrael crouched in front of him. "And why should we care?"

Lucifer crossed his arms over his chest. "Nikoli can destroy whatever he wants in his realm, and don't even think for a second you'll be allowed to live here. My need for an undead minion is nonexistent."

Azrael smirked up at Lucifer. "No one's need for an undead minion is nonexistent."

"I don't want to stay here," Winstin continued. "The Master took everyone who was fit to shift and left for Michael's realm. I was hoping you would repair me and send me the same way."

Lucifer's eyes glowed brighter, and his body went stone still for the briefest of moments. When his eyes dimmed, he fell into a crouch beside Azrael and hung his head in his hands. "Shit! He's telling the truth. Nikoli is in Falcroix with the Host."

"Better Falcroix than Salus." Azrael turned angry eyes on Winstin. "And why would we want you to join Nikoli in Falcroix?"

"Not Falcroix. Salus." He groaned at Lucifer and Azrael's confused expressions. How could they not be getting this? "I'm stronger than ten men when I'm at my peak. You said it yourself." He gestured to Azrael, "Any number of people would want me as a servant. I'm willing to bet Windstarr is one of them. I know you don't trust me, but she does. That has to count for something."

Azrael stood and raised an eyebrow. "And your allegiance to Nikoli?"

Winstin clenched his teeth and took a deep breath. "Fuck Nikoli."

He shivered, and his muscles relaxed. It was easier to say than expected. He toyed with the idea of letting it roll off his tongue a few more times, but his thoughts slowed and blurred together. It only lasted a moment before everything snapped back into focus.

"Heal him," Azrael told Lucifer. "I'll use Salus as a midpoint and drop him there while shifting between two places in this realm."

"You're sure?" Lucifer looked skeptical.

"I'm sure he's shown loyalty to Morghan in the past, he has no current inclination to join Nikoli's cause, and Morghan is going to need all the help she can get. Think about it. Nikoli isn't in Falcroix to forge an alliance. Why share power when he can easily have it all? He's about to take over one of the largest armies in the realm. An army he in no way needs."

Winstin nodded. "Which means whatever he's planning, he's in it for the long game. Being in the same realm as Morghan means he's close enough to be a threat."

Azrael sighed. "But far enough away he doubts we'd risk disobeying a cardinal rule until he made a move against her."

Lucifer's shoulders sank. "It keeps us here."

Azrael put a hand on Lucifer's arm. "We can go there now if you want, but Nikoli is unlikely to expect it. Right now, we can keep a close eye on him. If he lost control enough to kill members of the Host, he'll be taking things slow for a while to avoid a repeat performance. The three of us being together again might push him over the edge, and I can't predict his next move if he's stark raving mad."

"We'll stay," Lucifer agreed. He pulled Azrael close and caught his lips in a kiss.

Winstin's mouth hung open, and he barely brought his expression under control before Lucifer pulled away and reached for him.

Lucifer placed one hand behind Winstin's neck and the other over his injured arm. Winstin closed his eyes and waited for the warmth to spill over him. He was old enough that this was nowhere near the first time Lucifer was giving his body a tune-up. It was, however, the worst he'd been injured, since Nikoli punished him for helping Morghan centuries ago. The usual spiritual detachment overcame him, and a flood of warmth came along with it. He floated in a comforting abyss without a body, a name, or past.

The return to his physical shell was always a stepwise process, beginning with the hazy sorrow of leaving the darkness and ending with him sitting abruptly, as if waking from a sudden fall. His memory tricked him into breathing heavily, and his eyes flew open as he grasped his chest with both hands. Both working hands.

Winstin clamored to his feet and looked down at his body, as perfect as the day ages ago when Lucifer first reanimated him. Well, with the new addition of abs instead of the rounded belly he'd taken to the grave. Not to mention the dark skin covering his hands lacked the wrinkles he'd existed with for the entirety of his afterlife. "You made me younger," he said, running a hand along his cheek.

"I made you fit for battle," Lucifer said. "No offense to your more comfortable form."

Winstin pursed his lips and laid a hand across his flat stomach. "Can I have this back at least?"

Lucifer quirked an eyebrow. "You want me to make you overweight again?"

"I prefer the term endearingly rotund, thank you." Winstin patted the taut muscles he'd never had a day in his life, let alone the better part of a million years afterwards. "Who wants a new center of gravity after over six hundred thousand years anyway?"

Lucifer shrugged, and another short trip through the abyss later, Winstin retained the gift of youth but in the comfort of a body type that was his.

"Thank you." Winstin turned to Azrael, who was gazing at Lucifer as if no one else existed. "And you."

Azrael's gaze shifted from Lucifer to Winstin, and his expression changed to one of indifference. He didn't say a word as he took Winstin by the arm. The world went black for a moment before Azrael released him, and he fell to his knees in Morghan's room.

"She's not back yet." Azrael's voice startled him onto his feet, and he retreated a few steps.

"I thought you were dropping me mid-shift?"

"A few seconds won't hurt. I'm sure Nikoli has seen quite enough of me lately to keep his spying to a minimum."

Azrael closed the space between them so fast Winstin gasped. "Wait here for her, and I'll leave it to your better judgment if or when you break the news about Lucifer and me."

"I take it the relationship is new?" Winstin ventured. "Possibly even 'Nikoli losing his mind and ripping his servants apart' new?"

"It's as old and new as you want it to be. Just keep in mind that being alone in this realm is a source of great pain for Morghan."

"And it might cause her even more pain to know the two men she loves are fucking each other while she huddles in a corner every night too afraid of her dreams to sleep?" Winstin guessed, cringing even as the words left his mouth. The last thing he wanted was to anger Azrael, especially since he was the one responsible for Lucifer repairing his body. Still, Morghan didn't deserve to be left by the wayside.

Azrael took a step back, and uncertainty flashed across his face. "Only having access to Morghan skews your opinion. Don't presume to know the first thing about my life. Or Lucifer's. The three of us will be together again, but nothing is gained from everyone being miserable until that day comes."

"Keep telling yourself that." Winstin frowned. If he didn't watch out he would have a new body and a brain the consistency of scrambled eggs, but it was difficult to control his tongue. "One day you might believe it."

Azrael's jaw tightened, and his eyes flared before he vanished.

Winstin collapsed against the wall and stared at the ceiling. A sliver of guilt crept into his chest, but he fought it back with the same reasoning he'd thrown at Azrael.

Morghan was his master now, even if she didn't know it yet, and the cards had been stacked against her since the moment Lucifer resurrected her. He was sick of watching her fight for the right to breathe while the immortal titans in her life were so wrapped up in their own issues they either couldn't or wouldn't help her.

He stood and headed for the door. Morghan was still in Vahyir, at least for a few more weeks until spring took hold. Even then, it would be months until she reached Salus, and he wasn't going to sit in this room for half a year.

A flutter of excitement ran through him as he pressed his hand against the door. If he strained his ears enough, he could hear the conversations bubbling through the tavern. Civilization was out there, and for the first time in ages, he would be engaged with a group of people who weren't hell-bent on being pretentious assholes. His first order of business would be procuring one of those flashy drinks from the bar, and his second would be bedding a woman. He hadn't even seen a woman in person since before he died, except for Morghan, who absolutely did not count.

Winstin looked down at the bloody wreck of his robes and groaned, knocking all his priorities down a notch. First, he would have to find something new to wear. The rest would follow, and once he'd carved out a niche for himself in the community, his tasks would be familiar enough: to watch and wait.

Michael was certain blood must be leaking from his ears right along with his will to live. He opened one eye and glared past the smoldering embers of their campfire to where Dravyn rocked his nephew in a futile attempt to calm his screams. It had been two months since they set out from Vahyir, and while the chill of winter had been gone almost as long, the nightly screamfests continued. The only solace he took, was that more of the journey was behind them than in front.

He opened both eyes and propped himself up on his elbow before looking from the fire to where their horses grazed. Morghan was gone. Again. Probably not far this time, as she hadn't taken her mount.

"She went to get more wood for the fire." Dravyn's voice powered over the mind-numbing screams, the annoyance in his tone easier to discern than the actual words. And it wasn't directed at the baby. Michael wasn't sure why the boy hated him, but he made no attempt to hide his dislike.

"I didn't say anything," Michael answered defensively. But he'd been thinking it. Morghan traveled with them through the day without issue, but when their most vocal travel companion woke him every night, she was gone more often than not. He hoped she was enjoying herself while he was stuck watching her charges and wishing he was deaf. Somehow he doubted it, which was why he hadn't said anything to her about it. Yet. "Don't you have something to quiet him down?"

"Morghan does." Dravyn sighed. "But I'm not going through her bags to find the flask."

Michael rose to his feet and headed for Morghan's horse. He wasn't sure he would ever get used to the boy calling Morghan by her given name, but he imagined if she was going to make him stop, it would have happened already. How it would go over in Salus remained to be seen. Everyone knew her name, but until Dravyn, Michael was the only one who ever used it.

He reached her horse and stopped with his hand on one

of the saddlebags. It wasn't right to go through Morghan's things without permission, but he would lose his mind if the baby didn't shut up soon. Michael cursed and unbuckled the saddlebag. He flipped it open and immediately wished he hadn't. The scarlet cloak crumpled over the other odds and ends in the bag stole his breath away. He crushed the velvet folds against his palm to assure himself it was real. Alara's cloak. Morghan had come back from wherever she'd been with the signature wardrobe piece of their greatest enemy. His heart sank and soared at once. Did this mean Alara was dead? He didn't dare get his hopes up. After all, Falcroix's demands were increasing, the roads around the realm were more dangerous than ever, and there was nothing to suggest the legion was leaderless. But it meant one thing for certain: Morghan had been in Falcroix. Maybe she'd only snuck in and stolen it, or maybe she'd been there the entire time. Michael shuddered. She'd made a comment once about being rescued, but at the time he hadn't dared to ask what or where she had been rescued from. And she never offered the information.

"You're bound to find all kinds of trouble rifling through someone else's belongings." Morghan's voice cut into his thoughts. He turned in time to see her drop a small pile of wood on the ground by the fire, her eyes boring into him.

Especially mine.

The thought didn't so much push its way into his mind as pop there from his subconscious. He should have waited. It would have saved him her scorn, but more so, it would have kept him from the dark thoughts circling his conscience like vultures.

"The baby wouldn't stop crying," Michael stammered. "I was looking for the flask of tonic you've been using to quiet him."

A shadow of humor passed over Morghan's face, but it was gone as fast as it had come. In the six months since she'd returned, her body had healed spectacularly, but he wasn't sure the rest of her would ever recover. The dark humor that had always flickered behind her eyes and laced her words was all but gone. Every once in a while, Michael caught a glimpse of the woman who used to revel in dancing on his nerves, but she always retreated behind a veil of stoicism Michael had come to accept as permanent. Maybe returning to Salus would help. He hoped so.

Morghan walked to his side and shuffled through the bag, moving the cloak aside as if it was another random object. She brought out one of the metal flasks Michael had used months ago to seal the wounds on her back, but the blood had been replaced several times over by things far less gruesome. She unscrewed the top and threw back a swig.

"Feeling colicky?" Michael raised an eyebrow.

"Always." Morghan smirked, her breath hitting him like a wall of spices and heat.

"You're giving a baby rum?"

"I was fresh out of Benadryl." She tossed the flask to Dravyn, who went about rubbing some of the liquid around the inside of the baby's mouth.

Michael ignored her retort, assuming it was some sort of medicine from her time. When she closed the saddlebag, he laid his hand on top of hers to keep her from moving away. "You have Alara's cloak."

"I do." Her expression never changed, as if she had expected the words.

"You were in Falcroix."

"I was." Her fingers moved under his hand, but she wasn't pulling away, just digging them into the leather.

"Alara isn't dead," Michael said.

"Your powers of observation are astounding." Morghan winced and pulled her hand out from under his. "Sorry. My head hasn't been right for months, but no, Alara isn't dead. Whatever power you passed to her is stronger than the poison riding in my blood."

Her eyes were far away. She should have been sleeping instead of answering questions that could have waited for morning. Or forever. Honestly, he shouldn't have been asking after any of it. He didn't have the right to conjure painful memories for nothing more than to soothe his own aching heart. But he had to know. "How long were you there?"

"Long enough," she answered coolly before walking back toward the fire. The baby had finally stopped crying, but Dravyn watched them with the careful expression of someone who had seen one too many similar conversations go south in a hurry. After all, hyper-vigilance was the sure-fire sign of a rocky childhood.

Michael caught Morghan's shoulder and spun her around to face him. "How long?"

"I don't remember what day we were ambushed," Morghan bit out, striking Michael's forearm so hard his hand flew from her shoulder. Her face was all hard lines and sharp angles, betraying the fact she knew exactly how many days had passed. Maybe even how many minutes. Given her penchant for numbers, Michael didn't doubt the latter was true. "Ask Valerian. The day he lifted me from a ravenous horde just to challenge my immortality and throw me back to them is probably an Evenstar holiday."

Michael took a step back, and the concern burning in his chest cooled as icy fingers of anger snaked across his skin in its place.

"Valerian told me you abandoned the fight when you

saw it was hopeless." The words sounded wrong even as they passed his lips. "I believed him."

"It's not the worst lie you believed. It's not the one that damned over a thousand men and one very fucking hard-headed warrior queen to death."

Michael's anger slipped for a moment as the memory of Kayla came roaring to the forefront of his mind. He had buried her years ago, as had her kingdom—an empty ceremonial box in the cold ground. Still, the undeniable truth of her death from Morghan's lips brought a spear of pain, proving he hadn't quite shoveled the last bit of dirt on her grave after all. "Were you there when she died? Did she suffer?"

"It was a good death." Morghan's voice broke. "I'm sorry."

"Why did you kidnap her?" He'd wanted to ask her since their fight with the Vahyiran soldiers the night Falcroix attacked, but a few things had gotten in the way between then and now.

"Don't ask questions you don't want to know the answer to," Morghan warned. "Her death is on my hands, and I take full responsibility. How about you? You believed Valerian's lies, and I believed yours. Your dreams should be dripping with the blood of the dead as much if not more than mine are. I told you to go to Arden. Begged, even." Morghan's voice dropped an octave and her fists clenched at her sides. "You lied to me."

It had been a ridiculous request, or at least he'd thought so at the time. Why would Valerian lie? Why march into a battle he knew they would lose? Michael's gaze drifted past Morghan to the star-studded sky to the west. He barely acknowledged the anger as it swept through him this time, his skin chilling in the spring air, even as it hung with a warmth that whispered of summer. They were several days southeast of Falcroix, giving it the wide berth it undoubtedly deserved, which meant Arden was close. He could be there and back in a matter of hours. Maybe even before dawn.

"Don't." Morghan took a step closer and laid a hand on his arm. She jumped back and cursed as the static snap of electricity passed between them. "Damn it, Michael! Shock me again, and I'll have you burned to a fucking crisp."

Empty threat aside, he would have traded his powers for control of fire without a second thought. It would have made his current task that much easier. That much more mindless.

"This isn't the time, Michael. We can settle this later, when the betrayal isn't fresh and you've had time to think it through."

Michael kept his eyes on the sky. "You were taken prisoner over three years ago. I wouldn't call it fresh."

"You know what I mean. It is to you. This can wait. I'm not in Falcroix anymore, and I don't want you to do this to yourself on my account."

Michael stripped off his shirt, wondering why he even bothered wearing one anymore. His wings tore from his back, and his palm sweated against the hilt of his sword. "It's not just your account, Morghan." He spread his wings before turning tired eyes to her. "Hundreds of men will never return from where we sent them: their wives made widows, children orphaned. Because of us." His gaze shifted back to the sky. "Because of me. If I'm not back by dawn, keep moving southeast. I'll find you."

He took to the skies before giving her a chance to argue, and though a small part of him hoped it would be otherwise, the wind in his hair and against his skin did nothing to quell the storm raging within him. As Michael made his way toward Arden, the clouds flickered above him like hundreds of candles blazing to life and snuffing themselves out. The thoughts buzzing through his head deafened him to the thunder rolling along his path, and he landed without a sound when the verdant plains below him darkened to a sea of trees.

Michael walked through the dark in silence, intent on a small focus of light in the distance. As he moved through the forest, the light became brighter, the trees taller, until the sky burned with enchanted daylight, making it easy to forget the night looming a few steps behind him.

The border of Arden was marked by towering trees with silvery bark shining in stark contrast to the darkness of their lesser brethren. They were as ancient as the people who lived there, and not a single leaf was out of place.

Michael approached the gleaming giants, and two Evenstar clansmen with bows held across their chests dropped from low-lying branches. "Maritch," they greeted him, stepping forward and bowing deep.

Michael's sword was out and clean through their necks before they had a chance to finish the gesture. He stepped over the bodies and stained one of their silver tunics red as he wiped his blade and returned it to its sheath.

The dark clouds following Michael into Arden may not have been visible through the enchantment, but they were there all the same. He calmed his mind, letting the thought of those clouds and the power they held fill him like a vessel. He turned his left hand palm up, and when he snapped his fingers, a bolt of lightning cracked the illusion, feeding into his hand and plunging the forest into darkness for the briefest of moments. Michael rolled the white-hot light around his hand and between his fingers. He'd been practicing, and the more desperate he'd become over the past few years, the more he'd forced himself to do so. Both Morghan and his father had been right: he lacked control, but it was coming along. The light finished its run through his fingers before pooling in his palm once more. When the fingers of his right hand reached for the light, it stretched up eagerly to meet them. Michael split the ball of energy in two and forced it to the ground at the base of the trees to either side of him. The ground trembled before going still, and just as Michael began to doubt himself, the trees split asunder at the base, the light burning up through their core and devouring them from the inside.

Michael rolled his thumbs against the static-charged pads of his fingers before calling another bolt of lightning and sending it into two more trees as he made his way deeper into the Evenstar's territory. Fire crackled behind him in the smoldering ruin he left in his wake, and when more Evenstars abandoned their posts in the trees, they ran instead of facing him. Michael let them run. For now. When he was through here, there would be nowhere left to run. It might be years overdue, but the whole of Arden would burn.

Valerian startled awake in his study, his head coming up from the desk so fast it swam and almost took him to the floor as the room spun. He slouched in his chair and swatted at a piece of parchment stuck to his face. A decanter of wine sat within arm's reach, and he thought about draining it until a frantic line of knocks nearly split his head in two. Maybe three decanters of wine was a bit over his nightly limit. Then again, when this ritual of drunken, sleepless nights had begun after learning of Morghan's escape from Falcroix, he had only been able to tolerate one.

A shiver ran through him at the memory of standing before Alara's throne six months earlier. Varin had slouched in the throne beside her, and though his heart still beat, his face was slack, eyes unblinking, even when a fly landed on one of them and spent an obscene amount of time walking around it before taking flight.

As Alara relayed her displeasure at losing her most prized possession, Valerian's eyes never left his son, and his mind was elsewhere. Coming to grips with the loss of Vallos had been hard enough, but now his eldest was worse off than his dead brother. Valerian hadn't heard a word until Alara had forced him to look at her. She rambled on about how an unknown entity had swooped into the heart of her fortress and freed Salus's general. That had gotten his attention and snapped his thoughts away from his failing bloodline, if only for a moment.

The knocks on Valerian's door repeated, drawing him back to the present. The command to enter was on his lips, but the door flew open before the words left his mouth.

"Sire!" A wide-eyed guard burst through, chest heaving. "The Maritch is here, and he's furious."

Valerian struggled to keep his expression neutral. Michael not Morghan. This was the answer to every prayer he'd sent up to the Creator in recent years. He had sacrificed everything to keep the darkness of Falcroix out of Arden: his family, his morals, and the lives of so many men. Now he spent what little sleep he gleaned dreaming of a vengeful goddess coming in the night. She forced him to watch as she slit the throat of every last one of his people, saving him for last. Michael might be angry, but he was so much more level-headed. Perhaps he would listen to reason.

"Well, see him in." Valerian ran a hand over his face and frowned when dark ink stained his fingertips. He must have fallen asleep on a fresh letter, but he didn't even remember what he'd been writing.

The guard shook his head. "You need to leave. He's not in the building, but he's on his way. Everything is on fire. He's executing Evenstars as he goes and burning the forest to the ground."

Valerian's breath caught. So much for reason. His thoughts shifted to his two remaining children, neither of whom had come of age. "Where are Valera and Valek? Evacuate them immediately."

"Soldiers have already been sent to their quarters," the guard said. "But you must leave now."

Valerian grabbed his sword from where it rested against the wall behind him. "I am not leaving without my children."

"You will leave without at least one of them." Michael's voice froze Valerian mid-movement, his sword not yet secured to his belt.

Valerian turned his eyes to the doorway, and his sword clattered to the ground, forgotten. The guard who had insisted they leave was nowhere in sight, but Michael filled the doorway, his wings stretching out to either side beyond it. Valerian's youngest son and daughter stood in front of him, held by the collars of their nightclothes. Their cheeks were tearstained, and several strands of their fine blonde hair stood on end, waving in the air though no breeze ran through the room.

"Michael, please," Valerian begged. "They're only children."

"You pick the wrong time to be familiar, Valerian," Michael answered through bared teeth. He pulled Valek up by his collar until the boy choked and sputtered. "This one may look like a child, but he's lived longer than any human could ever hope. And her." He gestured to Valera with his head. In human years, she was just shy of eighty. "She would be well on her way to the grave if not already in one."

"Maritch," Valerian corrected himself, allowing a short sigh of relief to pass his lips when Valek's feet hit the floor and color returned to his face. "Show mercy. I beg you. The Legion came. They murdered my wife and took my eldest sons prisoner. If I hadn't worked with them, Arden would have fallen to ash, my people annihilated. Alara wanted immortal blood, and mine wasn't to her liking."

The light behind Michael's eyes dimmed, and his grip on the children loosened. Maybe the situation could be salvaged.

"I even did my best to save you from her," Valerian continued. "She was so set on capturing you, but I convinced her Windstarr would be easier to keep. I don't know what information she gave you after her escape, but everything I did the day of the ambush and for months leading up to it, was to protect you. To protect my people. I had no choice."

Michael's eyes blazed back to life and his grip redoubled.

"You have a choice now. Pick a child."

Valerian's eyes roamed from his daughter to his son and back up to Michael. "To live or die?"

"To keep the hope of your people alive," Michael said. "While the last of you languishes in whatever hell Alara has prepared for you."

Valerian steeled his expression and fought back tears as he nodded toward Valek.

Michael released Valera and shoved her into the room

before turning away and dragging Valek down the hall as the boy kicked and screamed for his father to save him.

Valerian stepped over his sobbing daughter and rushed after Michael. "Wait!" he called. Michael had already reached the far end of the hall, but he stopped and turned to face Valerian. Smoke crept from beneath the door frame, and Valerian could barely make out Michael's stony features through the haze. "You gave me a choice."

"And you chose. Keep your daughter. Your son is mine." Michael turned back to the door.

"No! Kill me instead," Valerian pleaded. "He had nothing to do with this."

Michael shook his head, his free hand flat against the door. "I've killed enough people for one night. You cast your lot years ago, when you came to me as a refugee from a broken kingdom. Now you will enjoy the truth behind your lie."

15

ALL THE COMFORTS OF HOME

"WHY ARE WE STOPPING? We're less than half a day's ride from Salus." Morghan attempted to hide her exasperation, but she'd been complete shit at controlling her emotions the past few weeks. Months, really, but ever since Michael had lost his mind and claimed Valerian's only living son as a spoil of war, her control had gone from bad to worse. "If this trip gets drawn out another night, I'm seriously going to lose my shit."

Valek jumped down from behind Michael and threw Morghan a backward glance as he disappeared through the trees.

"The boy is allowed to take a piss," Michael said. "Calm down."

"I am calm," Morghan snapped. "And isn't he over a hundred years old? He's not a boy anymore. He might look Dravyn's age, but he's not. You keep forgetting that."

"I'm not forgetting anything, and you're going to have to get used to him. He'll be living in Salus and eventually fighting with us. How are you going to train him, if you can't stand the sight of him?"

"That one's easy," she sneered. Train him? He had to be joking. If she had a sword drawn within ten feet of Valek, it would magically end up through his chest. "I'd rather slit my own wrists than train that shimmery little bastard. I don't care how many heart to hearts you have with him about atoning for the sins of his father. You burned his home to the ground and stole him away from the only family he had left. If I were him, I'd hate you and everything you stood for until the day I died."

"Thankfully, not everyone is like you." Michael flinched and held up an arm to deflect a partially eaten apple.

"Sorry," Dravyn offered, in one of the most unapologetic tones Morghan had ever heard. He adjusted the cloth sling holding the baby against his chest before taking the reins of his horse again in one hand. He pointed to the baby with the other. "Brennick moved, and my arm slipped. I meant to throw it into the trees."

Michael scowled at Dravyn and the baby who was, for once, asleep. He turned back to Morghan. "Valek is an orphan now. He should be in the Seiyaku with Dravyn."

"First of all, Dravyn is Seiyaku, not in it. Second, I'll be hand-picking orphans with the potential for loyalty. Kidnapped royal brats need not apply." Morghan eyed Valek as he emerged from the trees. He refused to meet her gaze as he made his way back to Michael's horse and climbed up behind him.

"Well then, I defer to you. We both know you're the expert on kidnapped royals," Michael said. He dug his heels into the sides of his horse, and it shot forward, nearly sending Valek to the ground.

Morghan closed her eyes and tightened her grip on the reins until leather bit into her palms. Kayla's beaten figure knelt in front of her, the dagger in her hand plunging through her heart over and over in a never-ending loop of death. Something touched Morghan's arm, and she gasped, her mind escaping to the present. Dravyn's horse was drawn up beside hers, and his hand rested on her forearm. Although she was thankful for the gesture, she needed to teach him not to touch her. Next time he could end up with his throat slit before she realized where she was or who she was killing.

"We don't have to stay with him. Sometimes family is better left behind." Dravyn leaned over until his head rested against her shoulder. "You taught me that."

"Sit up, and don't touch me." Morghan meant for it to be an order, but it came out as little more than a whisper. Still, Dravyn did as she asked, and when the chill of isolation spread through her, it took all her resolve to keep from reaching out to touch him or Brennick to be sure they weren't the dream. Instead, her hand went to the hilt of her sword, but it came up against her bare hip, as it had for the last half year. Maybe her real problem was that being away from her sword was driving her mad. She hadn't paid it much attention for most of her life, but until it was taken in Falcroix, it had always been close. Since coming to Michael's realm, it was a staple of her wardrobe, and she had a feeling her hand had gripped its hilt for a moment of clarity and peace more times than she realized. Her fingers dug into her thigh until she sucked in a sharp breath from the pain and let go. This was reality, and the truth was that even if she wanted to leave Michael, she couldn't. He may not have been aware of the countless debts she owed him, but even beyond those, the fact remained that now more than ever, Salus was Michael's. And Salus was the only home she had left. She urged her horse onward and motioned for Dravyn to follow.

The sun had just started its fall toward the horizon when Morghan and Dravyn reached the gaping mouth of a cave. For most it was a dead end, but not for Morghan. This cave would lead them into Salus as sure as any of its three gates.

Morghan hadn't made much of an effort to catch up to Michael, and he was apparently uninterested in holding back to finish the journey together. By now, he was likely relaxing in the tavern with a throng of patrons toasting his good health.

Morghan dismounted and unhooked her saddlebags from the horse, urging Dravyn to do the same. "Give them to me once you're done. You'll need both hands to protect Brennick if you fall. My quarters are farther away than any torch could hope to last, so we'll have to follow what light my eyes can provide."

"You live underground?" Dravyn finished pulling the bags from his horse and held them out to her.

Morghan shouldered both sets and started into the cave. "No, but I have an underground room connected to the one topside. The two of you will be staying there until I can figure out a more permanent arrangement. You should know where the room sits with regards to the cave mouth, in case you ever need to get out this way." Not to mention, she wanted some semblance of control over the people she met on her first day back.

While she was happy to be back, the idea of stepping through the tavern entrance turned her stomach. She hadn't abandoned Salus, but her time in Vahyir had taught her the truth was rarely as important as the presentation. Morghan was sure those in Salus thought her either dead, a coward, or a traitor.

In what she expected was an attempt to make her feel normal again, Michael insisted she resume command over the military, but it was the soldiers she dreaded seeing most. They knew her well enough to have scratched coward from the list of possibilities, and once she set foot back in Salus, only one option remained. If she had her way, she would train Dravyn and collect more Seiyaku to use as a special forces unit, leaving the bulk of the military to Michael.

"He would never agree to that," she muttered to herself as she continued to pick her way through the cave.

Dravyn stumbled and braced an arm against her back. Brennick whimpered. "What'd you say?"

"It's up ahead." Morghan ran her hand against the flat, smooth stone wall which had no place down here. She followed it until it turned and eventually met with the bumps and curves of the original cave wall. "You need something sharp to open it on this side."

She pressed the blade of a dagger at the junction between the natural and manmade walls and drew it downward until the blade slipped into a hidden recess. A series of clicks echoed around them as gears turned within, and a section of the wall that had been as smooth as glass moments before depressed and slid to the side, uncovering a looped metal handle.

"It's harder to open from outside, because you have to pull." Morghan grabbed the handle and braced herself against the cave wall as she leaned back from the door, her boots scraping against rock. She'd forgotten how heavy the door was. Dravyn would be lucky if he could pull it open once he was a grown man. "This isn't a good way to enter unless you're desperate, but pushing out from the other side shouldn't be a problem. Wait here."

Morghan dropped the bags to the floor, and her muscles relaxed as she walked through the familiar space. Or at least she thought it was familiar until her shin struck an object in the middle of the room. Her eyes flared enough to illuminate a large bed, which was a new addition since she'd left. She bent over it and rubbed her leg, catching the faint scent of matches and soot.

Redik.

He was the only person who had access to the room other than her. Was this some underhanded jab to suggest she needed more sleep? She could throw the same accusation his way. Had. On several occasions. She shrugged it off and crossed the room to the workbench that stretched the length of the wall closest to the stairs. Her hand fumbled through one of the top drawers until it landed on a cylinder of matches. She struck one and watched the blue flame burn until her fingers stung and she was forced to shake it out. When the second match blazed to life, she hurried to light the candles atop various dust-covered papers.

Her hand froze over the last candle as the light from the others illuminated the workbench, revealing another new addition—a wooden box the size of a small briefcase. A thin layer of dust had settled over it, but Salus's crest was still visible, meticulously burned into the lid. She winced as the flame met her fingers again, and the candle glowed when she dropped the remainder of the match on top of it.

Morghan hooked her foot around the front leg of a chair and dragged it forward. She sank into it and ran a tentative hand over the box, somehow afraid to open it. Which was ridiculous. Nothing the box contained could change anything. She grabbed the gold latch and flipped it open before pulling back the top.

"Can we come in yet?" Dravyn asked. "It's really dark out here."

Morghan tore her eyes away from the contents of the box. "Of course. Sorry, I wanted to get some light in here first."

Dravyn walked to her side and gestured to the box. "What are those?"

"Beautiful." Morghan smiled as she picked up one of the two shining black replicas of her handgun. Salus's crest was etched in silver along each of the slides, and three lines of bullets were embedded in the cushioned top half of the case. She popped the magazine out and barely held back a squeal of delight at the bullets stacked within it. The bullets in the magazine had hard grey tips, like the top line of bullets in the case, and on second look the base of the magazine was a similar color. She slammed it back into place and grabbed a bullet from the middle line. It had a soft gold tip, and she knew Redik well enough not to dare pressing on it too hard before asking what it did. The black hollow points in the lower line were easy enough to discern.

Morghan turned back to Dravyn. "They're weapons. Guns. They don't exist in this realm." She looked at the gun in her hand, and her happiness faded. "At least, they didn't until now."

She needed to talk to Redik and remind him how important it was not to make these for anyone else. It was never his job to make the gun, only the bullets, but desperate as she was for ammo, she'd given him full access to the weapon without a second thought.

Morghan's attention was drawn away from her thoughts

by the faint sound of scraping wood and a slamming door high above her.

"Stay here," she warned Dravyn.

She grabbed the second gun and headed for the stairs, taking them two at a time until she came to the heavy metal door separating the basement from the more conventional part of her quarters. She chambered the first round in both guns and disengaged the lock before kicking the door open. She turned first to one side of the room and then the other before dropping the guns to her sides. It was empty, but the desk and dresser were wiped clean where dust should have been, and the sheets were tossed about in a mess she hadn't left. She took a step toward the bed, and her grip tightened on the guns as the cloying aroma of vanilla and oranges hit her full force.

Impossible. Someone was fucking with her. Every last Hellion in Nikoli's realm had smelled like that, as did the sheets in the foster home of her youth.

Morghan stalked to the door and flung it open. The hall was largely empty, since most people were working. The only thing out of place was the crazy person flinging doors open and scowling at random people as they passed. She was about to duck back into her room and wait for whatever fool had decided to take up residence there, when she heard someone frantically calling her name. She tucked one gun into her belt and kept the other one out as she ran down the hall toward the voice.

When she rounded the corner of an adjoining hall, she nearly barreled into a toddler. Morghan jumped to the side and scooped the giggling boy up with her free hand. The girl chasing him stopped short, and it took Morghan a minute to recognize her. "Ralikaya?"

Bael's daughter nodded and took a hesitant step

forward, her eyes on the squirming ball of energy hanging from Morghan's arm.

"Here." Morghan deposited the boy in her arms. "I think you lost this. Were you the one yelling my name?"

Ralikaya held the boy against her chest. "It's his name, too. Well, part of it. Our parents had decided on Morgan, boy or girl, but when my father didn't return from battle, my mother added Bael."

Morghan raised an eyebrow.

"We only call him Morgan when he's misbehaving." Ralikaya blushed.

Morghan's day was getting better by the minute. Michael was pissed at her, an impossible entity had stolen her room, and now she had a namesake whose father was hacked apart and eaten by monsters on her watch. At least things couldn't get much worse.

"Is our father with you?" Ralikaya ventured.

"No." The flicker of hope in Ralikaya's eyes died, and Morghan reminded herself that things could always get worse. "I'm sorry."

Morghan took a few steps backward before turning and walking away as fast as she could without breaking into a run. Her feet carried her deeper into Salus's core, through the open-air markets and out the other side to the barracks. She wasn't sure when she made the decision to head to Redik's, but she found herself standing outside the smithy all the same.

Smoke billowed from several of the pipes jutting from the enormous circular building's roof. Despite the evidence of work being done within, a "Closed" sign hung from a nail at the entrance. It had never stopped her before.

Morghan tucked the second gun into the other side of her belt and rapped on the door. As a matter of safety,

Redik never locked it when the forges were lit, but after so long away, she thought it appropriate to knock. When a minute passed with no response, she gave up on being polite and opened the door, walking into the usual wall of stifling heat.

Two unattended forges burned brightly at the center of the room surrounded by anvils, a lathe, and various tools. Workbenches dotted the outer edge of the room, each one devoted to a different fragment of her friend's imagination.

At one of those, far removed from the fires, Redik's youngest son, Redden, hovered over a pair of boilers connected by a long, spiraling glass tube. One of his hands was on a stopcock and the other held a dish of multicolored powder directly beneath it.

Morghan slammed the door behind her to get his attention.

"Damnit, Dex!" Redden barked. "I told you to leave me alone. If this blows up in my face, I'm going to haunt the shit out of you."

"You'll have to take a number, Denny," Morghan said.

He froze in place before carefully moving the dish to the side and turning around. "Windstarr!" The smile he flashed could have been his father's. Thick copper frames wrapped around his face and several magnifying lenses, each one smaller than the last, projected over his right eye. He pressed a finger to the side of the frames and the series of miniature gears that lived there spun into action, the magnifiers swinging to the side and stacking along the arm until only the original lens of Redden's glasses remained.

Morghan couldn't hold back a smile. She owed Redik a week's worth of drinks for getting those damn specs to work. Drinks she'd promised to pay for instead of mooching them off his nephew.

Redden stood and walked toward her, the smile still plastered across his face. He stopped short, and his lips pulled into a tight line, as if considering a difficult equation. "Fuck it. Don't stab me, okay?" he said, throwing his arms around her. "Dad always said you'd come back. Wouldn't even let us sell to those bastards who talked shit about you."

Morghan tensed in his arms.

Redden gave her a hearty pat on the back before pulling away. "I see you found the guns. Looking a little sparse in the weapons department otherwise." He squinted at her waist. "Were those daggers made by children? The blades look like they'll snap if I stare at them too long. Follow me."

"The world is full of idiots making pointy sticks," Morghan droned as she fell in behind him.

"The least they could do is take some pride in their work," Redden scoffed. He pushed open the door separating the main forge from the room Redik often referred to as his dream factory.

Morghan imagined Da Vinci's workshop must have looked similar. Schematics papered the walls, marked up and drawn over in an array of colors, some of them singed at the edges. Several wastebaskets sat flush against the wall, overflowing with crumpled papers Redik rarely saw fit to part with despite the various degrees of failure to which they had led. The desk might as well have been a wall, as it held more of the same. It was constructed of one of the rarest metals in the realm, known for its strength and resistance to corrosion. The room contained no chairs, as Redik was morally opposed to them, likely due to his tendency to fall asleep the moment his ass touched a seat.

Redden walked past the desk to a series of chests lining the far wall. "I can grab enough daggers to fill out your belt from the main room, but I'm sure you'll want this, too." He flipped open one of the chests and brought out a hefty dagger with a black blade. The golden hilt was wrapped in oiled leather strips that shined in the lamplight. He held one hand against the base of the hilt and twisted it with the other. A blade sprang to either side, turning one into three. Redden pressed a button on the top of the hilt and handed the weapon to Morghan once the blades slid back into their original alignment.

"And these," Redden went on, moving to another chest and pulling out two long, thin swords by their sheaths. "Take both," he urged, pushing them into her chest. "When you need it, there's more where this came from." He gestured to several other chests around the room. "In his last few months, the only things he made were for you. I think he knew what was coming."

Morghan wrapped her hand around the sheaths before grabbing the hilt of one katana and pulling it free. The blade was beautifully acid etched and well-balanced. She expected nothing less from a man who had melted down "flawed" blades others could have only dreamed of crafting. Morghan sheathed the sword and leveled her gaze at Redden. "How did he die?"

He leaned against the wall and sighed. "In his sleep last autumn. I still half expect him to be here ready to bitch me out when I stroll in late every morning. When Mom came to tell Dex and me he wasn't breathing, we were certain his ghost would jump back into his body long enough to blow himself up with something." Redden chuckled, but the sheen of tears in his eyes wasn't lost on Morghan. Nor was the fact that as her life was beginning again, Redik's had ended. She should have made Azrael take her to Salus instead of Vahyir. Maybe she could have seen Redik one last time.

Morghan forced a smile. "Doesn't seem right for someone like him to leave without a bang."

"Dex and I begged for a funeral pyre, but our mother insisted we bury him. I think she wanted to keep some part of him, even if it was only to visit and eventually rest near when her own body gives out."

"Where is he buried?" Morghan attached one of the katanas where her longsword should have been and kept hold of the other.

"I can show you." He pushed off the wall and headed toward the forge.

Redex stood near the table where Redden had been working, and when his eyes met Morghan's, they held all the shock and none of the excitement of Redden's. He inclined his head the slightest bit. "Windstarr. Good of you to finally come back."

The cold welcome stole the last of the joy Morghan had left from Redden's warm one. Growing up, Dex had worshiped his father, and by default, her, but between her prolonged absence, the loss of his father, and the fact Bael and Merrick had been two of his closest friends, she wasn't surprised his reverence had soured. That didn't make the betrayed look in his eyes sting any less.

"Don't be an ass," Redden said before Morghan could come up with a response. He gave Dex a quick punch in the shoulder. "We're going to Dad's grave. You coming?"

"You're supposed to be working." Dex scowled.

"Work can wait. Anyone willing to pay our prices wouldn't even think to take their business elsewhere. She's been gone for years."

"Then she should have come back sooner. Or better yet, never left."

"I was held up." Above a monster's throne. Bleeding

and broken. Morghan turned her face to the ground and didn't bother defending herself further. She could tell him where she'd been, but it wouldn't turn back time, and it certainly wouldn't bring anyone back from the dead.

"Oh, I almost forgot!" Redden broke the tension and jogged to the wall where a vast array of weapons and armor hung. He grabbed five daggers of the same make and walked back to Morghan. "Take those shitty blades out of your belt and toss them. Use these."

"Those are bought and paid for," Dex grumbled.

"Yep," Redden replied, unconcerned. He held the daggers out to Morghan once her other blades had fallen to the floor. "Don't worry," he answered her skeptical look as he pushed the hilts into her hands. "I made all of these. I'll just work on my day off."

"You barely work on your days on," Dex said.

Redden ushered Morghan toward the door and held up a middle finger to his brother as they walked through it.

"I don't want to cause problems between you two," Morghan said as they headed down one of the paths leading toward the training fields. The clang of metal quieted as they passed, and Morghan put her head down in an attempt to ignore the stares.

"He'll get over it. Dad's death is still weighing on him, and he's been spending too much time with our mother. She really clung to the whole 'Windstarr betrayed us' craze when you didn't come home. I think it made her feel vindicated for all those years of disliking you so much."

"Most people dislike me," Morghan admitted. "Your mother flat out hates me."

"Well, it can't help that she's convinced you were fucking her husband."

"You can't force the truth on someone who's chosen to martyr themselves on the lie," Morghan said.

"I don't remember you being so philosophical."

"I had a lot of time to think." Morghan brought her eyes up from the ground, hoping to see the gates out of Salus. Instead, a line of soldiers blocked the path several feet in front of them. She put a hand against Redden's chest to stop him as she came to a halt. The line was made up infantrymen and officers alike, and the soldiers from the training fields collected along the sides of the path and filled in behind them.

Morghan's heart raced. She was trapped by her own men. Hopefully, they wouldn't be stupid enough to kill their best blacksmith. She pulled the katana she held in her hand, the tip of the blade hovering above the ground.

Grell, one of her finest strategic officers, stepped forward from the line in front of them. Under any other circumstances, she would have been glad to see him alive. He held up both hands, and his voice boomed. "Lay down your weapons."

Morghan's grip on the sword tightened, and she was about to reach for a gun when the sound of clanking metal rang in her ears. She glanced at the soldiers, now empty-handed, their swords discarded in front of them.

Grell drew his longsword and the short sword he kept at his back before tossing both to the side. He walked toward Morghan, his eyes shifting between her face and the katana she held at the ready. He stopped well in front of her and bowed at the waist. "It's good to see you, General."

"Is it?" Morghan wondered.

Grell stood straight and gave a terse nod. "The Maritch met with me a few weeks ago. It's hard to imagine you as a prisoner of war, but he has no cause to lie about such a thing."

So, this was where Michael had disappeared to after torching Arden. She'd almost killed him for leaving her alone with Valek. It had forced her to stay awake more than usual for fear he would kill Dravyn and Brennick while she slept. "Three thousand to one is shitty odds for anybody."

Grell's eyes strayed to her blade and back up to her face. "Since it was better than the alternatives, I wanted to believe it then, and I'm certain of it now. Can we expect you to return to your former position with us?"

Morghan thought for a moment before sheathing her sword. "Yes, but I need a few days to myself first."

Grell's grin stretched across his face.

"Of course, but don't take too long. Between you and me, the new recruits are shit," he said loud enough for the surrounding men to hear him. "And we don't want them getting jealous of how the rest of us could take them down in our sleep."

Laughter and taunts filtered through the crowd as the soldiers picked up their weapons and dispersed to the training fields.

Grell stepped closer and held out his hand to Morghan.

She took it, and he swallowed her hand in both of his. "Welcome home."

Morghan didn't remember the graveyard being so expansive. Then again, she'd only visited it a handful of times, all of which were before the city lost hundreds of soldiers in a span of hours. She'd bet most of these graves were empty, but not the one she was visiting. She sat in the grass, leaning against the side of Redik's grave and gazing over dozens of others. The tears had long since dried on her cheeks, and she didn't have any left to offer.

Grass crunched underfoot as someone approached the grave from behind her. Redden should be back at the forge already, but Morghan couldn't bring herself to care who it might be. It wasn't like she would die if they shoved a blade through her heart. If they could find it.

"Redex said you would be here." Redik's wife didn't need a blade. She was one.

Morghan's head thumped against the headstone before she rose to her feet and turned to face the woman. "It's been a while." Morghan offered a sad smile. "I'm sorry—"

"No." The woman cut her off. "The less I hear from you, the better." She held out an envelope so thick it stretched the seal holding it closed. Morghan could make out the –ghan across the front of it, the rest of her name hidden beneath the woman's fingers. Redik hadn't once called her by her first name, and she didn't doubt he'd used it on the envelope as an underhanded jab at the woman holding it.

Morghan took it, and Redik's wife withdrew her hand as if Morghan's touch might burn her. There was no point saying thank you.

"I never opened it," she went on, as Morghan broke the seal and pulled out a sheaf of papers. "I knew I would hate him otherwise, and I didn't want that."

Morghan shuffled through the pages, which were mostly schematics for the guns and each type of bullet. She smiled when she came to the gold-tipped ones which were, of course, explosive. Beyond the schematics, there was a single sheet with a few words scrawled across it.

I made the guns alone, but the boys can make bullets.

Take what you need from them, and tell my idiot wife I love her.

Morghan fanned out the schematics in front of Redik's wife, turning them over and making sure she could see them for what they were. She pocketed them and handed the last piece of paper to his wife before walking past her without a word. Morghan hadn't even made it to the next line of headstones before the woman's sobs cracked the silence.

Morghan looked up as she left the graveyard, but she stopped short, sure her eyes were in danger of jumping from their sockets.

"I should buy that woman a gift," Winstin said. He was dressed from head to toe in familiar clothes. Her clothes. "I thought you would never leave."

"Winstin?"

"I don't like graveyards, mostly because I should be in one," he went on. He looked down at himself and smiled as he tapped the toe of one boot against the heel of the other. "Good thing we're close to the same size. Everything's a little tight, but do you realize there isn't a single coin in your entire room? I turned that place upside down."

"How?" She couldn't get anything more coherent past her lips as she turned in a quick circle, making sure no one was taking advantage of her shock.

"It's just me, I promise. Nikoli lost his mind, and I reached out to your people for help."

"My people?"

"Lucifer and Azrael. Lucifer fixed me, and Azrael brought me here to wait for you. Congratulations, you've won your very own Hellion."

Morghan's spirits lifted. Finally, something to salvage this complete dumpster fire of a day. "Azrael is here?"

Winstin shook his head. "Months ago, for the span of a minute."

Her shoulders slumped, and she walked past him, heading toward the military quarter gate. "I don't understand why you're here. Nikoli is bound to come looking for you."

"Maybe, but he didn't seem to care overly much about me when he was ripping my eye from the socket and breaking half the bones in my body. Besides, he's already here."

Morghan stopped, and Winstin almost ran into her. "What did you say?"

"Well, not *here* here, but in the realm. Last I heard, he'd taken over Falcroix."

If anyone tried to shove another emotion down Morghan's throat, her body would explode. "Son of a—fuck! Seriously?"

"Yes, but from what I've gathered watching your travels, Falcroix is a good distance from Salus. Right?"

"The man can flash across dimensions in an instant!" she screamed. "I doubt a month's ride is much of a challenge."

Winstin shrugged. "In the grand scheme of things, it doesn't matter whether he's in Falcroix or a dimension away. You said it yourself; he's an instant from our throats no matter where he is."

Morghan continued the trek back to her room without another word. Winstin's reasoning was equal parts logical and terrifying, but she preferred to think about it from Nikoli's perspective—that as long as he didn't have a particular reason to kill her or the people she loved, he'd rather watch the game play out. After all, he had a lot of time invested in Luke and Azrael, and they were, for better or worse, invested in her.

She wished she didn't understand Nikoli as well as she did, but much of her last years in Luke's realm were spent going over his motives with Azrael. By the time Nikoli had dumped her in this hellhole of a realm, she knew more about his life than she cared to. And although it might make him easier to predict, it brought along empathy she'd rather not have.

When she reached her room, she directed Winstin inside before entering and closing the door behind her. She crossed to the far end of the room where Winstin's scent was less all-encompassing. "Nikoli being here makes no sense. The man spends half of eternity barely leaving his fucking room, and now he's a realm away commanding an army? What the hell happened?"

Winstin sat on the bed and pulled off her boots. He looked down at his feet and wiggled his toes. "I have to stop wearing these. If my feet end up ruined, I'm done."

"Winstin!"

He looked up and shrugged. "I don't know."

Morghan pressed her back against the wall and pointed an accusing finger at him. "You're lying."

He tried again. "I'm not sure, but it might have something to do with Azrael and Lucifer."

"What about them?" A thousand possibilities flashed through her mind, each more horrible than the last. She ran a hand over her face and gave him a pleading look. "Just tell me, Winstin. I'm beginning to think this day is never going to end. As long as they're not dead, I promise I won't go crazy enough to hurt you."

"They're not dead, but they are sleeping together."

Morghan let out a sigh of relief. That made a lot more

sense, and while Nikoli's reaction was dramatic, it could have been so much worse. "It's about damn time. At least I can stop worrying about them strangling each other. Although..."

"Morghan!" Winstin gasped when she started chuckling. "You're okay with that?"

"What, them strangling each other? Honestly, that's erring on the tame side, but whatever makes them happy." She slid down the wall and closed her eyes.

"What are you doing?"

She opened one eye, and when he started toward her, she held out a hand, signaling him to stop. "Stay over there. Your stupid Hellion scent already ruined my bed on the one night I could probably stand to sleep in it."

"You're going to sleep? You must be joking. Your reaction to Lucifer and Azrael fucking each other while Nikoli sits on Alara's throne plotting your demise is to go to sleep?"

Well when he put it like that, it drained much of the excitement out of Luke and Azrael finally getting their shit together. "I have strange sleep criteria. Now leave me alone. If I block out all the right things, I might get a good dream out of this."

"You're insane."

"Not at the moment, but wait it out. My sanity comes and goes. With all the time you spent in service to Nikoli, it should make you feel right at home."

"You are not like Nikoli," Winstin said.

"Sure I am. Our past lives have loads in common: murdered siblings, tortured childhood, Stockholm Syndrome, not to mention being abandoned or taken advantage of by the people we dared to care about after our lives went to shit. To be fair, no one maliciously hacked my wings off while pretending to be my friend. I'm kind of glad he got his back though, because that was too fuckin' sad."

Winstin looked like he was about to pull his hair out, but he apparently had no more words. Or maybe he had too many, and they were all so damning, he knew better than to speak them aloud.

"Listen, you need to lighten up or you'll drive yourself crazy," Morghan said. She hung her arms over her knees, and the lines on her forehead deepened. "And don't waste your time trying to figure out the emotional dynamic between Luke, Azrael, and me. I'm on the inside and still confused half the time. As far as Nikoli is concerned, you're right; he's plotting. Otherwise, he would have flat out killed one or more of us when they first slept together. So, let's sit back and enjoy the fact that the man is as old as time, and unless he's provoked again, his plans are more likely to come to fruition in decades rather than days. For now, I'm going to sleep. I'll figure out this mess another day, preferably when I don't feel like I've been run over by a bus several times in the span of a few hours."

"Fine." Winstin sat on the edge of the bed and scowled. "What should I do while you sleep?"

"Stare at the wall? I don't care. Whatever you've been doing." Morghan had no sooner closed her eyes than the muted sound of a baby crying met her ears. Her eyes popped open again. "Shit. The boys."

She really needed to get Dravyn set up to be self-sufficient, otherwise her inattention was going to cause them both to starve or worse. She rose to her feet and shuffled toward the basement door, dialing in the combination and turning the large metal wheel to unlock it. So much for sleep.

"The ones you picked up in Vahyir?" Winstin was by

her side before she had a chance to open the door. "I can take care of them. What do they need?"

"For now? Food, mostly, and to be let out of the dark for a while. You can show Dravyn around Salus, and if you find Michael, he can help you out with the food." She looked down at his feet. "And boots that fit. I'd keep the details to a minimum. Tell him it's a favor for me." She took her hand off the door but faltered as she turned back to the room. "You're sure?"

"We'll be fine." He pushed her away from the door. "Go catch your dream."

16

OLD HABITS DIE HARD

MORGHAN OPENED her eyes to the clear blue sky when the thwack of wood against flesh met her ears. A body hit the ground a second later. Some new recruits took longer to catch on than others.

"Why am I fighting with wooden sticks again?" the boy sparring with Dravyn grumbled.

Morghan sat up as the boy clambered to his hands and knees, blood pooling in the corner of his mouth.

Wrong.

A hefty wooden short sword cracked across his back, and his face hit the dirt again.

"Because she told you to," Dravyn barked as he stepped back. He rolled the practice swords over the backs of his hands before catching the hilts and regaining his battle stance. "Are you going to get up the right way, or are you done?"

Dravyn was sixteen by now. His voice had changed years ago, but the depth of it, especially when tinged with anger, still caught her off guard at times.

The boy across from him, four weeks in and stubborn as

a damn ox, started getting up the same way. Dravyn shot forward.

"He's done," Morghan said, and Dravyn's sword halted a fraction of an inch above the boy's back. He withdrew and faced her with a disappointed scowl. Dravyn knew his opponent would never step foot inside the barracks back home, and he loved nothing more than punishing those who wasted their time. It was possible the last five years had made him a little too much like her.

The group of boys sitting on the other side of the makeshift practice circle voiced their own disappointment with a short-lived stint of grumbles and frowns. Some of them no doubt wanted to see the boy beat unconscious, others worried they were next, but they all fell silent when Morghan looked their way. There were ten of them in all, including Dravyn. The others were recruits from the various cities and villages they'd visited over the past several months, all orphans between age ten and fifteen, with Dravyn's current opponent being the eldest. She'd brought four Seiyaku along for the trip, but the other three were gathering firewood and water with Winstin. They were only a day or two north of Sheltinata, which would be their last stop before heading back to Salus.

Morghan rose to her feet and walked over to Dravyn, leaning close and whispering in his ear. "Be glad I was the only one over there to see the look on your face, otherwise you'd be the next one bleeding on the ground. If you're going to challenge me, pick a battle worth fighting." His shoulders sank, and he mumbled an apology.

By the time she made it to Dravyn's opponent, he was standing, his practice swords back in his hands as he shifted from one foot to the other along the inside edge of the circle. "I'm good. I can go again."

"Sit down." Morghan pointed to the rest of the boys.

"But—"

"Sit down before I sit you down." She stripped the swords from his hands and pushed him out of the circle.

"If you gave me a real sword, I could fight just fine!" he shot back.

Sure he could.

Morghan drew one of the katanas Redik had made for her and dropped it at his feet. "Pick it up. You won't find a better blade. Step back in the circle when you're ready."

She was easily as tired of the little shit's temper as Dravyn, but until the boys openly defied her, she preferred to leave them be. After all, every soul in their company brought demons along with them. It wasn't fair to expect everyone to rise above them when her own dragged her down more often than not.

She walked back to Dravyn and held out her hand for the practice swords, which he turned over without a word.

"Break him," she rasped under her breath as she headed back to her spot outside the circle.

The boy wasn't in the circle by the time she sat down. "You didn't give him a blade."

"He doesn't need one." Morghan leaned back on her elbows and crossed her legs in front of her. "You shouldn't either."

"You have about ten!" he protested.

"I never said they weren't a nice addition, but I don't need them either. Would you prefer I take Dravyn's place and prove that to you?" A not insignificant part of her hoped he would say yes. She hadn't snapped a neck in years, and her moods had become progressively more volatile since her stint in Falcroix.

The boy paled and shook his head. At least he wasn't a complete dumbass.

She gestured to the circle with her hand. "We await your prowess."

Dravyn glanced over his shoulder before peeling off his shirt and tossing it to the side.

He was lean and muscular, his once fair skin long since vanished beneath the permanent tan that came with training outdoors in a part of the world which rarely fell below freezing. Scars peppered his arms and torso. A few of the smaller ones Morghan had put there herself, but the majority were jagged and thick, hailing from the life she'd carved him out of years ago. The silver brand on his right shoulder marked him as hers; it was a variation of Salus's crest, with vines that wound around the wings and stretched the length of the waterfall. They joined to form a star at the whirlpool's center before multiplying and branching out to the edges of the spiral.

The last five years had forged Dravyn's body into a finely-tuned weapon, and right now he was showing it off. But not for the boys and certainly not for her. Morghan looked past Dravyn, and her eyes fell on the person he was trying to impress.

Ralikaya walked beside Brennick and Bael. She had an axe slung over one shoulder and a cluster of wood under the other arm. Each of the boys carried kindling sticks against their chests, and Winstin walked not far behind, several large, gut-lined water bladders looped over either shoulder.

The elder Bael's wife had succumbed to an illness a few years after Morghan returned to Salus, and Morghan figured taking in his children might repay a small amount of the insurmountable debt she owed the family.

It hadn't taken long for her to remember why she had planned to recruit only male Seiyaku. The addition of Ralikaya had what few Seiyaku came before her falling over themselves to earn her favor. After a number of months, Morghan had tired of the bickering and taken Ralikaya aside, demanding she send them all a clear message of rejection. Ralikaya had followed through without complaint, but while Morghan had forbidden official romantic relationships, she'd ignored the furtive glances between Ralikaya and Dravyn for too long. By the time she realized how serious it was, the point had been reached where forcing them apart threatened to break more than leaving them to their own devices.

Which is why she'd decided to give the entire group a lecture on the female reproductive cycle and how to predict which days were less likely to lead to pregnancy. It was the only time she'd noticed any of them taking notes, and for those who were doing so, she made sure they wrote down the part about how she wasn't feeding or clothing any of their bastard children.

She only hoped Dravyn and Ralikaya wouldn't develop a reason to call her bluff.

"Morghan?" The boy who should have been fighting Dravyn stood beside her, head down, the sword held out to her hilt first. "I don't want to go back in the ring."

Morghan took the blade and returned it to its sheath. "That's the best decision you've made in weeks, and when we get to Sheltinata, you'll be staying there."

Winstin stood in front of the town crier's building, and his eyes roamed the various pamphlets papering the wall. Event announcements dotted here and there, but the majority were posts for goods, services, and odd jobs. He was fairly certain one of the help wanted ads was a thinly veiled call for an assassination, and yet another stated someone was willing to pay more money than he'd ever laid eyes on for a woman between the ages of fifteen and thirty-five. He ripped the last flyer off the wall and read over it again. Did it mean for a night? A week? There were no specifics, and for three hundred gold, he'd be willing to dress up and pretend for the rest of the advertiser's short, mortal life. With as busy as Morghan kept herself between the Seiyaku and Michael's new military overhaul, she probably wouldn't even realize he was gone.

He pocketed the flier and walked down the street, heading for the poorer sections of town. His goal had been to score a quick job, but the need to show Morghan the flier tugged at him more than the dwindling number of coins jangling in his pocket.

Sheltinata was all kinds of backward, with its gaudy gemmed pyramids spread throughout the north end of the city while the south existed in such abject poverty that the tropical climate was the only thing keeping the people from dying of exposure. Instead, disease ran rampant, leading to a strict caste system that preserved the power of the rich while trapping the poor in the slums. If any place in the realm allowed for the outright buying and selling of people, Winstin didn't doubt this would be it. Still, he couldn't see Michael or Morghan condoning the practice, and in a long-standing kingdom numbering in the tens of thousands, such a thing would be hard to disguise.

The smooth, shining stones below Winstin's feet gave way to jagged cobbles and eventually a packed brown slush he imagined was mostly dirt. The stench suggested otherwise.

There were several reasons Morghan took her lot from the realm's orphans, but it would be nice if once in a while they could pick them from an actual orphanage instead of the streets. Then maybe he wouldn't feel the constant need to douse the new recruits in lye, the only decent cleansing agent this realm had to offer. It was already hard enough to keep his body clean without scrubbing off skin that wouldn't heal.

Two royal guards burst from the hovel to his left, and wails of protest echoed through the door they slammed behind them. Their breastplates gleamed gold with an inlaid emerald eye hovering above a chiseled pyramid, and the sight was alien in a world of grays and browns. Between them was a flailing woman who fit her surroundings infinitely better. A dirty cloth was cinched between her teeth, and the coarse burlap dress she wore rode ever higher against her thighs as she struggled.

Winstin stepped to the side to let them pass. He turned and watched them fight to drag her down the street until one drew his sword and smashed the hilt of it against the side of her head. The woman went limp, and the guards adjusted their grips before moving along at a faster pace.

Winstin ran his hand over the fabric covering his left forearm and felt the contour of the dagger secured there. He was a walking corpse in a foreign land, and this was none of his business. Men and women disappeared all the time, even in Salus, although there it was by Morghan's command more often than not. Thinking of her made him remember where he should be going. So, why was he trailing the guards, moving in the wrong direction? He glanced around the streets filled with people going about their daily business and realized there was no way to dispatch the guards without making a scene.

If he made it a good one, maybe Morghan would be impressed enough to let the indiscretion slide.

Winstin slipped the dagger from its sheath and fell into the guard in front of him, sneaking the blade around his neck and slitting the man's throat as they hit the ground. He apologized profusely to the second guard, making sure to put most of his weight on the fallen guard's head to keep him from making noise while bleeding out. The mud they'd fallen into was dark enough that the blood spreading through it was almost invisible.

Almost.

The second guard stepped over the discarded woman and pulled his sword. Winstin rolled away from the blade as it sliced through the air. It narrowly missed his chest, but scored a deep line across his right shoulder. He stood and dodged another thrust, grabbing the guard's sword hand by the wrist and snapping it with ease. A rush of excitement bubbled through him, and if he didn't know better, he would have sworn his heart was beating again. The sword fell into the muck, and Winstin lifted the guard from the ground, flinging him into a side alley. He glanced around the main street, but those who hadn't fled were uninterested in helping the remaining guard.

"Touch her and you're next," he bellowed to the onlookers, pointing to the unconscious woman before disappearing into the alley.

The guard was halfway to his feet by the time Winstin reached him.

"Let me help you." He dragged him up by the arm and rammed the dagger into his gut, angling it upwards beneath his armor and using it to lift him higher. When the guard's screams exploded through the air, Winstin forced a hand over his mouth, shushing him as he followed the dying man's body to the ground.

"Don't ruin it." Winstin pulled the dagger free and caressed the broadside of the blade down the man's cheek, leaving a thick stroke of red in its wake. "This is the best part."

He ripped the two halves of the plate armor apart like tissue paper and was deciding which rib to peel back first when Morghan's voice interrupted.

"What the actual fuck!" she called from the mouth of the alley. "I thought I was pretty damn clear about this type of behavior."

Winstin groaned and rose to his feet. He turned to face her as she stalked into the alley, and her eyes shifted between him and the guard. "If you remember, I asked for those boundaries," he said.

"After almost carving up a couple hookers in the heat of the moment. Yeah, I remember." She knelt beside the guard and let a line of curses fly. A dagger was in and out of the man's chest faster than he could blink, and the excitement bled from Winstin's veins as the guard's eyes went blank.

Morghan stood and forced Winstin's back against the alley wall, one hand splayed across his chest and the other waving her dagger dangerously close to his face. "You cannot go around committing flagrant murder in a kingdom that is not ours. I have no authority here, and we're traveling with a group of new recruits who are untrained and vulnerable."

"I'm sorry, but they were hauling a girl away against her will, and I felt compelled to help her."

"From where I'm standing, your compulsion looks a lot different. And I don't care if they were carting twenty women away. Who are you to judge? How do you know she's innocent?"

Winstin reached into his pocket and held out the crumpled paper he'd snatched earlier. "I found this on the city message board."

Morghan replaced the dagger in her belt and took it, her brow furrowing as she read. "Why do I care about this? So, someone is looking to pay for a wild night? You should be familiar enough with the concept."

He stabbed a finger at the price. The woman had zero concept of money. "No one would pay three hundred gold for a night with an entire city full of women, let alone one. I think it's a call to buy women flat out, as in slavery, and by the looks of the criteria, sex trafficking. I was coming to show it to you, and when I saw the guards dragging a young woman away kicking and screaming, I worried they were somehow connected." He glanced down at the guard's body. "I may have gotten carried away."

"Ya think?" Morghan dropped the paper and gestured to his injured shoulder. "And what are we going to do about that? I don't have the power to heal you, and you sure as shit aren't healing yourself."

He looked at the bloodless slash across the front of his shoulder. "The arm works fine. It must not be as deep as it looks. Can't you just sew it up and swap the stitches whenever they get frayed?"

"What I should do, is sew your hands into your fucking pockets," she said. "But first, we need to get out of here. Fast. I found two new recruits, and now with this mess, we're going to have to find somewhere else to dump the flunky. He's a pain in the ass, but it's unfair to leave him somewhere he'll be hanged for murders he didn't commit."

Winstin rolled his eyes. "I said I was sorry."

The sound of metal ringing free from a wealth of sheaths tore his eyes away from her disapproving frown. Several guards stood at the open end of the alley, their swords at the ready. All four Seiyaku had their swords drawn in opposition, with Dravyn and Ralikaya between and slightly in front of the younger boys. The recruits huddled behind them with the woman Winstin had attempted to save.

"Oh, for fuck's sake." Morghan ran toward them. "Stop!"

The Seiyaku lowered their blades, and the guards turned their heads toward Morghan, most of their faces blanching when they recognized her. Winstin shoved his hands into his pockets and trudged toward the fiasco he had created. There was no point in hurrying, as any human who recognized Morghan would sooner run than fight her. He sighed. At least somebody around here had some sense today.

Morghan stood at the edge of a sprawling garden terrace atop the highest pyramid in Sheltinata. The view of the rest of the city and the fields beyond was breathtaking, but the height threw her off-balance. She was sure it had that effect on most people, which was no doubt why the royals wouldn't deign to meet with dignitaries any place else.

"General?"

Morghan turned toward the king's voice, her ragtag group splitting to either side so she could watch him climb the final steps onto the terrace.

"King Xale." Morghan inclined her head. "It's been a while."

The wealth of creases surrounding his eyes gathered together, and his bronze-tinted lips pulled up at the edges. "Nearly three years, but you've been expected. Although, I must say, it was under wholly different circumstances."

Morghan shot angry eyes at Winstin, who was conveniently admiring the view. She hated politics, and now she was stuck explaining to a king why her idiot minion saw fit to murder two royal guards. On a busy street. In broad daylight. "My apologies. There was a misunderstanding."

"What, exactly, was difficult to understand—the flash of gold in a squalid street or my royal crest on their armor?" Xale took a seat on the ground among satin pillows the color of blood, his legs crossed beneath him. A short glass table stretched in front of him, and a servant girl set a golden tray laden with fruit and cheese atop it. Xale toyed with her platinum blonde curls as she worked, and his olive skin took on an even deeper hue as he caressed her pale arm.

Morghan wondered what twist of fate had led a teenager from Vahyir into the service of a crown on the other side of the world. "I think he was confused by the screaming woman being dragged through the streets. My attendant is unaccustomed to such brutality."

"His skill with a blade would suggest otherwise." Xale turned his attention back to Morghan and gestured to the turquoise pillows on the opposite side of the table. "Please, sit."

Morghan stared at the pillows as if they were made of snakes, and who knew, maybe he'd hidden a few vipers in there just to be safe. After all, Sheltinata was known for its poisons as much as its jewel-laden streets. She did not want to sit, but if traveling the realm with Michael had taught her anything, it was to accept a common courtesy from royalty when it was offered. And not to insinuate they were trying to kill you in the process.

Morghan walked to the appointed spot. She nudged the pillows aside with her foot before tucking her legs beneath her and sitting on her heels.

"Let's move to more pleasant topics for now, shall we?" Xale suggested.

"What did she do?" Morghan meant to ask what he wanted to discuss, but these days her words rarely matched her thoughts. Or maybe they matched them too closely. The girl from Vahyir was tugging at the back of her mind. She hadn't even shied away—so young and already trained. "The one being dragged from her home."

Xale's smile faded. "Not a thing, but Falcroix requires weekly tributes now. It was her time." His eyes moved to where the young woman huddled in between the group of boys. "It is her time."

He had to be lying. "Most rulers send aged tributes. It's not prudent to send your young to slaughter."

"My apologies for yet another confusion. I forget some of us have the luxury of ignoring Falcroix's demands. They no longer accept the elderly, nor males. Alara has become more particular of late."

Alara was about as particular as a half-starved man at a banquet, but Nikoli had no trouble demanding very specific things. And he was used to getting what he wanted.

Morghan stared down at her knees. The problem was, the last thing Nikoli would want was a kingdom full of women. Trusting females hadn't worked out well for Nikoli in his youth, and he'd come to despise women so much over the years he'd even preferred Azrael wipe his memory of breeding with one.

Morghan's jaw went slack. Breeders. It was the only

way the version of Nikoli she knew had ever viewed women, the only reason Morghan, in her original incarnation as Lilith, had even been created. She doubted moving realms had caused a sudden change of heart. But what was he breeding? Humans with orcs? That made little sense.

"Shit. Angels," she rasped under her breath.

"Excuse me?" Xale leaned closer to the table.

Morghan cut her eyes to Winstin, and the look on his face said he'd come to a similar conclusion. Nikoli was breeding an army of Michaels. Well, not exactly, as she doubted, or rather hoped, he wasn't participating beyond his usual position of handing out orders. The spawn of the lesser angels wouldn't hold a candle to the power Michael had inherited, but increased strength, speed, and a superficial form of immortality were nothing to ignore.

From what Azrael had told her, he and Lucifer had taken millennia, and the other angels centuries to mold and breathe life into, with each costing Nikoli a piece of himself and his power he could never get back. This way would take less time, and he could have an army of lesser immortals in a matter of decades while retaining his power base.

And would these new soldiers have wings? If Michael was any indication, not unless Nikoli altered them, which meant they could blend seamlessly into society outside Falcroix. Morghan would have taken time to marvel at the genius of it all if she wasn't so busy having a fucking panic attack.

"General!" Xale was losing patience with her, but he had quite recently taken a tumble down her give-a-fuckometer.

Morghan stood. "I apologize, but we need to be going. Salus will pay for your guards. Calculate the loss and send a courier with the price. You have my word the Maritch will see it done."

Xale's dark eyes were not friendly. "What of our appointments to the Light? We've been honing our finest warriors for the past three years, and yet your first visit since the proposed alliance is to steal street urchins, murder royal guards, and then disappear after insulting me in my own home."

That sounded a lot worse when he said it than it had in her head, not to mention just referring to Michael's military pet project was enough to make her cringe. Apparently, the only advice he'd ever taken from her was her half-joke about tying his god-like status to the military in order to give alliances more widespread appeal.

Thus, The Light was born, which was his rebranding of Salus's military and the offshoots he planned to have in every allied city. Each city was charged with putting up its best soldiers, and Morghan's job was to hand-pick a few to train in Salus before releasing them back home as added protection and a symbol of Michael's favor. If she was honest with herself, it was a fantastic idea with a shitty name, and Morghan hated few things more than the loss of a creative naming opportunity.

"How many soldiers did you plan to offer?" Morghan asked.

Xale put his hands on his knees, bettered his posture, and raised his chin. "I handpicked ten for you to choose from."

"Send all of them." She hated the idea of favoring cities, especially this one, but in light of recent events, more than money was in order to pay the debt. "You will have three times as many members as any other city."

"And they will return with a piece of the Maritch's power?"

Sure, why not. "They will return as promised, an invaluable asset to your city, spiritually as well as in battle." Morghan had to get out of this place before she got too used to talking directly out of her ass. "Under two conditions."

"Name them." Xale's eyes shone hungry for the power she had promised Michael would grant him. Well, insinuated.

Morghan pointed to the woman Winstin had saved. After going through all this for his little screw up, they sure as hell weren't letting anyone cart her off to Nikoli. "She leaves with us."

Xale waved a hand in dismissal. "Done. And the second?"

"From now on you will sterilize each tribute before sending them to Falcroix." Morghan's stomach turned at her own request. She didn't want to think about the pain her words would inflict on a population doomed to a brutal existence no one should have to endure. "And be discrete about it."

17

THE TROUBLE WITH LOVE

MORGHAN WATCHED the soldiers practicing as she leaned against a post which could, in theory, be used to swing a weapon at, but, more often than not, was used for exactly what she was doing. Salus's morning training session was well under way, and while she was glad to be back home in her usual routine, her mind was on other things. Like how and when she was going to break the news to Michael that his father was living in this realm and had taken control of the Legion. Not to mention that he was turning Falcroix into an angel harem, the sole purpose of which was likely to infiltrate Salus and kill her with flair. Maybe she would leave out the last part, much like she would leave out any information relating to the act provoking this madness.

Something pressed against the side of Morghan's arm, and she jumped, unsheathing a dagger and slashing the air where it had been.

Redden jumped back, using the leather chest piece in his hands as a shield. "It's me! Put that thing away."

The tension in Morghan's muscles faded, and she returned the dagger to her belt. "How many times do I have to tell you not to touch me until I acknowledge your presence?"

He peeked around the armor. "I called your name several times. You weren't answering."

Since his response wasn't an improvement, she enunciated each word. "Until. I. Acknowledge. Your. Presence."

He shoved the leather armor into her hands, apparently in no mood for survival training. She looked down at it and smiled. The leather was a smooth, matte black with the Seiyaku's emblem embossed in silver across the front. It was light, but when she weighed it in her hand, she wondered if there was something more to it

"Just leather?"

"Just leather," Redden scoffed, rapping his fist against the armor. It didn't give at all. "What do you take me for? There's a thin sheet of metal between the layers. I used a low density alloy. I doubt you'll even notice the extra weight, but it's solid against a blade. And look." He traced a finger over part of the emblem. "It's inlaid with enough silver that if anyone bleeds on it, the blood will slide through the symbol so it shines red. I have the rest of the pieces at the shop, but when I saw you were back, I thought I'd run this out to you. What do you think?"

"Brilliant, as always." Morghan really looked at him for the first time: five o'clock shadow, red eyes, disheveled hair. She set the armor against the post. "You, however, look like shit."

"Long night," he mumbled, digging the toe of one boot into the grass.

"With that?" She pointed to the armor. The look he shot her said it had nothing to do with work. "Is there someone I need to kill for you?"

Her stony demeanor didn't falter when he chuckled. It

315

was cute how he thought she was joking. "Is Rhett still busy being an ass?"

"Rhett is busy being a newly married man with a child on the way," he said.

Well, that explained it. "So, yes. And you are, of course, not stupid enough to keep screwing him on the side?"

"Can I tell you to mind your own business without you shivving me?"

"You make the best weapons and armor in Salus and likely the realm. You could probably shiv me a couple times before I'd seriously consider killing you. That being said, I can't be held accountable for what happens if you sneak up on me."

He rolled his eyes. "It doesn't matter who I'm fucking, Windstarr. No one is awaiting my progeny, and I teach my niece and nephews as if they were my own. Dex is the settler, I'm a sampler."

"Oh, now we're starting in on the real bullshit. You've been chasing Rhett, and he's been letting you, since you were teenager. What are you now, like fifty?" She smirked. "That's a long time to be after one person if your goal is diversity."

"Fuck off," he seethed, apparently forgetting he was supposed to be afraid of her. "It's been nowhere near that long. I'm thirty-six, and you know it. Dad has been dead for years, but Dex and I still get some poorly wrapped metal scrap with our year on it every birthday."

"That's likely your mother."

"I'm missing my thirty-first, which should have come after he died but before you returned. Besides, my mother knows how to wrap a gift."

"So do I, but it's more authentic if it looks rushed. I'll stop."

"No!" He crossed his arms over his chest and looked away. "I mean, unless you want to. My point is, you keep up with more of the shit going on around here than you let on."

"And my point is, there are plenty of nice guys in this city who won't tap dance on your fucking heart. I can think of five or six off the top of my head, and one of them is an officer."

"Perfect. You can order him to ask me on a date. I understand what you're trying to do, but I can't help who I love."

"Whatever." Morghan hated him a little for being right. She leaned against her post and pulled a cigarette from her pocket. Pretending to care about the Light's training session was hard work today. She preferred her time with the Seiyaku, but she'd worn most of them out well before dawn. Her eyes wandered to where Dravyn was running Brennick and Bael through drills in the next field. "I have better things to do than keep up with who everyone's screwing anyway."

Redden shrugged. "No you don't. People mostly bicker over trade and city politics, but they kill for love."

"It's the easiest thing in the world to fuck someone without loving them, Denny. Think about that next time Rhett comes knocking. You'll inevitably wake up alone, but you have the choice to trade self-loathing for dignity. Trust me, it's liberating to take out the trash."

Until the trash comes back and murders you.

Morghan closed her eyes and picked through the memories she was channeling, tossing the majority of them back into her subconscious. She'd been spending far too much time in the past lately, lost in a life she'd literally died to leave behind. When she opened her eyes again, Redden was no longer beside her, but she spotted him walking along the side of the training fields.

"I need thirty more of these," she called after him, pointing to the armor. "I'll send the boys your way for fitting and come pick up the rest of mine later."

His response was a single finger raised high above his head, but after walking a few more steps, he turned back and nodded. He gave a half-hearted wave and continued toward the forge.

Morghan finished the remainder of her cigarette before grabbing the armor from the ground and signaling for a nearby officer to take the field.

Dravyn ordered the younger boys to stop when she approached. "Is something wrong?"

"What makes you say that?"

"The sun isn't high enough, and the boys have barely broken a sweat, but you're leaving," he said.

"I'm going for a walk."

"In the middle of a training session?" There was a hint of worry on his brow, right next to a gash she'd put there a few days earlier. She wasn't sure if he'd been distracted or she'd been moving at an unfair speed, though he swore it was the former. It had been a particularly off day for her, and she shouldn't have been in the ring. She didn't remember much between starting the match and the blood shrouding Dravyn's face as he lay on the ground.

Morghan pushed the thought aside. She'd already decided the Seiyaku would spar only with each other from now on. Nothing good would come from dwelling on it. "Do you know a man named Rhett?"

"The ass," Brennick said matter-of-factly, which, coming from a six-year-old, was borderline hilarious.

"Nicky, quiet!" Dravyn scolded, swatting the boy's short sword with the wooden practice sword in his hand.

Brennick bowed his head and kicked the broad side of his blade. "She says it. You say it. Why can't I say it?"

"It's not what you can or can't say. No one included you in this conversation," Dravyn said.

"It's nice to know you all are so familiar with him though, Brennick." Morghan tousled his hair, and the memory of doing the same to Dravyn when he was younger stung for the briefest of moments. "You and Bael should go grab a drink. It's hot out here."

The two boys sheathed their swords and sprinted away, chasing each other along the side of the practice fields and shouting as they went. Her words had essentially released them for the morning, and she was certain the least of their concerns was the drink they would down to honor her suggestion.

"So, is this an accident or an execution?" Dravyn wondered.

"Neither. I just want him watched. Closely." The disappointment on Dravyn's face made it hard to remain serious. "Don't look so put out. If we started murdering every narcissist in the city, half the population would be in the ground, and for the sake of fairness, I'd have to insist Michael run me through."

"You're sure we can't make an exception for him?" Dravyn pressed.

Morghan grinned. "I didn't realize hating him was so in fashion. He's a rich, thirty-something playboy. What did he ever do to you?"

"It's not important."

"I didn't ask if it was important."

Dravyn planted his hands on his hips and looked up at the sky. "He's used to getting everything he wants, and I don't always like what he wants."

"Has he been harassing Ralikaya?"

Dravyn turned wide eyes on her, and color rose in his cheeks. "Why would I care? She can take care of herself."

Morghan put a hand on each of his shoulders and leveled her gaze at him. "How stupid do you think I am?"

Dravyn's eyebrows pulled together. "Please don't make me hate you."

"Please don't make me have to." The urge to hug him snuck up on her, but instead she let go and took several steps backward for good measure. "Just keep it quiet."

"Our relationship or the spying?"

"What relationship?" She deserved a fucking medal for keeping a straight face. "I expect a weekly report on Rhett until I tell you otherwise. I want to know where he goes, who he fucks, and if he does anything at all that could be considered illegal. Use the others when you have to, but if someone misses training or classes, it's you."

"How committed am I to remaining hands off?" Dravyn was a little too interested in the question for Morghan's liking.

"Although I'd prefer this remain covert, the short answer is you are until you aren't." She shrugged. "When I give you an order, I expect it to be followed, but there are a thousand little decisions between the command and the action. Any fool can follow an order. It's the choices between point A and point B that will set you apart from the mediocre soldier next to you."

~

"Morghan, are you listening?"

Morghan turned her face from the ceiling and glanced across the desk Michael was sitting behind. She had tuned him out when the words "emotional instability" made their way into the conversation, so she hadn't heard much beyond a standard greeting. The room smelled like Winstin, and as soon as Michael got through lecturing her, the traitorous little bastard was going to regret he'd ever been reanimated. All the thread in Salus wouldn't be able to put him back together again.

"I've been meaning to tell you, it would be better to do business in another room." Morghan gestured behind her. "One where people don't have to walk through your bedroom to get to it. So unprofessional."

Michael slumped deeper in his chair. "So, I guess that's a no on the listening."

Morghan ignored him. "Are you trying to build alliances with people in here or sleep with them? I'm getting mixed signals."

"Those two things are by no means mutually exclusive." He made his own inspection of the ceiling. "Besides, most people around here think I'm a god. I like to think it's a little unnerving for dignitaries to walk past the bed of a god."

"I'm not biting on that one." She gestured to the empty corner behind him, where Valek often stood during Michael's meetings. "Your protégé has been gone to Predlitz for a while now. Did he run back to Arden when you weren't looking?"

"Politics doesn't suit him. He's staying in Predlitz to study as a healer instead."

Morghan rolled her eyes. "Those fanatical fucks will have him dancing in the moonlight and forcing people to drink their own urine to cure gangrene. My boys know a hundred times more about treating wounds than those charlatans in Predlitz."

"You don't get to bitch about that. It's not my fault you wouldn't train him."

She shuffled her feet against the floor and shifted in her chair. "Can I leave now? Are you through berating me?"

Michael scowled. "That wasn't my intention. I'm worried about you, and I'm not the only one."

She leaned forward. "All I need to know is if you brought Winstin here or he came on his own."

Michael pinched the bridge of his nose. "I should have waited for the stench to fade. That man is a walking perfume factory."

"Yeah, I'm aware. Vanilla and oranges. Answer my question."

"Lilacs, actually," Michael said.

"No, I'm pretty sure I know the scent of my own nightmares."

Michael's brow furrowed. "He smells like my mother."

Well, that was interesting. Morghan had thought Dravyn was nuts for swearing Winstin smelled like a tavern, but maybe that wasn't the case at all. "Whatever he smells like, I want to know how he ended up sitting here." She smacked the armrest of her chair.

"He didn't sit there. Dravyn did." When Morghan stood and turned toward the door, Michael reached across the desk and grabbed her wrist. "Sit down. I summoned them. Dravyn refused to say a word, but his expressions while Winstin talked were more than enough. That boy would rather slit his own wrists than disappoint you, and if you were in the right frame of mind, you'd know that."

"My frame of mind is pissed, summoned or not." And she was not sitting back down. "Let go of my arm."

"You're out of control, Morghan. It's getting difficult to ignore. How many people have you killed in the past month?"

That was four boring ass reports on Rhett ago. And Hell if she could remember. Five? Maybe ten? She never gave it a second thought when doing away with rapists, pedophiles, and murderers. Salus used to be peaceful, but since Michael had all but admitted he was a god, the nearer cities sent any fool pleading for mercy to Salus for judgement. "How many have you sentenced? I'm only the executioner."

"I rarely hand down such a punishment. Exile is not death."

She ripped her arm from his grasp. Evil spread like a virus because of soft rulers like him. "That depends on where you're being exiled from and who's doing the exiling."

Michael opened his mouth to respond, but a knock at his bedroom door interrupted him.

"Let me get that for you on my way out," Morghan said.

When she swung the door wide, she was met with Ralikaya's frantic, tearstained face.

"Thank the Creator! Dravyn said you might be here." She grabbed Morghan's hand and pulled her into the hall. "Please, hurry. You're needed in Redden's quarters."

"Morghan, what is it?" Michael called after her, but she was already running down the hall and didn't bother responding. Not that she had an answer. Maybe Ralikaya could fill him in, or better yet, stall him. It wasn't like she had any hope of matching Morghan's pace anyway, and with a disaster serious enough to bring one of her own to tears, waiting wasn't an option.

Morghan heard the scream a hall away. The length and pitch of it stole the breath from her lungs. She knew that sound, and it wasn't driven by physical pain or anger. It was the visceral cry of a mother who knows her child is dead, and nothing else sounded quite the same.

Morghan skid to a halt in front of Redden's open door. Dravyn knelt near the wall with Rhett's bloody, struggling form held flush against the floor. The man bucked below Dravyn with no hope of escape, one eye swollen shut, his arms wrenched at odd angles and pinned to his back. His good eye was wild, and he was screaming Redden's name, though it was difficult to discern over the wails of Redden's mother.

And there she was, kneeling in the middle of the room beside her son, who lay on his back with a dagger buried in his abdomen to its jeweled hilt. Blood oozed from the wound, and the way the blade was angled it could have pierced anything from bowel to aorta, likely both.

At least Redden was still conscious. One of his hand's laid atop his mother's arm in an attempt to comfort her despite his pained grimace and labored breathing.

Her screams deteriorated into ugly sobs when she noticed Morghan in the doorway. She gestured to the dagger and opened her mouth to say something, but no words came. She put one hand on Redden's chest and grasped the hilt with the other.

"No, don't!" Morghan yelled, diving forward to stop her from removing it. She landed on her knees beside them, and though she caught hold of Viela's arm, the blade was already out and dripping red.

Morghan turned back to Redden and thrust both hands over the wound, blood gushing through her fingers despite her best efforts to apply pressure. Tears slid down her cheeks and splashed onto her blood-soaked hands. In the span of seconds, Redden's life had become unsalvageable. The dagger had clearly been plugging the hole it created. If she had been able to open him up and remove the dagger herself, there might have been a small chance of closing the vessels before he bled out. As it was, she had no hope of tamponading a great vessel from the outside, and she had neither the tools nor the time to get to where the true damage had been done.

"I can't fix this, Denny." Morghan's voice came out as a fractured gasp. "I'm so sorry."

He let go of his mother's arm and placed his hand over Morghan's. His face was ashen, and his eyes were already far away. "It's okay. Dex can make your armor and weapons."

"I don't care about that, you dumbass," she sniffed.

He closed his eyes and gave her hand a weak squeeze. "I know, Morghan. I know."

His chest rose and fell once more before going still.

Morghan's hand painted a crimson line across his neck when she checked the nonexistent pulse. She bent forward and pressed her forehead to his as his mother's screams resumed behind her, this time with Redden's name and pleas to the Creator thrown in for good measure.

Morghan released Redden and moved to the side so the woman would have a clear path to her son's body. She didn't remember walking to Rhett or kicking his face so hard teeth clattered across the floor, but as her reality flashed like images from a faulty projector, the decision to snatch Rhett from Dravyn and drag him from the room by the leg was all hers.

Dravyn hurried along beside her. He glanced back at

Rhett before turning worried eyes on her. "He swore it was an accident about fifty times while begging Redden to live."

"How many people have you stabbed in the gut by mistake?" Morghan took a turn and flung Rhett against a wall in the process. People rushed to escape her path, and as she crossed from the living quarters into the thriving market, men gawked and mothers turned their children's eyes away from the spectacle. Despite Morghan's checkered reputation, she had always doled out punishment behind closed doors. This type of display was unprecedented, but at the moment she wasn't concerned with her popularity or lack thereof. Whispers of more serious consequences echoed in the back of her mind, but they were drowned out by the vengeful screams urging her onward.

When they entered the military side of town, Morghan turned toward the smithy. She pointed at the building and spoke to Dravyn. "Gather the other Seiyaku and guard that door. Michael will be here soon, and you are to keep him out until I'm finished."

"Finished with what?"

Her eyes flared, and Dravyn looked away. "Even with all of us, Michael will eventually get through. We can't kill him."

"And he won't kill you. Any of you. Just keep him occupied."

Dravyn peeled off toward the barracks as Morghan tore through the door to the forge.

Dex stopped at the top of an anvil strike and turned toward her, lowering the hammer to his side. He flipped up the protective mask he wore, and his brow wrinkled. "What's wrong?"

When Morghan didn't answer, he craned his neck to the side to get a better view of who she was dragging behind her. Recognition flashed in his eyes, and his lips pressed into a bloodless line. He tossed the mask to the floor and stripped off the heavy gloves and apron. "Where is Redden?"

Morghan shook her head, and by some miracle, she spoke without choking on her words. "Go see to your mother. She's in his room."

Dex's expression hardened, and he stalked toward them, pulling a glowing iron from a forge as he passed it. There was a sizzle of burning flesh, but Dex's face barely acknowledged the pain. "Give him here."

Morghan snatched the iron from his hand, grinding her teeth as the heat seared her palm. "Leave."

"He's my brother!" Dex bit out.

"Which is why you should go see him before his body gets any colder."

Dex put a hand on her shoulder and leaned into her. His knees buckled.

Morghan wrapped her an arm around him and pulled him close, keeping him on his feet. "Go," she whispered in his ear. Her eyes strayed to the forges and the wealth of tools scattered around them. She would use every last one. "I have work to do."

Winstin's nose wrinkled as he descended into the shadowy depths of Salus's prison. With the squalor he'd been born into, the dripping mold and creatures skittering around dark corners shouldn't have fazed him, but an eternity of marble walls and sunlight had spoiled him for the fineries of peasant life.

His boots squelched into the muddy floor as he took the

final step and continued past several empty cells until he reached a locked one. It had been the better part of a week since Morghan had made a scene by torturing Rhett. Winstin regretted missing it, but he'd gone in search of a quick lay, in case Morghan decided to relieve him of his genitals for talking to Michael. In the end, it wasn't his she was after, and by the time he and Michael made it past the Seiyaku, there was nothing left of Rhett but a gurgling husk the most creative minds wouldn't have recognized as human.

But that wasn't the surprising part of her latest bout of madness. It was the fact that, after Michael had marched her down to the prison and thrown her in a cell, she had simply stayed there.

The cell was locked, but the guards had all but abandoned their posts, making it clear they were unwilling to play a part in keeping their leader confined.

Winstin looked through the bars and cursed. Morghan lay on a rickety cot against the far wall, flipping a silver coin between the fingers of her left hand as she stared at the stone ceiling. He wondered if she'd moved at all since the previous day's visit.

"The least you can do is acknowledge my presence," Winstin said. "I'm not responsible for your poor choices."

She didn't bother looking at him. "If I had it to do again, I would—only more slowly."

"I wasn't talking about Rhett," Winstin huffed. "I regret missing the show, but you need to get the fuck up and walk out of here."

"I'm Michael's prisoner. It's not my place to leave."

Winstin hated this game. "Not that you need his permission, but your warden said you can have some time outside today." He held up the key Michael had given him and unlocked the cell, sliding the door to the side. "For Redden's funeral."

The coin fell from Morghan's fingers and she grabbed it midair, her fist blanching around it. She rose from the cot and walked toward Winstin until they were facing one another with only the metal track of the door between them. Her hand shot out and grabbed the door, slamming it into place. "No."

She turned back to the cot but must have thought better of it, because she returned to the bars and shoved her closed hand between them. Her fingers uncurled, revealing the coin resting in her palm.

Except it wasn't a coin. He took it from her and turned it over in his hand. It was a thin circle of shining metal with wavy beveled edges, the number thirty-one burned into its center with a substance that gleamed as blue as a summer sky.

"Do me a favor and put that in his coffin."

Winstin turned the odd trinket over in his hand. "There's no coffin. They're burning him."

"Then burn it with him. The fire will be hot enough; it's mostly tin."

"Do it yourself." Winstin thrust his hand back through the bars.

Morghan's eyes flickered to life. "You will do as I ask, or I will lock you in here with me."

Winstin withdrew his arm before she had a chance to grab it. "Fine. When you finish your tantrum, you know where to find me. I'm done coming down here."

"Perfect. Be sure to tell Dravyn, Ralikaya, and Michael they can stay the fuck out, too."

Winstin marched toward the steps, mounting them in a fury and emerging opposite the barracks. He would go to

Redden's funeral and do as she asked, but afterwards he would find his own release from the frustrations riding him. And there weren't enough whores in Malon, let alone Salus, to douse that fire. Not with sex, at least. He caressed a hand over the blade strapped to his forearm and grinned. Flesh and blood was another story.

18

ALL THAT GLITTERS

DRAVYN DIDN'T WANT to open his eyes when the cart he was laying in came to a stop. His mind had fumbled its way to wakefulness some time ago, but after more than a month of traveling, the last week without the aid of a horse, it was nice to be safe and warm.

Well, relatively safe.

Ralikaya's arm slid from around his waist, and the warmth against his side faded. He opened his eyes and smiled up at her, his lips inching downward when he thought of how close they were to their destination. And how she shouldn't be there at all.

He sat up and glanced to the front half of the canvas-covered cart, where four young women in various states of hopelessness sat with their feet and hands shackled to the floor.

"Out!" a gruff voice called from outside, banging on the side of the cart's wooden base. "I won't be blamed for smuggling in extras."

Dravyn pulled the dark green cloak tighter around him, making sure the symbol on his armor was well hidden. If they had been anywhere else, he'd be doing the opposite. He turned to remind Ralikaya to cover up, but she was already pushing through the fabric at the back of the cart, her cloak secured in place. He looked back at the shackled tributes and apologized before following Ralikaya.

His eyes narrowed against the harsh sunlight as his boots hit the ground. Ralikaya was paying the driver, a grimy, bald man from Bal Mek whose eyes were focused more on her than the last half of the sum they owed. Dravyn briefly considered murdering the man and driving the cart into Falcroix himself, but he couldn't kill him for a look. After all, if the man hadn't agreed to give them a ride, they'd still be trudging through the forest without mounts or supplies, all of which had been lost during an attack by a band of Legion scouts.

The bastards had snuck up on them the one time they were engaged with each other instead of keeping watch. The only things they'd escaped with were the armor and weapons they had snatched from the ground and the bag of coins they'd scraped together before leaving Salus. Between what the rest of the Seiyaku and a fair number of the Light's soldiers had contributed, the sum was more than Dravyn had ever seen. But the trees didn't care if a man held a bag of gold or dirt; they'd watch him waste away and die all the same.

Dravyn had never traveled in a part of the world so devoid of wildlife, especially given the lush nature of the forest. He and Ralikaya had been on their fifth day of eating grubs and other filth while remaining largely dehydrated when they'd become desperate enough to venture near a road.

Lucky for them, they encountered a man en route to deliver Bal Mek's tributes instead of more scouts from

Falcroix. Apparently, Falcroix had stopped sending soldiers to pick up the tributes and now expected them to be delivered. While being more efficient, it struck Dravyn as presumptuous of Alara to assume she was held in such high regard that her soldiers no longer had to show their faces to terrorize a city.

"Here, take this." Ralikaya handed him a water-filled skin and two thick crackers the size of his palm.

Dravyn took a few sips of water and shoved one of the crackers into his mouth. He pocketed the other one and secured the waterskin to his belt.

"You should eat both." Ralikaya gestured to where he'd hidden the cracker. "I have a few more for later."

While Dravyn had never felt compelled to hoard food, unlike so many of the other Seiyaku, after the past week he was intent on paying more attention to how much he had. "We ate well last night. I'm fine."

"One good meal in a week isn't enough. We're about to sneak into a city of enemies. We'll need our strength." She popped a cracker into her mouth and stepped away from the road as the cart rumbled forward.

"You shouldn't be sneaking in anywhere. What can I do to convince you to go home?" Dravyn took the cracker from his pocket and broke it in half. He ate one half and replaced the other in his cloak.

She stopped as they reached the tree line and turned toward him. "I'm getting tired of repeating myself. Come home with me." She pointed down the road the way they'd come. "Neither of us should be here. Morghan will be furious when she finds out, if she hasn't already."

"Not when we bring back her sword," Dravyn insisted, moving into the trees. He turned to the left and followed alongside the road toward Falcroix, being sure to remain hidden.

"This is insane. We don't even know what it looks like. It's just a sword."

"It's not just a sword." Dravyn was also tired of arguing. He doubted they would die today, but the potential was there. Fighting with the woman he loved was the last thing he wanted to do. "We've been over this a dozen times since you followed me out of Salus. It's like Michael's sword and somehow linked to Morghan's immortality. Winstin and Michael think the reason she's acting so erratic is because she's been away from it so long. It's been almost a decade since Alara stole it, and Morghan is getting worse. I don't expect you to understand. You haven't been with her as long as I have."

"I think it's nonsense. She's always been off. Everyone says so. No magical sword is going to make her any less crazy."

He hated it when Ralikaya badmouthed Morghan. Of all the Seiyaku, she was the only one who ever dared to do so, and he was sure it had something to do with her father's death. Funny how his commitment to Morghan stemmed from the same, but Ralikaya would always be different. Morghan had snatched her from one comfortable life and moved her into another. She'd never had to worry about someone ripping her out of bed in the middle of the night just to beat her over some drunken illusion of disobedience. Never had to dig through trash to find her next meal. "Damn it, Kaya, I have to do this! She gave me one job, and I failed. Redden is dead because of me. She might have been living at the edge of sanity, but I pushed her over it."

"Redden and Rhett always fought. How were you to

know when it was going to turn into a knife fight? You didn't do anything wrong."

"It was my job to know," Dravyn said. "And I was distracted. You shouldn't have been with me in the next room. Like you shouldn't be here now."

"You know, if you loved me half as much as you love Morghan, we would have been back home a long time ago."

Dravyn stopped and stared at Ralikaya's back as she kept walking. He had the urge to rub his hand over the place on his chest where it felt like she'd shoved a dagger. "I don't want to sleep with Morghan."

"I never said you did." Ralikaya stopped as she reached another tree line. "Well, great. How in the world are we going to get past this?"

Dravyn stalked to her side and looked over the grassy plain that stretched beyond the forest's edge. Falcroix loomed in the distance, but it wasn't what he expected. Every history lesson on Falcroix told of a once great city plunged into disrepair and ruin when taken over by the bloodsucking queen. Scaring the younger recruits with nighttime stories of crumbling walls packed with the bones of the dead and deformed orcs slinking through blood-soaked streets had become one of the Seiyaku's first traditions. Falcroix was a place filled with a darkness and evil so strong it had held their leader captive for a span of years. No matter how gruesome the stories became, Dravyn always found that particular aspect of it most frightening.

Which was why the multi-tiered city gleaming silver and white in the sunlight caught him off guard.

Ralikaya let out a frustrated sigh. "There's no cover!" She gestured to the left and right, where not a single tree dotted the space between the forest's edge and the distant outer walls of Falcroix. She pointed to the road stretching from the trees to the city gates. "There's so little traffic on the road. We don't have a chance of blending in enough to make it through the gates."

Maybe not here, but that was a good idea. "Let's circle around and see how many roads lead into it. There could be a busier one."

Ralikaya nodded, and they started moving parallel to the forest's edge. "If we hadn't spent the night in a cart full of Falcroix tributes, I would swear we were in the wrong place."

"I was thinking the same thing," he said.

"We're the good guys, right?" Ralikaya cocked an eyebrow.

How could she even ask that? "A white horse can throw you just as fast as a black one. Besides, how many shackled women do you see being carted into Salus?"

"True." Ralikaya pointed in front of them. "I think we found our road."

The western road was packed with carts of goods and people as well as foot traffic moving in either direction. It stretched from Falcroix's gate and cut through the side of a cliff.

He hurried ahead of Ralikaya. "It will take some time to make it over there. As the day wears on, the crowd might thin, and we'll already have to walk along the front of the cliff before getting to the road."

"From the city walls we would look like ants. We'll be fine," Ralikaya assured him. "We can blend in before getting closer."

Dravyn held his breath for much of the time they walked along the side of the cliff. He squinted toward the gate as they went, waiting for a swarm of orcs to rush in their direction, but the travelers continued to move in and out of the city with no discernible change in flow. He let out a sigh of relief when they made it to the road, and he pulled up the hood of his cloak as they tucked in beside a slow-moving cart.

"This place is huge, and we don't even know where to look," Ralikaya rasped under her breath. "We can still leave."

Dravyn wasn't leaving.

"It's too important to keep in the lower tiers. We'll start at the top and work our way back down." He dared to glance up as they reached the gates, but when his eyes met the soldier posted atop the wall, he pulled his hood down farther and looked away. "Don't look up."

Ralikaya turned her head to do just that. "Oh, shit," she whispered. "He has wings like Michael."

"And a sword like his, too. I didn't know there were angels in Falcroix. Morghan has mentioned Michael isn't the only one, but she always talks about them like they live in a different world." He looked back once they passed the gate, but the wall was empty where the angel had stood moments before. "He's gone. Look left, I've got right."

When their search yielded nothing, they broke off from the cart and moved through the crowded lower tier. They pulled their hoods back, since by then they looked more suspicious with them than without. The streets were crowded with orcs and humans alike, and a surprising number of human children wove through the masses. This tier should have been filled with Falcroix's poor and feeble, but Dravyn didn't see a single beggar, and despite being brushed up against several times, no one had attempted to pickpocket either of them. Still, something not quite right tugged at the back of his mind.

"This place is perfect," Ralikaya said, not bothering to

keep her voice low. Her brow furrowed. "But why are so many people looking at us like we have two heads?"

Dravyn paid closer attention to the faces in the crowd, but they weren't staring at him. It was then he realized what was so wrong. He reached over and snatched Ralikaya's hood back over her head.

"Hey, what the—"

Dravyn put a hand over her mouth and pulled her into the shadows of a side street, shushing her when she struggled to break free. "I'm going to let go, but don't scream. Turn around and watch the crowds. Tell me what's missing."

Her tense jaw and angry eyes didn't give him much hope she would do as he asked, but when he released her, she only bared her teeth before turning toward the busy street. "What's missing? Poverty. Sickness. Starvation. Not one of those little boys looks neglected, and there's nothing slinking around in the shadows but us."

"What about the girls?"

Ralikaya opened her mouth to reply but closed it again before saying anything. After a few moments of study, she turned to face him "There aren't any. No women at all."

"But they're carting them in from countless cities and towns on a daily basis."

"So, where are they keeping them?"

Wherever it was, Dravyn doubted it looked anything like this. He had the sneaking suspicion they were surrounded by orphans who had no idea what the word even meant. "All the children here are around Brennick's age or younger," he spoke mostly to himself.

"Fuck." Ralikaya stamped her foot and pulled her hood down more.

"Careful with the curses, or you'll start sounding like

Morghan." Dravyn threw her a sideways smile before step-ping back onto the main street.

They headed for the staircase to the next tier, relieved but more than a little confused to find it unguarded. They moved with the crowds until the staircase to second tier came into view. The top step was filled from one side to the other with a line of orcs, who stood in gleaming silver armor with perfect posture. Their black eyes stared over the third tier, a silent challenge to any who dared mount the steps without the appropriate authority.

Dravyn moved past the stairs to the shops lining the street. They ducked between two buildings and scaled one, creeping along the roof and vaulting over the wall between tiers. A similar tactic got them onto the top tier.

The sun sank close to the horizon, stretching the shadows to their advantage. A small group of angels left the main building, and despite being shrouded in darkness, Dravyn's breath caught when one of them turned and looked at him. At least, he thought it had. The angel's pace never faltered, and after what felt like an eternity, it faced forward and descended the stairs to the second tier.

Ralikaya ran for the door before it closed, motioning for Dravyn to follow her inside.

The door clicked shut at their backs.

"Trespassers!" a voice hissed behind Dravyn. He spun around to find a wiry man in a grey tunic and similarly colored leggings. The left side of his jaw hung at an odd angle, tendons showing through several lines of gaping flesh.

Dravyn didn't have time to reflect on the horror of the man's face. He drew a dagger and shoved it between the monster's ribs, forcing his free hand over what was left of its mouth and taking him to the ground.

The man wrapped his hands around Dravyn's neck, unfazed by the blade piercing his heart.

Dravyn abandoned his hold on both his dagger and the man's face, instead working to pry the hands from around his neck. The grip was so tight his lungs screamed, and his world dimmed at the edges.

Steel flashed, and air filled his lungs a moment later as the hands fell away. He rolled onto his side gasping against the thick red carpet.

Ralikaya knelt beside him, her sword gleaming. A scant line of blood darkened the blade's edge. "Are you okay?"

Dravyn forced his breathing to slow before turning toward the headless body beside him. "I'll be fine." He freed his dagger from the dead man's chest and rose to his feet. "I don't understand. There's no way I missed his heart."

Ralikaya gestured toward the head, from which little to no blood spilled. "I say we decapitate everything we see from here on out." She wrapped her arms around him. "I'm sorry."

He pulled away and frowned. "For what? You saved my life."

She took his hand and gave him a quick peck on the lips. "For questioning if we were the good guys."

"What you really mean, is that you're sorry for wondering if Morghan was evil incarnate," he chuckled. He headed down the empty hall and pulled her along with him.

"I confess nothing." She smiled, but it was short-lived. Her frown deepened as they passed a number of empty rooms with furnishings fit for royalty. All the doors were wide open, beckoning them to look inside. "This place is crawling with beings more powerful than we could ever hope to be. Angels and orcs walk the streets like normal people, and half-rotted monsters guard the doors. We're going to die here, Dravyn."

His gut told him the same, but he refused to admit it. And the deserted halls did little to quell his fears. "They have to catch us first."

Dravyn skidded to a halt outside one of the open rooms. A large bed covered in black velvet swallowed most of it, threatening to outmatch the opulence of the gilded walls. Wild streaks of silver and bronze chased one another through the gold, stopping only as they reached the open archways branching off the back corners of the room. While none of that was a striking difference from the other rooms they'd hurried past, the sword hanging above the bed was new. It hung parallel to the ground, and the hilt was almost identical to Michael's.

"That has to be it!" Dravyn pulled Ralikaya toward the doorway, but she resisted. "What's wrong? We can take it and get out of here. Hurry, before somebody comes."

"The hall is empty. The doors are open. There's a sword exactly like the one we're after hanging in a deserted bedroom. My instincts are screaming to run. Now. No sword. Don't tell me yours aren't telling you the same. We know better. We've been trained better." Ralikaya glanced into the room. "Besides, Michael's sword has an M on it. Shouldn't Morghan's? It could be a fake."

Dravyn didn't find the W embossed at the hilt's junction suspicious at all. He pulled his hand out of Ralikaya's. "No, that's it. Naming worked different in her world. Maybe when it was forged, she asked for her last initial to be put on it instead. Other than Michael, we're the only ones who call her Morghan. Even Winstin uses her last name." He strode into the room and climbed onto the bed. "It's coming with us."

He grabbed the sword by the sheath and removed it from the wall, his muscles tensing as he did so. But nothing happened. The heft of it shifted into his hand, but no blade swept from the ceiling. No battalion of monsters flooded the room.

Dravyn let out a relieved sigh and started to jump down, but a glint of metal in the corner of his vision had him turning his attention to the far side of the bed.

"Get down!" Ralikaya rasped under her breath, taking a step into the room. "Let's go."

"There are two more." Dravyn pointed to the gold and silver-hilted swords leaning against the side of the bed. He tilted his head when she took two hurried steps backward before her jaw went slack. She wasn't even blinking. "What is it? Do you think we should take these, too?"

"I would strongly advise against that."

Dravyn turned toward the voice, his eyebrows drawing together at the sight of the two middle-aged men standing before him. They wore nothing more than the white towels wrapped about their waists. Wet hair clung to their shoulders, and trails of water reflected off their bare chests and arms. Dravyn's eyes were drawn to the dark skin of the elder man, which was marred by a series of burns and gashes. His left arm appeared to have been mauled long ago, with chunks of flesh missing in a jagged line that ran from his elbow, across his shoulder, and finished with a particularly deep gash over the left side of his chest. Countless burn scars in the shape of forge irons papered the rest of his torso, and the letters FVG stood out as a thick, almost black scar high on the right side of his chest. In stark contrast, the younger man's pale skin was flawless, and by the smug look on his face, Dravyn imagined it was he who had spoken.

The scarred man glared at Dravyn before turning his

brown eyes to the swords propped against the bed. One minute he was standing across the room, and then he was gone. The swords disappeared, and the older man reappeared beside the younger, handing over the gold-hilted sword without a word.

Dravyn took a step back and nearly fell off the bed.

The younger man flashed in front of him, grabbing his shirt and steadying him on the bed. "Careful." He brushed off Dravyn's shoulders as if removing dust, eventually moving one of his hands to cradle Dravyn's cheek. "You mortals break so easily, and you're bound to get hurt straying so far from your mother."

Dravyn wanted to smack the hand away from his face, but he didn't dare despite the burning cold spreading across his cheek. "My mother is dead."

The man smiled, and his face looked oddly familiar. "I didn't mean the one who brought you into this world but the one who kept you in it." He patted the side of Dravyn's face and then, mercifully, removed his hand.

Dravyn rubbed his palm against his cheek and came away with bits of frost. He was torn between being happy he hadn't hallucinated the feeling and terrified the man standing before him had the power to create ice with the touch of his hand.

"Both reactions are suitable given the situation."

And he could read his mind. Shit.

"You're going to kill us," Dravyn stated. The bastard was toying with him, and any minute now he would shove his sword into Dravyn's chest before moving on to Ralikaya.

"Maybe." He turned to the older man and gestured toward Ralikaya, who still hadn't moved. She remained frozen in place as the dark-skinned man walked up to her and pressed the tip of his sword over her heart. "Maybe not."

"What did you do to her?" Dravyn growled, swapping Morghan's sword to his non-dominant hand and pulling a dagger from his belt.

The man raised an eyebrow, and Dravyn's blade flew across the room, clattering to the floor. "Temper, temper. I'm only giving her body a rest, but her mind is working fine." He turned to Ralikaya. "Speak."

"Run, Dravyn! Just go!"

"Enough speaking." The man rolled his eyes as he turned back to Dravyn, and Ralikaya fell silent again. "Neither of you has to die here. In fact, you can leave better than ever." He nodded to Morghan's sword. "And I'll even let you take the sword back to Salus."

"But?"

"No buts." He pulled open the towel around his waist and rewrapped it more tightly. "I have those at my command who could make you immortal. Both of you. All I ask is for you to keep me abreast of the goings on in your city." He rubbed a hand over his chin and turned a wicked grin on Dravyn. "Of course, immortality is a rare gift, and I'd reserve the right to call in a favor every now and again."

"I won't be your spy, and I don't want to be immortal. I just want us to walk out of here the same as we walked in."

"Well now, if we always got what we wanted, I wouldn't even be here. Choose. It will be immortality or death for the both of you. Although, I assure you her sentence will be much worse than anything I could devise for you."

Dravyn wished he could place why this asshole looked so familiar. He'd certainly never met him before, but something about the shape of his face, the line of his jaw, and the way his smile folded the skin around his eyes looked so much like—Michael. Dravyn's hand tightened around the sheath of Morghan's sword; if only he could use it. Was this Michael's brother? He looked at Ralikaya and his heart sank. No matter who he was, it changed nothing. "My answer is still no."

"Well, that's disappointing." The man's smile faded, and his arm shot out, grabbing Dravyn's cloak and pulling him forward until their chests touched. He leaned in, his lips brushing Dravyn's ear. "But only a little."

Dravyn shivered and tried to pull away, but there was no escaping the arm snaking around his back.

"And I am not Michael's brother." The man's damp hair slid against Dravyn's cheek as he turned his face toward Ralikaya. "But perhaps he needs one."

~

The discordant clang of metal and shouted curses met Nikoli's ears long before he reached the dungeon's lower level. If he was honest, he could almost hear the racket from his rooms on the top tier, but at this distance, it was impossible to ignore. He pulled at his linen shirt and adjusted the billowing white sleeves. After ages hiding his wings, he should have been used to wearing clothes above the waist, but even the robes he wore in his own realm scraped against his skin in all the wrong places. If he didn't hate being stared at so much, he would have gone shirtless, but the more skin one showed, the more eyes they collected.

He tugged on a sleeve one last time as he moved past the cells. Like those above, these were filled with the women delivered to him by Michael's population of cowards. The women pulled away from the bars as he passed, huddling with one another in the far corners and closing their eyes. As if that would save them.

Nikoli continued toward the last cell, at the far end of the dungeon. The only one from which anything more than a wayward sob emerged.

"Good morning," he greeted Dravyn. It had only been a few days since his capture, but the boy's face had already turned drawn and sallow. He wouldn't last long.

Dravyn lunged forward, and Nikoli took a step back as blades slid between the bars. The daggers pulled back, and Dravyn flipped them over in his hands. The silver emblem on his armor flashed in the torchlight. "Where's Ralikaya?" he demanded.

"Indispose." Nikoli yawned. "She is no longer your concern."

Dravyn's eyes narrowed. "Either kill me or let me out of here so I can die trying to kill you!"

"How could I possibly refuse such a polite request? But no, you are right where you belong. For now."

Dravyn slammed his daggers into his belt and clenched his fists at his sides. "Can you at least have someone bring me some damn food? All I get is water."

"Your benefactor sits in a cell refusing to eat. Are you better than her?"

Dravyn rolled his shoulders, and fear flashed behind his eyes. "I need food. I'm not immortal."

"A pity, but an easily remedied defect. My offer stands, but this is your last chance to accept."

When Dravyn's blades slipped through the bars again, Nikoli sprang forward and grabbed both of his wrists.

"Morghan is going to kill your ass," Dravyn rasped.

"Wrong answer." Nikoli twisted Dravyn's wrists until bone snapped and the daggers clanked to the floor. He shoved Dravyn away from the bars before retreating a few steps and straightening his shirt. "You will continue to receive water, but your meals will coincide with those of your petulant leader. When she eats, so will you."

Dravyn leaned against a wall, his hands held limp against his chest. "That's not fair. How will you even know? She's nowhere near this place."

"I'll know, and it's perfectly fair." Nikoli smirked. "I'm always fair, but depression is a fickle mistress. It causes some to eat to bursting while others deem themselves unworthy of sustenance."

Nikoli turned away from the cell and headed for the stairs. "What should concern you most is that in six weeks she has yet to accept a single meal."

"This is ridiculous! Kill me or set me free. You can't just let me rot here forever."

"You know nothing of forever." A smile spread across Nikoli's face as Dravyn's vehement curses echoed off the walls behind him. Dravyn was wrong on every account, though Nikoli imagined the boy would be a stain on his city for no more than a few weeks to months. Certainly not forever.

He placed a booted foot on the first step before thinking better of it; the last thing he wanted was to push through the throng in the lower tiers. He closed his eyes and concentrated on the throne room, and when he breathed in next, the scents of decay and human waste were replaced by the overwhelming aroma of peppermint.

Nikoli bowed his head, and his hands flexed on the arms of the throne. A pair of cold, sparkling green eyes hovered at the forefront of his mind, and his back burned. He winced and swallowed the memory as his eyes opened.

A small group of Hellions looked up from where they

were scrubbing the floors of the dais. Their eyes were wide and afraid, as they were by no means allowed so close to him.

Nikoli stood, and they scattered to various corners of the room as he stepped down from the dais and made his way to the main hall. It was empty, with the exception of Phanuel striding toward him. Blood painted his chest, and broken handprints of the same scattered across his arms and wings.

"Master." Phanuel bowed.

"Is there anything left of her?" Nikoli was surprised by how much he wanted the answer to be yes.

Phanuel gave a terse nod. "She's unconscious, but her wound healed. I'll have Raphael carry her down to the dungeon."

"That's won't be necessary." Nikoli ran a hand down Phanuel's arm, and the blood came away warm. He touched his thumb to the bloodied fingers and it slicked across them like a dream. "Krishna and I will tend to this one. She deserves a gilded cage."

19

WHEN THE WHOLE WORLD'S AGAINST YOU

MORGHAN STARED up at the ceiling, and her mind was blissfully clear. There were no thoughts of death or torture, no worries over commitments or failures. Even the loneliness associated with memories of Luke and Azrael was missing. Her only thought revolved around the angry pangs of hunger radiating from her stomach.

It had been over three months since Michael threw her into a cell, and she had no more reason to step out of it now than when he'd first dumped her there.

The clank of metal against the bars of her prison interrupted her study of the ceiling. She imagined it was probably another soldier trying to force food down her throat, but her brow furrowed when Winstin appeared. His dagger pressed against one of the bars, and several slices of flesh were carved out of his left cheek.

She sat up and swung her legs over the side of the cot. "What the hell happened to you?"

Winstin frowned. "Occupational hazard. I need your help."

Morghan walked to the bars. "Your occupation consists

wholly of following my orders, of which I've given you none. Well, other than leaving me alone. You're doing a fantastic job, by the way."

"While you've been brooding, I took up some old habits." He ran his free hand over his cheek and winced. "You should see my back."

"How many people have you killed?" Morghan didn't really give a damn, but depending on the number, Michael may or may not have noticed.

"One."

Thank God.

"Every few days."

Morghan's jaw clenched. "Winstin! If Michael gets wind of this, he'll banish you or worse."

"Calm down. They weren't even from Salus." Winstin crossed his arms over his chest. "You didn't want me around, so I took a vacation. Bal Mek and Malon had a sudden reduction in their population of rapists and murderers. No one will miss them. But this?" He pointed to his face. "I can't stay like this. People will wonder, and the gashes will get dirty and wider until half my face is gone."

While Morghan was relieved his adventures in flesh carving had taken place elsewhere, fixing the injuries he acquired during them was not on her list of priorities. Though to be fair, the list was pretty short these days. Nonexistent even.

She turned away from the bars and waved him off. "Get Dravyn to fix you. He knows how to sew."

"That would be great, if he wasn't still gone. I can't wait for him to finish whatever task he's completing for you. I need this fixed now."

Morghan stopped in the middle of the cell and turned back to him. "What did you say?"

"I said I need this fixed yesterday, damn it!"

"No." Her hand sliced a line through the air, parallel to the ground. "About Dravyn. I didn't send him anywhere. I haven't even seen him since before Redden's funeral."

What was left of Winstin's face dropped into a confused frown.

Morghan strode to the bars and slammed her hands against them. "How long has he been gone?"

Winstin looked at the ground and mumbled something under his breath.

She reached through the bars and grabbed his shirt, pulling him closer. "How long!"

"He left after Redden's funeral—Ralikaya, too. I thought they'd come down here one last time, and you'd sent them on an errand to some other kingdom. The remaining Seiyaku didn't seem concerned."

Which meant they knew where the other two went.

Morghan let go of Winstin's shirt and grabbed the bars of the door, pushing them upwards and to the right. A metallic snap rang through the prison, and Morghan reached over and flipped the switch that popped from one of the bars. The entire door released from its track, and Morghan tossed it to the side. She pushed past Winstin and headed for the stairs.

"I knew you could get out if you wanted to," Winstin grumbled.

Of course, she could. She'd designed the damn prison herself.

Winstin hurried along at her side as she made her way across the moonlit practice fields. She jumped up the steps to the Seiyaku barracks and ripped the door clean off its hinges before stomping into the building.

Every boy in the room sprang upright in bed, and a few tumbled to the floor.

She headed for Brennick, who sat beaming at her from his bed. "You're back!"

"Where is Dravyn?" Morghan didn't bother softening her features when his excitement bled into fear. Instead, she grabbed him by the shirt and lifted him until his eyes were level with hers. "Where?"

Tears slid from Brennick's eyes, and he shook his head. "They should have been back by now."

"Back from where?"

"Falcroix."

No.

"They went to find your sword. To help you."

No. None of them even knew about her sword. This was a dream. A nightmare. As soon as she woke up from it, she would leave her fucking cell for real and make sure nothing like this would ever come to pass.

Morghan lowered Brennick into his bed and walked out of the barracks. She stopped and turned toward the group of boys crowded in the open doorway. "Go back to sleep."

The doorway was empty a moment later, and her gaze shifted to Winstin. "This isn't real." She held out her arm. "Cut me. Wake me up."

"I'm not cutting you. You're already awake, and you know it."

Morghan grabbed a dagger from her belt and slid it across her forearm. Pain sang along the wound, and blood welled up, spilling to the ground. The world around her never wavered. Winstin was right; it wasn't a dream.

"Shit, Morghan." Winstin ripped off a section of his shirtsleeve and tied it around her arm. "Why do you have to be so damn self-destructive? I'm real. You're real. And as much as neither of us wants it to be true, Dravyn and Ralikaya being stupid enough to sneak off to Falcroix is real, too."

Morghan glared at him. "My sword was lost in Falcroix years before I met Dravyn. Years! I've never mentioned it. How would he know it existed, let alone its importance?"

Winstin looked away from her. "It doesn't make a difference how he found out. If they made it to Falcroix, then they're already dead or worse."

Morghan grabbed Winstin from behind and pressed her dagger to his neck. "How did he know?"

"It may have come up when Michael and I were discussing your recent unpredictability."

Morghan released him and stormed toward the market.

"Where are we going?" Winstin hurried after her.

"I don't give a damn where you go," Morghan shot back. "I'm going to have a pointed conversation with Michael."

"He's bound to be asleep."

"I'm sure I don't care." She stalked past the dark shops and deserted carts.

Michael's quarters weren't far beyond where the market ended and the residences began. She banged her fist against his door, but other than the whisper of sheets shifting on the other side, nothing happened. Morghan collected what thoughts she could grasp from the maelstrom raging in her head and pulled a gun from the holster at her hip. She released the silver magazine and exchanged it for a gold-plated one before chambering the first round.

"Stand back," she warned, although she didn't bother giving Winstin much time to move before aiming at the doorknob and pulling the trigger. The right side of the door exploded as the bullet hit its mark, and Morghan stepped through the splintered remnants.

Michael stood against the far wall, eyes wide and wings out. Recognition lit on his face, but his fight or flight posture never faltered. "Morghan? You blew up my fucking door!"

"I knocked first."

"This is not the appropriate response when someone doesn't answer their door in the middle of the night!" Michael's eyes flared to life, and he took a step toward her.

She brought the gun up and aimed it at his chest. "Don't tempt me, motherfucker, or we'll find out exactly which body part regenerates first when a ranking immortal get blown to shit."

Michael stopped and put his hands up. "And to think, I'd been looking forward to the day you left that cell."

"Oh boo fucking hoo," she sneered, gesturing toward the next room with her gun. "Follow me. We have things to discuss."

Morghan took a seat behind Michael's desk, leaning back and propping her feet on top of it.

Michael scowled and opened his mouth, but he shut it when she waved her gun at him. She used it to point at the chair across from her. "Sit."

She turned to Winstin. "You. Traitor. Stand wherever you did the day you two fuckers gave my boy a death sentence. I want the image burned into my memory so I can bring it up time and again to remind myself how much I despise both of you."

"What are you talking about?" Michael's eyes hadn't calmed since they moved from the bedroom.

Winstin stood beside Michael's chair and turned his face to the floor. "Dravyn went to Falcroix. Ralikaya followed."

The angry light in Michael's eyes dimmed. "What? Why? And holy hell what happened to your face?"

Morghan hit the table with the butt of her gun. The only part of her body she could feel was her chest, and there was a rabid animal somewhere inside ripping it to shreds. "Tell him."

"Someone fought back a little too hard while I carved the beating heart from their chest."

"Not that!" Morghan yelled before turning back to Michael, who looked more baffled than ever. "From the conversation you two had in front of him, Dravyn not only learned about my sword, but where it was and how being away from it might be causing me to lose my mind." She looked at Winstin. "Do I have the gist of the conversation right?"

Winstin nodded, and Michael paled.

"And now Alara has him?" Michael asked.

Morghan pulled her feet off the desk and leaned forward over it. "I could almost live with that, but Alara doesn't rule Falcroix anymore."

Michael cocked his head to the side. "You said you didn't kill her."

"I didn't." She leaned back in the chair and turned her eyes to the ceiling. "I have no idea if she's alive or not, but your father took over Falcroix around the time Brennick was born."

The room remained silent, and eventually Morghan looked back at Michael to make sure he was still there. He was, and he was staring at her, his expression blank.

"You never told me that." Michael's voice was far too calm for the topic they were discussing.

"It wasn't important." Morghan decided it was a good time to holster her gun. After all, he had a ranking sword in the next room, and she did not.

"How long has it not been important? How long have you known?"

She pointed a finger at Winstin. "Since he showed up in Salus and told me."

Michael stood and his chair clattered to the floor behind him. "Six years? You've known my father was our greatest adversary for six years and deemed it unimportant to tell me? What the fuck rates as important to you, Morghan? The apocalypse?"

Maybe.

"Dravyn being trapped in Falcroix by your sick fuck of a father rates as important right now. Nikoli has been my greatest adversary for over half a million years, closer to four million by more loosely interpreted versions of our history. I apologize if, up to this point, it's been same shit, different dimension by my standards."

"I don't know who the fuck you are anymore."

"Neither do I, but all you need to know is you're flying my ass to Falcroix. Now."

"Absolutely not. There is no love lost between my father and me, but for the most part I don't even know him. This could be a good thing. It's hard to imagine worse than what Alara was doing."

Winstin cleared his throat, and Michael cut his eyes toward him. "He's currently enslaving women to breed an army of nephilims, with the most likely goal being to infiltrate your army and kill Morghan, along with anyone else who may get in his way. This is a man who destroyed everything you loved and cast you into a desolate dimension just to watch you suffer in the inexplicable hope you would become like him." He gestured to Morghan's side of the desk. "Forgive me, if I find it hard to understand how you would ever take his side over hers."

Michael's nose wrinkled. "What is a nephilim?"

Morghan rubbed the heel of one hand against her forehead. Behind all the rage, she knew she wasn't thinking straight, but there was no telling if she would ever have that luxury again. "You are—half human, half angel. Your father has dozens of angels at his beck and call. With all the women he's dragging into Falcroix each month, God only knows how many of those little bastards they're popping out."

Michael righted his chair and dropped into it, scooting closer to the desk. He leaned forward and folded his hands on top of it. "Can we beat him? Be honest."

Morghan's hands fidgeted atop Michael's desk. "No. Not with every man in the realm at our back could we hope to kill him, but we can break his ranks and force him from his comfort zone. Believe it or not, that would be worse than physical pain. And maybe I can save Dravyn and Ralikaya, if they're still alive."

Michael placed his hands over hers and his eyebrows drew together. "I'm still not taking you there."

Morghan pulled away and stood, leveling a gun at his head. "You will take me."

Michael leaned back in his chair. "I will not. Put the gun down."

"Agree to fly me to Falcroix, and I'll think about it."

"We both know you're not going to shoot me with exploding bullets." He yanked the gun from Morghan's hand by the barrel and slammed it onto the desk. It was a wonder it didn't discharge. "And I'd sooner fly you thirty thousand feet up and drop you than take you back to Falcroix. The next time we go there, it will be with an army. An army that isn't outnumbered and at odds with one another."

Morghan hated him for his logic. Of course, she wouldn't shoot him—with those bullets. She drew her second gun and shot him in the thigh. The silver-tipped bullet went clean through his leg and buried in the hardwood floor.

Michael hit the floor not long after, and his screams echoed through the room. "You shot me!"

"Your fault." Morghan grabbed the gun on the desk and replaced both at her hips. She kicked her chair out of the way before stepping over Michael and heading for the door. "Winstin, with me."

"Where are you going?" Michael called after them.

"To explore other options." She walked through Michael's shattered door and turned toward the outer halls.

Winstin walked beside her. He opened his mouth to speak, but Morghan silenced him with a shake of her head. She knew what he was going to ask. She didn't want to discuss the options she was exploring, because there weren't any. Michael could fly her to Falcroix in a matter of days or she could sit in Salus wondering what piece of Dravyn would be delivered to her first. There were so many reasons why trying to sneak into Falcroix alone was a bad idea that the blind rage couldn't even convince her to try it.

She needed a drink. A strong one. Or ten.

Morghan pulled her coat tighter when she entered the tavern. She dropped into a chair around one of the many deserted tables. Too far from midnight but not close enough to dawn, this was the only time of day the place was more empty than full.

Winstin took a seat on the other side of the table but didn't say a word.

Raelyn rushed from behind the bar, well as much as a man in his seventies could rush. "Windstarr! About time

Michael let you out. Absolutely ridiculous he put you there in the first place."

Morghan nodded but couldn't bring herself to look up from the table. "Just bring me some of that disgusting grey shit Michael drinks, okay?"

She was never so thankful for Raelyn's ability to judge his patron's needs as when he dropped a large bottle with two clean glasses in front of her without another word.

Morghan opened the bottle and filled one of the glasses halfway. She slid it across the table to Winstin.

He took a healthy swig and grimaced. "I can't believe you really shot him."

Morghan draped an arm over the back of her chair and tilted the bottle up to her lips, downing half of it before coming up for air. A shiver passed through her, and Winstin's features weren't quite as crisp as they had been moments before. While the drink tasted like wet cement, its effect was swift and potent. Unfortunately, her metabolism would make certain it lasted a fraction of the time it should. "Regular bullet. Straight through the muscle. He'll be fine. Probably almost healed by now."

"You can only hurt him so much before he stops caring about you." Winstin took a smaller sip and scowled at his glass. "How can you drink this shit?"

She drained the rest of the bottle and set it on the table. "I'm family. He'll always care about me a little whether he wants to or not."

"Not everyone thinks like you."

The empty bottle disappeared and a full one replaced it. Morghan reached for it, but Winstin pulled the bottle to his side of the table. "Bad idea."

"Fuck you." She stood up too fast and had to grab the table to keep from falling flat on her ass. This probably wasn't the best choice for a first meal after starving herself for months.

Winstin stood and took her arm. "Need a wall?"

She glared at him. "No." Her stomach reeled, and she barely managed to swallow the vomit surging up her throat. "Maybe."

She let him guide her out the door and around the side of the tavern. "I don't really have other options, Winstin. I was being dramatic."

He leaned her against the cold stone wall and stepped away seconds before she vomited. "I can understand how you'd think shooting him wasn't dramatic enough. Your brooding lot back home would be proud."

She spat in the dirt. "Sometimes I talk to them at night. No hope of a response. I know I'm crazy. I wish I could forget them. I think it would be easier."

"The only crazy part about that is wanting to forget them. Loss is a part of life. It makes us appreciate things more when we find them. Lucifer and Azrael aren't gone; you've only temporarily misplaced them."

"That's a nice bit of coddling, but I doubt they're even watching me these days."

They were no doubt preoccupied with watching each other.

"I was with them for a whole five minutes, and over four of them were spent worrying about you. If you think they aren't watching, you're fooling yourself."

"Then why didn't they help? Why not bring Dravyn back to me, or at least tell me he was gone?" She wiped the back of her hand across her mouth and stood up straight.

"I doubt Azrael deemed it important enough to risk the trip," Winstin said. "Nikoli is full-force fucking with us right now, which means he's watching all of us. A lot. Your men left you hanging in Falcroix for years. You think they're going to risk your life over some mortal kid? As much as it pains me to say it, I agree with Azrael on this one."

"Luke should have come anyway."

Winstin shook his head. "Azrael is captain of that ship. Believe me."

A heavyset man stumbled toward them and leaned on the wall behind Morghan. His bowed head pressed against her back, and she jumped forward, landing in a pile of her own vomit.

"Fucking great." She spun around, ready to rail against the man, but the pitiful form before her made her think twice.

He was doubled over, and though there seemed to be no vomit in him, his body heaved every few seconds all the same. His clothes were dirty and threadbare, his scant brown hair finger-combed hastily across the shining dome of his head.

"Sorry," he mumbled, looking up at her through a few wisps of misplaced hair. His brown eyes were bloodshot, but they opened wide at the sight of her. "I've never met you."

"Not everyone can be so lucky." Morghan gave him an empathetic pat on the shoulder and headed past him. "The wall is all yours, pal. Try not to fall down. There are better ways to die than drowning in piss and vomit."

"No, wait! Please." The man staggered after her, grabbing at her coat.

Winstin peeled him off her and held him up by the scruff of his neck. "Are you too drunk to realize who you're talking to? Leave her alone."

Morghan turned back and raised an eyebrow. "Put him

down, Winstin. What's he going to do, dry heave me to death?"

"Don't bother with him." Winstin dropped the man and moved to her side. "Just some idiot from Bal Mek whose been running around the city for days insisting he has a delivery for someone who doesn't even live here."

The man sniffed and hung his head. "You don't understand. I can't leave until my job is done."

"Stop bothering everyone. There is no Lilith here."

Morghan grasped Winstin's shoulder with her left hand and leaned on him so hard he shuffled a half step to the side. Any illusion she had of rescuing Dravyn from Falcroix vanished.

Lilith. Fuck. Did Nikoli even think of her as anyone else? That jackass clung to the past so hard he was going to obliterate all their futures. She pushed off Winstin and took a knee in front of the man's huddled form. "There is. Where's the package?"

The man smiled, and several broken teeth appeared between his cracked lips. "You're Lilith?"

She rose to her feet and pointed for Winstin to assist the man to his. "I guess today I am."

The man wasted no time heading through the trees toward a series of hitching posts. Morghan followed, and Winstin kept stride with her. "Shit. How did I forget Nikoli called you that sometimes? I mean, to be fair, it's been a ridiculous amount of time, and he referred to you as Lucifer's whore ninety-nine percent of the time."

"Shut up, Winstin."

"Got it." His lips pressed together for only a moment. "This can't be good."

"You're not shutting up." Morghan stopped behind the covered wagon the man had jumped into. As her heart rate picked up, she found it increasingly difficult to breathe. "And no, it's not good."

Wood scraped against the floor of the wagon as the front end of a rectangular box slid partway out.

"Stop!" Morghan placed her hands underneath the wooden box before it tipped over the edge. "Winstin, help me get this down."

Morghan pulled her end of the box until the slender length of it came into view and Winstin grabbed the opposite end.

"On the ground. Careful." Morghan could barely get the words past the knot in her throat as she looked down at the simple pine box. It was child-sized, and there was no way Nikoli could have fit Dravyn's entire body into it. A single crimson word spread from one end of its lid to the other in a thin, flowing script.

Lilith.

Morghan closed her eyes and concentrated on taking deep, even breaths.

"Thank the Creator I'm rid of it." The courier's voice shattered Morghan's concentration. "Thought it was haunted when I first loaded it. Would have sworn it moved."

Morghan gasped when an explosion went off so close that the heat rushed across the side of her face and the ground shook beneath her feet. She blinked through the smoke and frowned at the gun in her hand. The covered wagon was a flaming ruin, and the scent of burning flesh permeated the air.

Morghan turned to Winstin, who looked like he was about to piss himself, if he hadn't already. "Go get Michael."

His voice trembled. "I think we burned that bridge for

the night. He's not going to come here just to get shot again."

Morghan knelt beside the box and traced a finger over the letters. She grabbed the lid and pried it up until the nails started to give. "That was an order, not a request. He'll come whether you listen to me or not. The only difference will be how much of the city I raze before he stops me. You can tell him I said that."

One moment Winstin was at her side and the next he was gone. She blinked, and he was there again, but when she wiped a hand over her eyes, he wasn't. Either time was jumping, or she was hallucinating, neither of which was a good sign.

Morghan ripped the lid off. She'd been wrong; it could fit all of him. She stared at the emaciated husk folded inside it. Dravyn was nude, and the size of the coffin had forced him into the fetal position. Paper-thin skin stretched tight across his frame, giving prominence to bones that should never have been visible. She reached inside and ran her hand through his hair, imagining the annoyed look he would give her if he was alive. Her hand strayed down to his shoulder, and her fingers brushed the silver brand there. It was the only thing left with any life to it. Packed around him were the weapons Alara had stolen: her belt of daggers, katana, gun. Even her coat was there, spread out beneath him like a blanket. The only things missing were the only ones that mattered—Dravyn's life and her ranking sword.

When she removed her katana, a folded sheet of paper peeked out of the coat pocket below it. The smart thing to do would be to leave it, shred it, or better yet, have Winstin burn it. Nothing good could come from reading whatever message Nikoli had for her, as if Dravyn's wasted corpse wasn't message enough.

Morghan ripped it from the pocket all the same. It fell open in her hands, the familiar blood-red script shining up at her.

Waging war with mortal children? And somehow, I'm the monster. At least I gave him shelter and offered to feed him whatever meals you consumed. I can't be blamed for your hunger strike. Enjoy your time-locked boy, and if you want your sword, come get it yourself.

Morghan crumpled the paper and threw it into the smoldering ruin of the wagon. Her katana's blade gleamed in the firelight, and she was oddly calm as she pulled a gun from its holster. She wondered how many people were in the tavern, and thought about their blood splattered across its worn wooden floors.

"Morghan." Michael's voice came from behind her, and when a hand touched her shoulder, she spun around and snarled. He took a step back and glanced past her to Dravyn's box. When he looked at her again, his eyes gleamed with unshed tears. "I'm going to enjoy this more than I should."

Michael's fist flashed through the air so fast Morghan didn't have time to move. Or maybe she hadn't wanted to do so. The punch connected with the side of her face, and her world went dark.

20

INTO THE MOUTH OF MADNESS

MICHAEL HATED this part of the day. Dawn was a few hours off, and the whole of Salus was asleep. Except him. Instead, he was stalking through the forest outside the city in search of an ass-kicking. Bed sounded infinitely better.

A twig snapped, and Michael froze. It took him a minute to realize the twig was beneath his own boot. He let out a long, slow breath and waited for his heart to fall back to its normal pace. He drew his sword and pushed onward through the trees. If he strained his ears, he could hear the river gurgling ahead. He'd be safe if he made it to the river.

A black streak flashed in the corner of his vision, and he spun toward it. Nothing.

A line of pain erupted along Michael's lower back, and he reeled forward, falling on hands and knees. He turned and threw up his sword to ward off the next attack, but there was nothing there to meet it. Morghan stood several paces away with her katana in one hand, its sheath still in place over the blade. That explained why he had an aching back instead of a bleeding one.

He jumped to his feet as she unsheathed the blade and

charged him. His sword came up again, but Morghan threw hers at his feet as she neared. Michael made the mistake of watching the sword instead of her, and his lungs deflated when her boot connected with his chest.

Michael skid through the grass and skirted a tree. His wings emerged somewhere between her boot and the tree—not a good sign. He rubbed his chest as he climbed to his feet, but no sooner had his knee left the ground than Morghan was on him. Her fist angled for his jaw, but he dropped his sword and grabbed it before she landed the blow.

She glared at him and brought her other fist around, but he ducked and pulled her down by the hand locked in his. As she fell forward, he buried his other fist in her gut before letting go and stepping away as she hit the ground.

She was back on her feet before he could grab his sword, and for every step she stalked toward him, he took an equally large step backward. Steel flashed as she drew daggers from her belt, and when her eyes moved to Michael's wings, a wave of panic washed through him.

He was faster than her, especially in angelic form, but every move Morghan made in battle was calculated. She took each step with the knowledge of where her foot would be five steps from that one in any of several scenarios, and her blades rarely missed their mark. Between her strategic advantage and the fact he was loath to hurt her, his superior speed meant nothing.

Michael's wings spread out behind him, and the urge to take to the sky almost overrode his good sense to stay on the ground. The last thing he needed was a dagger through his wing while in the air. He put his hands up in front of him and backed away faster. "Not the wings, Morghan. Please."

She cocked her head to the side as she continued toward

him, but the glazed, sleepy look in her eyes gave him little hope she acknowledged his plea. He didn't know where she was, but it certainly wasn't in that moment. Since Dravyn's death nearly two decades earlier, her mind was rarely in the same place as her body.

In the beginning, he'd kept her confined to his quarters, forsaking his duties to the city in exchange for babysitting her around the clock. That had lasted a few weeks, until she escaped during one of the five minute naps he scattered throughout each twenty-four hour waking nightmare. He thought she'd run off to Falcroix to find Ralikaya, but he'd found her asleep in a tree, the blood dripping from her fingers giving her away. Whose blood was anyone's guess, as she hadn't remembered a thing when he woke her. Not even being imprisoned for the previous month. They'd been cycling through different methods of keeping her functional ever since.

And they didn't talk about Ralikaya, who was clearly dead. At least, everyone really hoped she was dead considering the alternative for women in Falcroix.

For the past few years, sparring each morning had worked wonders for Morghan, but lately, Michael was taking such a sound beating his body still ached when it came time for the next match. So far, today was tame, but that would change if she targeted his wings.

Winstin's voice interrupted his thoughts. "Not the wings. Stop."

Morghan stopped moving toward him and sheathed her daggers. Her posture relaxed, and she threw him a tired smile so devoid of joy it hurt. "Sorry."

Michael let out a long, slow breath. As much as Winstin's walking corpse status disturbed him, he was relieved to hear his voice. There were only two signals to stop: Winstin's command or Michael making it to the river before Morghan found him.

He never made it to the river.

"You don't need to apologize. I'm not even bleeding this time. How do you feel?"

"Calm." She rolled her shoulders. "Exhausted."

"You should take a nap," Michael said.

She picked up her katana. "It's almost dawn. I have shit to do."

"I still vote nap. The officers know how to do your job, and even your boys will train by themselves if you're not there."

She turned her eyes to the ground, and her smile disappeared. Michael was so busy these days, that sometimes he forgot having nothing to do could be worse than having too much.

Winstin's eyes narrowed at Michael as he emerged from the trees, but when he spoke it was to Morghan. "Do what you want. You don't have to listen to the dumbass who brought his wings out during a knife fight."

"I'm stronger with them out," Michael protested, but Winstin was right. Anyone with skill would exploit a weakness, and while he could stand and take a hundred beatings in human form, an injury to his wings would bring him to his knees in an instant.

"You're both right." Morghan tapped the back of her shoulder. "You rely on them too much for balance; it makes a big target. Keep them close to your back, and shift your weight as if they were frozen there. You can have the power surge from having them out minus the big red bullseye." She sheathed the katana, and her fingers played along the hilt. "Can we start doing this at night?"

"I never turn down sleeping in," he chuckled. "Swapping to evenings is perfect."

"I meant twice a day. I can't sleep anymore, and I'm starting to, you know..." She waved her hand in the air. "Slip. Earlier."

Michael groaned. This wasn't the best time for him to be limping through the days like a wounded animal. He'd spent years pulling the realm together one fragment at a time, and in a few months, the armies would finally begin to move. By this time next year, one way or the other, their world would be a lot different.

"Never mind." Morghan shook her head. "I'll figure it out. Winstin doesn't need to sleep. He can watch me, and if things go south, he'll get you."

If he could escape. "I'll think about it."

And he would. And as much as he didn't want to, he would probably agree.

Winstin slouched in one of the tavern booths, spinning a copper piece on edge and catching it before sending it across the table for another whirl. Morghan was right; she was getting worse again. And as exciting as it was playing referee while she and Michael beat the shit out of one another, he wasn't sure increasing the frequency would solve anything.

The copper piece spun the wrong way and went careening over the side of the table. Long, dark, delicate fingers snatched it from the air.

Winstin knew those fingers. They'd slid across his skin enough times in recent years. He looked up and smiled at the woman standing before him. Her skin was darker than

Dex's, which was hard to get, but it had nothing on the velvety black of her irises, only a shade or two lighter than her pupils. "Ilena, to what do I owe the pleasure?"

She slipped into the seat opposite him and tucked the copper piece down the front of her shirt. Ilena didn't dress like most whores. She was never done up or showing more skin than not, but then again, she was a collector first and foremost. Michael may have forbidden Rothert's family from running a brothel in Salus, but it only meant the world's oldest profession was a bit more privatized. As Salus's foremost pimp, Ilena didn't need to fuck people for money, but everyone needed a hobby.

"It's been awhile," she said. "Surprising how much some of us can miss sex with the dead."

Winstin leaned across the table. "Ilena, you know better. Keep it down."

She ran her fingers over the frayed stitching on his cheek. "About time for new thread again, Love. I can fix it, and I'd wager I'm better than the General. At any number of things."

Winstin wrapped a hand around hers and placed it firmly on the table between them. "Spreading those types of rumors are how people end up with a knife in their chest. I may serve her, but not like that."

Ilena pulled her hand away as she leaned toward him. "Then who have you been fucking, dear?"

No one. That was the sad truth of it. His plate was piled a little too high with crazy to have time for pleasure. He shouldn't have even been taking a breather in the tavern. Morghan may have looked fine when he left her at the practice fields, but with sleep deprivation added to her already tenuous state, who knew how long she would stay lucid. "I've been busy with other things."

The dark violet tattoo covering the right half of Ilena's top lip slid upwards, while the matching one on the left side of her bottom lip never moved. She caressed a hand down his arm. "Well, when you have a moment, let me know. After such a pitiful drought, the first one's on me. Maybe the second. I'm not starved for coin."

Morghan could surely hold it together without him for another hour or two.

Winstin reached across the table to cup the side of Ilena's face, and the stitching in his back pulled. He roughed the pad of his thumb across her cheek and pushed Morghan from his mind. It would be her job to fix his back when the stitches broke, as they did every time he was with a woman. She never complained. Hadn't even asked questions after the first time.

A shadow fell over the table, and a man slid into the booth beside Ilena. She turned and scowled at him.

Black hair, dark eyes, and skin so pale it in no way matched the other features—not this asshole again. Xayne was one of King Xale's bastards, no doubt from the Vahyiran girl they'd seen on top of Sheltinata's pyramid years ago. He'd been hounding Morghan and Winstin for weeks, because, as a typical male in his prime, he was bull-headed and couldn't get it through his thick skull that both the Seiyaku and the Light were vetted and chosen by Morghan, not tried out for by entitled idiots.

"So, I know becoming one of the Seiyaku isn't possible," he started right in, not acknowledging Ilena in the slightest. "I'm too old."

"By easily five years," Winstin droned.

"And technically I'm not an orphan, but the Light—"

Ilena let out a frustrated sigh and stood in her seat. The

woman hated all things political and war-related almost as much as she hated being backed into a corner. The tall, wide heel of a black leather boot shook the table, followed by another as she walked across it and hopped to the floor. Tight, jet curls bounced around her face when she turned back to Winstin and threw him a wink. "Come find me when you finish with the boy." She gave Xayne a once over with her eyes, and a wicked grin crossed her face. "Or before you're done with him, if you think he's capable of something more worthwhile than talking."

"Winstin!" Xayne pounded his fist on the table.

Winstin glared at him. He stole a sideways glance as Ilena made her way up the stairs to the inn. "That woman offered to bed both of us, and you didn't even look at her."

Xayne waved a hand in dismissal. "I can have a whore like her any day. This is important."

"Really, it's not. Windstarr only needs to deny you once, and I've heard her turn you away half a dozen times. Leave it alone and be glad you're alive." Winstin stood and Xayne mirrored his action. "Follow me, and that last bit will no longer apply."

Winstin headed toward the middle hall, which would take him to the city's center fastest. This was the perfect reminder of why he should be with Morghan. If Xayne had approached her first, who knew what the added annoyance might have sparked.

He found her with two of the newer Seiyaku on one of the few empty practice fields. Morghan stood between them in the sparring circle, demonstrating an appropriate battle stance. When the boys attempted to copy her, she moved to one of them and repositioned his hands on the hilt before pushing his practice sword into the correct position. She backed away and signaled for them to start. They began fluid and beautiful but quickly devolved into a chaos of kicks, punches, and random sword swipes.

Winstin made sure to approach Morghan from the front. He stood beside her and bumped his shoulder against hers. "Shouldn't you stop them?"

"They're learning."

"To do what, scratch out each other's eyes with their fingernails?"

"I've scratched out my fair share of eyes." She shrugged. "Then again, who knows how much of that was real. I had so much heroin shoved into my veins, it was always hard to tell. Either way, I learned to do better. So will they."

Winstin fought to maintain a neutral expression. They'd traded any number of mortal stories during their time watching Michael together in Nikoli's realm, but this wasn't one of them. It crawled under his skin, because between the two of them, he was the addict. Morghan had never missed the chance to taunt him about the various ways he'd sent his mortal body spiraling into ruin, and as far as he knew, she hadn't even started smoking until Lucifer reanimated her.

Michael believed if they knew where she went when she slipped, bringing her back would be easier. Winstin didn't agree. He was sure it would only give both of them a new set of nightmares.

One of the boys fell down and stayed there. Morghan called the fight to a close and walked to the fallen boy. She helped him to his feet before returning to Winstin's side.

The victor headed toward them, a twelve-year-old they'd fished out of a ditch in Malon. "Can we swap sides? The sun is in my eyes over there."

Morghan nodded and gestured toward the other boy.

"But only because he needs to learn to fight with the sun in his eyes."

The boy from Malon smiled. A small red vial hung from the silver chain around his neck, the majority of it hidden beneath a wealth of carefully crafted golden vines. The vines provided protection, while being soft enough for a desperate man to bite straight through. And if they were breaking the vial and dumping Morghan's blood down their throat, they were truly desperate.

Morghan had disappeared not long after Dravyn's body arrived in Salus. During a frantic search, Winstin found her in the basement workshop with several bound men on their knees before her. He'd thought she had lost it again and had nearly gone for Michael. However, as he watched her slice lines along her arms and force-feed the men her blood one drop at a time, he found the action too calculated for madness. It was a sadistic experiment to see how much of her blood was needed to kill a man. The weakest one began convulsing and foaming at the mouth after three drops, the strongest after five. The vial around the boy's neck held ten drops, just to be safe, and every Seiyaku was required to carry at least one. Some, like Brennick, wore so many hidden away on their person Winstin had lost count.

Morghan took a step toward the boy and tucked the vial beneath his shirt.

"Thank you, Windstarr." He ran one of his hands over the contour of the vial before heading back to the practice circle.

Winstin always felt a twinge of sadness when the boys called her Windstarr. Like so many other things that had changed after Dravyn's death, Morghan had forbidden new recruits from addressing her by her first name. And now, with Brennick and Bael aged out and splitting their time between protecting Malon and Bal Mek, the name had vanished from the lips of everyone in Salus but Michael.

"We have three aging out in the next year," Winstin thought out loud. Since she recruited various ages, the list of the thirty Sciyaku training in Salus was a dynamic entity, much like the list of older members who served in other cities. Many of the ruling families believed the Seiyaku in their territories belonged to them, an added benefit of their alliance with Salus. Morghan let them believe it, but no matter their age or location, the Seiyaku bowed to only one person.

"They've already chosen the cities they'll serve in, and they can leave at twenty, like all the others. We won't replace them until after the attack on Falcroix."

Winstin didn't see the logic. "Those cities won't need the added protection. Nikoli will know we're coming weeks, likely months before we make it there. He'll probably stop attacking them to keep his numbers high in Falcroix."

"I don't doubt he has the month we plan to attack circled in red on his calendar, but that man wouldn't know a real threat if it bit him in the ass. He'll be business as usual. Falcroix hasn't missed a quarterly attack on a city since we stopped their flow of tributes over a decade ago. Nikoli is overconfident and predictable; it makes him weak."

"He's confident with good reason," Winstin reminded her. "He could rip the soul from your body and eat it if he wanted."

Morghan cut her eyes to Winstin. "I think he knows better than to try that shit again. I'm a ranking immortal now, and ripping my soul out wasn't listed under 'ways to die' in my ranking immortal user's manual."

"What do you mean again?" Winstin quirked an eyebrow.

He lost all hope of receiving an answer when Morghan screamed at the sparring boys and ran into the practice circle. The boy from Malon was writhing on the ground, and a short steel blade glinted in the hand of the other.

Winstin rolled his eyes and strode toward the boy who was still standing. He ripped the bloody dagger from his hand. "You're going to be in a shit load of trouble if that boy dies."

No sooner had the words left his mouth, than a shot rang through the air, and the boy fell to the ground, a gaping hole between his eyes and a widening pool of blood collecting behind his head.

Winstin whirled around and glared at Morghan. "You almost took off my fucking ear!"

The eyes she turned on him were stormy and wild. She holstered the gun and looked from one dead boy to the other. "I either do something, or I don't. There is no almost."

"Well, if you don't get your shit together, Michael will chain you up again until we figure out something new."

Morghan shrugged. "Don't care."

"You do. Fighting Michael isn't working anymore. We need a different strategy."

Morghan turned to one of the other practice fields and whistled, gesturing for someone to come pick up the bodies. The whistle was unnecessary, since the eyes of every last person in the surrounding fields were trained on them. "It's not like our attempts have lacked variety. I'm open to suggestions."

A group of soldiers picked up what was left of the boys and carted them away. "I stand by what I've said from day one," Winstin said. "You need to get laid."

"And I stand by my original response: fuck, no." She

followed the soldiers at a distance, and her hand clamped down on her katana's hilt.

"You're so on edge, a stiff breeze could annoy you into a murderous rampage. You need to relax, and you're denying yourself one of the most basic ways to do so."

"If Luke or Azrael stroll into Salus, give me a yell. Otherwise, fuck off and mind your own business."

"It's everybody's business when you murder a child in public."

"You won't get an apology for that. He killed a boy two years his junior by cheating during a practice match. I can't risk someone shanking half the Seiyaku in the middle of the night over petty bullshit, so stop trying to guilt trip me into fucking random strangers just because I exacted more justice in half a second than Michael has in the past several decades."

"It's the means, not the end." Winstin wanted to wring her stubborn-ass neck. "Your discretion is nonexistent. And I'm not saying to go out and fuck random people. Pick one, teach him what you like, and fucking pretend he's the person you really want. You act like half the sex in the world doesn't take place while screwing one person and thinking about another."

"This is a non-issue. Michael will agree to fight twice a day, and everything will go back to normal."

Her definition of normal varied greatly from his. "What makes you think Michael will agree? You beat the shit out of him nine times out of ten. If it was me, I would have told you to go straight to hell as soon as you suggested it."

She pulled out a black cigarette and shoved it, unlit, between her lips. "You said it yourself, I murdered a child in broad daylight. The poor bastard cares way too much, and he's running out of options."

Alara sat on the plush linens of her bed, and her gaze swept across the white walls of her prison. There had been a time when she looked forward to being in this room. Her room. It had been the one place none of her foolish minions would disturb her unless she willed it so.

But that was forever ago, and the walls had gleamed onyx back then.

A fly buzzed around Alara's face. She swiped at it, and the chains attached to her shackled wrists slid through the holes in her metal headboard before catching hard. They snapped back through their feeders, forcing Alara onto her back.

The fly continued to the other side of the room, where it taunted her by scurrying around the open window before taking leave of the room.

Alara glared at the ceiling and didn't bother trying to sit again. These days, what freedom she had was earned one slow inch at a time, and any sudden movements brought the chains snapping back to their shortest length. Once, she'd made it halfway to the door, but now her wrists hung at awkward angles against the headboard. The chains would hold their current position for hours before allowing her to earn their trust again.

Between glaring and dozing, she wasn't sure how much time had passed before the lock on her bedroom door clicked out of place and Raphael walked in. He closed the door behind him and gazed out the window.

Over two decades ago, when the daily ritual began, Alara was certain he did it to be cruel. He came into her room with the sole intention of stripping her dignity, yet he couldn't be bothered to acknowledge her existence, instead focusing on the window and the freedom she was so viciously denied. The imagined slight had infuriated her almost as much as the act that followed. Months had passed before she realized Raphael only abandoned his study of the window once her heart rate slowed, and by now she was certain he did it more to give her time to collect herself than anything else.

Raphael's hand rested on the bronze hilt of his sword, his wings held tight to his back.

"You can look at me if you want." Alara's heart had stopped racing in fear years ago. Now, it raced for other reasons. The sad truth of it was Raphael was as much Nikoli's pawn as she, and once she'd come to terms with that, his visits became more a welcome break in the monotony than the torturous experiment they were meant to be.

Raphael turned from the window and approached the side of her bed. The usual sad smile curved his lips, and his green eyes flashed in the torchlight. Unlike most of the other angels, whose eyes were as pale and empty as hers were dark, Raphael's eyes were bright and soulful. Shades of green layered in his irises, producing the illusion of leaves and draping vines. "Do you want to fight today?"

She shook her head and held out her arms as far as the chains allowed.

He bent to remove the shackles but jerked upright when the door swung open.

Phanuel strode into the room, the leg of a screaming, blood-covered infant grasped in one hand. "You haven't even started?"

"I just got here," Raphael lied. His upper lip twisted as he glanced at the child, who was likely minutes from the womb. "What are you doing?"

"Being more productive than you. This is not your only task, and you draw it out more and more each day. I hope, for your sake, you haven't started enjoying it." Phanuel scowled and held up the baby in front of him. "I wanted you to take this down to the monsters, but I guess I'll have to do it myself."

Raphael frowned, and his wings rustled the slightest bit. "You might want to double check. If I'm not mistaken, that one has a penis."

Phanuel's cold blue eyes flared to life. "I know how to do my job. He's changed his mind. Now, he wants twins."

Raphael tucked his clenched fists behind his back. "Of course, he does. I'm sure the twenty-fifth try will bring more luck."

Phanuel moved across the room so fast Alara lost track of him. His free hand balled into a fist and hit Raphael's side hard enough for bone to crunch beneath the skin. Raphael collapsed to one knee. "Control your tongue, or next time it won't be me punishing you. Now get this done, and then meet me on the second tier. Don't make me come in here again."

Phanuel swept out of the room, screaming child in tow, and the door slammed shut behind him.

Raphael pushed to his feet and turned back to the shackles.

"Leave them," Alara insisted. "Hurry, so you don't get in trouble."

Raphael steeled his expression, and the shackles fell away a moment later.

Alara ran a hand through the soft brown curls framing his face. She leaned forward to kiss him, but he pulled away and stood.

"You're right; we don't have a lot of time."

Alara's chest cramped. She'd become accustomed to kissing him, even if it never felt like his heart was truly in the act. She nodded and turned onto her stomach; he liked it better that way.

Raphael stripped off his pants and climbed onto the bed behind her. "If you ever do fall pregnant, I'll steal you away from this place. Your creator is more benevolent than mine. If we make it to Salus, I'm sure he'll give us refuge."

She was certain Michael and Morghan wanted to do many things to her, and none of them involved opening their home as a safe haven. But there was no point worrying over things that would never come to pass. From the beginning, she'd told Raphael's master she was infertile, but he'd insisted on torturing her on the off chance she was incorrect. Or lying. Years later, it was obvious she'd been doing neither. After all, the poor soul down the hall had born twenty-four children in significantly less time, not that they had ended up as anything more than monster fodder.

Raphael pulled her hips backward, before leaning over and offering his wrist. "I hate this, and it's still the best part of my day."

As she opened his vein and drank him in from both ends of her body, she couldn't help but think the same.

Michael's screams crashed through Morghan's head. She pressed one cold hand to her ear and braced herself against the ground with the other. If she sifted through the screams, Winstin's frantic voice was a whisper beneath them. "Stop, Morghan! Stop! For fuck's sake, why do you have your guns?"

Guns? She didn't bring her guns when facing off against

Michael, and with good reason. She never remembered much between passing through the city gates and coming up for air when Winstin called for the fight to end. Bullets, especially the type she carried, had no place being used if she wasn't consciously choosing where to direct them. In return for the kindness of not accidentally blowing his head off, Michael promised not to electrocute the ever-living shit out of her. She always left her guns in her room before heading for the gates with Winstin, just like she had this morning.

Except it wasn't morning, and she hadn't returned to her room before stalking out of Salus to find Michael for their first evening session.

The haze shrouding her thoughts rolled away, and she recognized the cold hand against her ear for what it really was—cold steel.

Michael lay beneath her, his breathing quick and labored, the screams reduced to groans and the occasional whimper. His left hand, slick with blood, lay across the corresponding side of his abdomen.

Morghan jumped to her feet, the blood dripping from her pants adding to the crimson pool expanding behind Michael's back. She brought the gun around and checked it. Black clip—hollow points. Fuck. Granted, it could have been worse. She glanced at the gold clip of the gun still hanging at her side. Way worse.

"We have to turn him over." Morghan spoke to Winstin, who was kneeling at Michael's side. "I need to see his back."

Winstin looked to be at a complete loss. "Last time you shot him, he healed in a matter of minutes. Why is he bleeding so much?"

"Last time, it was a regular bullet through the leg. This was a hollow point through the gut." She knelt across from

Winstin and hovered over Michael. "We're going to turn you, together. Try not to move."

Michael's sweat-drenched face stared up at her. "Did you blow off my legs? Shit, I'm going to have to regenerate the entire lower half of my body."

Morghan looked at his unmoving yet perfectly intact legs. "Your legs are fine." His spinal cord, probably not so much. "I have to see how wide the hole is in your back. These bullets expand as they move through the target." She positioned Winstin's hands on Michael's shoulder and the upper part of his chest. "You take shoulders, I'll take his hips and legs. This is a three-man job, but his neck is fine. On three, roll him toward you.

She counted to three and Michael screamed again as they rolled him. Her breath caught when she saw the gaping hole in his back; she could have fit her entire open hand in it. Nets of leaking vessels were already stretching to join one another, and Michael's exposed organs knit together as if she was watching a time-lapse video.

"Is it bad?" Michael asked.

Morghan pulled her eyes away from the miracle in Michael's abdomen and focused on the more important thing —the havoc that exact process was wreaking on his spine. There was enough of it exposed for her to count up from the sacrum to the last two thoracic vertebrae, which were shattered. Shards of bone stuck out from the exposed spinal cord, clear liquid dripping around it to settle in his open abdomen. To make matters worse, those same shards were weaving together with the new tissue that stretched from the intact vertebrae above and below them. "You'll be fine, but we need to get you back to one of our rooms. The faster the better."

She ordered Winstin to collect the backboard they used

to cart injured soldiers off the practice fields. He was almost out of view when a few other things crossed her mind. "Get a bunch of the grey shit from the bar, too. And Dex. Bring Dex."

"It's called Grau," Michael mumbled. "Like the color, but in German. Only damn thing I remember from those stupid classes is colors."

She knew what it was called, but "grey shit" was a lot more fun to say. Morghan put a hand on Michael's side when he started to move. "Don't. I know it hurts, but right now there's only one thing not healing well. Let everything else finish, and then I'll see what I can do about your spine." She pulled a black cigarette out of her pocket and tucked it between his lips. "Try this."

Michael took the cigarette from his mouth and held it out to her as she struck a match. "You know I don't smoke. Especially not these minty-ass ones you make."

She lit it and took a draw before shoving it back into his mouth and pinching his nose shut. Michael breathed in quickly through his mouth and coughed out a cloud of smoke.

"The peppermint is to make it smell better to some people and worse to others. Trust me, it will help with the pain."

"The pain was already getting better," he insisted, but he took another drag on the cigarette all the same. "I still can't feel my legs though."

"Lucky for you, most of what's on the inside doesn't have nerves, but like I said, your back is fucked up. Don't worry, I'll fix it." By cutting through layers of healed muscle and breaking it again, but he didn't need to know that right now. "It's going to be a long night, so smoke up, and when

Winstin gets back with the liquor, just drink that shit like water."

Morghan worried the wait for Winstin would stretch on forever, but eventually he came back and they moved Michael to his quarters.

Morghan popped the stopper on Michael's second bottle of Grau and pushed it into his hand as Winstin rolled him onto his side.

Dex's daughter, Redra, barreled into the room, a full tool belt wrapped around her waist, and a large satchel slung over her shoulder. She held out a pair of magnifying specs in one hand while leaning over to catch her breath. Apparently, Dex was getting a little too old for late night wake-up calls.

Morghan walked to the other side of the bed and grabbed the glasses, deciding to save that depressing thought for another time. She dropped into a chair beside Michael's bed and sighed at the flawless skin covering his back. Such a waste. The laceration repair kit she used for Winstin was lain out on a table beside her.

She situated the glasses on her face and pressed the buttons on the arms. A single magnifying lens flipped around for each time she pressed a button. "These things will never stop being fun." She pressed a separate button, and the magnifiers swung back to their respective homes against the arms. They would be useful later. Her gaze shifted to Winstin. "Hold him down."

"Who, me?" Michael wondered an instant before she sliced into his flesh, and his screams exploded through the room.

"Yes, you." She held her hand out, and Redra turned over a tanning tool they often used for stretching hides. Morghan inserted the apparatus and twisted a handle at the center, causing it to expand until the thin opening in Michael's back stretched to expose the muscles over his spine.

Michael sobbed as she pared away the muscles and ligaments. The two shattered vertebrae had healed into a rounded mass of bone. She handed Winstin another black cigarette and tipped her hand up to her mouth so he would make Michael drink more.

Morghan plucked a chisel and ball peen hammer from Redra's belt. She turned back to Michael and counted to thirty, hoping it allowed enough time for the painkillers to dull his senses without missing the short window during which they'd be active. "Hold him, both of you."

Michael bucked as she cracked the malformed bone and fished the fragments out until his spinal cord was lain bare beneath it. She reached toward her glasses, but the blood dripping from her hands gave her pause. Instead, she stood and leaned over Michael's body toward Redra. "Give me five lenses on both sides."

Once they were in place, she grabbed a pair of forceps and went to work digging the original fragmented vertebrae out of his spinal cord. A few pieces were the size of a fingertip, but the miniscule, needle-thin splinters of metal and bone were the most time-consuming. Dawn was fast approaching, and they'd gone through fifteen bottles of Grau and Morghan's entire stock of minty-ass cigarettes before she was satisfied enough to let the cord heal on its own. She aligned the vertebrae above and below the healing cord as well as she could and secured them with two metal plates and a handful of screws Dex's youngest son had forged for them during the night.

The bone filled the gap, but it healed much more slowly than the previous time. Morghan removed the makeshift retractor, and Michael's spine disappeared behind a wall of skin and muscle as it mended several times faster than the bone below it.

Morghan's stiff muscles protested when she stood, and she stumbled backward before catching her balance. "I don't want him rolled or moved in any way until this time tomorrow."

She walked to the other side of the bed and crouched in front of Michael, who was barely conscious. His mouth moved, but nothing coherent emerged.

Morghan assessed him over the top of her specs. His screams echoed in the back of her mind; they probably would for a while. She reached out to touch his face, but her bloody hands stopped her yet again. "Get some rest."

Michael grabbed her wrist when she tried to stand. "No more night fights, okay?"

Morghan bent close to his ear and placed a light kiss at his temple. "No more fights. Period. I promise."

She stood and handed the specs back to Redra. "Thanks for your help. I'll drop by and see your father later today."

Winstin cleared his throat when Redra took her leave. "And me?"

"Stay with Michael. I made up half of that shit as I went, and from my brief experiences with orthopedics, I didn't curse enough by half to expect a good outcome. If he can't feel his legs when he wakes, come find me. I'm going to clean up." And hopefully remain sane once the reality of the situation set in. She didn't say that part, but she may as well have given the concern on Winstin's face.

"Be careful." He pointed to Michael. "Right now there's no one to stop you."

"I'll stop me." Morghan's coat was already on the ground, discarded hours earlier along with her sword and guns. She unlatched her belt and her daggers clanged against one another as they hit the ground as well.

"I'm serious. We both know you don't need weapons."

"It will slow me down, if nothing else. Besides, there's only so much I can take off. Don't worry. After I take a shower, I'll just get drunk enough to pass out." Or drunk enough to give Winstin's earlier suggestion a try.

Morghan left Michael's room and hurried to hers, shutting the door against the prying eyes of those she passed in the halls. Seeing as every inch of her was caked or dripping with blood, she couldn't blame them. She entered the bathroom and stepped into the shower fully clothed. Her shoulders hunched forward, and she rested her head against the wall as Michael's blood swirled down the drain. The water turned cold before it ran clear, so she stripped to make sure at least her skin and hair were clean. A fresh set of clothes later, she was back in the hall, headed for the tavern.

"General!" An all too familiar voice assaulted her as she entered the tavern.

"Go away, Xayne." She concentrated on the bar across the room and didn't bother looking at him.

He kept talking, and when she took a seat at the bar, he sat beside her.

Her first instinct was to grab his neck and snap it. Instead, she pushed his useless chatter to the back of her mind and placed a fair amount of effort into ignoring the drone. Winstin would have been proud, or at the very least, relieved.

Morghan ordered a bottle of Grau and waited while Raegan, the current owner of the tavern, and if push ever came to shove the ruler of Salus as a whole, disappeared into the storeroom. She hoped to God Michael hadn't finished off the Grau.

Several minutes passed before he returned and set three bottles in front of her. Raelyn had been in the ground more than a few years now, and his son had gone before him. While Raegan was nowhere near as efficient as his predecessors, what he lacked in speed he made up in forethought and creativity.

Morghan opened the first bottle and drank it down so fast she nearly fell off her seat. She opened the second bottle and tossed the stopper across the bar. It bounced off the far wall and landed in the trashcan. She raised her hands in the air and gave a silent cheer.

In the corner of her vision, she noticed Xayne staring at her as if she had lost her mind. Maybe he was more intuitive than she gave him credit for.

"You." She took a swig from the second bottle and pointed at him with the hand holding it. "Go the fuck away. You're ruining my moment."

He glanced from the empty bottle on the bar to the one in her hand. "How are you still conscious after drinking so much so fast?"

"You don't know when to shut up. Has anyone ever told you that?"

"Yes." He frowned. "You."

She nodded and took a small sip. Unless she wanted to end up outside puking instead of slipping gracelessly into a coma, she needed to slow down a little. "I give good advice. Occasionally I even take it." She shooed him away with her free hand. "Now leave before you end up with more trouble than you can handle."

"I can handle plenty, but you won't give me a chance."

She turned to face him, and his features were softened enough by the liquor to make her do a double-take. He was way shorter than Luke, but with a little help from the third bottle, she could probably ignore the difference. She looked at the bottle in her hand and sighed. She couldn't pretend passing out drunk was a real answer to her problem. What was she going to do, sleep through the next seven months until she could go ballistic on things in Falcroix? Besides, if Michael woke up and needed more work, she should at the very least be conscious. "How old are you?"

His brow furrowed. "I know, I'm too old—"

"Just answer the damn question." This asshole would be the end of her. She looked around the tavern; there had to be someone else. The problem was, everyone else probably knew better, and at least Xayne was nice to look at.

"Twenty-three."

Morghan finished the second bottle and set it down hard on the bar. "Listen, I'm never going to give you what you want, but how do you feel about sex?"

A glass shattered behind the bar, and Morghan turned around so fast her head spun. Raegan dropped to his knees and made a valiant attempt at pretending to mind his own business as he cleaned the floor. Once her brain stopped bouncing around inside her skull, she turned back to Xayne, who had paled from the color of a sheet to nearly transparent. "Well?"

"I like it?"

Morghan was a second away from slamming her forehead into the bar. She was awkward enough with this shit, but it was going to be painful if he was just as bad. "You have had sex before, right?"

The color rushed back into his face. "Of course."

Her next thought was to ask for a list of his partners along with how many of them had been paid for. Aside from being ludicrous, it would have no doubt convinced her to run back to her room and scream into a pillow, instead of going through with anything productive. "So, you interested?"

He nodded, his mouth hanging open the slightest bit. Morghan put a finger under his chin and closed it.

The third bottle of Grau slid across the bar and pressed against her shoulder. Raegan was holding it, and he gestured to the bottle, on which the words "Him? Really?" were scrawled in charcoal pencil.

Morghan smiled so wide she was sure her face would crack. She grabbed the bottle and was about to wipe it clean when something brushed against her thigh and stayed there. Her muscles tensed, and her hand flew to her hip. She cursed under her breath when it came up against her pants and nothing more.

Her eyes shifted to where Xayne's hand lay atop her leg. The excitement in his eyes died when she slapped it away. "Don't touch me in public, or I'll rip your heart out and shove it down your throat."

Xayne's heart rate skyrocketed, and Morghan was more than a little relieved she'd scared him. Regret was already tugging at her, and she hadn't even done anything yet. If he ran off, it would be better for everyone—except whoever was on the receiving end of her anger next time.

Xayne cleared his throat, his hands fidgeting in his lap. "When can we go to your room?"

Morghan stopped with the bottle halfway to her mouth. She could smell the fear on him, but either his excitement or lack of common sense was overriding it. She stepped off her seat, taking the bottle with her and trying to ignore how much his fear aroused her. "You're never going to my room. You have a room at the inn."

It wasn't a question. She made a wide gesture toward the stairs with her arm.

"The bed is barely wide enough for one person," he protested.

She grabbed the front of his shirt with her free hand and dragged him down from the stool, heading toward the stairs with him in tow. "I'm interested in fucking, not sleeping. The room is mandatory. The bed is not."

21

SOME SLIPS ARE HARDER THAN OTHERS

MICHAEL PURSED his lips at the three cards in his hand. Complete shit, as usual. He glanced around the table, but between Winstin, Ilena, and Raegan, he couldn't spot a single tell. Morghan sat across from him, her heel tapping against the floor so fast the rest of her body vibrated along with it. Still, it wasn't a tell—not to do with cards at least.

He shifted in his seat and winced as pain shot down his leg, a constant reminder of why it was so important Morghan had traded her aggression for anxious melancholy. Michael wasn't sure what Morghan had done to his back, but when he woke the next day he could walk. That should have been miracle enough, but along with having feeling and strength in his legs again, he also gained shooting pains along the back of his thighs and a constant, dull throb in his lower back. He'd hoped the pain would work itself out, but in the four months since the incident, nothing had changed.

Michael threw a few coppers into the middle of the table and Winstin did the same. Ilena tossed in a few extras, which earned a groan from Raegan. He folded and pushed his cards to the center of the table before his time to bet came around. Morghan threw a run-of-the-mill cigarette onto the pile, but Ilena picked it out and insisted she exchange it for a black one. Instead of agreeing, Morghan swiped the cigarette from Ilena and folded.

Winstin threw the extra coins into the center of the table and set down his cards. "Can't say I'm disappointed. I don't put anything on fire in direct contact with my body anyway." He draped an arm around Ilena's shoulders and leaned in for a kiss.

Ilena hid her cards and pushed her palm against his face. "Stop trying to cheat. It won't help you anyway."

Winstin feigned offense as Raegan passed out a fourth card. Ilena eventually gave in and kissed him.

Michael smiled and relaxed in his chair. It was nice to have some time to unwind. If he concentrated enough on the banter between Winstin and Ilena, he could almost forget several of their allies had already started the slow march to war. Being one of the closer cities gave them the luxury of mobilizing later than most.

His gaze slid back to Morghan, and his good mood bled out. "Morghan, are you okay?"

She crossed her arms over her chest and glared down at nothing in particular. "I'm fine."

The glances exchanged around the table didn't agree.

Winstin cleared his throat. "You can always run upstairs if you need to. I haven't seen Xayne leave since you came down."

Morghan pulled her coat tighter despite the sweltering heat blasting through the tavern doors each time someone opened them. "I said, I'm fine. Besides, he's recovering from earlier."

Michael folded his cards and leaned over the table. "He's a young guy in his prime. I'm sure he's capable of going more than once a day."

Morghan stood and jammed a finger into the table. "It would be great if people could mind their own damn business. I'm not a threat to society anymore. Can't you all leave me the fuck alone?" She stalked a few paces toward the hall before turning around and heading for the stairs.

Michael watched her stomp up them and hung his head. "I don't understand her. The anger I got, but this is depressing."

"For you or her?" Winstin folded his hand.

"Both, I guess. I don't know what this is or how to fix it. I'd rather her go back to the aggression and shoot me once in a while. Preferably with normal bullets."

Ilena raked in her winnings. "I'm well acquainted with the many faces of shame, and she's worn most of them over the past few months. If I didn't know better, I'd think the woman employed instead of choosing a lover."

Winstin slouched in his seat. "It's not like she wants to fuck him. She's doing it so none of us ends up with a bullet or blade where it doesn't belong, but I didn't think it would be like this."

Ilena separated her winnings into two piles and slid one in front of Winstin. "It's no different than the women who pledge their bodies to me in order to feed their children. Of course, since the act lends itself to creating extra mouths to feed, they rarely leave. If she's fluctuating between anxiety and shame, each breeds the other. Some cycles are hard to break."

Winstin pocketed the coins and gave Ilena a quick kiss on the cheek. "This conversation needs more alcohol. I'll be back."

Michael took the deck from Raegan and shuffled the cards as Winstin left for the bar. There had to be another way. Hopefully reuniting with her sword would help, but between the depressed moods and her drinking until she was sick most days, he wasn't sure he could let it go for another few months.

As Michael thought through his options, the chair across from him scraped against the floor. He guessed Morghan had changed her mind.

"Well, hello there," Ilena purred.

Michael's eyes shot up. Winstin wasn't back yet, and Ilena's greeting was in no way meant for Morghan. His brow knit together when he spotted the man sitting in Morghan's chair. His features were close enough to Xayne's they could have been related. Maybe he'd come to reclaim his brother.

Ilena leaned over and whispered something in the man's ear.

His eyes widened, and he jerked away from her. "No. Just no."

Ilena shrugged and sat back in her chair. "Your loss."

The man didn't look like he'd lost anything.

Michael set the cards on the table. "Can I help you?"

"Not at all." He draped one leg over the other and stared past the table.

Michael turned around, but there was nothing behind him aside from the stairs on the other side of the tavern. He faced the man again. "There are other places to sit."

"Deal the cards, Michael. This chair still smells like Morghan, and I'm not moving until she comes down those stairs."

Michael's hand drifted to the hilt of his sword. "Who are you, and what do you want with Morghan?"

The man shook his head and lifted his sword by the sheath until the golden hilt peeked over the table.

Another ranking immortal.

The man opened his mouth to speak, but he was interrupted by Winstin, who walked up to the table and promptly began choking on his drink. He dropped into his chair, and his mouth hung open. "Lucifer?"

"As in the devil?" Michael's eyes widened. The devil being a ranking immortal made an odd sort of sense.

Lucifer glared at him. "No."

Winstin sucked some of the ale from his shirt before abandoning the task and taking another drink. "Well, you do live in an odd sort of hell."

"I'm confused," Michael mumbled.

Lucifer nodded. "Trust me, we all know."

Winstin choked on his drink again. He gave Ilena a cryptic look, and the woman disappeared from the table, pulling Raegan along with her. Once they'd gone, he turned back to Lucifer. "Why are you here? I can't imagine what unpleasant circumstances would warrant a visit."

"Don't worry. It's not all bad."

Winstin braced himself over the table. "Really? You let Morghan rot in Falcroix for years and sat idly by as Nikoli tortured and killed her adopted son. What makes you think I'll believe you strolled into Salus and risked Nikoli's rage for something that's 'not all bad?'"

Lucifer's eyes flashed red. "Shut up, Patches, or I won't fix you before I leave. I shouldn't fix you anyway, as this is all your fault."

Michael was having a difficult time following the conversation, but that got his attention. "You can heal the dead?"

Winstin sat back and took another drink. "Sure. Lucifer here is a grade A necromancer. Pretty much the only thing he's better at than your father."

"I'm not a necromancer," Lucifer seethed. He raised his hands palm up, and a flame sparked to life atop each one. "Besides, I'm better than Nikoli at a few things."

Michael was impressed.

Winstin, not so much. "I know there aren't dictionaries anymore, but you are, by definition, a fucking necromancer."

"Can you raise the dead?" Michael wondered.

"No." Lucifer paused. "Well, yes, but only if a soul is nearby."

Winstin finished his drink, and the glass clanked against the table. "He raised me. He raised Morghan. He can build a body and reanimate it with a soul, but he can't create a soul or give life. Only your father can do that." Winstin thought for a moment. "And I guess you."

Michael shook his head. "I have no idea how to reproduce what I did. It was an accident, much like everything else I've created since. I don't even know what a soul looks like."

Lucifer tilted his head. "You can't see them?"

"No, can you?"

"Of course," he answered, as if it was the most natural thing in the world. He tapped a finger over his heart. "Yours is here." He looked at Winstin and smirked. "His is significantly lower."

"Ass." Winstin chuckled. "So, where's the other half of hell?"

"Brooding back home. It's too risky for both of us to be here. Given the circumstances, I was the safer choice."

"You're never the safe choice. No one believes Nikoli would kill Azrael. You, on the other hand?" Winstin pointed at the ground. "Six feet under with glee. Especially now you and Azrael are, you know, romantically entangled. Or whatever the two of you are calling it."

"Definitely not that." Lucifer glanced past Michael again, and he sat up straight in his chair. His brown eyes disappeared behind a bright, swirling red. He stood and took a deep breath. "I'd say we'll finish this conversation later, but you're already drowning in enough lies." He clapped a hand on Michael's shoulder as he passed. "I owe you, but don't worry. I'll pay up soon."

Michael turned around as Lucifer walked to where Morghan stood at the foot of the stairs. "She looks terrified. Should we do something?"

"The best thing would be to stop staring at them." Winstin turned his chair so he had a direct view of the stairs. "But where's the fun in that?"

Lucifer made it to Morghan, but she barely acknowledged him, continuing her study of the ground. She shied away when he placed a hand on her shoulder.

Michael stood and took a step toward the stairs, but Winstin grabbed his arm. "Sit. Give them a chance to work through this. She's his hybrid."

Michael stopped moving forward, but he didn't sit. "They're life mates? But I thought you two were talking about him being together with someone else?"

"Don't break your brain on that one. It's literally the love triangle from hell."

Michael sat down hard in his chair and glanced at Winstin. "Still, he's sleeping with someone else. He shouldn't be angry with her for doing the same."

"I'm hoping he's not. If he does anything but—" A grin spread across Winstin's face. "There we go. Now, we can stop watching."

Morghan and Lucifer were locked in one another's arms, kissing as if they were the only people in the room. She pulled herself up against his neck and wrapped her legs around his waist, but Lucifer held his balance without moving a step.

Most of the tavern was staring at them, but neither seemed to care. Lucifer pulled away from Morghan's lips and laughed before pressing his mouth close to her ear. Morghan nodded and slid down him until her feet hit the floor. She took his hand and led him back in Michael and Winstin's direction.

A spear of jealousy ripped through Michael as they walked past. Whatever was going on between Morghan and Lucifer, there was love in it. He wanted that, the kind of love that could watch one party rip it apart at the seams while the other patiently waited to mend it.

Winstin gave Michael a light punch on the shoulder. "I haven't seen her smile like that in ages."

Michael watched until they disappeared from view. "I've never seen her smile like that."

Morghan didn't even care that Winstin had used the bed before them. Whatever remnants of his scent lingered had been ghosted away by the feel of Luke's skin against hers. She sighed into his chest and closed her eyes. Being close to him was like having her own personal space heater, and she'd been cold for so long.

"Morghan?"

She grumbled and pressed her face into the side of his chest. Opening her eyes was the last thing she wanted. For the first time in years she was at peace, like she'd reached down to grasp the hilt of her sword and it was right where it was supposed to be. She wanted to sleep, and if she opened her eyes only to find this was a cruel dream, it would be weeks before she'd get any rest.

"Morghan, look at me. Are you hurt?"

"Why would I be hurt?" She opened her eyes. They were in her bed, and it was still Luke. The real one, not the pretend one she'd fashioned from Xayne and an ocean of alcohol. Thinking about Xayne made her heart race and her throat close, as if the very thought of the betrayal might chase Luke away. Morghan sat up and struggled to breathe. She leaned over the edge of the bed and grabbed her coat, rifling through the pockets until she found a black cigarette.

Luke touched her shoulder, and her body tensed. He wrapped an arm around her, pinning both arms to her sides as he pulled her upright. She wanted to believe she wouldn't have punched him without the restraint, but it probably wasn't true. He whispered against her ear, and though she only grasped every few words, it comforted her all the same.

"You can let me go," she assured him once the room came back into focus. When his arm loosened, she fell back onto the bed and frowned at the ceiling. "Sorry."

"You don't have to apologize. It's my fault you're broken."

Broken was a good word for her, but it wasn't Luke's fault. "Don't blame yourself for all the poor choices I've made over the last century."

"I let you suffer. I should have brought you home instead of leaving you in Falcroix. The three of us could have made a stand against Nikoli then, for better or for worse."

"It would have been for worse." She held up the cigarette. "Can you light this?"

Luke pulled her closer. "No. I want you to stop smoking."

"Really? We're going to have this argument now? I know you hate it when I smoke, but at least it's appropriate timing." She gestured to the bed.

"Please. For me? You've been smoking and drinking way too much. You need to take better care of yourself."

Morghan's temper flared. "I'm immortal, goddamn it. I can smoke and drink as much as I want and it's not going to do shit to me. It's not like I'm..."

Morghan sat up and leaned against the headboard of the bed. Her vision blurred as she waited too long to blink while trying to convince herself she was wrong. Luke was worried he might have hurt her during sex. They hadn't seen one another in close to a century, and she'd gone half mad in the meantime. Yet he was pressing her on something as petty as her smoking and drinking habits. "When you look at me, how many souls do you see?"

Luke turned his eyes away. "It's hard to tell with you. Your soul moves around and changes color sometimes."

Talk about a non-answer. She threw the cigarette on the ground and glared at Luke. "Why did you come here? You said it yourself—you left me in Falcroix for years. I'm sure you watched Dravyn die, and you no doubt saw me being driven to the breaking point.

"Today I was miserable, but I've been miserable. There

was nothing so earth-shatteringly awful that you, of all people, should risk coming to this realm."

Luke hunched forward. "I don't want you to go to Falcroix."

"You haven't answered my question. I don't want to go to Falcroix either, but we can't afford to let Nikoli continue raising an army of immortals until the realm is overrun. It's taken two decades to gather enough men to have any hope of putting a dent in his numbers. Many of the nephilims have surely come of age already. The longer we wait, the more he'll have."

Luke took her hand. "Just postpone the battle a year or two. It won't make a difference in the grand scheme of things, but it will for you."

"There is no postponing. Half the armies are already on the move. We're going to Falcroix. I'm going to Falcroix."

Luke ran his free hand through her hair, and his eyes glistened. "Two."

"Two what?" He'd come this far, risked all their lives. The least he could do was say the words.

"Two souls, Morghan. When I look at you, I see two souls. That's why I'm here. We wanted to warn you. Stay as far away from Nikoli as possible. The baby may not be ours, but Nikoli's rules are never clear cut."

Morghan thought about ripping her hand from his, but she couldn't bring herself to do it. "Didn't you and Azrael already destroy about a hundred rules by getting back together? Maybe this one has become irrelevant."

"Nikoli loves pinning responsibility on others. You know that. He would rip the child from your womb while convincing you he had no choice. Rules are rules."

She looked down at her flat stomach. "How far along am I?"

"I've never had a reason to know at what point a soul appears, but it's been there for several weeks. At least two months. Winstin might know more about timing, but I doubt his job involved watching conception."

Morghan ran a hand over her face. "So what you're saying is I'm bound to be six or seven months pregnant by the time we reach Falcroix? This is fucking ridiculous, Luke. I wanted a child with you for as long as we lived together, even after Nikoli's stupid ass rules and you confessing you might be infertile. Hundreds of years and nothing. I sleep with some dumbass and get knocked up in the first few weeks. And you know the worst part? If Michael's theory is right, I'm only pregnant because I was thinking of you while I fucked the bastard. And of course, my goddamn enemy would find out before me."

Luke shrugged. "I'm not sure Nikoli knows. Nothing has changed in the past couple months to suggest he does."

Morghan froze. "What do you mean you're not sure? Luke, we just slept together."

"I remember, and maybe if you're not too pissed off at me by the end of this conversation, we can do it again."

She pushed away from him and stood, pacing a short line along the side of the bed. She never thought she'd be hoping for attention from Nikoli. At least then, he'd know the child wasn't Luke's. "Azrael didn't give you strict instructions not to sleep with me?"

Luke moved to the side of the bed closest to her. "No. Azrael never tells me anything."

Morghan glared at him. "That's bullshit."

Luke rolled his eyes. "He does, but you know him. He answers one question, and I end up with five more. I was concerned about the same thing as you. For once, I was the one worried it was a bad time to risk the trip, but he told me to come anyway. When I asked about sex, he did everything short of demanding I sleep with you."

Morghan stopped pacing and sat on the edge of the bed next to Luke. "That's bad. Worse than bad. Did he tell you what he saw?"

"He can't always tell the difference between what little precognitive talent he has and nightmare logic."

She slumped forward and threaded her fingers through Luke's. "He wouldn't tell you what it was."

"No, but I agree it can't be good. He's on the verge of losing his shit every time I mention Falcroix." Luke laid his free hand over her womb. "But he didn't see this coming. I'm using it to convince myself that whatever else he saw was only a bad dream blown out of proportion."

"Maybe we shouldn't have slept together."

"What's done is done, and I'm not sorry about it." He moved his hand to her cheek and leaned in for a kiss.

Morghan backed away and smiled. "Neither am I."

Luke pressed his forehead to hers. "I shouldn't stay long. You have Michael and Winstin, but Azrael is alone. He's already a wreck. I can't abandon him."

When Luke had shown up alone, she'd never entertained the idea it was permanent, but her heart sank at hearing the truth of it. "Can I keep you a few more hours?"

He mumbled an agreement as she nipped his ear with her teeth.

"I'm still going to Falcroix," she whispered.

"Then so are we."

Krishna stood before the ornate double doors leading to Alara's prison. Dragging her to the throne room where

Nikoli awaited them would no doubt lead to death and destruction; he only hoped it wasn't theirs.

Neither he nor any of the Host had been alive when Lucifer was stripped of his original form, but everyone knew it had been an accident. Just like when Nikoli created the expansive void in Lucifer's realm.

The thought of Nikoli channeling so much negative energy on purpose was terrifying. There was no precedent for it, and as much faith as Krishna had in Nikoli, he doubted much thought had been put into how much power would rise, not to mention where any excess might go. If it went anywhere at all.

The last thing Nikoli needed was a new internal demon to fight; he had plenty of those already. Nikoli had always been particular and quick to anger, but since moving realms he'd gained a twisted cruelty the likes of which Krishna had never seen.

At first, Krishna thought the move a blessing. Nikoli hadn't shown him so much attention in ages, but it didn't take long to realize the added attention was tied to Nikoli's anxiety and increasing obsession with scheming and vengeance. Nikoli had been his refuge since he was a boy, but now that Nikoli needed him to return the favor, he was unable to quell the storm.

If he'd been enough for Nikoli, they never would have come to this realm in the first place, and maybe it wouldn't feel like they'd started a slow march to the end. Krishna pushed Alara's doors open and prayed this latest act of insanity wouldn't send them sprinting toward it.

Krishna was so wrapped up in his thoughts, it took a moment to process the scene before him. Alara lay draped across Raphael's lap, her open shackles hanging against the headboard.

Raphael pushed Alara off him and hopped down from the bed. "It's not what it looks like."

It was exactly what it looked like. An array of punishments fluttered through Krishna's mind, but if Raphael was at all attached to the woman, he could think of nothing worse than what her future held. "Get dressed and meet me outside. Both of you."

Raphael and Alara looked at each other and then back to Krishna, but he didn't bother giving an explanation before walking out of the room and closing the doors behind him.

Not long after, Alara walked into the hallway, her wrists bound with a short length of the chain from her bed. Raphael emerged behind her, guiding her by the shoulder.

Krishna quirked an eyebrow. "Are we pretending she's your prisoner now?"

Raphael's wings twitched. "She is my prisoner."

"How long have you been removing her shackles?" Krishna's hand drifted to his sword when Raphael only glared in response. "You can tell me, or you can tell your master."

Raphael's wings stilled as fear replaced the anger in his eyes, but he didn't say a word.

"Over a decade," Alara spoke up for him. She hissed and bared her fangs when Raphael's grip on her shoulder tightened. "What? If he takes us to your master, they'll know anyway. He can read minds."

Krishna grabbed Alara's free shoulder and tore her from Raphael's grasp. "Don't be mistaken, he's already waiting for you."

"Give her back!"

Krishna glanced at the angel, whose hand grasped the hilt of his sword. "How attached are you to your wings,

Raphael? At this moment, you've done little worth reporting. Think hard before you draw your sword."

Alara shook her head at Raphael. "Let it go."

Raphael dropped the hand from his sword and trudged along to the throne room without another word.

Krishna's heart raced as they crossed the threshold, and Nikoli turned to face them. He stood at the bottom of the dais with Phanuel, wearing nothing but a pair of linen pants. Every Hellion in their employ gathered against the wall to the right, while the left side of the room was packed with mortal women from the lower tier prisons. An image of Azrael walking alone through Eden shimmered on the wall above the Hellions, while Lucifer and his woman lay in bed above the cowering mortals.

Nikoli beckoned Krishna with a wave of his hand. "Lucifer will only be preoccupied for so long. Put her on the throne so we can begin."

Krishna hauled Alara to the throne and forced her into it. He and Phanuel layered chains around her body until most of her skin disappeared beneath them.

She made a halfhearted attempt to escape before going still. "Is this supposed to be ironic?"

Nikoli mounted the steps and pulled on the chains. "Only if you want it to be."

Nikoli beckoned Phanuel, who handed him the ivory-hilted sword that had hung above his bed since their move to the realm. Nikoli lodged it between the chains at Alara's back, the hilt standing out at an angle above one of her shoulders. He stepped back and turned to Krishna. "You should leave."

"But, Master—"

Nikoli cut him off with a disapproving frown. He laid a

hand against the side of Krishna's face before leaning in to kiss him. "I can make this quick."

"Please, don't do this." It wasn't his place to request anything of Nikoli, but he couldn't stand leaving him to drown in a room of living nightmares. Krishna closed his eyes and waited for Nikoli to strike him, surprised when the blow never came. He opened his eyes again when something jostled against his side, and the overwhelming smell of rotting corpses choked his senses. The Hellions crowded around them, and Nikoli's hand clamped down hard on Krishna's shoulder.

"Go." Nikoli's eyes pulsed with light, their brilliant blue irises swallowing his pupils. Tears slipped down his cheeks, frost glittering along their paths until they froze against his skin. "Now!"

Nikoli slammed the palm of one hand into Krishna's chest, but Krishna grabbed his forearm, and instead of hurtling through the air, Nikoli fell forward with him. Nikoli's wings burst from his back, and Krishna braced for the impact of Nikoli crushing him against the stone floor.

But the sensation never came.

Krishna opened his eyes to a cold, grey sky, and as he dragged himself to his feet, the muddy ground wavered, rippling as if he'd disturbed still waters. He turned around slowly, taking stock of his surroundings. Dozens of angels slogged through the mud, their shackles jangling as they dragged stones and various pieces equipment across the bleak expanse of land to his left. But Krishna had never seen these angels, nor did he recognize the humans walking free alongside them. The laboring angels cowered from the crack of their master's whips, shifting away wings in various states of disrepair.

If there was one thing Krishna knew all too well, it was

slave labor, but why would Nikoli send him here? Wherever here was.

Krishna's gaze was drawn to a lanky figure slinking along the chain-link fence to his right. The man was filthy, from the fraying bandages wrapped around his otherwise bare chest to the dirt caked beneath his jagged nails.

He didn't have wings, but the gnarled knots beneath the bandages on his back led Krishna to believe he had at one time. Still, the lack of wings made him inconspicuous enough to be overlooked by his captors, at least for the short distance he stalked along the edge of his cage.

Krishna followed him at a distance until he realized the man's goal. A woman walked on the other side of the fence. She was dressed in a long silver gown set off with thin, swirling accents of gold thread. A handmaiden traveled at her side, holding a parasol to block the nonexistent sunlight. The regal woman pointed at a large piece of parchment a man beside her was holding, before shooing him away and continuing her walk.

The wingless slave picked up his pace until he was even with the woman.

"Marette." The man's voice was a harsh rasp, but it was familiar.

"Master?" The word caught in Krishna's throat. He moved until he had a clearer view of the man's face, and sure enough it, was no different than the youthful version of Nikoli he'd seen the day they left for Falcroix.

Krishna's stomach turned. He wasn't sure what was more upsetting, Nikoli's clipped wings or his disheveled state. He would have never guessed Nikoli came from such beginnings, and as much as he mourned for the younger version of his master, it made Krishna feel somehow closer to him. This was a past they shared. A kinship. Though he doubted Nikoli would ever allow a discussion about it.

"Marette!" Nikoli dared to raise his voice. He cleared his throat and stood up, walking closer to the gate as the woman turned toward him.

"Niko? What a surprise!" She raised the back of her hand to her nose, likely to block the stench of sex and sweat radiating from Nikoli, though Krishna found the sharp scent of peppermint wafting from her side of the gate infinitely more offensive. "You're looking well. The life of a laborer suits you."

Nikoli's features drew downward, and shame passed over his face as a shadow. "Sasha hasn't come yet. It's been weeks."

"You boys and your childish nicknames," the woman scoffed, though the tremble in her top lip gave away the hint of a deeper emotion. "Felix isn't coming for you. He has more important things to do than fret over a broken pet."

"Please," Nikoli pleaded, and the pain in his voice, in his expression, made Krishna's chest cramp. "You have no idea what they do to me here."

"The Keepers know their boundaries. They won't punish you unless it's deserved. Do you deserve it, Niko?"

Nikoli's muscles tensed, and the bandages stretched across the short, bloody stumps protruding from his back. Krishna wondered if he missed his wings, and even more he wondered how his master had gotten them back. "It's the other angels. They give me no rest."

Marette waved a hand in dismissal. "So you've tired of your angelic lovers and wish to crawl back to Felix's bed? I won't allow you to put such a pressure on him, just as I wouldn't allow you to ruin his life with your foolish idea of running away together."

"No, they're not my lovers. They—Wait." Nikoli brought his face up from the ground, and his eyes widened. "It was you who betrayed us."

Marette stabbed an accusatory finger in his direction. "I betrayed no one. Felix is married to his kingdom as much as he is to me. I saved him from your demonic wiles. So many of us fell prey to them, but bestiality is as sure a sin as murder."

Krishna stepped through the fence and wrapped his hands around the woman's throat. As expected, his fingers slid right through her, but it was worth a try. He turned back to Nikoli, who had wrapped his fingers around the metal wires of his prison, but the fence was so much more than metal. His body arched as electricity snapped across the wires, and Krishna wasn't sure if Nikoli meant to hold on or was simply unable to let go.

Marette backed away from the fence and screamed for the guards.

Krishna moved through the fence again as thick, barbed hooks buried in Nikoli's shoulders and dragged him away from the fence. It took four Keepers to subdue him. After administering a sound beating, one held each arm as they dragged him to a large wooden block at the center of the camp.

Krishna turned back to find Marette's green eyes smiling from the other side of the gate. He had never hated anyone more.

The Keepers smashed Nikoli's face into the wooden block and blood gushed from behind his lips.

"String him up." Marette's voice was so close. She had deigned to cross into the camp and stood before Nikoli, surrounded by a small army of Keepers. "I haven't all day."

A rush of polite responses followed, and Nikoli's

captors wrenched his arms so far above his head it shouldn't have been possible. One of the Keepers stepped to the side and unraveled a massive whip from around his waist while another ripped off Nikoli's threadbare pants, leaving him completely exposed aside from the sparse bandages layered over the ragged stumps of his wings.

Leather snapped and Krishna flinched as a line of red blossomed across Nikoli's stomach. The whip bit flesh more times than Krishna could count, but Nikoli didn't make a sound. His mouth remained closed, his eyes open as they bored into the cold green ones watching from the audience.

The light in Nikoli's eyes dimmed until the pale blue morphed into something more sinister. Nikoli's head jerked to the side, and their surroundings wavered as black sparks crackled across his face, fed by the dark, depthless pools of his eyes.

Krishna took a quick step back and fell through the faltering dreamscape. He woke with blood caked in his hair and drying beneath him on Falcroix's throne room floor. The Hellions were back in their place along the wall, and Nikoli stood on the dais, his wings radiant in the fading sunlight. A few mortals cowered on the right side of the room, but most lay strewn at Nikoli's feet.

He turned toward Krishna and his eyes lit, clear and blue, as a smile spread across his face. He held out a hand and waved Krishna forward. "Come and see."

Krishna rose to his feet and tried not to stare at the countless bodies he walked past. Most of the necks were ripped open, but little blood marred the floor. He mounted the steps and took Nikoli's hand.

Alara remained chained to the throne, though there wasn't much resemblance between the woman he'd brought his master and the twisted creature struggling against its restraints. Glittering black scales covered her bare chest. They swept up her neck and over her shoulders, where they gathered and rose to form thick spikes. Beyond her shoulders, the smooth scales returned, ending only as her clawed fingers began. Blood covered her face, and her subtle fangs had been replaced by a mouthful of long, jagged teeth protruding beyond dark, tattered lips.

Nikoli leaned into Krishna and breathed deep. He laid a kiss behind his ear, and Krishna shivered as Nikoli's lips curled against his skin. "This one is more than skin deep," he whispered. "When it was done, I let her drain Raphael first, then Phanuel. Their blood had no effect on her. She's devoured over half the room since, and her eyes remain black as pitch. Even her response to telepathic commands is tenuous at best."

"That's good?"

"It's enough," Nikoli assured him. He withdrew from Krishna and took a step toward the throne, ripping Alara's head back by the hair. She hissed and opened her mouth, drops of thick, black liquid oozing from the tips of her razor-sharp teeth. Nikoli pressed a finger to one, and a black map of vessels spread beneath his skin. He pulled his finger away and put the wound to his lips, sucking the darkness from his veins and spitting it onto the floor.

"It can be transferred." Krishna's eyes widened. "How much?"

"Under the right circumstances, perhaps all of it." He squeezed Krishna's shoulder and nodded to Alara. "Her soul is unrecognizable, but we need to clear the rest of the room before Lucifer leaves the realm. You grab Raphael, and I'll take Phanuel."

Krishna knelt by Raphael and hoisted the pale, unconscious angel onto his shoulders. The Hellions and remaining mortals had already left the room by the time he and Nikoli started toward the door. "How much do we feed her after this?"

"Nothing. No one speaks of her, and no enters this room once we leave it." Nikoli grinned. "Well, not for a few months at least."

22

SELLING THE DRAMA

MORGHAN LAY on her back in the grass, the early morning mist cool against her skin. She might have enjoyed the sensation if the rest of her body wasn't a fireball of agony.

"I'm dying," she moaned, as she unlatched the clasps holding the front and back pieces of her chest armor together. The release of pressure eased the pain in her abdomen, focusing her attention on the leaden quality of her limbs and a headache which hadn't subsided for weeks.

Winstin scowled down at her. "You're not. Get up."

Brennick's face appeared next to Winstin's, his grey eyes smiling. "I don't know. She looks done for."

Morghan rolled over and sat up. She took the hand Winstin offered and rose to her feet. "I can't fight in this armor anymore. I'm too fuckin' fat."

Brennick rolled his eyes. "You're not fat. You're pregnant."

Bael dropped from a nearby tree and sheathed his sword. His father's wedding band flashed on the chain where most Seiyaku kept their vials. "Nah, there's definitely some fat. He's just waxing poetic because his girl in Malon is about to burst any day."

Morghan knew Tryn well, and she doubted the matriarch would find Bael's description flattering. "Either way, we'll get to Falcroix in a few days, and I don't see myself getting any trimmer between now and then."

Winstin gestured toward her rounded belly with his hands. "You were a doctor. Don't you know how to pop the kid out a few weeks early?"

Morghan ripped off her chest piece and slung it over her shoulder. "Sure, let me grab my secret stash of steroid shots and a portable ventilator. We can leave Brennick alone in the middle of the forest to guard it. I have two to three months to go, Winstin. That's a little more than a few weeks early, and the kid is safer inside me than anywhere I'm not. Once it's born, Nikoli will be waiting to snatch it the first time I blink too long."

Winstin started toward camp. "I see it's going to be one of the many days I miss the drunk, stoned you."

"Since we're getting nostalgic, let me see your face." Morghan drew a dagger and beckoned him closer with the blade. "You're missing a few marks."

The boys laughed, but Winstin ignored her and shoved a waterskin against her chest. "Put the pointy stick away and drink this."

Morghan took a small sip and held it out to him.

"More." He refused to take it back.

"I'm already pissing twenty times a day. I don't feel like making it forty."

"When Lucifer sweeps through here and takes off my head, you'll have no one to blame but yourself. I can only do so much to keep your stubborn ass healthy."

Morghan dropped the waterskin. "Luke talks a big game, but those threats are empty."

"I've watched him rip a man in half with his bare hands." Winstin swiped the waterskin from the ground and shoved it toward her again. "So you keep believing his threats are empty, and I'll keep making it clear I'm doing my best to save you from your own stupidity."

"Good luck." Morghan's thoughts flashed to an underground corridor a lifetime away in another dimension. The doors along it were ripped from their hinges and body parts of the men who frequented the rooms were scattered from one end of the hall to the other. Her bare feet left bloody footprints on the stairs as she climbed toward freedom.

Morghan took a long drink and let the chill of the water wash the memory away. She knew what Luke could do, but he wasn't about to do it to anyone on their side. She tossed the skin over her shoulder to Brennick.

He caught it and strapped it to his belt. "Do you think Michael could rip a man in half?"

Winstin plucked the armor from Morghan's shoulder and swung it over his own. "Michael is strong, but it'd be hard to pull off without the claws. Not to mention the temperament."

Bael reached beneath one of his bracers and brought out a cigarette. "I can't wait to meet this Luke guy. Bat wings, claws, ripping people in half—he sounds badass. I think we'll get along just fine."

Morghan grabbed the cigarette and threw it on the ground. "Don't smoke when I'm this close, and stop talking about Luke like he's some type of hulking death machine. He's not, and you won't even see his angelic form unless he's in over his head."

Winstin glanced at the boys. "Either way, if you see a

hulking death machine on the battlefield, he's on our side. It's the breathtaking rainbow wings you have to watch out for. Don't stare, just crunch down on a vial or three and pray the blood is still potent enough to end you."

As much as Morghan wanted to argue with everything lately, Winstin's logic was sound. So, instead of contradicting him when the boys looked to her for an opinion, she nodded in agreement.

Morghan turned her eyes to the sky when a shadow swooped past and leaves rustled high above them. She sheathed her dagger and drew both guns. They were close enough to Falcroix that they could no longer rely on Michael being the only one approaching from above. The fact the men around her had blades drawn, assured her they'd made a similar connection.

Michael dove through the trees and landed in front of them, his golden breastplate gleaming. Morghan had no idea how he could fight in that thing. It might have been sturdier than leather, but plate was too heavy and restricting for her. It didn't slow Michael down though, and Redra had forged his armor with openings in back so his wings could expand and retract without removing it.

Morghan lowered her guns. "We need a signal for you. The closer we get to Falcroix, the more likely I am to shoot your ass on accident."

"I could just yell our battle cry before landing," he said. "What is it these days? 'My father's an asshole!'"

"Solid choice," Morghan snickered. She replaced her guns in their holsters as they fell into step beside one another. "How are the other armies?"

"On track, and the way to Falcroix is clear." Michael frowned. "I couldn't even find a scout."

That wasn't shocking; Nikoli had no real need for scouts. "How far did you go?"

"I met with most of the commanders and then flew out to Falcroix and circled it." He stopped walking and put a hand on her shoulder. "I didn't believe you about the city being restored, but Luke was right. It's more than restored—it's immaculate."

Michael had a hard time believing any information Morghan had gotten from Luke during his short visit. He'd originally been intrigued, but once Morghan had called him Luke instead of Lucifer, things got dicey.

Luke may not have looked like a child anymore, but the resemblance was there. Michael had demanded answers, and for once, Morghan couldn't see the point in lying. She'd left out the bit about Luke being partially responsible for his mother's abuse and wholly responsible for burning their world to the ground, not to mention the part where she had murdered the love of his life. Come to think of it, she hadn't told him much of anything, but he was still pissed to find out the brother he'd mourned for so long was not only alive, but not his brother at all.

"Falcroix is dark inside. Trust me." Morghan ran her fingers over the bullet clips lining the outside of her thighs. As her pregnancy progressed, her endurance waned, making her guns more important than they'd ever been in this realm. There were more clips lining the back of her chest piece, if she could ever get the damn thing to fit around her again. "How many men do we have?"

"So many I can't count them all. Adding the estimates from their respective leaders, over fifteen thousand."

Morghan's mouth hung open. "Shit. I didn't know you had that many people in the entire realm."

Michael laughed. "There are close to twenty thousand

people living in Vahyir alone, Morghan. And Falcroix has a century-long history of terrorizing everyone from the largest kingdom to the smallest village. It didn't take much beyond a show of magic, a flash of wings, and throwing in the promise of a little protection. What did you think I was doing flying around the realm for the past two decades?"

"I always thought diplomacy was useless, but I stand corrected. Fifteen thousand. Damn. You've done amazing work with this."

Michael stopped and eyed her as if she'd grown a second head. "I think that's the first real compliment you've ever given me."

That couldn't be possible, could it? Maybe she was a little too hard on him.

Michael shrugged it off. "Falcroix became more oppressive, which helped. It doesn't matter how pretty it looks on the outside. Most of these soldiers will only see the memory of their loved ones being carted away to a fate worse than death."

Morghan took a step forward and wrapped her arms around Michael, pulling him into a hug. It was awkward, since her head only came up to his shoulders. Then again, Luke was taller than Michael, and hugging him was never awkward. "I'm sorry, I don't treat you as well as I should."

Michael returned the embrace and assured her she wasn't so bad, but she knew better.

Morghan glared at the shocked faces of the other men. "One word about pregnancy hormones and someone's getting stabbed."

"A little stabbed or a lot stabbed?" Bael wondered. He put his hands up when she pulled back from Michael and pointed a dagger at him. "What? You're the one who taught us to weigh our options."

Morghan sheathed the blade and stomped toward camp. The sun was up, and if they didn't get back soon, the armies would move on without them. Sure they could catch up, but after staying out all night, Michael would want to ride in a cart instead of falling asleep on horseback. She would probably do the same.

Reaching camp took no time at all, but the next few days felt more like a month. Every moment was an emotional dance between the anxiety of going to war and the excitement of a reunion with Luke and Azrael. If they showed up. She didn't envy Winstin or the others who were forced to spend time with her.

Morghan sat in her tent and fidgeted with one of her guns. She'd even driven Brennick away in the end. They were about to push out of the forest and onto the plains surrounding Falcroix, and she hadn't seen him in two days. Maybe she'd pissed him off enough that he was heading back to Malon where he belonged.

Winstin ducked into the tent and held out her chest armor. "Try this. Sheltinata brought a smith, and I had him replace the clasps. It should be a little looser now."

Morghan didn't like the idea of someone else working on Redden's armor, but she held her tongue as she tried it on. The armor latched in place, and while it wasn't as tight as she liked it to be, it wasn't painful either. "Thanks," she mumbled, running a finger along the shiny new clasps. They weren't the same.

Winstin dug in his pocket and set the old ones on the ground in front of her. "In case you want to replace them once your girlish figure returns."

Morghan dumped the clasps into the saddlebag beside her and pulled out Alara's cloak. She secured it at her neck and stood. "Ready?"

Winstin smiled, but it didn't reach his eyes. "As I'll ever be."

She clapped him on the back, and they exited the tent together. There was no point in breaking camp; they would either make it back or they wouldn't.

Brennick stood outside the tent waiting for them, and the twenty-five Seiyaku who still lived in Salus stood behind him. "Ah, we're going for big red bullseye today," he said. "Gutsy."

Morghan wanted to throw her arms around him and yell at him to leave all at once. Him being there meant the world to her, but she didn't deserve his loyalty or his sacrifice. The past few weeks aside, she'd been a complete disaster of a human being for most of his childhood, not to mention the last few years of ignored letters and missed life events. He'd married the damn matriarch of Malon a year ago. The match had strengthened the bonds between their cities more than any treaty could have hoped to do, and Morghan hadn't even shown up for the ceremony.

She didn't deserve Brennick, and more to the point, he didn't deserve her. The instability. The chaos. She'd ruined his childhood, and the last thing she wanted to do was ruin his future, too. He deserved better, yet she couldn't bring herself to dismiss him.

Not that he would have left if she had.

Morghan started toward the edge of camp closest to Falcroix. Winstin and Brennick walked beside her while the other Seiyaku fell in behind them. "We're fighting a man who can sense my exact location from another dimension. It doesn't matter what I'm wearing, so it might as well be fashionably ironic."

Winstin leaned toward Brennick as they left camp. "She's not wearing it for him."

Morghan scowled as they reached the back line of soldiers waiting to advance. The soldiers moved to either side, clearing a path for them to walk to the front. "Luke can see me as easily as Nikoli."

"I never said it was for Lucifer."

Morghan didn't have an answer for that. Was she wearing it for Azrael? She had no idea why she'd brought the cloak, but it felt right to do so. The same way wearing it now felt right. She pushed the thought to the back of her mind and continued to the tree line separating the forest from the plain surrounding Falcroix.

She stopped when the soldiers parted to show the front line of men. Michael was a golden flicker in a sea of leather identical to hers. Morghan's eyes ran over the faces of those who had left Salus over the past two decades.

Brennick leaned close and put a hand on her shoulder. "Don't look so shocked and stop counting. Including the ones behind you, it's all ninety-seven of us."

"I thought you went home." Morghan kept her voice to a whisper so it wouldn't crack.

He gave her shoulder a squeeze and flashed a smile she would always see as Dravyn's. "I am home."

She turned her face to the ground. If she looked at him again, she would burst into tears, which would no doubt instill the utmost faith in those about to risk their lives under her command.

Winstin pulled the hood of her cloak onto her head. "C'mon, Red. Let's go kill some shit."

Morghan couldn't help but laugh. She walked through the Seiyaku and stood beside Michael. Falcroix gleamed in the distance, and flecks of silver dotted the ground in front of the city gates.

"Orcs, mostly." Michael pointed toward Falcroix. "There are regiments of them surrounding the city."

Morghan had to take his word for it. Her eyesight wasn't good enough to see a mile away with any type of clarity. "Rough estimate?"

"Five thousand? There are men mixed in with them, although I'm guessing they're not really men."

Morghan shrugged. "As much as you are. They just don't have the benefit of your age and lineage."

Brennick interjected his usual optimism. "Three to one odds in our favor isn't half bad."

Winstin snorted. "Five thousand orcs, thirty-five lower angels, and four ranking immortals most of us can't even harm, let alone kill. Seems fair."

Brennick's smile faded. "Your morale boosting needs work."

"We have as many ranking immortals as they do." Morghan turned to Michael. "The troops know not to fight the ones with swords like yours, right?"

Michael nodded. "And I briefed your men a few minutes before you arrived. I doubt I'll be with you for most of the fight. I'll go where I'm needed."

Morghan had expected as much. "Have you fought in the air before?"

"You know damn well I haven't."

Morghan gave him a hearty smack on the back and started toward Falcroix. "Don't start today."

Michael took off and flew along the tree line as Winstin and Brennick fell into step beside Morghan. The sound of footsteps and clanking armor followed.

"Don't look now." Winstin pointed to their left. "But I think you're leading the largest army this realm has ever seen."

Morghan's gaze followed his finger to where the trees disappeared behind a swath of soldiers which stretched as far as she could see around the forest's edge. She turned back to face Falcroix, and her heart raced as the outline of Nikoli's army gained definition. They stood in their neat, even lines like slumbering giants waiting to be woken.

She was a little over halfway to the gates when flecks of silver moved at the upper edge of her vision. Angels launched skyward from the top tier and turned to fan out over the plain like spokes from a hub.

Gasps and frightened murmurs rose from behind Morghan until they overpowered the clanking of armor. The soldiers knew Michael wouldn't be the only one in the sky. At least they should have. But being told something and seeing it first-hand were two different things, especially where gods and monsters were concerned.

Morghan pulled the guns off her hips and swapped the black clips for gold as two angels headed in their direction. She chambered the first rounds as they descended. Neither of their swords had a bronze hilt.

Small miracles.

Morghan aimed and fired, blowing the left wing clear off one angel and taking the right arm with the wing of the second. Both screamed their way to the ground and created flaming craters where they landed.

Swords unsheathed at her back and the whispered fears transformed into an enthusiastic roar. The angels could be killed—that was enough for them. Morghan drew her katana. She held it high above her head and pointed it toward Falcroix. If Nikoli wanted dramatic, she would give him fucking dramatic.

~

Azrael's hand slipped from Lucifer's as he fell to his knees. His thoughts were scattered before the shift, but now the rest of him was just as upended. He got one foot beneath him before the ground shook, and he sat down hard.

Lucifer staggered but caught his balance. "Was that you?"

Azrael sat back and pressed his hands into the grass. It felt wrong, like the earth beneath him longed to be elsewhere. Maybe he should help it get there. He closed his eyes and struggled to collect himself, but the world shuddered around him again.

"Azrael!"

Azrael opened his eyes when Lucifer's hands pressed against his shoulders. Lucifer knelt before him, his eyes on fire. His hands moved to either side of Azrael's face. "If you can't calm down, then you need to go home."

"I'll be fine." Azrael laid a hand over one of Lucifer's before pulling away and standing. He walked to the edge of the cliff they stood on and gazed over the land between them and Falcroix. The battle raged far below, and though they were well out of earshot, a thousand thoughts pushed into Azrael's mind. Fear and pain were chief among them, but there was a whisper of hope beneath the misery. Azrael clung to that hope and shut out the rest.

Lucifer draped an arm over his shoulders. "Using me to shift is one thing, but you can't go around causing random earthquakes. Most of those men are on our side, so let's try not to hurt them while we're taking out Nikoli's brood."

Azrael hadn't realized the ground had really moved. He'd imagined it was an after-effect of Lucifer's terrible shifting. "I'll be more careful."

Lucifer raised an eyebrow.

"I promise. If things get out of hand, I'll leave." If he

could muster the concentration to shift. He hadn't been able to concentrate on much of anything recently.

Lucifer spread his wings. "Ok, then let's go find Morghan."

"Go ahead. I need some time."

"I can wait."

Azrael sighed. "I meant I need time alone. I can take care of myself, and it's easy enough to call you when I'm ready."

"Or when you're in trouble," Lucifer insisted.

"Of course."

Lucifer gave him one last look of disapproval before launching skyward and heading for Falcroix.

Azrael frowned at the spot where Lucifer had stood, and his chest ached. Despite the countless voices fighting their way into his head, he was desolate. The wind kicked up behind him, and he turned in time to see Lucifer land on the edge of the cliff.

"Just in case." Lucifer wrapped his wings around Azrael and bent forward, pulling him into a kiss.

Azrael leaned into him, and the voices faded until there was nothing left but the two of them. His knees buckled, but Lucifer kept him on his feet. Once his legs saw fit to work again, Lucifer pulled away, and it stole the breath from his lungs.

Lucifer backed toward the cliff, a lazy smile tugging at his lips. He wrapped his wings around his body and fell backward over the edge.

Azrael stepped forward as Lucifer's wings unfurled mid-fall, his angle changing as he swept toward the battle-field. He tried to hang onto the warmth of Lucifer's embrace, but a familiar chill overtook him. He pulled his jacket tighter. "Reliable to a fault."

Nikoli stepped up beside Azrael and clasped his hands behind his back as he joined Azrael in his assessment of the battlefield. "I have no faults."

Silence stretched between them before Nikoli spoke again. "It was a good joke."

"Forgive my poor humor. The last time you were this close, you were shredding the most sensitive parts of my body."

Nikoli crouched and dug his right hand into the ground, coming up with a handful of dirt. Blue light pulsed down his arm, and when it reached his hand the soil shifted. Thin green tendrils stretched up from it, twisting around one another and coalescing into the stem of a rose that bloomed full and red in a matter of seconds. He plucked it with his free hand and let the dirt scatter on the wind. "We all make mistakes, Azrael."

Nikoli could create life in an instant, yet somehow he managed to destroy it just as fast. When his old world had died, Nikoli had been entrusted with the power to make a new one. A better one. "You are such a waste. It's painful. Whatever you want, the answer is no."

"If you knew that for sure, we wouldn't be standing here."

Azrael hated him for being right.

Nikoli offered the rose to Azrael. "This world isn't for us. Come home with me, and we can start over. I'll release Lucifer to do as he pleases, and we'll never think of him again. He can stay here and raise Lilith's bastard if it suits him."

That was a deal Nikoli was unlikely to offer twice. Morghan and Lucifer could be happy. They could be a family. "Until you tire of me."

"My love has never faltered. It was you who broke us."

Nikoli gestured to the battle. "This show is for you. Say the word, and it ends."

Azrael wanted Lucifer and Morghan to be happy. He did. But he couldn't spend an eternity with this man again, biding his time until Nikoli became bored enough to force him into some new monstrous act he'd regret until his dying breath. "No. Only you can stop this, but you won't. I could restart the cycle, but I'm so tired of running in circles."

"Circles aren't so bad." Nikoli shrugged. "There will be no love in the line I offer."

"The only thing you have ever loved is the idea of me." Azrael gestured to his face. "It's not my fault I look like this."

Nikoli's expression hardened, and frost crept up the rose's stem. "No, it's mine. I should have had the strength to finish the breath when you first rose from the earth as I named you, but the shock was too great."

Through some cruel twist of fate, Nikoli had created him in the form of the man he'd loved and lost in his original realm. When Azrael's eyes had first opened to the world, there had been only pain and the view of his stunned creator hovering overhead. Nikoli hadn't finished breathing life into Azrael until his wings had decayed and his body began wasting away along with them. Some days, he could still feel death clawing through his veins when he woke, but that was neither here nor there. "You know that isn't what I meant. I am not Sasha, no matter how much I resemble him. It's not like Morghan and Lilith—there is no shared soul between us."

"I'm well aware."

"Then act like it, and leave us alone! You already have someone who loves you more than I ever could, and from what I've gathered, you aren't even decent to him."

Ice covered the last of the rose, and it shattered in Nikoli's hand. He took a step back and drew his sword. "Krishna is not your concern. I will continue to do as I please, and I would rather see you dead than with Lucifer and his demonic whore."

Azrael unsheathed his sword. He backed toward the edge of the cliff and sent out a silent call to Lucifer. "Empty threats don't flatter you, Nikoli, but know this: I would have murdered you a thousand times over if I thought success a possibility."

Nikoli lowered his sword. He put a hand to his heart, and his lips curled into a smile. "How you wound me. Although to be fair, of all the things I excel at, existing is chief among them. If you weren't so stubborn, you'd see I'm trying to improve upon your ability to do the same."

Azrael sheathed his sword and made a point of ignoring the frantic responses Lucifer pushed into his mind. "I've existed far too long, Nikoli. It's time to live."

Nikoli's smile faded. "Living is dangerous, my love. Life doesn't care how old you are or how much power you command. It will rip you apart and spread your remains about like so much carrion. This realm, these people—they will destroy you more than I ever could."

"I've made my choice." Azrael leaned back as he took the final step off the cliff, mimicking Lucifer's fall. Except he had no wings wrapped around his body, and as he plummeted toward the ground, his thoughts were far too chaotic for his powers to be of any use beyond causing a catastrophe. He closed his eyes and wondered how much pain he would suffer before losing consciousness.

No sooner had the thought crossed his mind than his body connected with something solid, but it wasn't the ground. Arms wrapped around his chest, and Lucifer's scent slammed into him. Azrael opened his eyes when his stomach dropped with the changing trajectory. Lucifer skirted the side of the cliff as they rose, and they were so close, Azrael feared if he breathed in too deep he might scrape against it.

Azrael looked up and caught a glimpse of Nikoli leaning over the edge, his wings out and spread wide behind him. As they rose higher and passed him, he staggered backward and fell to the ground.

Nikoli's anger roared through Azrael's mind, but when he glanced back to the cliff, Nikoli was no longer there.

Luke grabbed a nephilim by the throat and snapped his neck. He flung it into an oncoming orc, who fell to the ground under the weight of the corpse. Luke stepped forward and rammed his sword downward so hard it cut through both sets of plate armor. His boot smashed into the top body, and he pulled the sword free.

He retreated until his back came up against Azrael's, and he squared his shoulders in preparation for whoever dared to walk through the low-burning ring of fire he'd built around them.

Azrael should have been concentrating on the orcs he was controlling: the two fighting along the opposite side of the ring and a third standing in front of him ready to defend if the need arose. Instead, he looked over his shoulder and frowned at Luke. "Isn't the situation a little too dire to stay angry about something so trivial?"

Luke elbowed him hard in the back. Their sword hands touched, and Luke cursed when a jolt of energy ripped through his left arm. It went numb for a moment, and the hilt almost slipped through his fingers. He shook it off and glared at Azrael, who was readjusting the grip on his own sword.

Trivial? Azrael had sent him a single, calm telepathic message that he was falling off a cliff, and then had, in fact, jumped off said cliff without knowing if Luke had any hope of getting there in time to catch him. "If you had jumped a second or two earlier, I would be scraping your ass off the ground right now."

"If you hadn't gotten there, apparently Nikoli would have."

Was Azrael trying to rile him on purpose? If so, it was working. Luke turned his head to the side until his neck cracked as his thoughts strayed to creative ways to kill whatever being attacked next. "You're sure Morghan's on her way here?"

"No. Pointlessly standing in the middle of an ever-expanding graveyard is one of my greatest joys in life." Azrael smiled. "See, I can be angry over senseless things, too."

Luke stifled a laugh, but he couldn't save his scowl from turning into a grin. When all of this was over, he was dragging Azrael and Morghan into a room and not letting them out of bed for days. Weeks maybe. With any luck, Nikoli would be dead and they wouldn't even have to worry about the consequences.

The flames to Luke's left cooled and died as Morghan walked through them with Winstin, Brennick, and a healthy number of Seiyaku at her back. Her face was streaked with a mix of new and drying blood, and the emblem on her armor shined the same color as the cloak billowing behind her.

Luke could barely spare the attention to torch an oncoming orc as she walked toward them.

"Hello, boys." Morghan threw Luke a wink before stopping in front of Azrael and pulling him into a kiss.

Luke almost didn't notice when Azrael's hold on the orcs snapped. The two falling in battle didn't faze him, but when the third turned on Azrael, there was no time to react.

Morghan saw it first and pulled back from the kiss. She grabbed Azrael by the arm and backed up so fast she ran into Luke and lost her balance. Her free hand found Luke's left arm, and her grip slid down as she fought to keep her footing.

When her hand covered Luke's his breath caught, and no matter how hard he fought to breathe, his lungs refused to work. He fell to his knees, and the other two followed as his power waned and his angelic form rose to the surface. He turned toward Azrael, who was faring no better on Morghan's other side. She knelt between them, head down and hands locked over theirs. Light rippled from her in waves, the color alternating through green, gold, and red.

Luke tried to drop his sword. Tried to pull his hand from Morghan's. Anything to sever the bond and stop the pain.

Despite Luke's best efforts, it was Morghan who ended it. Her hands slipped from theirs as her body pitched forward, and she collapsed in the blood-slicked grass.

Luke let go of his sword and fell to his side, thankful when air filled his lungs and the burning in his chest subsided.

Winstin knelt beside Morghan and rolled her onto her back. She was still unconscious. He looked to Luke and then at where Azrael sat with one hand planted firmly against the ground. "What the fuck was that? You three dropped half the goddamn field!" He swept his arm in a wide arc, gesturing to a large circle around them without a single person on their feet. Except Winstin.

Luke sat up and waited a few more breaths before doing away with his angelic form. His

wings stayed. "Are they dead?"

"No," Azrael answered. "Unconscious."

"It's like everyone's in a damn coma." Winstin dragged Morghan into a sitting position. He held up his right arm. "Me, I just got healed. Five minutes ago this arm was useless and one of my knees was torn to shit. Now, good as new."

Luke put a hand to the side of his aching head. "Is she okay?"

Winstin shook her a bit. "Morghan, wake up. Stop taking a nap in the middle of a fucking war."

She groaned, and her eyes fluttered before closing again.

"She's fine," Winstin assured him a moment before before he hauled off and smacked her across the face.

Luke growled, and he would have made Winstin wish only his arm and leg were injured, if Morghan hadn't woken up and screamed at him.

"Ow! What the Hell, Winstin?" She rubbed her cheek. "I'm pregnant!"

"You're not pregnant in the face." He rose to his feet and offered her a hand up. "Well, maybe a little."

She took his hand, but once she was standing, she shoved him to the ground. "That's for the underhanded comment."

Luke stood and wrapped his arms around Morghan. "Are you hurt?"

Morghan shook her head. She looked down at Brennick, who was starting to wake. "What happened?"

Azrael rubbed his eyes. "Your hands got too close to our swords. It incapacitated everyone around us and nearly took the three of us along with it."

Morghan rested her head against Luke's chest. "Is that supposed to happen?"

Azrael shrugged and looked away. That was one of Luke's least favorite reactions. It meant he knew damn well if it was supposed to happen or not, but the topic wasn't up for discussion.

Morghan pulled Luke down by the shirt and gave him a quick kiss. "I'm going to make sure my boys wake up safe before anything else does, but then we should go to the top and find my sword. You know, so I'm not so tempted to use yours."

Luke was so focused on Morghan as she picked her way through the Seiyaku, that he didn't notice Azrael at his side until fingers threaded through his.

Azrael squeezed his hand. "She lives. At all costs. Understood?"

Luke imagined it was time he accepted Azrael's visions of this place as more than random nightmares. "Let's not pretend I'm the one who needs convincing."

23

TWISTING FATE

MICHAEL PRESSED his back against the wall surrounding Falcroix. He nodded along with whatever the officers in front of him were saying, though he doubted he'd be able to repeat it if asked to do so. If he could get a minute to rest, then maybe he could pay more attention. His back had been screaming for hours, but the wall helped. It vibrated as the combined forces of Vahyir, Predlitz, and Sheltinata rammed the western gate, but he couldn't stand there forever.

The gate would fall soon, and their forces would flood the lower tier in a matter of minutes, moving up from there. The advantage was theirs, but while several of Nikoli's angels had fallen in battle, Michael had yet to see a single ranking immortal. Aside from his father, there should have been three others, including two angels who, according to Morghan, lacked the ability to hide their wings.

Thinking of Morghan reminded him it was time he checked on her. Last he'd seen, she was cutting a steady path through Falcroix's southern forces, surrounded by enough of her men he hadn't bothered to land. He wiped the sweat from his brow, and his hand came away with fresh red streaks over the darker, dried blood that covered most of his body. When this was over, he was going to scrub his skin raw and sleep for a week.

But first, Morghan.

Michael excused himself and peeled his back from the wall. He was in the air and banking south when a body crashed into him, sending him hurtling sideways into the wall. Michael's legs went numb, and the pain in his back was so overwhelming, he couldn't control his descent. Michael closed his eyes and braced for more pain as the ground rushed toward him.

His eyes flew open when instead of pain, fingers curled over the top of his breastplate. Cold blue eyes stared back at him, and white wings stretched behind his assailant as they fell. The angel grabbed the bottom of Michael's breastplate with his free hand and pulled them into a barrel-roll before flinging Michael skyward and launching after him.

Michael spread his wings and rolled to the side, narrowly escaping another hit. He angled up and sped to the top of the wall as the other angel hit the side of it and ricocheted toward him.

Michael landed on the wall and staggered backward. He took a knee, and a thousand needles stabbed down his legs as he tried to rise and failed. While there was some strength left in his legs, it would never be enough to stand and fight. Michael pulled his wings close to his back, and darker clouds had already started to roll over Falcroix by the time the angel landed on the wall in front of him. The bronze-hilted sword hanging from his belt sent a wave of panic through Michael. His only hope was to send enough of a shock through the angel to allow time for escape.

The angel strode toward Michael and held out his hand

as if they were meeting on polite terms. "I am Phanuel, chief among the Host. Your father would like a word."

A bolt of lightning struck the ground between them, and Phanuel jumped back as thunder rumbled overhead.

Michael reached toward the sky, and the next bolt fed into his hand, coming to rest as a coil around his forearm. "I have several words for him, none of them pleasant."

"If you're smart, you'll listen to his offer." Phanuel gestured to the energy coiled around Michael's arm. "Put that away, so we can go. He demands an audience with you. Now."

"So he sends someone to maim me and drag me to his feet? No. He can come to me if he wants to talk."

"It wasn't I who maimed you. That weakness was waiting to be exploited." Phanuel placed a hand on the hilt of his sword. "Come. My master despises being made to wait."

Michael glared at Phanuel. He was right. Morghan was responsible for his back, but it had been an accident. An accident she'd done her best to fix and apologize for in her own way. Nikoli had done so much more damage, and it was doubtful he was being summoned for any type of apology.

Michael unsheathed his sword, and the line of energy on his arm snaked up the length of the blade. His heart sank when he caught sight of another angel circling high above them. He was far too tired to fight off two of them. "My father watched me suffer for hundreds of thousands of years. I don't give a damn about his five-minute inconvenience. Either you tell him I said he can go fuck himself, or he can come out and hear it first-hand."

Phanuel's eyes flashed, and his sword rang clear of its

sheath. "He had so much to offer you, but that woman corrupts everything. Such a shame."

When their blades met, the energy surrounding Michael's sword transferred to Phanuel's. As it fed up his blade, the light dissipated until only a single spark remained to jump harmlessly onto Phanuel's skin.

Michael tried to rise to his feet one last time, but he collapsed on hands and knees when his legs refused to support his weight. He gripped his sword and held it up to parry when Phanuel raised his sword for the killing blow. It wasn't a strong enough stance to hold. He would lose at least his arm, likely his life. When the shadow of the second angel fell over them, Michael closed his eyes and prayed for a swift death.

The angel landed with such force that the wall shuddered beneath them. Michael opened his eyes when a sword clanged against stone, confused to see a blade sticking out of Phanuel's chest.

The sword withdrew and Phanuel crumpled to the ground. He touched the wound on his chest and held the bloody hand in front of him before gaping at the other angel.

"Raphael? What are you doing?" Phanuel rasped. He reached for Raphael with one hand while the other clutched his chest.

Raphael's stony features betrayed no remorse. He took a step toward Phanuel and raised his sword high above his head, bringing it down in an arc aimed at Phanuel's neck. "Being more productive than you."

~

Morghan stood on the top tier flanked by Luke and Azrael, their presence the only thing between her and a complete nervous meltdown. Winstin peered over her shoulder, his eyes locked on the main keep looming before them. She'd tried her best to leave him behind with Brennick, but he'd grabbed Luke's arm at the last second as they shifted.

Winstin nudged her. "You think it's locked?"

The three turned to him with equally critical expressions.

Morghan's eyes never left Winstin as she raised her gun and blew a flaming hole in the door. "The world will never know."

"The hitchhiker doesn't belong here," Azrael said. "Can't we throw him down to the lower tiers?"

Winstin glared at Azrael's back. "Honestly, Windstarr, I'll never get how you can stand these two." He pointed to Azrael. "Especially him."

The remainder of the door blew aside as Azrael approached it. "How do you know I wasn't joking?"

"I don't. That's part of the problem."

Morghan grabbed Azrael's shoulder and pushed him behind her as she crossed the threshold. "It's usually safe to assume he's not joking."

"Especially today," Luke said as he pulled his sword and followed Morghan. "We've had a rough start."

"It's not getting any better," Azrael said as he reached for Morghan's hand. "Let us go first. You're pregnant and without the means to protect yourself."

Morghan turned on him and pulled her hand from his. Out of the corner of her eye, she saw Luke and Winstin take a step back. "This is my show, and on the whole, I've been protecting myself just fine for the better part of a century. Thanks."

Azrael's indifferent expression never wavered. "I meant your sword, but go ahead and be offended if it makes you feel better."

Morghan recognized his flat affect for what it was, and wondered which masochistic nightmare Azrael's subconscious was playing out this time. She stepped up to him and straightened his jacket. "I don't know if we can do this with only half of you."

"I wish I was strong enough to give you half." Azrael took her hand and placed it over his heart. It thundered beneath her palm at a rate so high she could scarcely discern one beat from the next. "You're the one we need whole. We can't end this without you."

She moved her hand to the side of his neck and ran her thumb along the line of his jaw. "All the more reason for me to go first. If I walk into a world of shit, the two of you can do something about it. As much as I hate to admit it, the opposite isn't true, and then where would I be without you?"

Luke laid a hand on each of their shoulders. "She has a point."

Azrael looked from Lucifer to Morghan and gestured for Morghan to take the lead. "She usually does."

Morghan hurried down the hall, passing one closed door after another.

Winstin pushed past Luke and Azrael to walk beside Morghan. "Shouldn't we check these rooms for your sword?"

"No. It's not in any of those." But it was close. She could hear it calling to her, a psychic whisper tugging at her soul like the gravitational pull of a planet. "Trust me, I'd know."

Winstin looked from one closed door to the next before dropping behind Luke and Azrael. "This place feels wrong, like there are a million people screaming behind those doors."

Morghan stopped in front of the first open door. An enormous black bed swallowed the room, and a set of shackles lay abandoned in the far corner. Her sword wasn't there, but it had been.

Azrael stopped at Morghan's side and grimaced. He took several quick steps away from the door. "Or one person screaming a million times."

Morghan's brow furrowed. "Alara?"

"Wrong room," Azrael said. The left side of his face was paler than it had been moments earlier.

"Ralikaya," Luke elaborated. "Phanuel bled her as his hybrid, and Nikoli has been using her as his personal broodmare."

Morghan's jaw clenched so hard her teeth hurt. She had hoped Ralikaya was dead, but she should have learned by now that hope was never enough. "And how many siblings does Michael have?"

Azrael pointed down the hall. "Let's keep moving."

Morghan glared at him. "How many?"

"Cronus swallowed his children—Alara's monstrosities swallowed Nikoli's for him. None have survived thus far. Now, can we please go? She's beyond our reach, and I need to be away from this room before I lose what little composure I have left."

Winstin snorted derisively as they continued. "I'd like to see that. You always look the same. Would it kill you to let a real emotion slip through?"

"It wouldn't kill me," Azrael said. "Which would be unfortunate for everyone else."

They turned down a few more halls before Morghan realized where the sword was leading them. She made the final turn and pulled her katana as the doors to the throne room came into view. Of course, it would be there, and she imagined Alara and Nikoli were on the other side ready to pounce. If that was how they wanted to play this game, so be it. While Nikoli might kill her, Morghan would be sure to skewer the blood-sucking bitch before his sword found a home in her chest.

Morghan's pulse quickened as the doors drew nearer. Her sword was screaming for her now. It needed her as much as she needed it. The doors opened, though no one was close enough to touch them. Her vision tunneled when the ivory hilt flashed into view, and she sprinted for the throne room. The warning screams at her back were whispers in comparison to the pull of her sword, but as she crossed into the throne room the screams vanished. The walls flickered blue, and a net of light spread around the room, stretching upward until even the ceiling was covered with the web of Nikoli's energy field.

Morghan's trance fell away, and she wondered if the final pull had anything to do with her sword at all. She spun toward door. Unlike the rest of the room, the net of light merged into a solid sheet of blue to cover the entrance.

Her three companions stood on the other side. Winstin and Luke's mouths moved as if they were screaming at her, but no sound made it past the barrier. Luke had already brought out his angelic form, and the cracks in his charred skin burned as brightly as his eyes. He raged against the energy field, attacking it with everything from claws to sword. Bright bursts of fire layered over the blue, but the trap never wavered.

Azrael stood in front of the barrier, still as stone. His right hand pressed against it, wisps of golden light stretching from his fingertips. He turned his head to watch

Luke for a long moment, and when he faced Morghan again his eyes were wild and desperate.

"Stay calm," Morghan pleaded. She wasn't sure if her poor excuse for telepathy would work across the energy field, but he could surely read her lips for something so simple. She pressed her hand against the barrier to match his, but she jerked it back when the light seared her palm.

Azrael shook his head and placed his other hand against the blue wall. His eyes narrowed, and his mouth opened in a silent scream as light exploded from his fingers.

The stone floor shook beneath Morghan's feet, and she stumbled backward before catching her balance. When she looked back to the door, Winstin was pointing at her with increased fervor. She pointed at herself and shook her head, unsure what he was trying to tell her.

Morghan heard chains sliding against one another and the clang of metal hitting stone behind her.

"He said, 'behind you,'" a silken voice whispered in her ear an instant later.

Pain ripped through the back of Morghan's neck as Alara's claws wrapped over the top of her armor, and the next thing Morghan knew, she was in the air. Her back came down hard against the steps of the dais, and when she rolled to the side, the hilt of her sword flashed a few feet away. She crawled toward it, and a deafening crack sounded when her hand wrapped around the hilt. She stared at the sword, and it took a few seconds to realize the sound had nothing to do with her. The ground shook again, and the net of light above her wavered as pieces of the crumbling stone ceiling rained down and smashed against the floor. Morghan made a quick survey of the walls, noting an array of widening fissures racing up from the ground. If Alara didn't rip her to shreds, then Azrael would bury her.

Morghan struggled to her feet and decided to concentrate on one disaster at a time. She faced Alara and took a step back when her eyes met the monstrosity stalking toward her. The voice was unmistakable, but whatever Nikoli had done to her, it hadn't been kind. Alara grinned, and black sludge slid over her teeth and oozed past her lips.

Morghan ducked and rolled away when Alara pounced. She would have finished on her feet if she hadn't been forced to pitch left in order to miss another piece of the ceiling as it shattered beside her. Instead, she ended on her back, and when she tried to rise again, a cramping pain ripped through her abdomen, sending her back to the ground. Morghan gritted her teeth against the pain, which refused to subside, and she realized she wasn't moving anywhere for the next several seconds. She pulled her guns and unloaded them in Alara's direction without much thought toward aiming—all she needed was time.

Fire blossomed against the energy field on the other side of the room, sending ripples through the web. Alara howled when a bullet skimmed the spikes on her right shoulder, the explosion causing enough damage to leave her arm hanging by a thick slab of muscle and nothing more.

Morghan holstered one of her guns and grabbed her sword from the ground as the pain faded. She rose to her feet and prayed it wouldn't return. She managed a few steps toward Alara before it came roaring back, taking her to her knees. She keeled over and pressed a hand against her belly. How dare her kid try to be born over two months early in the middle of a goddamn battle.

Alara's injury must not have been as grave as it looked, because she was on Morghan as soon as she fell. She grabbed the front and back of Morghan's chest piece, and the clasps snapped as she pulled them apart and flung them across the room. Alara pinned Morghan's hands to the ground and squeezed her wrists until she had no choice but to release her gun and sword.

Morghan tried to pull away, but Alara's one good hand was somehow stronger than both of Morghan's.

Fetid breath filled Morghan's nostrils as Alara's head dipped toward her neck, and thick black ooze dripped onto her shoulder.

Morghan screamed when Alara's teeth sank into her neck, and what little strength she had mustered beyond the pain, siphoned off with her blood. The floor lurched beneath them, and Alara clung to her as the throne room collapsed in on itself and they tumbled to the tier below.

Morghan landed on her back atop Alara. She began to fade from consciousness as her heart hammered in a futile effort to perfuse her brain with what little blood remained. She was on the verge of passing out, when the sharp pain in her neck subsided. A throbbing pressure replaced it, as if someone was trying to blow out her veins with a large, swift injection.

Morghan's vision blurred, and the pain in her abdomen was nothing in comparison to the icy claws that wrapped around her heart and tore through the rest of her body.

Alara shoved Morghan to the side and straddled her. The monstrous form hadn't changed, but the eyes glaring down at Morghan were brown and alert, unlike the soulless pools of black from moments earlier.

Morghan reached for her remaining gun, but her fingers were clumsy and numb. Pain bowed her body, and black waves crashed inside her head, pulling her down until they flooded every thought and drowned her.

~

Winstin threw up his hands in a pointless attempt to shield himself from the stone raining down upon them. His eyes were closed, but the image of Morghan falling through the floor with Alara locked to her neck was burned into the back of his mind. And while Azrael may have doomed them all to a world of pain, the three ranking immortals would recover. He, on the other hand, was a few blows to the head away from being sent straight back to his own personal hell. A twinge of shame rode in with the thought that, in the midst of everything, he dared to fear for his own well-being. Morghan would have dismissed it as natural. Morghan, who was buried under a mountain of stone because she refused to risk the lives of those she loved before her own. It was nice to be loved, to have a friend. Friends were something his mortal life had sorely lacked.

An arm cinched around Winstin's chest, and his feet left the ground. He opened his eyes and screamed as Lucifer swerved through chunks of falling stone. By the time they rose above what was left of the top tier, he had narrowly avoided being pulverized no less than a dozen times. If Winstin's heart had been beating when he left the ground, their wild ascent would have remedied that.

Winstin took in the view as they hovered above Falcroix. A mountain of broken stone piled high where the main keep once stood, and their soldiers packed the lower tiers. He glanced to his left, where Azrael hung from Lucifer's other arm. Azrael's disheveled appearance, from the skewed hair to his blank eyes staring down at the wreckage, did nothing to quell Winstin's anger. He would have screamed at the bastard if Lucifer's frantic voice hadn't interrupted before he had the chance.

"I've got her!"

One moment they were high above Falcroix, and the

next they were in a dark corridor, though Winstin was certain random parts of his body were still in the sky. He reeled forward and hit the ground, his head pounding and his stomach tied in knots. How Lucifer and Azrael shifted from place to place so easily was nothing short of a miracle. The first shift had been disorienting enough, but this time, he felt the need to make sure all his organs were on the correct side of his skin.

Fire spread along the sides of the corridor, illuminating the hall, its ceiling a low-lying mass of broken stones packed together from the upper tier's wreckage. Morghan lay on her back with Alara poised above her, long claws fumbling with the clasp of Morghan's cloak.

Winstin pushed to his feet and ran toward them, drawing his sword as he went. Lucifer flashed past and barreled into Alara, sending the two of them tumbling down the hall. Winstin slowed, unable to pull his gaze away as Lucifer tore Alara limb from limb before shoving a clawed hand through her ribcage and ripping out her heart.

Azrael was kneeling at Morghan's side by the time Winstin made it to her. Her eyes were open wide, the irises a thin, glowing ring of emerald in an expanding sea of black. Aside from the war waging in her eyes, she lay still as death, and her skin shone pale against the black blood spreading through the map of veins beneath it.

Winstin crouched near Morghan's head when Azrael pried Morghan's lips apart, revealing perfectly normal human teeth. "What are you doing?"

Azrael didn't bother responding. He pulled a dagger from Morghan's belt and dragged it across his wrist.

Lucifer ripped the dagger from Azrael's hand and flung it down the hall. He knelt on the opposite side of Morghan and grabbed Azrael by his injured arm. "Let it heal!"

"No. Her teeth haven't changed yet. I can take it, but it'll have to be funneled straight from the vessels."

"And then what?" Lucifer growled. "I can't stop you, Azrael. Only Nikoli has the power to do that. Maybe. And why would he? It would thrill him to watch you torture and murder us to a man. And you would."

Lucifer bent forward to kiss Azrael, and when he pulled back, the sharp edges of his teeth left Azrael's lips torn and bloody. "Now let your wound heal, and help me channel this madness from her veins to mine."

"We can share it," Azrael pled, but the blood pumping from his wrist had already slowed. "Between the two of us. Or even the three of us."

Lucifer ignored him. He unsheathed one of Morghan's daggers and tapped the blade against each of her wrists. "Morghan's blood into me on my left, my blood to her from my right. She's my hybrid, and our blood was made to heal each other, so if you don't keep things flowing, her wounds might close."

Azrael shook his head. "Even if I wanted to, I'm all over the place right now. I can't."

"You can, but you have to force yourself to want it bad enough," Lucifer insisted. He pressed his forehead to Azrael's. "This is going to happen just as we planned. We reclaimed Morghan's sword. Now it's time to get her out safe. Afterwards, you'll take her and Winstin to Nikoli's realm for Jessimine's soul, then retreat back to Michael and stand your ground. The only difference is I won't be there."

Tears streamed down Azrael's face. "But—"

"No buts," Lucifer cut in. "Now that I can't atone for my own sins, you'll have to do it for me. This is how it has to be. Don't act like we haven't suspected it for months. You'll do as I ask, because you love me. And I love you."

Lucifer pulled back from Azrael and used Morghan's dagger to slash both her wrists before turning it on himself and doing the same. He pressed his left wrist to Morghan's right. "Winstin, hold our wrists together here. Azrael, the other side."

Lucifer nodded to Azrael. "At all costs, remember? Start pushing the blood. Everything will be fine."

Everything was not going to be fucking fine. Winstin did as he was told, tears of blood leaking from his eyes all the while. The charred skin of Lucifer's angelic form made it impossible to tell when the transfusion began, but the darkness in Morghan's veins faded a shade at a time until Winstin would have sworn the deed was done.

Winstin redoubled his grip when Morghan's arm threatened to pull away. He glanced at her face and was relieved to see her eyes bright and alert with only a few wisps of black lingering near the edges.

Her eyes darted from one of them to the next. "What's going on? Let me go!"

Lucifer hunched over Morghan's body. Red and black chased each other through the cyclones in his eyes. "Keep her down. Finish it."

"No, Winstin. Let me go!" Morghan demanded.

Winstin's grip wavered, despite his best intentions to keep her still. Lucifer had given him a direct order, and at the core of the magic that drove him, he should have moved at his animator's command. So why was he torn?

The compulsion to follow the orders of Lucifer and Morghan warred in his head until a third voice smashed through the confusion and his hand tightened around Morghan's arm.

Morghan bucked beneath them, screaming obscenities Winstin had never heard pass her lips, which was impressive. The final wisps of black left her eyes, and new skin knit together over the ragged wound at her neck.

Azrael released her arm, which she promptly used to punch him in the face. She rolled toward Winstin and grabbed his neck, slamming his head against the floor as she rose to her knees.

The world went dark for what seemed like a second, but when Winstin regained consciousness, Lucifer was no longer kneeling beside him. He lay on his back, not far down the hall, with Morghan and Azrael standing over him screaming at one another. As Winstin gained his feet and stumbled toward them, his thoughts had less to do with the tragedy unfolding before him and more to do with why they weren't running. As far away and as fast as possible. Whatever evil they had pumped into Lucifer, it didn't have the added distraction of giving him a physical makeover. Winstin expected its job would be short and to the point.

Winstin came up beside Morghan, and her eyes blazed when she turned to face him. He didn't blame her for the betrayal shining in their depths, and his chest was a little emptier knowing this act was unlikely to be on her long list of forgivable ones.

Winstin only had a moment to mourn their friendship before Lucifer's body burst into flames, and his voice boomed through the hall. "Go!"

Somehow, despite Lucifer's flaming, evil-infused, demonic form yelling for them to leave, Azrael still appeared conflicted. Nonetheless, he reached across Lucifer's body and wrapped a hand around Morghan and Winstin's wrists.

The corridor faded, and Winstin fell flat on his ass near one of the terminals in Nikoli's control room. Though the walls were blank, the keyboard and dials on the main console glowed beneath a thick layer of dust. It had been a quarter century since Nikoli burst into the room with wings and the face of a teenager. A quarter century since Winstin had crawled his way to Lucifer's realm to choose a new path, and he didn't miss a single thing about the old one. Least of all this room.

Morghan's voice pulled Winstin away from his thoughts. "I love you, Azrael, but it's hard not to hate you right now."

Winstin stood and moved to her side. Azrael didn't seem to think her comment warranted an answer, but given the emptiness in his eyes, it was possible he hadn't heard a word of it.

Despite the anger rolling off her in waves, Morghan grabbed Azrael by the shoulders and crushed him against her chest. She buried her face in his neck and breathed deep. "Remind me to yell at you more when we're not in a hurry."

Morghan threaded her fingers through Azrael's and headed for the door. She stopped short when Azrael didn't move. "C'mon, let's get this over with and get the fuck out of here."

Azrael pulled his hand from hers. "I can't."

"Can't what?"

"I can't leave him like that." Azrael backed away from her and shook his head. "I'm so sorry. I thought I could."

Morghan reached for him, but he vanished before she could make contact. She stood there staring at nothing, her eyes wide and unblinking.

Winstin's aversion to Azrael came flooding back. "Did that bastard seriously just abandon us?"

Morghan's expression blanked as she turned toward the doors and pulled them open. "He has his priorities."

"Priorities?" Winstin stomped along beside her. If he ever saw Azrael again, he was going to go straight for that asshole's throat. "He dumped us in the middle of Nikoli's realm with no way to leave! We're as good as dead."

"You're already dead, Winstin. So was I." She pointed to the maelstrom of souls above their heads. "We're on bonus time."

Her lips pressed into a thin line, and a shadow of pain swept across her face. She gasped and grabbed her abdomen. "Goddamn it."

Winstin put a hand on her shoulder. "Are you okay?"

"No, I am not fucking okay! Under none of the currently fucked up circumstances am I okay, and the last thing I need right now is preterm labor. It's gonna be a goddamn miracle if this kid isn't dead already, but I thought whatever Luke did to me had at least stopped the contractions."

"Maybe the power he gave you is fading?"

"Maybe, but I can still see your soul, and I'm having a really hard time controlling the urge to set this whole place on fire." Morghan stood up straight and started walking again.

"Is my soul really in my genitals?" Winstin couldn't help but ask. He'd been wondering since Lucifer had commented on it back in Salus.

"No, it's in your chest. I think they're always supposed to be in the chest." Morghan's brow furrowed, and the anger in her eyes faded as she let out a short snort of laughter. "In your genitals? Dumbass."

Winstin was a little disappointed. "I know we're stuck here, but do we even know where we're going?"

Morghan tapped her temple. "Soul vision."

She waved to the souls overhead. "Whatever the Hell

that is, I don't know, but there is only one spot in this place that feels the same. If nothing else, after we grab Jessimine's soul and use the control room to ship it to Michael's realm, we can take the shifting chamber to Luke's realm."

"Which is just as empty as this realm," Winstin pointed out. "And if Azrael deigns to come get us, he wouldn't know we'd gone there."

Morghan turned down a side hall and ducked into one of the rooms. It was empty aside from the swirling blue orb on a pedestal at its center. A pedestal surrounded by an icy blue net of energy. "One problem at a time, Winstin."

Morghan's shoulders sank as she examined the pedestal. "Well, if Nikoli doesn't know we're here, he will as soon as we touch this energy field."

There was no point touching it. The energy field in Falcroix had held until the floor dropped out and room imploded. There was no ceiling here to bring crashing down on it, and if Lucifer and Azrael's combined powers hadn't been able to take one down, Winstin didn't have much hope for Morghan.

"I've got an idea. Stand still so I can try something." Morghan pressed her hand to his chest, and her eyes flared red.

Winstin's breath caught, and the room spun. He placed a hand over hers and mumbled a plea for her to stop. His knees buckled when she removed her hand, but she caught him before he hit the ground. She was grinning from ear to ear, but he wasn't sure why.

Morghan set him on his feet and turned back to the pedestal. "I don't need to touch it. I can call it."

"Please tell me you didn't test this theory by trying to rip my soul from my body."

"Ok, I won't tell you. Now quiet, I need to concentrate."

Morghan held her hand in front of the energy field and concentrated on the soul on the other side. At first nothing happened, but as time passed the soul inched toward the edge. "I probably should have asked this beforehand, but do souls bounce?"

He didn't have time to answer before the orb rolled off the pedestal and fell through the energy field. Morghan lunged to catch it, and her shoulder came up against the net of light as her hand closed around it.

"Shit!" Morghan held the soul close to her chest as she rushed for the door. "We have to get this damn thing gone before Nikoli shows."

Winstin followed as they turned down one hall after another until the control room doors came into view. They burst through them, and Morghan headed for the main console. She pushed the soul into Winstin's hands and looked at him expectantly.

He glanced at the soul, which was streaked with so much blood he could barely tell the original color. "What do you want me to do with it?"

She leaned on the console and fought to catch her breath. "Send it out."

"To where? I need a person, a place, something."

Morghan clutched her abdomen and waved her free hand toward the console. "Vahyir. I know you have a random generator somewhere in that system. Send her to some random woman in Vahyir. We'll find her."

Winstin placed Jessimine's soul into the console and started typing. "Really? Vahyir is about as far as you can get from Salus, and it's cold as shit up there."

"Azrael will come back. Nothing will be far from Salus, and she'll look more like Michael remembers if she's born to a family there."

"Well, first of all, let's hope she's a she." Winstin finished plugging in the codes, and as he pressed the final key, the swirling blue light within the orb disappeared along with the blood covering it.

"Wait, what? Why wouldn't she be a girl?"

"Please tell me you didn't really think souls had sex chromosomes."

"Well, fuck, I don't know. I'm still a girl the second time around."

Winstin rolled his eyes. "And with such long odds."

Morghan ran a hand over her face. "What if she's a guy? Michael isn't interested in men."

Winstin shrugged. "If I had mourned the love of my life for over half a million years, the last thing I'd worry about was whether or not they had a vagina. Soulmates are soulmates. If they're meant for each other, it will work itself out."

"I'll keep my fingers crossed for two X chromosomes. It would be nice if something was easy for once." Morghan pointed to the console. "Does that thing keep a record? Can you erase it?"

"Why bother? Nikoli knows her soul well enough to seek it out in an instant."

Morghan held up a bloody hand and wiggled her fingers. "Camouflage."

Winstin had no idea if that would really work. No one had fused a blood sample with a soul before as far as he knew, especially not blood from God only knew how many other people. There was a way to bring up the last soul destination, but there wasn't a way to clear it. With one exception.

Winstin balled up his hand and slammed it into the console. The metal bowed, and sparks flew through the air.

Morghan jumped back. "What are you doing?"

"Destroying this monstrosity so Nikoli can't access the last destination. Want to help?"

Morghan pulled her ranking sword and brought it down on the other side of the console. She glanced around the room. "Do we have to break all of them? We don't have a lot of time."

Winstin shook his head. "All the others feed into this one with no backward communication. Its creator was a little single-minded, if you can believe that."

Morghan backed up and leaned against one of the side terminals while Winstin continued to destroy the main one. "Fantastic. Let's get the fuck out of here and head for the shifting chamber. I'd rather die in Luke's realm a thousand times than be cut down once in this shithole."

Winstin turned from the console as Morghan headed for the doors. She pulled them open and stopped short. Her knuckles went white against the handles, and her body bowed forward. She took an unsteady step back and fell to the floor.

Krishna stood in the open doorway, gaping at the blood on his outstretched blade, as if he didn't understand how it had gotten there. The confusion morphed into excitement as Morghan writhed on the floor with her hands pressed to her bleeding abdomen.

Winstin sprinted from the console and dove for Krishna's legs as the blade came down to take off Morghan's head. The two of them went to the ground, and Winstin grabbed the dagger from his forearm, shoving it deep into Krishna's heart.

Krishna flung Winstin into one of the side consoles and was on his feet before Winstin had any hope of recovering.

Krishna stalked toward Winstin, ripping the dagger from his chest as he went.

Winstin wasn't sure what part of his body was broken, but none of his limbs obeyed when he willed them to move. So, instead of dodging when Krishna's sword angled for his neck, he used his last moments to do the only thing he could think of that might help—he screamed Azrael's name.

THE DEVIL'S IN THE DETAILS

MORGHAN LAY on the icy marble floor, her life pouring out between her fingers. There wasn't a single part of her that didn't hurt, and when she left this place—if she left it—she doubted the pain would ever stop.

When Luke had shown up in Salus, her world had made sense again. There was a purpose and a real plan to move beyond the misery. But that was gone. Her future was gone. It had died in a shadowy corridor, when Luke had forced his choice on all of them.

And now, Azrael had abandoned her. She couldn't blame him. Even when they lived together, she would have put money on Azrael driving his sword through her heart if it meant saving Luke. She was fine with that, but now the deed was done, and her heart kept right on beating while the act saved no one.

The bite of Krishna's blade wasn't nearly as painful, and if it landed a second time, she was bound to stop hurting all together. Nothing would have been easier than closing her eyes and waiting for the end, but as Winstin sped past her and took Krishna to the ground, she remembered some things were more important than her macabre pity parties.

Morghan grabbed her gun when Krishna's blade swung toward Winstin's neck, but it clicked uselessly in her hand. She cursed and checked the black magazine, which was disengaged and lodged at an odd angle. Winstin screamed Azrael's name as she slid the magazine out and forced it back between the grips. She hoped Winstin's expectations were low, because she'd been silently screaming Azrael's name since he'd disappeared.

Winstin's scream stopped short, and her eyes darted up to find his headless body slumped against a side terminal. The brilliant mahogany light in his chest began to fade, and panic set in. She couldn't stand the thought of him being thrust back into a spin cycle of his worst nightmares. Winstin was far from perfect, but she had experienced Nikoli's version of hell firsthand. It was nothing like Luke's realm, and no one deserved that kind of eternal torture.

Morghan pulled the trigger before Krishna had a chance to turn his attention back to her. The bullet went wide and shattered the marble wall, earning her a mocking grin as Krishna moved toward her. She swapped to point shooting, since her gun's sight was clearly skewed to shit, and the second shot sent Krishna reeling backward with the force that hit his right shoulder. His sword clattered to the floor, and she fired a third time, skirting the right side of his abdomen as he fell.

Morghan cursed at the gun trembling in her hand. Maybe it wasn't the sight after all. She tried again, but the gun clicked, this time from lack of bullets. It would have been nice if her remaining bullets weren't buried in Falcroix with her armor and second gun.

She cursed and tested her strength to rise, but even

sitting was an impossible task. So, she flipped over and crawled arm over arm toward Winstin's body. His soul had reduced to a dull glow, but she was determined to make it to him before the light vanished. Not that she had any idea what to do with it once his soul was in her possession.

"One problem at a time, Winstin," she whispered as she reached his body and pressed her palm to his chest. The grey light flared, and she pulled the swirling orb from his corpse. She rolled onto her side and cradled it against her chest. Across the room, Krishna struggled to his feet. "One problem at a time."

Krishna grabbed his sword from the ground with his left hand and stalked toward her. After a few steps, the satisfied smirk on his face faded, and he came to a halt. He took a step back and let his sword fall to his side, his eyes glowing with a hatred so fierce it in no way matched his actions.

"Good to know I'm still off limits."

Morghan had never been so happy to hear Azrael's voice, even though she still planned to strangle the shit out of him when this was all over. "Now, run along before I convince Nikoli you're the one who did this to me. Or maybe I'll change my mind altogether, and we'll find out how little he really cares for you."

Krishna's grip tightened on the hilt of his sword, and he took a hesitant step forward. The doors swung open, and Krishna doubled over as his feet lifted off the ground, and he flew out of the room. He hit the floor and skid a ways before the doors slammed shut.

Morghan rolled over to face Azrael when a chair creaked behind her. He sat hunched over one of the side terminals, blood oozing from a deep, gaping wound that ran from the bottom of his left ear to the top of his shoulder. His jacket was gone, and his shirt was little more than strips of fabric clinging to his shoulders by dried blood. "What happened?"

He turned his head to the side, and the left half of his face was so pale it matched the walls. "I made a mistake." His eyes slid from Winstin's corpse to her wound. "A terrible mistake."

Morghan touched the side of her neck. "Luke did that?"

Azrael stood and braced himself against the terminal. He rested his hand on the hilt of his sword and his chest heaved. "Lucifer no longer exists."

Morghan wasn't sure what that meant. Had Azrael killed him, or was he referring to the rise of whatever monster Nikoli's power had turned him into? She was about to demand an answer, when her breath condensed on the air. "Fuck, Nikoli!"

Azrael sank to his knees in front of her. "We need to leave. Now."

Morghan held out Winstin's soul. "No, we have to send this first."

"There's no time."

Morghan pulled away from him before he could touch her. "Make time. Drag me over to that side terminal you were at. Maybe I can get it to send something without the main console being active."

"Just give me your hand."

Morghan drew her sword and pressed the tip against his chest. It was so heavy in her hand she almost dropped it. "You lost the right to an opinion when you left me for dead. Shift us out of here before I say so, and there won't be a Lucifer or an Azrael."

And a few minutes after that, no Morghan either.

She clutched Winstin's soul more tightly when her body floated through the air and came to rest in the chair

Azrael had been in. She set the soul in the appropriate recess and swiped her hand and arm across every button she could reach.

Nothing happened.

"Morghan, please." Azrael's voice was desperate. "Neither of us knows how to use this, and the main computer is a wreck."

Morghan shook her head. What did they have to lose? Nikoli would never kill Azrael, and she was as good as dead anyway. The baby was going wild inside her, but even if the sword had missed it, being born so early was a death sentence in Michael's realm. They were all fighting against the inevitable, and the only meaningful thing she could do with the time she had left was to give Winstin another chance. She glanced at the main console, and while most of it was destroyed, one button glowed blue.

Thank God for hurried, half-assed jobs.

"Part of the main console is still glowing. We can try that. If it doesn't work, we can leave."

Azrael held his hand out for the soul. "I can do it faster."

Morghan handed him the soul and immediately regretted it when he hesitated. If he crushed Winstin's soul instead of trying the main console, she would make damn sure they both died in this room. "If—"

"I heard you the first time." Azrael walked away from her, leaning on the side terminals as he went. When he reached the main console he placed the soul into it and pressed the glowing button.

Morghan let go of the breath she was holding when Winstin's soul disappeared into the system. "Break it."

Azrael's shoulders deflated, but a moment later metal groaned and the main console folded in on itself, the last bit of light fading. He spun around and fell back against what was left of the console when the doors swung open.

Nikoli stalked through them dragging a battered and broken Krishna by the back of his robes. "Honestly, Azrael, breaking things that don't belong to you? What are we, savages?"

At least now, Morghan knew what had taken him so long. She looked away from Krishna—the poor bastard. She despised him with every fiber of her being, but that was no way to live.

Azrael disappeared from the room, leaving Morghan to contemplate if Nikoli would ever agree to hunting him down and killing him with her. She was about to propose the idea, when Azrael flashed into existence in front of her, grabbed her arm, and pulled her into the void.

They emerged in Michael's realm, on a cliff overlooking Falcroix. Even at this distance, she could see Salus's banners hanging from the wall of the lower tier. She rolled onto her side and smiled; at least Michael was having a good day.

Thinking of him made her chest ache, and she wished she could see him one last time before she died. She had so much left to tell him, so much she should have already confessed.

Morghan rolled onto her back and turned her attention to where Azrael knelt at the cliff's edge. "I need you to tell Michael about Jessimine," she said. "We sent her soul to Vahyir, but you two will have to figure out who it went to once she's born."

Azrael rose and staggered a few steps toward her before collapsing in the grass at her side. "You can tell him your-self, but I have to get us to him first. I didn't mean to shift here. I must have been thinking of something else."

Morghan wondered how much blood he had left in his body, seeing as he could barely walk and his wounds had yet to start healing. "So, clear your mind and shift again."

"In a minute. I'm spent." He placed a hand over the one she held atop her wound. "Your blood was on Krishna's sword."

She nodded. "Survived a raging battle to be skewered as I walked out of a damn room."

"I don't have any blood to give you, Morghan. Your wound will heal so slow, and the baby..."

Nikoli's voice rode in on a cold gust of wind. "That child was mine the moment it was conceived."

He stood a few paces from them with Krishna by his side.

Azrael tightened his grip on Morghan's hand, but Nikoli flashed forward and wrapped a hand around Morghan's opposite wrist.

"Wherever you go, Azrael, I will follow," Nikoli rasped. He grabbed Azrael by the throat and flung him toward Krishna before standing and drawing his sword. He gripped the hilt with both hands and raised it high above Morghan's chest. "You go alone."

Morghan brought her arms over her eyes and braced for death. She heard a blade connect with flesh, but the pain never came. Instead, warmth spread across her chest, and she opened her eyes to see Azrael hovering above her on hands and knees. Nikoli's sword peeked out from the right side of his chest, and what little blood he had left slid down the blade, adding to the pool of warmth on her chest.

"No!" Nikoli and Morghan's voices echoed one another.

Nikoli pulled his sword from Azrael's body and flung it over the cliff. He fell to his knees, and the grass froze in a circle beneath him. "I couldn't stop!"

Morghan didn't give a shit about Nikoli's sudden attack of conscience. She pulled Azrael against her chest and buried her face in his hair. "Keep your breathing slow and shallow. Relax. Everything will be fine."

"Don't." Azrael's breath caught, and the warm trail of his tears slid across her neck. "I've heard enough lies today."

The hair on Morghan's arms stood on end, and golden sparks skittered across the ground until they came up against Nikoli's icy blades of grass. From there, they climbed into the air and built a low, solid, glowing dome of light around her and Azrael.

"Azrael, stop." Nikoli's voice was high and panicky. He moved to reach through the barrier but pulled his hand back at the last second. Maybe he was remembering Azrael's energy fields did more than burn your skin if you touched them. He turned to Morghan. "Don't let him do this. Please."

If Azrael wanted to protect them until his dying breath, so be it. Nikoli could wait his happy ass until Azrael's energy field dissipated, by which time she would be good and ready to die along with him.

Morghan glared at Nikoli. "Wait it out, you self-right-eous prick."

Nikoli's eyes blazed, and he slammed his fists into the ground. The cliff shook beneath them, and wings tore from his back as the soft lines of his face sharpened until a boy stared back at her. A terrified boy. She knew he'd been young when his world was ripped out from under him. What she hadn't realized was, unlike Michael, who was eternally stuck in his mid-twenties, Nikoli's body hadn't aged. "I can help him. Give him back!"

Morghan squeezed Azrael's shoulder. "Can he really heal you?"

Azrael pressed his face harder against the side of her neck. "I'd rather die here with you than go with him."

Morghan was convinced angels had a genetic predisposition to never answer her questions directly. Or maybe it was just Azrael.

Morghan turned back to Nikoli. His next move would be to attack the energy field, consequences be damned. She was certain of it, because she would have done the same. It was only a matter of time until the desperation shining in his eyes overruled logic, but until then, she had no doubt Nikoli would promise her the moon to get what he wanted.

All she had to do was feed Azrael to the wolves.

"He's yours, but it's time for new rules. My rules." Morghan forced a grin. This was something Nikoli would understand, but if she proposed too many, he would bend them all while picking which would be better off broken. Too few? Well, that would be her loss.

"First, you will not try to kill me when the energy field falls. This wound might do the trick, but if not, you'll leave me alone until I'm healed." She didn't dare shove never into the mix, as the word only existed with an asterisk in their world. Nikoli's rules had proven time and again that the longer you demanded, the shorter you got.

Azrael sobbed, and his body shook against Morghan's. He clung to her arm, but the strength in his grip was nonexistent. "No. Morghan, please."

"Trust me," she whispered against his ear. "And let me play the game."

Morghan turned back to Nikoli. "Next, Salus is off limits. I don't want you setting foot in my city."

Nikoli's eyes never left Azrael. "Those requests are reasonable. Drop the shield."

"Do I look like I'm fucking done?" Morghan seethed.

She was so fucking done. Her world was dim around the edges, and with Azrael on top of her, it was so much harder to breathe. "You will give Michael a chance to be happy. Let Jessimine grow up without torture and death hanging over her head."

"Anything else?" Nikoli snapped. "Or are we waiting until he dies in your arms?"

"Jealous?" Morghan smirked, but it didn't last long, and her lips tugged into a frown. Nikoli was right, and she wouldn't have time to get through half of what she wanted. "Finally, you will do your best to heal Azrael. Unless you have some magic to heal a wound from a ranking sword, you'll start by covering his chest wounds and sticking a tube between his ribs to suck out whatever air and blood is building there.

"Don't look at me like I've lost my mind. If you can make people from dirt, you can figure out how to put in a fucking chest tube. Do as I say, and once he's healed, you will not force him to stay with you, in your realm, or any combination of the two."

Nikoli's fists clenched for a moment before his lips curled into a serpentine smile. "Agreed." He held out his arms. "Drop the shield."

Azrael shook his head. "No."

Morghan had really hoped he wouldn't force her hand. She pulled his face up to hers and gave him a quick kiss on the lips. "I love you, and I'm sorry." She grabbed his shoulders and rolled him off her, toward Nikoli.

Azrael screamed when he hit the ground, and the energy field flickered long enough for Nikoli to reach through and grab him.

Nikoli cradled Azrael in his arms and stood. He beckoned Krishna to his side and transferred Azrael to him. "I'm sending you home. Cover his wounds, and I'll be along soon."

Krishna nodded, but he didn't look happy about it. Neither was Morghan, as nothing good would come from being alone with Nikoli.

Nikoli took Krishna's chin in his hand and forced him to make eye contact. "If he dies, so do you, and when death settles over you, it will be a mercy."

A moment later Nikoli stood alone. He held out his hand, and his sword flew over the side of the cliff, above Morghan's head, and came to rest in his hand. "What am I going to do with you?"

"Not kill me. Rule one." Morghan had zero confidence in Nikoli's word now that he had what he wanted, but Azrael had always been adamant that beyond the manipulation and rule-bending hypocrisy, Nikoli believed himself to be fair.

Nikoli sheathed his sword and took a knee at her side. He pulled a dagger from her belt and weighed the blade in his hand. "Not yet, but you still have something of mine. Now, hold still."

Morghan tried to roll away from him, but he grabbed the front of her shirt and held her back to the ground. Her legs kicked uselessly behind him as he sliced a fresh wound across her abdomen and plunged his free hand inside it. He turned and replaced the hand on her chest with a knee so he could use both hands to rip the child from her womb. The baby lay pale and limp against Nikoli's chest as he used the dagger to cut the cord. A faint green light shimmered in its chest, but the only sound echoing around them was Morghan's screams.

The pain was so sharp and unrelenting she could scarcely breathe past it. The wound may not have been a mortal one, but blood surged from it nonetheless, and the added loss was bound to make her true wound worse. "You lying bastard," she said.

Nikoli rose to his feet. He breathed deep, and his wings melted into his back as he regained his usual, middle-aged form. "The dagger shouldn't have the power to kill you. I can't be blamed for your poor ability to heal."

Nikoli smiled down at the child in his arms before turning his eyes to Morghan. "Even in death, a boy should have a name."

Had he said it was a boy? Morghan's thoughts were as blurry as her vision, her body heavy and numb aside from the fire burning in her emptied womb. And why was he looking at her like he expected something?

"A name," he said.

Oh, that made sense. Or did it? She wasn't sure. "Elijah."

"Your optimism is admirable." Nikoli laughed. "Unfortunately chariots of fire aren't really my style."

Morghan closed her eyes, and she wasn't sure if she had blinked or passed out, but when she opened them again, Nikoli was gone. She struggled onto her side, one hand dangling over the edge of the cliff. She didn't want to die, but if she did, the last thing she saw would be Salus's crest billowing against the walls of the fallen city. She could almost imagine a group of men on horseback riding toward the cliff, the emblems on their armor gleaming red in the setting sun. She clung to the image, a last bastion of hope as she faded from consciousness. Maybe she could live. Living was important.

On the following pages, is an excerpt from *Vahyir Rising*, the third installment of the *Eternity's Hourglass* series. Available late November 2021.

Want to keep up with all of E.A. Blackwell's upcoming releases? Visit the author's website at:

WWW.EABLACKWELL.COM

VAHYIR RISING

Nikoli shifted in his chair and glared at the bed across the room. Azrael's wounds had healed weeks ago, not that it mattered. His chest rose, his heart beat, but his eyes had yet to open. Nikoli had delved into his mind any number of times to force him awake, but that route was blocked. At least, Nikoli hoped the wall of nothing he came up against each time he tried was a barrier, because he couldn't quite bring himself to entertain the alternative.

He shouldn't care one way or the other. The defeat at Falcroix had left him with a number of other issues that needed addressing, and Azrael's death would have given Nikoli a freedom he hadn't enjoyed since before the traitor's creation.

But some freedoms were no more than well-disguised prisons. He was well-acquainted with that truth, as was the woman whose privacy he was currently invading.

Nikoli hunched over in his seat and gazed out the window at the lower tiers of Galmedea. Michael had wasted no time returning the city to its previous name, but that didn't bother Nikoli. This place had never been his home. It was a means to an end. An end that had only been half-realized before he'd managed to ruin his own victory by being too greedy. And so, for now, he was reduced to this.

Nikoli returned to his study of the bed and pulled enough energy from the room to send the temperature into free fall.

Morghan rolled toward the wall and pulled the blankets tighter. "Freezing me to death isn't winning you any brownie points, jackass."

The woman wasn't even scared of him anymore, or maybe she'd never had sense enough to be so. "Azrael still won't wake."

She turned away from the wall and pulled the blankets up to her chin. Her breath spiraled on the air. "Yeah, I got that by the fact you're sitting in my damn room. Again. I've helped you all I can. He lost close to a body full of blood, and then, thanks to you, he lost a little more. There's no way to know how much of what was left fed his brain once he went unconscious."

"He's still there," Nikoli insisted. "Such a mind doesn't go away just like that."

"I've watched countless great minds go away—just like that. Trust me, in an instant is better than long and drawn out."

Nikoli wanted to believe she was saying that to rile him, but the sad gleam in her eyes had him worried. "We'll pretend, for the sake of your life, that he's in there. Is there anything else that might keep him from waking?"

The gleam in Morghan's eyes morphed into a flame. "First off, I'm not fully healed, so stop threatening me. And what do I look like, the fuckin' Azrael whisperer? If I was him, I wouldn't wake up either. As far as he knows, I could be dead, Luke is dead or worse, and he's being taken care of by a man who only knows how to love him through torture."

The heel of Nikoli's boot tapped a staccato against the floor. "I told him you're alive."

"If he can hear you. Did you also tell him that you killed my son by ripping the child from my womb seconds after sending him to your realm?"

Nikoli gripped the armrests of his chair. "I saved you from dying while giving birth to a child who would have perished in this realm, anyway. You never would have managed hours of labor with that true wound gushing the way it was."

Morghan was out of bed and lording over him a second later, her eyes blazing. "Don't you dare turn yourself into the fucking hero! You destroyed the only men I've ever loved and topped it off by murdering my unborn child."

Nikoli pushed the chair back and rose to his feet. "For someone so gravely injured, you're awfully spry. I'd wager you're fully healed and sulking."

Morghan's laugh was humorless and irritating. "Then go ahead and kill me. Solve all my problems, and give Azrael another reason not to wake up. But here's the truth, Nikoli—you're bothering the wrong person. We're beyond anything my medical knowledge can touch, and where Azrael is concerned, you and I, we've always played second fiddle."

ALSO BY E.A. BLACKWELL

Eternity's Hourglass Series

Eternity's Hourglass

The Falcroix Legion

Vahyir Rising (Late November 2021)

Shattered Skies (December 2021)

The Third Tenet (January 2022)

Eternity's Hourglass Standalone Stories

Granite Windstarr

Eden Eternal

Short Stories

The Messy Business of Wolves

The G.A.M.E.

Hard Knocked Up: A Billionaire Zombie Romance

ABOUT THE AUTHOR

E.A. Blackwell is an author of dark to grimdark fantasy and dystopian fiction.

Blackwell resides in Florida with a dog named Cerberus, a snake named Crowley, two children, who are fast becoming snarkier than their parents, and a husband who has likely stuck around the past two decades for entertainment value alone.

Made in the USA
Monee, IL
09 November 2021